CW00502053

# Mountain Daddies

The Complete Collection

Lucky Moon

# Contents

# Keep in Touch

Thanks for stopping by!

If you want to keep in touch and receive a **FREE BOX SET** as a thank you for signing up, just head to the link here: http://eepurl.com/gYVLJ1

I'll shower with you love and affection, giving you **insider information** on my series, plus all kinds of other **treats**. My newsletter goes out once a week and contains giveaways, polls, exclusive content, and lots more fun besides.

Also, you can get in touch with me at luckymoonromance@gmail.com or find me on Facebook. I love hearing from fans!

Lucky x o x

# Chapter One

# TRAPPED WITH DADDY

# JOEL

'**I**T'S NOT APPROPRIATE TO meet a guest with my top off, is it?'

No reply.

'Come on Tina,' I say, turning away from my work. 'Give me a hint here.'

Tina looks at me for a moment, blinks, then raises her paw up to her mouth and gives it a long, deliberate lick.

'Thing is Tina,' I continue, turning back to the roof panel, 'I have to work with my top off 'cause of this damn heat, and I've got no way of knowing when this guest is gonna be here.'

I've always found it easy to talk to animals. I guess it's the way they don't talk back. No arguments, no back-chat, just simple, no-judgment listening.

Summer in this part of Colorado means one thing. Well, two things. Heat and mosquitoes. Heat in the day, mosquitoes at night.

'Not just heat,' I say to Tina, absentmindedly. 'We've got thunderstorms, too. Don't know what the tourists see in the place.'

Tina meows.

'Exactly. Only thing crazier than vacationing in a rickety cabin in the middle of the Rockies is livin' here. I mean, what kind of maniac would give up a perfectly good job in the city, just for the chance to live off-grid up here?'

It's a rhetorical question, of course. I'm the kind of maniac who'd do that. For four years now, I've been living out here on my own, forty miles from the nearest town, two miles from the nearest road. If I want to go anywhere, I've got to trek through the woods, avoiding bears and mountain lions, before I can even start the engine of my car.

Tina gives another, thoughtful meow, then slinks out of the cabin. I watch her tabby tail swishing from side to side. Probably off to chase some squirrels.

'Sorry for boring you,' I call after her.

Despite the complaints I make to my cat, I love my life out here. I lived the city life for years, earning money, being a slave to my boss, and all I felt was a gnawing sense of emptiness, like there had to be something else out there for me. Now, I think I've found it. It's not perfect, of course, but that's part of the charm.

It's stimulating, too. Had to learn a whole bunch of new skills. Out here, if something breaks, no-one's gonna fix it except me. So I'm not an investment banker anymore. I'm a plumber. And an electrician. And a carpenter. And there's no internet here, of course. I learned it all from old books.

The cabin I bought — an old ranger's place — was tiny. But you don't exactly need planning permission here to extend, so after a few months of living in the tiny shack, I started adding to it. Building extra rooms, and reinforcing the roof. Then, when I was done with my place, I thought to myself: why not make a little extra cash?

So, I started on the biggest project of my adult life. Building a house. Well, a cabin.

Planning it was the hardest part. I wanted to make sure that it was the perfect vacation spot for those with an adventurous spirit. I picked a little patch on the top of a hill, a couple hundred yards from my place. The view from the hill is incredible — a sweeping vista over

Purple Lake and the surrounding ink-green pines. I cleared space and sketched out the floor plan with cut logs over the course of a few weeks. When I was sure of the layout, I got to work.

There's an art to chopping down trees.

*Look twice, chop once.*

That's the advice I read in an old book about it. It's advice that chimed with me. I'm naturally cautious, ever since what happened between me and Sadie. When I was young, I was slow, impulsive. Now though, I'm methodical, careful.

Boring.

'Come on, Joel, you're not boring. You're a strong, silent, mountain man: exciting and enigmatic.' I give a wry grin.

I'm not even talking to Tina anymore — just myself.

Crazy *and* boring. What a combination.

At least I built a good cabin. Made from local pine, with a solid fuel stove and artisan fixtures, the guest cabin's been popular on Airbnb ever since I built it.

Mostly, couples come out here for fresh air and a dose of the wilderness. Today though, I'm expecting just one visitor — a young lady called Ella, who's making her way here from Denver.

She's due any time now, so I'm scrabbling to make sure that the roof is totally waterproof. We're due a big storm over the next few days, and the last thing I want is for Ella to get soaked in the night.

I lay a final plank down onto the roof, then take a nail out of my pocket.

'Should I be worried that you're only just making the place now?'

I'm so surprised that I almost fall off the ladder.

'Jesus!' I splutter, struggling to grab something solid.

'It's Ella, actually.'

I look round, and see her, right next to the path which leads to my place. She's petite, curvaceous, pale. I can't help but scan up and down her body, taking in her smooth, toned legs, the curve of her hips. Then, when I see her face, I feel something I haven't felt for years.

My Daddy radar. It's going berserk.

Looking at her smiling eyes, and her small, pouting mouth, I can sense her soul — tender, gentle and free.

'Ella,' is all I can say.

She looks at me, curiosity twinkling in her eyes. Wonder if she's scared — a big man with lots of tattoos. Hope I'm not making her uncomfortable.

Finally, I manage: 'I'm Joel. And, for the record, I'm not just building this place now. I'm just—'

'Repairing the roof?' She's chewing gum. She tucks her thumbs behind the straps of her rucksack. Damnit, being this cute shouldn't be legal.

'You got it.' I hesitate a moment. 'But it's just a precautionary measure. We're due some rain, so...'

'No problem. It's so beautiful here. Bet it's even pretty in the rain.'

I press the nail into the plank and hammer it in with three sure strikes.

'Sure is. Lots to discover, too, if you know where to look.'

'Maybe you could help me with that.'

I feel my heart start to pound in my chest. The thought of spending time alone with this gorgeous creature is getting me all hot and bothered. The intensity of these feelings has taken me by surprise.

'Sure,' I say. 'Tour of the local area is all part of the service.' I wipe my brow. 'You want a look around? Got some ground rules to go over with you.'

'Ground rules? Yes sir!' she gives me a little salute. 'I respond well to rules.'

'Good,' I say. 'Because these rules are important.'

*

'I guess I didn't think there would *actually* be bears.'

'Oh yes,' I reply. I've got my t-shirt back on now, and I'm carrying Ella's bags. 'They're harmless, usually. But just to be safe, it's crucial that no food is left outside, at any time.'

'Got it.'

I push open the front door of the cabin.

'So, here it is. Hope you have a great time here.'

'Holy crap, it's beautiful!'

If I was her Daddy, I'd tell her off for swearing right about now.

Why am I letting these thoughts run around my head? I'm not her Daddy, and I'm not gonna be her Daddy.

She surges ahead into the cozy space.

'Frick, did you hunt that yourself?' She's looking up at an elk head that's mounted above the fireplace.

I shake my head. 'Nope. Bought it at Target.'

She lets out a snort of laughter. It's just about the happiest sound I've ever heard. Her laugh is amazing — like pure, bottled sunshine.

'You're really destroying my wilderness fantasy here.'

'Well, if it helps, I did catch *that*. Killed it with my bare hands. Skinned it too. With my teeth.' I point down at the bearskin rug under her feet.

'Oh my god,' she gasps. Then, she pauses for a moment. 'Hang on...'

'Yeah, that was Target, too.'

'One thing I know is that you didn't buy this view from Target.'

She's standing at the feature window of the cabin. It's a floor-to-ceiling pane of glass, and it looks out over Purple Lake. It's the entire reason I built this cabin.

'Glad you like it,' I grunt.

'Feels like a whole different world to Denver. Which is exactly what I needed.'

There's something about the way she says that, in a sad, strange voice.

'Most people don't come on wilderness vacations,' I say, putting her bags down on the ground, next to the couch. 'Most people like comfort. Like beaches and convenience. What made you decide that this was the vacation for you?'

She purses her mouth for a moment, then looks at me with those sharp blue eyes.

'Oh you know, just running away.'

Maybe she's joking, maybe she's not.

'You want to talk about it?' It's a crazy thing to say — we only just met. But for some reason, I feel this instant link to her, as though I understand there's a tenderness underneath her bluster. A vulnerability.

She shakes her head. 'Nah, I'm fine. Think I'll just get unpacked then go for a little walk somewhere.'

'No problem,' I smile. 'There's food in the fridge. Nothing fancy, just beans and sausage. Plenty of bread on the sideboard. All baked by me.'

'You bake your own bread? You don't exactly look like a baker.' Is she impressed?

'Kinda have to be. Don't head to town so often, so I just buy flour in bulk. Stores way longer than bread that way.'

'Makes sense. The one time I tried to bake something, I burnt it so bad I almost set the oven on fire.' She lifts a hand and runs it through her hair. As she does so, I notice that she's wearing a silver ring shaped like a snake. It shines in the low light.

'Well,' I say, 'that settles it. I'll make breakfast for you tomorrow. Seven thirty in my cabin, which is just down that track.'

'Oh, I d—'

'No ifs, no buts,' I say. 'I want to make sure that you get a good breakfast before you head out into the wilderness. Can't have a delicate thing like you rambling on empty.'

She looks genuinely touched. 'Thank you, that would be lovely.'

'It's nice to get looked after, sometimes.'

She nods. 'It sure is.'

*

After I show her around the rest of the cabin, I point her in the direction of a local trail that's totally safe, and should only take her about an hour or so to walk.

'If you're lucky and quiet,' I say, 'you might see some deer. Take this.' I hand her a sturdy, professional-grade walkie-talkie. 'Phone reception's not so hot round here, but this will be able to reach me, no trouble.'

'I haven't used a walkie-talkie since I was a kid,' she says. 'Kinda fun.' Her eyes flash a mischievous blue. I'm getting such strong Little vibes from her. I think back to the last time I was with a Little.

*Don't go back to that place, Joel. Don't fall for her.*

'Glad you think so,' I grunt, trying not to be too encouraging.

There's no way she'd be interested in me, anyway. She's still in her early twenties. I'm ancient, compared. Almost forty.

'Well, see you soon,' she says. 'Wish me luck.'

A sudden, overwhelming urge grips me, to stay with her, to make sure that she's safe in the woods. But it's not appropriate. Not now. This isn't how an Airbnb host acts. But there's something about Ella. Something that's making me want to be a big Daddy bear.

I hold back. I need to let her be independent now. Tomorrow, we can talk. Then I'll see if there's anything between us.

I wave her off, then head back to my place. Tina's waiting for me by the front door.

I watch Ella make her way into the thick wood, then I turn to my cat.

'I think I just fell in love, baby.'

# ELLA

OH MY FREAKING GOD. This is meant to be a vacation to help me forget about men. So of course, the host is the most gorgeous man I've literally ever seen in my entire life.

Why did he have to have tattoos?

I've counted three so far. An anchor on his powerful chest. A skull on his thick, impossibly strong bicep. And a tiger on his back, curled up from the base of his spine, all the way up to his broad, muscular shoulders.

It's not just his body that's got me all twisted up, either. He's got thick stubble, almost a beard (the *perfect* length, by the way), and strong, soulful eyes. But his lips are the most amazing part of him. They're so... generous. So thick and warm-looking.

I went for a little trek yesterday evening, and the whole time I should have been looking at majestic pines and dappled sunlight, all I could do was imagine those beautiful lips working their way down my body, making me feel all yummy inside.

Joel makes Pete, my ex, look like a twig. And not a thick twig, either. A tiny, wretched, sickly-looking stick.

*Don't think about Pete, Ella. Don't let him ruin this vacation for you.*

I roll over in the bed. Last night was chilly, and I've got a buckskin rug pulled up over me. It's so snuggly and cozy in here that I don't want to get up. But equally, I'm desperate to spend more time with Joel. He put me so immediately at ease yesterday.

It might not be obvious when you first meet me, but I suffer pretty badly from anxiety. Always have done. There's nothing that really causes it, but I definitely have triggers. And being in the wilderness, near potential bears and god knows what other nasty creatures? Turns out that's an anxiety trigger.

That's partly why I booked this break. I wanted to challenge myself.

Pete always told me that I was pathetic, that I never pushed myself, that I always took the safe option. I guess he was right, most of the time. But I wanted to prove that I'm tougher than he thinks. I may be a Little, I may act cute, I may like to wear diapers and sleep in an adult-sized crib, but that doesn't mean I can't be a brave Little.

That's the thing that freaked me out about Joel — he seemed to know exactly how to talk to me to get me to relax. With confidence, tenderness, and understanding. And when he asked me if I wanted to talk to him about why I was running away, I almost did. I almost opened up to him.

And that's just something I don't do.

I can hear a weird noise, somewhere nearby. It's a rhythmic thunk, and it sounds like someone's hacking into something. Intrigued, I finally pluck up the courage to lift myself out of bed.

After a very quick diaper change and a new set of clothes, I'm ready to explore. I check my phone, which, without a connection is basically only good as a watch right now. It's seven o'clock — not quite time to meet Joel for breakfast.

I have a sudden worry that maybe the sound is some kind of wild animal, and I'll be putting myself in danger by heading outside. But I master my fear. It's too regular to be a wild beast. This has to be something else.

Outside, the dawn has broken. The sun's barely visible through the tree canopy, just casting golden, shimmering rays across the clearing between the two cabins. This is the most beautiful place I've ever been. I can't believe that Joel gets to live here all the time. I wonder what it would be like to be so far from society, to be out in the woods, with just the chipmunks for company.

'Quiet,' I whisper to myself. 'It'd be very quiet.'

I'm caught up in the peace of the moment, and I imagine, for a second, stepping out into the view, traveling somehow on a sunbeam, flowing like the light across the trees, over the surface of lakes, up, up, into the clear blue of the sky.

Then there's another thunk from behind me, and I turn, creeping behind a tree to hide.

I think back to playing hide-and-go-seek as a kid. The thrill of fear, that prickle of anticipation as the hunter moved closer toward you.

When I discover the source of the thunking, my jaw hits the floor.

It's Joel. He's clutching a huge ax, over his head. He pauses for a moment, and then brings the gleaming blade down with terrifying force, hewing a thick log in two. The pieces of wood zip through the air, landing with a clunk.

Joel takes another log and places it on the chopping block. As he moves, I watch his body as it ripples and shifts. He looks so heavy, so powerful. Is he always topless? It's not even that hot yet. His body is so tan and smooth, it's making my mouth water. Imagine what he'd feel like to touch. Imagine how strong he could push up against me.

This swing is even easier than the first, and the ax bites into the chopping block as it sunders the log.

There's a rustle down by my feet and I glance down.

It's an animal, brown and gray and black, and it's moving around my legs. I shriek before I have time to fully take in what I'm looking at.

The sound echoes out, hollow among the trees.

'What's wrong?' Joel's voice bellows out, as he turns to look at me.

'Oh my god, it's a cat!'

She's beautiful, a silvery, slinky tabby.

Joel's next to me. 'What are you doing over here?'

'Nothing, just coming over for breakfast.'

He leans down and strokes the cat, which has started to purr and rub herself against his legs.

'What do you think, Tina, was Ella spying on me?'

I feel my cheeks start to burn. The cat lets out a soft meow and looks at me, as though she's keeping a little secret.

'I wasn't spying!' I say. I'm a terrible liar.

'Funny, that's not what Tina says.'

'Well maybe Tina is trying to make trouble. She seems like a troublemaker.' I bend down and stroke Tina. Her fur is smooth and warm. As I stroke, I accidentally touch Joel's hand. There's a spark of electricity between us, and I jerk my fingers back.

'Come on, I'll show you my place. Breakfast won't take long.'

*

My cabin's beautiful, but Joel's is ridiculous.

'It's so tall!'

'Yeah,' he says, looking up. 'It used to be a fire-watch tower, so it needs to be tall. The view from the top is incredible.'

'Fire watch?' I ask.

'Yeah. In the old days, some poor bastard would sit up there during fire season, and call in reports so that the fire service can put them out.'

'Sounds romantic.'

He nods. 'I guess so.'

'So they don't do that anymore?'

He opens the front door.

'Oh, people still do fire-watching, it's just that they don't use this tower anymore. In fact, I know a fire watcher. Travis. He's an interesting guy. Anyway, how do you like your eggs?'

'Cooked!'

He grins. 'I think I can manage that.'

Joel leads me up a staircase to the top of the old tower. He's doing amazing work here, converting the space into an incredible dining and living area. Everything is super-rustic, with a simple red and white checked tablecloth over a handmade, wooden table. The chairs look handmade, too. The view is truly sensational. The landscape spreads out like an endless carpet of green and blue.

'Did you make everything in this place?'

'Can you tell? You're the first person who's ever seen this place.'

'Honestly?'

He nods. 'Mmmhmm. Not everyone gets a special breakfast.'

'I'm honored.'

'I'm gonna go finish breakfast. You just relax.'

He heads down the stairs and I have a few minutes to myself. I guess this isn't normal. I wonder whether Joel feels the same weird tension I'm feeling between us.

If only I wasn't a Little.

If I was a normal person, I'd consider making a move. But even with all the Daddy vibes I'm getting from Joel, there's no way I'm gonna risk freaking him out. And there's no way I'm ever going to start a relationship — or even flirt — with anyone who doesn't know I'm a Little ever again.

Not after what happened with Pete.

This vacation had been my friend Julie's idea. She'd come out to visit from New York, to help support me after Pete and I fell apart. Julie's a Little too. I met her online and we've been penpals for years, but this was only the second time we'd met in the flesh. She'd recommended this cabin to me, saying that her husband knew the owner, and that she thought a little wilderness time would do me good.

As I sit here in this comfy chair, looking out across the vast expanse of country, I wonder if she had another reason for recommending it to me.

Maybe Joel *is* a Daddy. Maybe he'll respond well to me.

No. I can't take that chance.

I hear the tramp of Joel's feet on the staircase again, and now a heavenly scent rises up with him. The smell of bacon, of toast, of all the good things life has to offer.

'Well, I didn't burn anything, thankfully.' I love his voice. So kind and gentle, at the same time as being strong and confident.

'Glad to hear it,' I say. I'm squirming with excitement.

He puts down a plate in front of me that's stuffed with so much food I've got no idea how I'm gonna finish it.

'Colorado breakfast,' he says, sounding pleased with himself.

'So you don't cook this for every guest?' I ask, lifting a forkful of hashbrowns to my drooling mouth.

He shakes his head, sitting down opposite me. He's thrown on a red and black check shirt, much to my dismay. 'Look, Ella, I've got something I need to admit to you. I hope it's not weird for you.'

This takes me by surprise. I don't quite know what to say, so I say nothing.

He purses his lips, as though preparing for something. Then he continues. 'While you're here with me, I'd like to look after you. Coddle you, in a way. I'd like to make sure that you're safe and having fun. I'd like to show you around the woods and the lakes here, protecting you from the wildlife and making sure that you have the best possible time it's possible to have.'

The more he talks, the faster and shallower my breathing becomes.

'You want to look after me?'

'That's right. Because I get a sense from you, that it's what you need.' He leans forward and takes my hand in his. His skin is warm, and as he squeezes, I can feel his heartbeat in my fingers. 'But if it's not what you want, I understand. You can go back to the guest cabin and carry on with your vacation and I won't bother you again.'

'No.' I say. 'Please. Bother me. I mean. Yes, you can look after me.' My voice is Little now. 'That would be nice. Like. Super nice.'

He smiles a warm smile and gently strokes my hand. 'Good girl. Now eat up your breakfast, because we've got a long day ahead of us.'

# JOEL

I CAN'T BELIEVE SHE agreed to my idea. She wants me — actively wants me — to look after her while she's here. I mean, I'd have been looking out for her, anyway, but now I get the chance to spend more time with this gorgeous, precious girl, with her blessing.

I've just got to remember myself. I mustn't give in to temptation. This isn't a sexual thing, I just want to look after this lost soul. I don't want to make myself vulnerable again. Because in just a few days, she'll be leaving me and the cabin.

'Have you put on insect repellent?' I ask as gently as I can.

'Ooopsie! I forgot. Are there skeetos?'

I pass her a can of bug spray. 'Get this all over yourself. It's not just skeeters, we've got fleas and ticks out here. Don't want any nasty critters taking bites out of that cute body.' I know I'm straying into dangerous ground talking like this, but I can't help myself. It's like there's some invisible connection between the two of us, strange and irresistible.

We're standing outside her cabin, and she's prepared for a day in the woods. I'm going to take her to a favorite spot of mine, down by Purple Lake. She's looking gorgeous, wearing tiny little hiking shorts and a tight sports top that leaves nothing to the imagination.

She starts to spray the solution over herself, but she's doing a pretty poor job.

'Have you never used bug spray before?' I ask.

'Nope,' she says.

'Want some help?'

She nods, those big blue eyes like wells in her cute little face.

I walk over to her and take the can.

'You've got to be methodical.' I take her hand in mine and lift her arm before I spray. Left arm, then right.

'It's tickly,' she says, giggling for a moment.

'Got to get every bit, or you'll be itching, not just tickly.'

Legs next. I follow the lines of her body, spraying up from her ankles to her thighs. As my eyes scan over, I notice that her shorts are actually quite puffy — they don't fit her as sleekly as her top. I wonder why that is.

Soon, I've covered her in the stuff.

'Do you need to rub it in?' Her voice is quiet and cute. It's an innocent question, but I can't help but think filthy thoughts. She's practically inviting me to touch her. I want to so badly. But that's not why I'm doing this. I just want to look after her, not actually do anything with her.

It's been so long since I've touched a woman. I could reach out now, rub that slippery solution into her soft skin. I could allow myself to get closer to her, open myself up to her. But I know that it would be a mistake.

'Don't need to with this stuff,' I say, averting my eyes. 'Should work just fine like that. Right, time to go.'

We head out to the East. There's a rough track that winds its way down through the pine and spruce. It's only a track because I love to walk this way so much. There are no other humans around for miles. It's a beautiful day, but rain is forecast for later. For the first few minutes, we walk in respectful silence. Ella seems to be taking in our surroundings, and I can hear her smelling the air.

'Everything's so fresh!' she finally says. 'In the city, you forget what greenery actually smells of, don't you?'

'Sure do,' I say.

'Have you ever lived in the city?' The question takes me by surprise.

'I thought it was totally obvious. I was born and raised in New York.'

She balks at me. 'You mean you weren't like, raised by grizzly bears in a cave?'

I let out a low, booming laugh. 'Seriously? Damn. My few years in the wilderness must have changed me beyond all recognition.'

She obviously thought I was some kind of wild man. Not a former investment banker from Wall Street. I still think of myself as a kind of city slicker.

'Well, you coulda fooled me,' says Ella, treading carefully. 'You've got a whole rugged, untamed thing going on. Plus, you're so handy. I just assumed you'd been living in this cabin forever.'

'Nope,' I say. 'I left New York a few years ago, and my friend Carl told me this place was gonna be available. He's a sheriff in the local town: Little Creek. Carl's a real frontiersman. Born out here in the middle of nowhere. I don't think he's ever left the state.'

Carl's a Daddy, like me. A very old friend of mine in New York — Dylan — got me in touch with Carl. He's about the closest thing I've got to a friend in this new life. He's a good guy, but I can never quite get him to open up.

'How come you left the city?' she asks, her voice innocent and curious.

'It's a long story.'

'We've got all day.' She smiles.

I consider for a moment. 'You know what. It's not a long story. It's just an old story. A cliché. I left 'cause of a woman.' I can't help but open up to her. She's so disarming, so charming. And it's like she actually wants to listen to my boring old stories.

'I'm sorry,' she says.

'It's OK. Ancient history now.'

Her hand is on my arm. 'It's something we've got in common. A break-up's why I'm here. That's what brought me to the wilderness, too.'

I smile a wry smile. 'It's a story as old as these trees. Pain drives people to loneliness.'

There's sadness in her eyes, and she nods.

'Not that that has to be you,' I continue. 'You're just here for a vacation, for a break, to get your head straight, right? You're not dumb enough to stay out here like me.'

'I dunno,' she says, thoughtful. 'I'm dreading going back. I was meant to be getting married.'

'Aw, shit,' I say, then instantly regret it. 'Sorry for cussing. Can't help myself sometimes.'

'It's OK,' she says. 'I've heard worse.'

We walk together in silence for a few minutes, listening to the calls of crows and burr of crickets on the breeze.

There's a feeling bubbling up in me, a tenderness towards Ella. Finally, when I can't take it anymore, I say, 'You know, I feel sorry for the guy.'

'Huh?'

'The guy who was meant to be marrying you. Poor bastard.'

She laughs. 'Believe me, he doesn't feel that way. Nope.' She pauses a second, considering something. 'Truth is, he only loved the idea of

me. When he found out who I really am, he got cold feet. Not just cold
— frozen.'

Damn. It's like she's telling me the story of my own life.

I'm about to tell her as much when I see it. Quiet and still, behind
a mask of trees. I crouch down.

'Look,' I whisper, instinctively pulling Ella in tight. 'Can you see?
There.'

'Is that...?'

I nod. 'It's a deer. Look.' The creature takes a tentative step forward,
its slender limbs testing the forest floor before it commits its full
weight down.

'It's beautiful.'

'Look, it's a momma.'

A moment later, two tiny fawns trot out from behind their mommy. They reach up to tender green leaves, their cute necks straining as
they chew.

'It's magical,' Ella says. I feel her warmth next to me, her own slender
body pushed into mine. Her hand rests on the small of my back.

I could kiss her. Right now. Maybe she'd kiss me back. Maybe she
can feel this insane energy between us too. I turn, look at her face, and
she does the same, looking back at me. I can feel her breath against my
cheek. Up close, I notice tiny details about her face: the true shape of
her eyes; the way her eyelashes stick together at the edges; a tiny chip
in her front tooth.

She moves forward, her face so close to mine that we're practically
touching. Her lips are just about to graze mine.

Then, there's a rustle from in front and a cry from somewhere far
away.

'Mountain lion,' I say, standing bolt upright.

Ella grabs me instinctively. 'Are we safe?'

'Uh-huh,' I confirm. 'It's miles away. Won't be bothering us. But look, the deer have gone.' Weird. They wouldn't normally be spooked by something so far away. I look up. Through the trees, I see that the sky is looking suddenly ominous. We're due rain, but these look more like storm clouds. 'Come on,' I say, 'we should get moving. I want to show you Liberty Falls, and we don't want to get caught up in whatever's coming.'

Ella glances up. 'I thought summer in Colorado is meant to be hot.'

'Either bright sunshine or thunderstorms from hell. Nothing in between.'

*

Even though the sun has well and truly disappeared by the time we reach Liberty Falls, it's still a beautiful sight. It's the highest waterfall in this part of the Rockies and it's gorgeous. Water cascades over a curved, sheer drop into a crystal-clear basin. On sunny days, you can see rainbows in the water. Today though, it's kinda moody at the same time as being striking.

'I love it,' Ella says. 'I wish I could bottle this feeling and take it back with me to Denver. I could take a sip of this crazy, free feeling and just feel close to nature again. Makes me feel like one of those fawns.' She turns to look at me. 'Although I guess that would make you my Daddy deer, not a momma like the one we saw.' There's a wicked look on her face.

*Don't give in, Joel. You nearly made a mistake back there on the path, almost gave in and kissed her. Don't do it. Nothing good will come of it.*

'Shame I don't have antlers.' It doesn't really mean anything. I'm just so flustered by Ella that I'm scrabbling around for something to say to reduce the heat.

'You don't have... any kind of horn?'

As soon as she speaks, I feel my cock tugging at my pants, reminding me that I *do* have a horn, and that there's nothing I'd like more than to use it.

'This is real naughty talk,' I say, shifting from foot to foot.

'I could do with some discipline,' she says, biting her lip and stepping towards me. 'Someone big and strong to make sure I stay in line.'

'Maybe you could,' I grunt, looking down at the ground.

She huffs. 'I can't believe I didn't bring my bikini. I'd love to have a dip in the water. What a missed opportunity.'

I try not to think about her in a bikini, try not to think about the curves of her body, tumbling from skimpy fabric. I fail.

'Well, it's a shame we didn't think to bring anything,' I say. I wish I could bite my fist, scream, do anything to dissipate this pressure, this intense crackle of sexuality between us.

Ella's eyes widen. 'What about skinny dipping? You ever done it? You seem to like taking your top off. You could show me if you've got any other tattoos.'

I've never met anyone like her. She's so vulnerable but so fierce. So tender, but so forward.

She's perfect.

'Ella, I—'

I'm about to say yes, that I'd love to go skinny dipping with her. I'm about to give in, to follow my cock, follow my heart, follow my head. But I don't get the chance. Because there's an almighty crack from the sky, and a moment later, rain starts to fall, hard as bullets, from the silver sky.

'We've gotta go,' I say, wiping the rain from my face.

'Now?'

'Now. This isn't like a normal thunderstorm. It's dangerous. There'll be fire.'

She pauses. Then nods. Then her eyes widen with fear. 'Look. Smoke.'

# ELLA

I DON'T LIKE THUNDER. I like lightning even less. Put the two together, and you've got one terrified Little girl.

The weather changed so quickly that I didn't even realize. I was enjoying spending time with Joel so much that I barely looked up at the sky.

I even suggested that we go skinny dipping, which is kind of insane when you consider that I'm wearing a fricking diaper right now. I don't know what my plan was. Maybe I'd have hidden behind a tree somewhere or something. Who knows?

Maybe I'd have just showed him who I really am. I get the feeling that he wouldn't mind. That he wouldn't judge. I promised myself I'm never getting involved with anyone who doesn't know I'm a Little ever again.

But those thoughts can wait. Right now, I'm dodging lightning bolts in a torrential downpour.

'Keep going,' says Joel, as I cower from another flash. Almost instantly, the sound of thunder rolls around us.

'That was close,' I say, my voice tiny among the drumming of the rain. The smell is so intense. I always love the scent of rain, but this is ridiculous. It's like I can smell the whole planet coming alive. All the trees, all the ferns, all the tiny organisms in the mud underfoot. It's a rich, musty smell, and for some reason it's linked in my head with Joel.

We're both soaking wet now. He, of course, looks incredible. His plaid shirt is stuck to his hard body, and his hair is plastered onto his forehead. Rivulets of water stream down his cheeks and into his thick stubble.

I, on the other hand, must look awful. Just my luck. I can imagine my mascara trailing down my face and my hair stuck to my skin like a drowned rat.

Ugh.

Another crash of thunder, and this one's so close I let out a scream.

'You OK?' Joel stops, looking back at me with concern in his eyes.

'Yeah,' I say, 'just not good with storms.'

He walks over to me. 'Don't worry,' he says, putting his hands on my shoulders, 'you're safe with me, I promise. I said I was gonna look after you this holiday, and I always keep my word.'

Even though they're just words, and I know there's no real way that he can stop a random bolt of lightning from zapping me into oblivion, but there's something about the way he says it that fills me with warmth.

'Come on,' he says, rain pelting his handsome face, 'let's keep going. We can watch the storm from the lookout tower if you want. Nothing better for curing fears than facing them.'

He holds out a hand to me and I gladly take it. Then, he starts leading me up the hill, through the trees, back towards the cabins.

As we get closer to the cabin, I can feel his anxiety growing a little. Because the closer we get, the thicker the smoke.

And when we finally reach the top of the hill, Joel pauses, his face a mask of horror.

'Oh no!' he cries out.

I follow his gaze up to the guest cabin, and my own face mirrors his shock and surprise. The smoke *isn't* coming from either of the cabins. It's coming from a nearby tree trunk, which smolders and glows, despite the driving rain.

But that's not the reason for Joel's dismay.

The body of the tree that must have been struck by lightning has completely flattened the guest cabin. My cabin. The huge trunk of the fir tree lies across the cabin, and all of Joel's hard, careful work is strewn all around the place. Glass shattered. Walls splintered. Dreams destroyed.

'Your stuff!' Joel says. It's not what I expected him to say at all. Is he really more concerned with my possessions than he is with the destruction of his cabin?

'Never mind my stuff,' I start to say, but Joel's already sprinting towards the cabin. He wrenches open the door and heads in. I follow him in. It's a tragedy. The roof of the cabin — the roof he was repairing just yesterday — is totally destroyed. Rain pours in through the hole in the roof, drenching the inside of the space. The bear rug is soaking wet, and the deer head lies on the floor, one of its antlers is broken off.

'Ella, what's this?' There's a note of surprise in his voice.

I duck under a cracked, splintered beam, and join him in what was the bedroom. When I see what he's looking at, I feel a tremor of fear and self-disgust that almost knocks me flat.

The tree smashed the wardrobe where I'd put all my things. Including my diapers. Now, the white, puffy things are strewn around the room like confetti at a wedding. Joel has picked one of them up — it's covered in tiny tiger cubs, dressed in sports uniforms. His face looks so confused, so surprised, that I think I might just pass out right here and now.

I try to speak, I really do, but I can't bring myself to say a single word.

What must he be thinking about me? It's like Pete all over again. Joel was into me — I could tell. Now he's just going to think that I'm a freak. A pervert. I can't deal with it. I'm trembling, rain still pouring down my face. And then, I do the same thing that I always do when I feel ashamed and vulnerable. I turn around and I run.

As I stumble my way down into the forest again, I don't know what's going on in my mind. I'm not acting rationally, I'm just acting on instinct. Adrenaline's pumping around my body, and it's making me run.

I pass trees and roots, and somewhere behind me, I hear Joel running after me, shouting my name, telling me to stop. But I can't stop. I don't want him to catch me. I don't want anyone to ever catch me.

The rain makes everything slippery, and I keep almost falling, my hiking boots sliding over soaked logs, over patches of slick mud. I can feel flecks of dirt coating my legs as I run faster and faster. I can't handle it, can't deal with being humiliated like this again.

'Ella, please, wait,' Joel bellows, his voice even closer to me now.

I don't reply, I can't. My breathing is hoarse and quick. I can't keep up this pace for long. My legs are getting tired.

There's another crack of thunder, and it's so close that I freeze, then shriek. It's like my emotions are being assaulted, like I'm at the mercy of raging forces out of my control. When I try to move again, my tired legs can't manage it. I fall forward, and as I do, my shorts catch on something sharp, a jutting, splintered tree branch. There's a hideous tear, and as I fall, my humiliation is complete. I land, my diaper on full display, sodden and caked in muddy filth.

I feel tears pricking my eyes, and I think about those tears, about how they'll get lost in the rain. Then, before I have too much chance to feel sorry for myself, he's there, right next to me.

'You poor, sweet creature,' he says. 'It's not your day, is it?'

'I'm not sweet,' I say, the rain beating down on me. 'I'm a freak. A weirdo. A p-pervert.' I'm sobbing now, head hunched over and body covered in mud.

Suddenly, I feel Joel's hand on my shoulder. 'Sweetheart,' he says, 'if you're a pervert, I don't know what that makes me.'

I sob again.

'Come on,' he continues, squeezing my shoulder. 'I need to get you back up to the house. And you need a change.'

The way he says change sends a thrill down my spine. Is he just talking about my clothes, or could he mean something else?

I sniff as he helps me up.

'You got so dirty, didn't you, baby?' His voice is soft and tender, like he's wrapping me up in his words.

'Uh-huh,' I say. I instinctively pop my thumb in my mouth and suck it. I feel calmer. I wish I had my pacifier right now. It's back at the cabin. Mind you, it's probably been crushed by the fallen tree.

'If you put some trust in me,' he says, stooping to pick up my shredded shorts, 'then I can make you feel a lot better. You see, I know something about Little girls like you.'

I'm using his strength to walk, leaning in on him as he guides me back up the steep, slippery hill. 'You know about Littles?'

He grunts in the affirmative. 'I know what you need. Affection. Guidance. Firm boundaries. But right now, I know that you need a bath, and you need a new diapee. Then, maybe, if you're good, you can have a nice hot cup of cocoa.'

'You'd do that for me?' I ask.

His face, damp from the rain and streaked with mud, breaks into a wide, satisfied smile. 'Of course. It's what Daddies are meant to do.'

'Thank you.'

'So,' he says, pausing for a moment, 'are you gonna put your trust in me?'

*

'You built this, too?'

'Not exactly,' he says, 'but I installed it, if that's what you mean. I think you kind of need to be an expert to design and install a hot tub.'

The bathroom in Joel's cabin is absolutely incredible. It's so modern and light, and it's the only part of the place that doesn't feel like it's a rustic, ramshackle cabin. No, this feels like I'm in the luxurious surroundings of some five-star hotel somewhere.

'It's really nice,' I say.

'Come on now, let's get you out of those muddy things. Daddy's gonna look after you now, Ella.'

I nod.

Joel steps forward. 'Arms up, sweetie. Let's get that filthy top off you.'

I do as he asks, relieved that he's taking control of the situation. Then, I feel his fingers as they take hold of the bottom of my top. He lifts it up, peeling the soaking wet fabric away from my skin. As his fingers touch me, I tremble in excitement.

'Feels nice,' I mumble.

'Good,' he says, tugging it up, over my chin, and then, with a final move, whisks the dirty old rag away from me. 'Do you want me to take that fiddly bra off?' he asks. He looks at my breasts for a moment, and I blush when I see lust in his eyes.

'Please,' I say. 'It's too complicated.'

He comes in close and reaches his arms around behind me. He's so close I can feel the heat of his body, a nourishing, reassuring wave of warmth. He unclips the bra and I feel my breasts relax. If I had my way, I'd never wear a damn bra. So much better to be free and comfy.

I'm impressed by how respectful Joel is being. He barely looks at my bare form. All he seems to care about is putting me at ease, making sure that I'm happy. It's a wonderful feeling.

'OK sugar,' he says, 'now why don't you lie down on this towel and I'll get that diaper off? You must be so uncomfortable in that thing. It looks like it's gonna burst.'

He lays a big yellow towel down on the ground, and I lie down on it as he asks. As this is all going on, I'm getting so fricking excited. Everything he's doing, every word, every expression — it's everything I've always wanted in a Daddy. It all feels so innocent, but there's a burning flame of attraction between us, fueling everything we do.

'I'm gonna undo this now, sweetie,' he says, resting his hands on my diaper and looking me in the eyes. The pressure of his hands on me makes me think some naughty thoughts.

Then, without another word, he undoes the tabs on the diaper and frees me from it. It's such a relief to have cool air on my skin.

'Thank you,' I say.

He leans in, kissing the top of my head. 'You're welcome, baba. Now, let's get you in the bath.'

# JOEL

I HAVE TO KEEP pinching myself. You know, figuratively. The most beautiful woman I've ever met is in my hot tub right now. Naked. And, to top it all off, she's a Little. It's crazy. It's unbelievable. And yet, it's happening.

'Head back, sweetheart,' I say. 'We don't want any shampoo going in your eyes.'

She leans her beautiful head back, lengthening her smooth neck, closing her eyes as I run the sponge over her hair.

'Can I have some more bubble bath?' she asks, her voice as sweet and innocent as can be.

'Sure,' I say. 'But this is the last bit, OK? Don't wanna overfill the tub.'

She nods. I grab the liquid and pour a capful into the frothy water.

'I feel much better now,' she says, stretching out in the tub. 'Thank you for helping me.'

'It's the least I could do,' I reply. 'And I'll reimburse you for all the stuff that got smashed in the cabin.' I feel a pang of sadness. 'Can't believe it got crushed like that. Of all the things that coulda happened to the cabin, I honestly never thought it'd go out like that.'

'I'm sorry,' she says. Then her face brightens. 'Hey, now you've got the chance to rebuild it. Make it even better.'

I let out a snort of laughter. 'I guess you're right. Every cloud has a silver lining. Just that this silver lining involves six months of hard work from me.'

'Sorry, Daddy,' she says. She scoops up a handful of foam and blows it toward me. The bubbles float through the air. 'I didn't know it would take so long to re-make.'

'Ah, it's OK,' I say. 'I'll have to cancel my other Airbnb bookings for the foreseeable future, of course. But who cares? It's not like I need the money.'

She looks confused. 'Then why do you let people stay?'

'I wanted to share this place with the world,' I say. 'It's so beautiful here, I want people to be able to see it. But tourism in this area needs to be carefully managed. If too many people come, then the wilderness would be ruined.'

'Big words,' Ellas says, her brow knitting.

'That's alright, pet,' I say, stroking her hair. 'It's boring, grown-up stuff. What do you do for money?'

She holds out her hand toward me. She's still wearing the silver snake ring I noticed the first time I met her.

'I make jewelry,' she says. 'Like this.'

'You made that?' I ask. It's so beautiful, so intricately detailed. The craft on this thing is incredible.

'Yep,' she says, nodding enthusiastically. 'You like it?'

She looks so damn beautiful. It's been so hard for me to not stare at her. Just looking at her face, with those big, wide-open blue eyes, those soft lips, it's enough to make me bristle with lust.

'It looks amazing.' I say.

She loosens the ring, removes it, and puts it into my hand.

'It's an ouroboros,' she says.

'Tail-eater,' I say.

She nods. 'I wear it to remind myself not to eat myself up.'

I laugh. 'Is that a problem for you?' I move the snake in my hand, marveling at the way the light plays off the silver surface.

'Silly Daddy! Only meta...me... only in a way. I mean, it reminds me not to over-analyze myself. That it's OK to just be me.'

'Yep. 'Cause if you over-analyze yourself, it ends up destroying you,' I say, nodding.

'You get it.'

'Course I do. I feel the same way.'

'Maybe I'll make one for you,' she says.

'That would be wonderful.'

She holds up her fingers to the light. 'Look, I'm turning into a prune.'

'We better get you out then,' I say.

I hold up a towel to the side of the hot tub, and Ella steps out. I wrap her up in the warm, soft thing.

'I feel human again!' she says, stretching up. Her skin has gone a cute pink color, and her cheeks look all rosy.

'Good,' I say. 'Because I only really let humans stay at my place.'

'Hey!' she says, suddenly worried. 'Where am I gonna sleep? Do I have to sleep in the guest cabin? With all the... trees and rain?'

'No way,' I say. Somewhere in the distance, a low growl of thunder reverberates around the world. The storm is still going strong. 'You can sleep in my bed. I'll take the couch so that you can get a good night's sleep. Obviously, if you'd rather just get away from here, I can walk you to Little Creek tomorrow.'

'No way,' she says. 'I want to stay.' Her eyes flick down. 'As long as I can.'

'Well, OK,' I say. I hope she can't hear how excited I feel. Don't want to put her off.

'Now Daddy, I think I need my diaper.'

We managed to retrieve a few diapers from the cabin. There were about four that weren't completely trashed by the falling tree. I haven't ever put a diaper on a Little before, and I've got to say that I'm a little nervous. I'm gonna stick to the old adage: fake it 'til you make it.

'Lie down for me, Little girl,' I say. I manage to keep the excitement out of my voice.

She lies on a fresh towel, and then, without me needing to ask her, she undoes the towel around her body, and it falls to the ground. Her body is slim and lithe but with incredible curves. My eyes stray to her stomach, to the soft mound of pubic hair beneath it.

'OK, lift your legs up, darling,' I say.

With a cute little grunt, she rolls her legs up and grabs them with her hands.

'Good girl,' I say, then I slip the diaper under her butt. It's a big piece of fabric, but so far, I think I'm doing a good job for her.

She wriggles a little then lets her legs fall down to the ground with a thump.

'Time to strap you in. I'm gonna pull this tight, OK? I don't want you having any accidents. I want you safe and secure and confident tonight.'

I lift the central flap up, pulling it hard, then I secure the diaper so that there's no way that she's ever going to get out of this.

'Feels tight,' she says, grimacing a little. 'It's good.'

'Now, I think you should relax while I sort things out in the guest place. I'm gonna bring your stuff in and clear away some of the debris. Why don't you head into the snug and I'll be in soon? After that, I'll make us some dinner. I bet you're hungry as a horse.'

She nods, raising herself up onto her butt. 'I'm hungry as a really hungry horse.' She says. 'A giant, really hungry horse.'

'I bet.'

*

My priority is Ella's stuff, and I bring it over as quickly as I can, putting it by the fireplace in the lounge. After I've got everything in, all her clothes and bags, I arrange split logs in the hearth, before stuffing old newspaper in between them. When it's crackling and warm, I arrange all the wet things so that they'll dry quickly. Ella is curled up on the couch, watching me work.

'You're clever,' she says. 'Lighting a fire is hard.'

I shake my head. 'Nah. I'm just stubborn. When I first got here, I couldn't do any of this stuff. Couldn't split logs, and all the fires I started fizzled out in minutes. But I don't give up. It's a strength, but a weakness, too.'

'A weakness.'

'Yep. I don't know when to quit.'

She must be able to sense the sadness in my voice because she's quiet for a moment. Then, in a tiny voice, she says. 'You wanna talk about it?'

I purse my lips, then I throw another log on the fire. I can't believe I'm about to tell someone about this, but I can't help myself. 'Well,' I say, sitting down next to Ella on the couch, 'it's a long story. Or maybe it's short. I guess it depends.'

'You're stalling, Daddy,' she says, smiling, resting her head on my lap.

I'm nervous because I don't want her to think I don't know what I'm doing. That I'm not the experienced Daddy I seem to be. She's clearly experienced with ABDL stuff. You don't wear nappies all the time if you're just dipping your toe in. 'You got me,' I finally say. Then,

I decide to just come clean. 'Look, I'm nervous because you seem so confident about yourself, so sure about your, well, your sexuality, I guess. Your identity.'

She looks up at me. 'You're kidding, right? I'm terrified of people finding out.'

'Well, I mean, thing is...' I'm struggling to think of the best way into this. 'OK. I've never been in a DDlg relationship before. The woman I told you about, the reason I left New York, she wasn't into it. I told her about my fantasies, about the type of relationship I wanted to have, and she was disgusted. It took months to convince her that I'd only been joking.'

'But you weren't joking, right?'

'Of course not. But I didn't want to lose her. And I didn't want her to think I was a freak.'

Her hand strokes my thigh, urging me to keep going.

'So,' I say, 'we stayed together for years. The whole time, I knew it was wrong, that it was going to end. I wasted my time. I wasted her time. I cared for her, but because I wasn't honest with myself, I hurt her. And then, inevitably, she ended up hurting me.' A heavy sigh. I don't like to think about that time. 'Of course, she ended up cheating on me. It was my fault. I was living a lie, and I couldn't pretend to be happy. But I wouldn't quit. I was stubborn.'

'You poor thing,' she says.

'Poor thing?' I ask, raising an eyebrow. 'It was my fault.'

'Nah,' she says, yawning. 'It was no-one's fault. You two just weren't right for each other. But obviously, there were deep feelings. And you *were* honest with her, at the start. That must have been hard.'

I've been so scared of being judged for so long that hearing Ella's sensitive, thoughtful take on the situation is deeply moving. 'It was rough. I kinda knew she'd be surprised, but I hadn't been prepared for how *disgusted* she was. It was like I'd told her I was a murderer or something.'

'At least you told her,' she says. Her voice is quiet and tired, and I can feel her slipping into sleep. 'You tried. Not like me.'

Then she turns over, and I hear her breathing change, and I know that she's drifted off. I lean in and kiss her hair. Her head is heavy on my lap, and my heart is heavy in my chest. There's a slow-building tenderness in me, equally exciting and terrifying. Could I have really found *my* Little Girl? Could she be the one?

I sit like that for half an hour, until I feel Ella is deep enough into sleep for me to move. Then, like in that scene at the start of Indiana Jones with the golden idol, I replace my legs with a bulky cushion. She mumbles something but stays asleep. I grab an old bearskin blanket and throw it over her, then I lie down on the floor in front of her.

*

When I wake the next morning, it takes me a moment or two before I realize where I am. Then, a moment more before I remember to look up behind me to see Ella. But when I do, she's not there.

It's only one more moment before I hear sounds coming from outside the cabin.

A male voice. Shouting. And then, a panicked sob.

# ELLA

WHEN I WOKE UP this morning, I felt happy for the first time in months. All my niggling worries, all the problems I'd been dealing with seemed totally insignificant.

I was covered in a thick, soft blanket, and Joel — that beautiful, fierce, sensitive man — was lying down on the floor beneath me. Felt like he'd been up all night, protecting me.

I guess he was probably sleeping though.

Technically, I'm Joel's paying guest here, but I had an urge to make breakfast for him this morning. He gave me exactly what I needed last night: space and understanding. He was honest with me, too, and I could tell it was difficult for him. Something happened between us: the birth of trust.

I could hear the sounds outside. The birds, the rustle of leaves in the warm breeze. Thank goodness the storm was over. I decided that before I made breakfast or did anything else today, I was gonna head outside, and catch the end of the sunrise.

I carefully shuffled off the couch and tiptoed my way out. Joel looked so damn cute on the floor. It's kinda funny to think of a man as big and strong as Joel looking cute, but it's true. I think it's his long eyelashes. As he quietly breathed, they gave him the look of a beautiful deer — strong and masculine, but also lithe and elegant.

The view outside was sensational. Life is always best after a storm. The clouds skitter away, the sting of the rain is just a memory, and birdsong replaces rumbles of thunder. I took a big lungful of air and sighed. Today was gonna be a good day.

I'm still standing out here, enjoying the view, when suddenly, I hear a voice.

'I found you.'

The blood in my veins turns to ice. Because from the shadows underneath the trees, emerges a lanky, tall figure. It's Pete. And he's here.

I'm so shocked, it takes me a second to realize I'm just standing there with my mouth hanging open. Then, my senses come rushing back to me like water over a cliff.

'What the fuck are you doing here?'

My heart is pounding, my mouth is dry. What's wrong with Pete? He looks really bad. Haggard and exhausted. There are heavy shadows underneath his pale blue eyes, and three-day stubble on his chin. It's not like the thick, prickly stubble on Joel's chin, though. More like bum-fluff. Still, this is the worst I've ever seen him look.

He steps forward, totally in the sunlight now. It's almost like he's swaying a little.

'What do you *think* I'm doing here?' he asks, his eyes crazed, his brow pricked with sweat. 'I'm here to find you. And I'm here to save you.'

I look around me, raising my hands up in a gesture of utter confusion. 'Save me from what, Pete? The trees?'

I'm furious and I can't hide it. At times like this, I lash out with sarcasm.

He snorts. 'I'm here to save you from yourself.'

How *has* he found me? I didn't tell him where I was coming. He's the last person I would have told.

'Well, thanks for your thought and your consideration,' I say, my voice dripping with sarcasm, 'but I don't think I need protection from myself. Feels more like I need protection from you.'

He looks down, shakes his head, hands on hips.

'I've been thinking, Ella, and we're not breaking up.'

'Excuse me?'

'You heard me. We're getting back together. I'm going to change you. Help you realize that you're not a baby. You're a fully-grown woman, and you need to wake up. It wasn't easy for me to get here. And I'm not leaving without you.'

He's talking quickly, and there's a manic edge to his voice. Then it dawns on me. He must have hacked my email. That's the only way he could have found out that I'd be here, in the forest.

'I need to change my passwords, don't I?'

He looks at me with rage in his eyes. 'I had to check up on you, babe. I can't have you doing something stupid.'

'Listen,' I say, trying to meet his anger with my own. 'I'm going to ask you to leave now. Did you honestly think that I would take you back? All you've done is confirmed all my suspicions about you. All you've ever wanted is to have me as a pet. You say you want me to grow up, but you don't. You want to dominate me, but the trouble is, I'm not interested in that, not unless it's on my terms.'

He laughs — a sick, twisted sound.

'You'll never find someone who wants to be with you, you fucking freak. I'm doing you a huge favor by coming here and rescuing you.'

'You're not rescuing me,' I say.

'I am.'

That's when I see it. He brings his arm out from behind his back and he's holding something. A long, silvery thing, sharp and terrifying. A blade.

'Pete, wha—'

'Shut up,' he spits, lips thin and teeth glinting. 'You're gonna come with me now. I need you, Ella. I'm taking you back to Denver, and then we're gonna pay our rent, and we're gonna carry on as though everything's normal. Everything's good again.'

I'm trembling. No-one's ever pulled a knife on me before. Seeing it there, the point so close to me, the thought of what it could do to me so, it's paralyzing.

'P-Pete,' I stutter, 'don't do this. It's... insane.'

'You leave me no choice. You think I can tell my parents that you dumped me? A month before the wedding? You think I can tell my friends? All of them told me you weren't good enough for me. And now, you're the one that gets to dump me? I don't think so. We're getting married.' He lunges toward me. 'Say it!'

I cower backward, my arms trembling. There are sobs lodged in my throat. I feel so powerless again. But I'm not. I'm not going to let him bully me like this. I think about Joel. Think about how brave he'd been yesterday, showing himself to me. He's not ashamed of who he is. And neither am I.

'No,' I say, standing up tall. 'You don't scare me, Pete. And we're not going to get married. I'm a Little. Can't change. Don't want to change. It's not just something you can pretend isn't real. It's not just part of who I am. It *is* who I am. And I need a Daddy who can look after me. A real man. Not a pathetic wretch like you.'

His eyes are narrow and rat-like, his hands twitchy and anxious.

'You're filth,' he says.

'Whatever I am,' I say, 'I'm proud to be me.'

Pete is right next to me now, so close that I can smell his breath. It's laced with booze — a filthy, acrid stench that hits me like a wall. It's starting to make sense. The pieces are falling into place. He's wasted, probably has been since I broke up with him. Doesn't have the money to pay the rent anymore, now that my income is gone, and besides all that, he obviously can't handle telling the people closest to him what happened between us.

He holds the knife up to my throat. I'm frozen, like a rabbit trapped in headlights.

'Now what the fuck do you think you're doing, Pussycat?'

The voice behind me is low and rolling, a guttural, dominant growl that fills my heart with hope and strength. Pete's eyes widen.

'Who are you?' His voice has changed. All the confidence that was there a second ago is gone. Now it's hollow — the voice of a little boy being told off by his mommy.

'I'm the guy who knocks the knife from your hand then smacks you so hard you forget which way is up and which is down.'

A sickly grin spreads across Pete's face. 'Get back inside o—'

I can't see what happens behind me, but I see what happens to Pete. It's a small stone, nothing that's gonna cause him any permanent damage, but it zips hard into the side of his temple. It's enough of a distraction that he drops the knife away from me, just for a moment. Long enough.

Joel surges past me, and I see the muscles of his bare back bunch and flex as his hand smacks into Pete's gut. He drops the knife, lets out a deep yowl of pain, and within seconds, Joel is behind him, holding him tight, making sure that he can't move.

'Ella, in my bedside table there are handcuffs. Grab them for me.'

Shaking but steady, I head into the house, get the handcuffs, and come back out again.

'How come you've got handcuffs?' I ask. Pete is struggling a little, but there's no way that he's gonna break Joel's iron grip.

'Exactly for situations like this,' Joel says. 'Cops aren't coming out to a place like this, so if anyone breaks into the cabin, I have to apprehend them and take them to Little Creek.'

'You're taking me to the police?' Pete says, his voice a pathetic whine.

Joel lets out a wry laugh. 'You're lucky I don't just leave you out for the bears.'

The handcuffs make a snappy click when they fasten around his wrists. It's the sweetest sound I've ever heard.

# JOEL

LITTLE CREEK IS A picturesque town, nestled between two mountains, covered in green coats of fir trees. The Sheriff's office is a squat, square building. I park my pickup straight outside.

'Please,' Pete pleads, 'Ella, there's things you don't know about me. You can't take me into the cops. I'll go to jail.'

'Maybe that's what you need,' Ella says. Her voice is soft. I can tell that even though Pete shook her, she still cares for this guy. Not in a romantic way — that much is obvious — but in the way all of us care for the people in our lives. A quiet, empathetic tug of feeling. 'Maybe you need a reality check.'

He sobs.

'Look, son,' I say. I don't mean it to sound patronizing, but I'm sure that's the way it comes out. 'There's no way that I'm not gonna take you in. You pulled a knife on my Little Girl. You trespassed on my property. And I can tell from the way you keep twitching and sniffing that you're high on something.'

Ella looks shocked.

'Is that true, Pete?'

He can't meet her accusatory gaze, but he nods, eyes down.

'Why?'

'There's a lot you don't know about me.'

It's kind of crazy that Ella could be in a relationship with Pete and not realize that he's got a drug problem. But then again, when you care for someone, it kind of makes you naive. That's what happened with Sadie. I trusted her. She cheated on me for years. Never woulda found out if she hadn't told me.

There's a look of deep sadness on Ella's face. It's painful to see those big eyes look so despondent. I hope I can cheer her up soon. I've had enough of thunderstorms and crazed exes. I just want Ella to have the chance to play and relax. She came to Little Creek for a vacation, but her problems just followed her here.

'Pete, you're coming with me. Ella, honey, I want you to stay in the car, OK? You just relax. Everything's gonna be OK.'

She nods and gives me a tiny little smile. I know she must be hurting now, poor thing.

Pete shuffles out of the car. A few people on Main Street watch as I march him out of the pickup and into the front of the Sheriff's office. His hands are cuffed behind his back. I guess I must look kinda like a bounty hunter, bringing in a bail bond. I wonder what they'd all think if they knew I was just an ex investment banker.

I explain the situation to Angela, the receptionist.

'You're in luck,' she says. 'Carl was just about to head out on patrol, but I'm sure he'll want to deal with this personally.'

Carl's an interesting character — you can tell from the way he decorates his office. From what he tells me, until around five years ago, he was a bare-knuckle fighter. He'd travel around Colorado, challenging other fighters to underground, mostly illegal boxing matches. That all changed, though, when he almost died. Had a change of heart. Ever since then, he's been more philosophical, and he's dedicated his life to law and order, making his little part of the world as safe and reliable as it can possibly be.

The space is *full* of plants. Succulents, flowers, trailing vines; there must be twenty different shades of green in here, all vying for attention. It's not exactly to my taste, but it's kinda beautiful too. In stark contrast to the elegant shoots and leaves are the boxing posters. Iconic images of Mohammed Ali, Mike Tyson, Tyson Fury. The powerful men look down on the room, scowls on their faces, muscles bulging, sweat on their brows.

'So this punk pulled a knife on a lady?'

'That's about the size of it,' I say, nodding grimly.

Carl's even bigger than me, and even though he's sitting down, his bulk is clearly visible. Pete is quiet as a mouse right now. He must be coming down off whatever upper he took earlier this morning, whatever substance gave him enough courage and dulled his reason enough to make the crazy move of threatening Ella the way he did.

'Trespass too?'

'I'm sorry,' says Pete.

'You're responsible for your actions,' says Carl. 'Just like all of us. Doesn't matter how sorry you are. Although, if it makes you feel any better, I'm *sorry* that I have to arrest you. Don't like doing it. You're obviously struggling with a few things. Got issues, huh?'

Pete nods. I unlock the handcuffs at his wrists.

'Trouble is,' says Carl, standing up, 'we've all got issues.' He strokes one of his plants. 'How you deal with those issues is what makes you a man. Maybe you should take up horticulture. Damn near saved my life.'

\*

Before long, Pete is being processed by one of the deputies in the station, and Carl and I are alone. I'm gonna head back out to Ella, but I just want a minute with my friend.

'Carl, can I ask your advice on something?'

'Sure you can, Bud.' He leans back in his chair, between the ferns and fighters.

'The girl he threatened, the girl who's staying as a guest in my cabin...' I trail off.

'You care about her, don't you?'

'Is it that obvious?'

He grins. 'As obvious as the fuckin' thunder from last night's storm. No — more obvious. What's more obvious than thunder? A volcano?'

I shake my head. 'I dunno man, but the point is: she's a Little, too. Lives in Denver. I feel like she's perfect for me. It's just, I can feel it happening again. Like, I'm opening my heart to her, and I don't know if I can handle it getting broken a second time.'

He looks me in the eye, his cool gaze as confident and self-assured as a mountain lion.

'Joel, what's the point of having a heart if there's no risk of it getting broke?'

*

'Roll down the window,' I mouth, miming with my hand.

Ella does as she's told then looks up at me with a soft smile on her face. 'Is it all done?' she asks in a tiny voice.

'It's done. I asked Carl to go easy on him. I know that he's got problems, that kid. But he does need a shock. Something to let him know that he needs to change his ways. '

She nods and purses her lips.

'You know what,' I say. 'It's been a long morning already, and we haven't had any breakfast.'

'I was gonna make you something,' she says, looking disappointed. 'To say thank you for looking after me last night.'

'Well that's very kind, sweetie, but since we're here, in civilization, what do you think about getting a huge stack of pancakes? Ice-cream, strawberries, maple syrup, whatever you feel like.'

Her eyes light up. 'Ice cream for breakfast?'

'Is that all you heard?'

'Ice-cream for breakfast!'

We head for a little diner called Tracy's. It's the only place to get breakfast in town, but, lucky for us, it's damn good. It's a rare treat for me to come into town, and, even though I enjoy my isolation, it's kinda fun to be around other people, too. It's a shame the circumstances of our visit aren't different, but if there's one thing I'm good at, it's making the most of a crappy situation.

We sit in a booth by the big windows, and we watch the people of this quiet mountain town walk up and down the street. Ella orders her pancakes, and I get eggs and bacon with a large black coffee.

This morning the weather's so beautiful that it seems almost impossible to remember yesterday's storm. Ella looks relaxed as she tucks into her breakfast.

'I hated seeing you scared this morning,' I say.

'I hated being scared.'

I reach out across the table and take her hand. 'I don't ever want to see you scared again.'

She squeezes my fingers.

'Look,' I say, 'I know you're meant to be heading back to Denver tomorrow, but I was thinking, maybe you don't have to go back so early.'

'Maybe.' She takes a sip of her chocolate milk.

'Maybe,' I say, drawing in breath sharply, 'you don't have to go back at all.'

I see the excitement in her eyes.

'I don't even have to rebuild the guest cabin,' I say, stroking her soft fingers. 'I could build you a special place next to the cabin. Like, a play-room. Or a big nursery. And not just that. I'd build you a workshop for jewelry-making. I bet you could run a business from out here if you wanted to. We could head into Little Creek once a week, and post your masterpieces off all over the country. Bet we can get supplies for you without much trouble.'

She waits for a moment. There's a little chocolate mustache on her top lip. She licks it away.

'That sounds w—'

'Breakfast!' It's Tracy, carrying two huge plates, full of food. Talk about crummy timing. She puts the plates down in front of us, and Ella's eyes light up. She's an amazing woman, with such a free spirit. Now that her food's here, she can't tear herself away, even for a second, even though we were just talking about something so important. It's a bit frustrating, but as I watch her rip into the fluffy stack of pancakes, I realize something.

She lives in the moment, every moment. She's in Little Space right now, carefree and happy, and it must mean that she feels comfortable around me.

While we eat, all she can talk about is how delicious everything is and about how happy she feels. The instant she finishes her chocolate milk, she looks up at me with innocent eyes. 'Can I get another one?'

I shake my head. 'No way, cutie. One chocolate milk is quite enough for now. Too much is bad for your teeth. You know that.'

She gives a sulky look, but I can see a hint of a smile, too. She's testing her boundaries, seeing what she can get away with. And even though they might not admit it, every Little *loves* boundaries. 'OK, Daddy.' Then, she mumbles under her breath: 'Boring, silly teeth.'

'Nothing boring about good dental hygiene,' I say.

'If I live with you, will I have to brush my teeth every day?'

'Twice a day,' I confirm.

'Ugh,' she says. 'And floss?'

'One hundred percent. And if you skip it, there will be consequences, young lady.' I make my voice a little stern to let her know I'm serious.'

'Good consequences?'

'Sometimes they'll be good. Sometimes you might have to do something for Daddy that Daddy really likes. But if you keep being naughty, there will be more serious repercussions. Do you understand?'

'And if I'm a good girl, can I have a gold star?'

'I tell you what,' I say. 'Why don't we go back to the cabin, and I'll show you exactly what you'll get if you're a good girl?'

Her eyes sparkle, her mouth is fixed in a wide grin. 'OK,' she says. Then she licks her lips and pushes the last bit of her pancake into her hot, sticky mouth.

# ELLA

As WE DRIVE BACK to the cabin in the pickup, I feel like something momentous is going to happen. I've got the windows down and the breeze is blowing in my hair. The forest smells incredible — like life itself. It's been a crazy morning. Seeing Pete and being threatened like that was horrendous. But ever since we dropped him off at the sheriff's place, it's like a weight has been lifted from my heart.

It's not like I expected Pete to show up and brandish a knife at me. I could never have guessed that. But I had *known* that things with Pete weren't over. Now, hopefully, they are.

At breakfast, I felt myself deep in Little Space. I was being myself. And that lovely, yummy, cute glow is still with me, still making me feel like I'm living each moment to the full.

'You OK there, baby?' Daddy asks, looking over at me. He's got one hand on the wheel and the other rests on the rim of the rolled-down window.

'Mmmhmm,' I say. 'The air tastes yummy.'

'That's all the bugs,' he says, grinning.

'Yuck! It's not the bugs. Silly Daddy. It's the flowers and the trees.' I breathe in deeply. 'Smells nice.'

'Hopefully soon it's gonna smell like home to you.'

My heart starts to pound. Could I really leave my place in Denver and just come out here to live? Even though I've only just met Joel, I feel like I trust him implicitly. I get the impression that if I did agree to live with him, and then changed my mind, he'd be really cool about it.

You know, he wouldn't show up to my new place and pull a knife on me, is what I'm saying.

'Did you ever miss city life?' I ask.

'I didn't,' he says. 'But I know that not everyone's like me. You know, I was thinking about setting up something special here, Ella. A vacation cabin, especially for Bigs and their Littles. A cabin where people can come and stay, get away from their normal lives, and stay in Little Space the whole time.'

'That's a wonderful idea.' I say. 'We could have a nursery and a hot tub. Oh, oh and we could build a jungle gym!'

'We?' he asks.

Damn, I hadn't meant to say *we*. It had just come out. But when I think about it, I hate the thought of Joel living out here without me. It would be so much fun to set up the ultimate age-play vacation cabin. We'd meet so many cool people! Make some friends who are into the same lifestyle as us! And when we don't have guests, I can use it, too.

I shrug and blush. 'Maybe I could stay a little longer. See how things go. I'm not good at making big decisions. They're scary.'

'I understand, sweetie. This is all very quick. You take all the time you need. And in the future, if you want, I can help you with any decisions you need. I'm going to do my best to be a good Daddy for you. Helping with structure and discipline if you need it.'

'Thank you,' I sigh. Then I let my hand rest on his, as he changes gear. He feels warm and strong. 'You make me feel... loved.' It's a big word, but I mean it. That's something that Pete never made me feel.

And honestly, in the past few days, Joel and I have been more intimate with each other than I've ever been with any other partner.

'I'm glad,' he says. 'You deserve it.'

We're silent with each other for the rest of the drive. It's not too long before we arrive at the lock-up where Joel keeps his truck, just at the edge of the National Park. We park up and get out. Now there's just the trek back to the cabin.

Joel leads the way, ducking under branches and stepping over roots. I made this trek by myself just a couple days ago, but today, doing it again, I feel like a brand new person. I feel empowered. I feel accepted. I feel free.

As we head deeper into the shady grove, I start to feel really free. I watch Joel as he powerfully steps through the undergrowth. And as I watch him, watch the gorgeous shape of his body and the manly confidence which flows through him.

I want to spend more time with this incredible, intoxicating man. And I want him to know that. But I'm not going to tell him with words. I'm going to tell him with my body.

It's time for this good girl to get naughty.

Quietly, without stopping moving forward, I slip my hands down and lift up my t-shirt. I lift it up over my breasts, then over my head. The forest air is chilly against my torso, and I feel my skin pucker in the mid-morning breeze.

My next move is tougher. I undo the buttons on my tiny shorts, bulging because of the bulk of my diaper beneath. I do my best not to grunt with the effort of tugging the shorts down, and thankfully, I manage OK, and when I slip them down past my shoes, I keep my footing.

Now the most difficult part of my little trick. I stop for a moment, just a moment, and rip both sides of my diaper away from the center.

Joel is still going strong. And I'm almost naked. I lean back and swiftly unclip my bra. Then, I let it drop to the floor.

With each of my breaths in, I let the cool air into my lungs. I'm naked as the day I was born — well, except for my shoes of course. I don't want to get prickles in my feet!

Then I stand there. Nude. Thrilled to be close to the wild, with the man of my dreams.

'Daddy. I think I lost something.'

Joel stops and twists around. As soon as he sees me, his eyes widen and his mouth opens. There's a wicked look in his eye as he takes me in. Then, he says, 'Oh really? What have you lost?'

I return his smile. 'My clothes, silly! Can't you see?'

'Hmm,' he says, lifting a hand to his strong chin. 'I better come take a closer look. I'm not sure exactly what you mean.'

As he approaches, my heart beats faster, harder, making my whole body shake and tremble. My nipples harden in the cool breeze, and as I imagine how his body's going to feel against mine, I feel my pussy start to moisten and bloom, as my lust begins to grow.

He's right next to me now, examining me.

'You know, I don't see what you mean.' He lifts a hand and lets it brush against my shoulder. 'Hang on, you're right. That's your skin, isn't it?' His hand starts to stroke me, his fingers gently resting on my body. 'You know what I think?' he asks, eyes flashing, white teeth grinning. 'I think you took your clothes off on purpose. I think you want to get your Daddy's cock hard so that he can't resist you. Is that right?'

'Sorry, Daddy,' I say, biting my lip. 'I'm so horny. Being this close to you is so hard for me. It makes my pussy feel funny. But I know it's naughty.'

'It *is* naughty,' he says. 'But it's working.'

My breathing is so heavy now. I keep glancing over Joel's shoulder. Even though there's no one around for miles, the threat of someone finding us is intoxicating.

'And look' he says, glancing down at his crotch. 'You got Daddy hard in public. Anyone could walk by here, couldn't they? Anyone could see your naughty, naked body, couldn't they?'

'Uh-huh,' I say, squirming. I can see a bulge there. It's big. Really damn big, pushing up against his blue jeans, making the fabric surge outward. I'm desperate for him to touch me again, desperate for his hands to stray down further to my chest, to my pussy. 'That looks big, Daddy.'

'How am I meant to look after you when you pull this kind of trick on me, huh? Being this hard, needing release like this is kinda distracting.'

'Sorry, Daddy.'

'Down on your knees.' His voice is cool, totally in command. Dominant. 'I want you to take my pants off. Then, Daddy needs you to suck his cock.'

As I drop down to my knees, I feel twigs and dirt under them, pushing against my skin. I love the freedom of being told what to do, and my body is trembling with anticipation. 'I hope I do a good job, Daddy,' I whisper.

'I'm sure you will.'

His pants are tight, and I tug at the buttons. As I undo the second one down, to my surprise, his cock, thick and hard and powerful, springs up out of his pants.

'Holy c—'

'No swearing,' he says. 'Or there'll be more punishments.'

'Sorry, Daddy,' I say. His cock is inches from my face now. Precum seeps from the tip, moistening it, making it glisten. I can't wait to taste it. I lick my lips and look up at his eyes. 'Be gentle,' I say. And then, I close my eyes and lean in, planting a kiss on him. As soon as my lips meet his skin, he groans.

He tastes good, earthy, and masculine. As my lips slip over his thick tip, I twist my tongue around him, submitting to the power of him, to the taste of him, to the salty, deep scent.

'That's good,' he says. 'You feel really damn good.'

I suck gently, keeping my tongue moving. Rhythmic, slow, languorous. I feel his fingers, threading through my hair. I can tell that he wants me to move more quickly, that he wants release. But I'm not going to give him that. Not yet.

I take more of him in now, let more of his probing cock fill my mouth, then dip into my throat, but I keep the pace slow. He's groaning, straining, and I can feel him gently pushing into me, trying to speed me up. I tug his pants all the way down, move my hand around, moving over his butt, feeling his hot, muscular flesh beneath me. Then, slip my fingers down, over his balls, cupping them, rolling them around in my fingers.

'Fuckk, Ella, you're so fucking good at this.'

I feel a flush of pride, of excitement. He's losing control. He's lost in pleasure.

So I give him what he wants. I move faster, twisting my tongue around, pulling my lips tight, showing him just how desperate I am for him. And as I increase my pace, I can feel the dew drip from my pussy, slippery juice, dripping down to the forest floor.

'I can't take much more of this,' he grunts. 'I need you, all of you.'

I close my eyes again, enjoy the sensation of him in my mouth, think about just how good it's going to feel when he finally pushes my pussy open with this monstrous thing.

Then, I slip my mouth off his cock and look up into his smoky eyes. 'I want you too, Daddy. I'm hungry for you.'

Then he leans down and grabs me. I can't believe how strong he is, how powerful his arms are, how easily he lifts me up. He carries me, his cock swinging left and right with each step, and pushes me up against a thick, dark tree trunk. I feel the bark against my butt cheeks, against my smooth, bare back.

Joel's hands are all over me, pushing my arms back, moving across my breasts, my thighs. He buries his mouth into my neck, kissing, gently biting, and then, I feel his thick, hard cock, resting against the entrance to me.

'Do I still have to be gentle?' he growls.

'No Daddy,' I say. 'I want you to tear me apart.'

With a moan of desire, he pushes his length into me, splitting me apart with a surge of delirious pleasure. My mouth opens wide but I make no sound, throwing my head back in a silent howl of joy.

'Oh fuck,' he says, as he starts to pound into me. I grab the tree as he slams into me, feeling nature behind me as he claims me, making me entirely his. I feel like he's sharing me with the earth, sharing me with the life force of the planet, and as he takes me hard and rough and deep, I surrender entirely to it.

'Just like that,' I groan, 'do it just like that.'

He pushes a finger into my mouth and I suck it, letting him fill every orifice. I'd let him do *anything* to me.

'I'm going to do this to you again and again,' he says, 'until you scream with pleasure. Until you let go so completely that you're reborn.'

His fingers entwine with mine, his cock surges up into me, and he bites down on my shoulder. My eyes roll back, and I look up at the sky between the trees. And as we come together, somewhere, not far from here, I hear the clear, clean cry of an eagle.

# JOEL

## SIX MONTHS LATER

THE FIRST SNOW OF the year starts to fall from the dark winter sky. I'm chopping logs, trying to preempt the coming chill. It looks like I'm gonna be done just in time.

'Ella, baby,' I shout out. 'You were right, snow's coming.'

I look back towards the cabin. Ella's in her workshop. I can see her crouched over her desk, working on some new piece or other. She tells me that since she joined me out here, business is booming. Turns out she finds our life together inspirational. She says it's the scenery, but I know that it's because she's finally found herself.

She glances up at me through the huge windows of the workshop. I see that she's got her earbuds in. She smiles at me and takes them out. Then, she sees it.

'Hey,' she shouts out, through the open window, 'it's starting to snow! I knew it!'

'Don't you think you should have that window shut, young lady? I'm gonna have to get the fire on, and you're letting all the heat out.'

'Sorry Daddy,' she says. 'I just like to be able to smell the cold.'

I know exactly what she means. There's a crispness to the air — a snappy, piney scent that's intoxicating.

I pick up the crate of logs I've been splitting and drag them to the cabin. I'll definitely need to get the fire on. I consider lighting it in the new-built guest nursery, too, just to try it out. But I know that would just be a waste of wood.

I'll get a chance to try the fireplace in that place out soon, anyway. Carl's coming to stay. He's bringing someone, too. Someone new. Carl's been single the whole time I've known him, so this is a big deal. Kinda nerve-wracking that the guest nursery is going to be used for the first time during a cold snap, but it should be fine.

I mean, what could go wrong?

It's not like another tree's gonna fall on the damn thing.

Tina's waiting for me inside, curled up on a pillow next to the couch. She likes Ella so much that I get jealous.

'I'm surprised you're in here, cat,' I say. 'You're normally in with Ella about this time. I guess you must know that the fire's about to get lit.'

A meow. A purr. A stretch of the back.

I light the fire with practiced slickness, and when it starts to crackle, the door opens from the workshop and Ella comes in.

'Young lady!' I gasp, as I see what she's wearing. 'It's far too cold for that.'

Her gorgeous body is nude, save for her puffy diaper. It's a thrill every time I see her like this. So innocent, yet so sexy at the same time.

'Can you think of any way to warm me up, Daddy?'

'One or two,' I say, grinning from ear to ear.

As we fall into each other, I'm struck by just how far we've come in such a short time. It's like we're two halves of the same whole now, two lost souls, now reunited. And as her tongue slips into my mouth, and I feel the fabric of her diaper crinkle against my body, I feel a swell of pride and happiness. She's my Little Girl. And I'm her Daddy.

* * *

**Read on for Carl and Diana's story: *Lost with Daddy*!**

# Chapter Two

# LOST WITH DADDY

# DIANA

'YOU CAN'T PULL OUT now; you already agreed.'

Liv's looking desperately at me.

'Yeah, but when I agreed to help you,' I say, 'I didn't realize that you were asking me to break the law.'

She scoffs. 'You're not going to be the one breaking the law, dummy. All you've got to do is talk to Mandy. There's no way that you're going to get into trouble.'

I cringe. She's talking so loudly, and we're standing right outside the store she's planning to steal from.

'Liv, just, cool down, OK?'

'I am cool. I just don't appreciate you pulling out at the last minute.' She purses her lips. It's a little gesture she's done ever since I've known her. For just a second, I'm sent straight back to high school, to remembering the willful, rebellious girl who's always been my best friend.

Liv hasn't changed much. She's still a gorgeous girl with jet-black hair and bright green eyes. She's still attracted to danger and loves to break rules. She's still almost impossible to say no to.

'I'm not pulling out,' I say. I feel so bad about what we're going to do. I know Mandy, the owner of Cartwright's. It's the only clothes store in my hometown, Little Creek. Stealing's always wrong, but it wouldn't feel as bad if Liv was about to steal from, I don't know, a big chain store like Walmart or something.

'Good,' she says, smiling. 'So, remember the plan? All you have to do is keep Mandy chatting while I take a few items of clothing. I'm not taking a lot, and remember, these guys have insurance. It's not like it's actually gonna cost Mandy anything. Or the store in general. Just some wealthy asshole, miles away from Little Creek.'

I keep telling myself that, but there's a nagging voice in the back of mind that's telling me this is just wrong, totally wrong.

'OK,' I say, steeling myself. 'Let's do this.'

Maybe if Liv wasn't my only friend, I wouldn't be doing this. Maybe if I had a stable home life, if I still had my folks, I wouldn't be doing this. Maybe if I hadn't stopped auditioning for dancing work, I wouldn't be doing this.

But none of that matters now. Because I'm here, and I'm doing it.

We head into Cartwright's. There's dull muzak playing over the speakers, and I can smell the weird, stuffy scent that this place always has. Kind of like a mix of lavender and oak. I've been in here so many times. But never to do this.

Liv gives me a look and then heads across to the dresses. She starts flicking through rails, trying to decide on what she might like.

To steal.

The words stick in my head like red-hot daggers.

Lots of people have a shoplifting phase. I understand it's kinda like a compulsion, like an addiction. I've never shoplifted, ever. In fact, I don't think I've ever broken the law at all.

What would Miss Ranger think? My dance teacher, ever since I was a little girl, is one of the most wholesome, downright good people I've ever met.

'The only way to become excellent,' she always used to say, 'is to practice. There's no such thing as talent. It's a myth. Talented people just happen to love what they do, and have the time to practice it.'

I know what I love. Dancing. And I've got time to practice. I work at the town's diner, a place called Tracy's. But it's only part-time. Up until a few years ago, I was totally dedicated to dancing. I knew, just *knew* that it was going to be my career. My life.

Then, everything fell apart.

'Diana!' Mandy is giving me *that look*. I've gotten so used to that look over the past two years. The look of benign pity. She's not just saying my name, she's asking — with those narrow eyes and those pursed, concerned lips — just how I'm coping with my grief.

I get it. People don't know how to ask how I'm doing since my mom and dad both died. Of course they don't. It's hard, and obviously, it's a taboo subject. But I always prefer it when people just come out and ask me.

'Hi Mandy,' I say, waving sheepishly. Mandy's nice, really. Not exactly a family friend, more of an acquaintance. Little Creek is a small place, and I know almost everyone in the place. Mandy's involved with the local Scout troupe, and she also is involved with the Thanksgiving cook-off in town each year. She's been the manager here at Cartwright's for long as I can remember. 'How are you doing?'

'I'm fine, dear. In fact, I've got that Friday feeling!' Her eyes make happy little crescents.

'Glad to hear it.' This would normally be the point where I'd break off the small talk and start looking around the store. I wonder if she'll notice that I'm as nervous as hell. I can feel sweat on my forehead and my heart starts to pound. 'So... you got any plans for the weekend?'

She looks a little surprised. I rarely come into the store — I do most of my shopping online — and I think I can count the number of times

I've had anything resembling a conversation with her on the fingers of one hand.

'Thank you for asking,' she says. She seems sincerely touched that I've shown interest in her. Guilt stabs at my heart. I glance over at Liv, just in time to see her stuffing some kind of item under her top. There's no backing out now.

To my horror, Mandy follows my glance over toward Liv. Has she seen what she's doing?

'Oh, you're here with Liv,' she says, her voice dropping a little.

'Yeah,' I say.

'She's a wild one.' She's trying to be polite, because she knows that the two of us are close.

'Yeah, she's fun.'

Liv sees that the two of us are looking at her, thank goodness, and she's wise enough to stop her stealing spree. She gives a goofy grin, which to me is clearly full of nerves.

'So, what are your weekend plans?' I ask, trying to take attention off of Liv.

'Oh, not much. A bottle of wine and a romcom, probably.' She sounds distracted. 'You know, Diana, I hope you don't mind me saying this, but I always thought that Liv was a bad influence on you.'

I'm surprised to hear her say this. I didn't think she'd be this honest with me. I feel a pang of anger. How dare she judge me — and Liv? Then, I realize that I'm literally here to help my friend steal from Mandy's store.

The anger is replaced by something else. Sadness.

'Liv's nice,' I say, but I sound sheepish. Mandy must realize I'm not entirely convinced.

'She may be nice to you, but she's got you into a lot of trouble over the years. Look, I know life's been unkind to you. But people like Liv, they aren't the answer. I know it can be tempting to give in to bad thoughts, but there's another way.'

As she talks, I start to get angry again.

She's being incredibly patronizing. And what's worse, what makes me even angrier, is that she's definitely right.

I look over at Liv again, and she gives me an intense look that tells me that it's time to get out of here.

'OK Mandy, well, thanks for the *advice*,' I say, trying not to sound too confrontational. 'I think I'd better go.'

Mandy looks a little despondent but doesn't say anything. She nods and gets back to pricing t-shirts.

I'm a nervous wreck. I'm doing this thing I always do when I get like this — wringing my hands together. It's not something I can really control. I can remember doing it when I was a kid, and I never really got out of the habit. Squeezing each of my knuckles in turn, feeling the reassuring pain as I squeeze a little too tight.

Mandy glances down at my hands, and then over at Liv. Has she realized something's going on?

I turn, and I'm about to head over to my friend, when I see a figure, moving across the store.

Oh no. Not Sheriff Carl.

He's tall, well over six foot, and broad too. There's a strength to each of his steps that betrays the power that must reside in him. It's easy to see that he's totally confident — exactly the opposite of me.

He's wearing the dark gray shirt and navy pants of a town Sheriff, and he's heading straight for Liv.

I know Carl, all too well. While my dad was alive, Carl was his deputy. Dad loved Carl, and they spent a lot of time together. He'd come round for dinner, and I know that they'd go for drinks together too. Carl always has this embarrassing effect on me, because I had a crush on him basically since the first time I ever saw him.

I know, I know. Such a cliché. Having a crush on your dad's hunky best friend. But it's not my fault. Carl is, like, objectively perfect-looking.

Carl used to be a prize fighter. He doesn't like to talk too much about those days, but he doesn't need to talk about it for it to be obvious. His body is cut like cold steel. I once saw him with his top off in the summer and nearly passed out. It's not just his body, though. He's got this strong, angular jaw. Piercing blue eyes. But it's his smile that really gets me. Probably because it's so rare that he actually smiles. When he does, it's like a dawn breaking. Like rain after months of drought. It's heaven.

Trouble is, he's not smiling now. He's looking straight at Liv with a grim look on his face. He doesn't look angry, just hugely disappointed. I freeze, stop dead in my tracks.

'What's going on?' Mandy says. She sounds genuinely hurt.

'I-I don't know,' I say. I can't tear my eyes away from what's going on across the room.

Carl stands in front of Liv, hands on hips, face totally impassive. He says a few words that I can't hear, and Liv looks furious. She even stamps her foot. Then Carl says something else, looking even more serious.

Mandy looks at me and then bustles over to join Carl and Liv. Eventually, Liv takes out the clothes she's got stuffed under her shirt.

Adrenaline spikes in my veins. I glance over at the door. I should get out of here. This is bad.

Then, with tears in her eyes — and I know that these are crocodile tears, Liv doesn't cry unless she's up to something — she turns to point over at me. Mandy's eyes burn with anger, and Carl's face is impassive.

My heart almost stops.

How could I let my dad's best friend down like this? How could I let myself down like this?

I turn, run out of the store, tears streaming down my face. And unlike Liv's, my tears are real.

When I get home, I look up at the photo that's hanging above the fireplace. It's my family having a barbecue with Carl. As I look at the happy faces, I slump down onto my knees, the hard floor hurting me.

What am I doing with my life?

# CARL

T HERE'S A PAIR OF scissors in my hand. I'm kneeling at a low
table, looking intently at the tiny, twisted tree in front of me.

'Where do I cut you?' I ask the tree. 'What do I need to do to make
you realize your potential?'

Bonsai trees didn't save my life. That would be ridiculous. But they
helped. They definitely helped.

I'm trying to save the tree I'm working on right now. The poor thing
had a run-in with my German Shepherd, Prince. Prince has got a taste
for trouble, especially when it takes the shape of one of my miniature
trees. This particular specimen is a Chinese plum, less than a foot high.
Ten years old, I think. All that time, and not even a foot tall. Some
things just grow up slow, I guess.

There's an ugly wound in the trunk, where Prince's teeth pierced
the bark. If I'm careful with strappings and trimmings, I should be
able to save it, though. Trouble is, I won't know whether I've been
successful for years.

Shaping miniature trees demands total focus. That's something
that I'm struggling with today. Ever since I caught Liv shoplifting in
Cartwright's, my mind's been buzzing like a bee in springtime.

I've been expecting Liv to get in serious trouble for a while. She's always been wild. What surprised me was the fact that she insisted that Diana Jennings forced her to do it.

Obviously the accusation is nonsensical. The store decided not to press charges against Liv in the end, so neither girl is actually going to get into any trouble. I kept Liv in a cell overnight. Hopefully that'll scare some sense into her. Honestly, though, it's not the first time she's got into trouble. There's even a chance she might do some jail time. But Liv isn't who I'm truly concerned about.

I trim a couple leaves from the right-hand side of the tree, taking to reduce the pressure on this side of the little thing.

After Diana's parents died, I made a promise to myself. I promised to look after that wonderful creature. To watch from afar, to make sure that she has a good life, full of the kind of experiences someone as talented and beautiful as her deserves.

I hear the skittering sound of paws against carpet, then, a moment later, Prince bounds into the workshop, tongue lolling and tail wagging.

'Whoa, boy,' I say, forming a physical barrier between the excitable dog and the vulnerable tree. This thing definitely wouldn't withstand another toothy embrace.

Prince listens, thankfully. For the most part, he's a really good boy, and — without wanting to sound big-headed — I'm a good trainer. He lies down, looking up at me with those big brown eyes.

'We'll go for a walk later,' I say. 'I gotta finish this first.'

I don't know whether I'm talking about finishing my work with the tree, or whether I'm talking about what to do about Diana.

Maybe it's time to stop watching over her, and intervene in her life. If it wasn't for the confusing feelings I have for her, I'd go talk to her. But the fact is, I've felt... a lot for Di for a long time. In fact, before the incident with her folks, I'd been working up to asking her dad, Chris, if I could take her out. I never got the chance.

She always felt like forbidden fruit. I mean, me and Chris were close. But I was much younger than him.

I take out a little roll of tape and start to patch up the wound in the tree. I'm careful, holding the split branch carefully. It doesn't take long. The key is to be confident, to commit.

'That's what I need to do with Diana,' I say, to no-one in particular. Prince lets out a sympathetic whine and cocks his head to the side. 'I need to commit to helping her.'

Unlike this tree, I know exactly what I'd do to help Diana.

She needs looking after. She needs structure. She needs someone to help her see just how much she has to give the world. She needs someone to be proud of her.

She needs a Daddy.

Not a father. I would never be that. But she does need a caregiver. And I know that I could be that person.

'Trouble is,' I say, this time definitely to Prince, 'not everyone likes being told to act like a kid and let someone else take care of them.' And that's the reason that up until now, I haven't spoken to Diana about my idea. But seeing her with Liv today, realizing just how serious her situation is, well, it shocked me.

That look on her face — that haunted, lost look — just before she turned and ran out the store, it reminded me a lot of how I used to feel.

Before I settled in Little Creek, before I became an upstanding member of society and joined the Sheriff's department, I was a wild kid. A streetfighter, a bare-knuckle boxer. My face still bears the scars of that lifestyle, and so does my soul.

My last fight was in Little Creek. It was a crazy night, and, as usual, I was drunk. Off my head. I don't remember much of the actual fight, but I remember the carnage at the end. Cops broke it all up. People running, fights breaking out all over the place.

I shoulda been put away. But Chris took a chance on me. He saw that I didn't want to live that life anymore.

So, bonsai trees didn't save my life. That was Diana's dad.

The trees came later.

Satisfied that I've done my best to give the little plum tree a fighting chance at life, I put it all the way back up on the highest shelf of the workshop wall. Just enough light from the wide window, and at the perfect temperature.

'You won't be getting at that,' I say to Prince.

I've got so much nervous energy zipping around me, I need to find a way to channel it. I head into my home gym, start to pump iron. I may not fight for a living anymore, but I keep myself in good shape. There are times in my job that strength comes in handy. Normally, a good workout gets rid of my anger, leaves me feeling calm and relaxed. Not today though. Today, every time I lift the dumbbell over my head, I feel myself getting more and more angry and disappointed with myself.

Because I know I've reached a tipping point. And if I don't do something now, there's a chance that Diana's gonna waste her life. And I'm not willing to risk that.

I decide to call someone. A friend of mine. Joel's an interesting character. He used to be a banker in New York, but now he lives in a cabin, out in the Colorado wilderness, about an hour from Little Creek. Joel is a Daddy, just like me. He believes that women should be cared for, coddled, and treated with love and respect.

In fact, he believes it so much that he runs a special cabin getaway for Bigs and Littles. It's the kind of place that I've always dreamed of taking a special someone. But I've never had anyone who'd appreciate it.

'Carl,' he says. 'Good to hear from you.' The line is a little crackly, just like it always is when I talk to Joel. He gets almost no reception out where he lives.

We exchange pleasantries. I ask him how his Little, Ella, is doing.

'She's a handful,' he says, 'but things are good.'

Ella visited Joel's place before he set up the ABDL cabin, when it was just a normal Airbnb place. She loved it so much and fell for him so hard that she ended up staying.

'Look, I'm calling for some advice,' I say, my voice hardening.

'Of course.'

'There's this... girl. She's an old friend. Couple years ago, she lost both her parents. A car accident. Bad business.'

'Damn, that's rough.'

'Uh-huh. Anyway, since then, she's been having a hard time. I think she needs some help.'

'Regression?'

Damn. He's smart. Maybe it's obvious from the way I've been speaking.

'I'm not sure. But I think it might help her. Help her connect with the sweet Little Girl she used to be. Not just that though. Maybe if she's allowed to play, if someone takes care of her, she might get some focus back.'

'Maybe. Is she a Little?'

'I don't know. I mean. I don't think so.'

'That's tough.'

'So, you think I should talk to her?'

He pauses for a moment. I can hear the sound of his cat, Tina, meowing in the background.

'You know,' he says. 'I don't know if it's my place to say. You know this girl, not me. But I do have some advice for you. If you do talk to her, you have to be honest. Totally honest. Honest about who you are. Honest about what you're going to ask of her. Because the only way to build a relationship like this — or any kind of relationship — is trust. You can't fake it.'

As he talks, I start to feel more confident. Because he's right. Honesty is the only way to solve any of life's problems.

And if I'm honest with myself, right now, there's only one option, only one path I can take.

So I shower. I change. And I step out into the cool evening air.

Little do I know just how much my life is about to change.

# DIANA

I'M IN THE BATH when there's a knock at the door. Ever since the shoplifting incident, I've been obsessed with cleaning myself. I've been having at least two showers a day, and today, I decided that maybe a bath is the thing to go for. Plus, it's cold outside. Feels like snow.

I shout out, 'Coming,' and quickly spring out of the bath. My skin's all pink and my hair is wet. It's probably just a delivery, but as I wrap a thick towel around my torso, I can't think of anything I'm waiting for right now. I wrap another, smaller towel around my hair, then I head to the front door.

When I look through the peephole and see Carl out there waiting for me, I freeze.

He's here to arrest me. I knew it. My heart rate spikes. I knew this would happen. Liv sent me a message to tell me that she wasn't in trouble. I'm wringing my hands again, back in that bad place.

What should I do? Should I run again? Where would I go?

I look at Carl. His face is so close to mine. I wonder if he knows that I'm looking at him now. Even though I'm freaking out, I can't believe how damn handsome he is.

He's rugged at the same time as being wholesome. Sexy at the same time as being kind.

My dream man. Shame there's no way someone like him would ever be interested in a loser like me.

Just when I'm about to head back into the house to pretend I'm not in, Carl says, 'Di, I know you're in there. Listen, I'm not here to punish you. Not here to arrest you or anything like that. I'm here to help.'

Why is he interested in helping me?

'I don't believe you.' I shout the words loudly and I almost surprise myself. I sound angry. I hadn't realized that I'm angry.

'It's true,' he says, leaning into the door. 'I don't want you to make the same mistakes I did.'

The same mistakes he made? What's he talking about? He's nothing like me.

But something about the way he says it makes me pause. He sounds sincere. Like he really does want to help.

I unlock the door. He hears the click and gently pushes.

As soon as he's inside, he puts his hands on his hips and gives me a serious look. 'OK, you have the right to remain silent, you have the right to an attorney.'

'But you—'

'Got you.' Now he's smiling. Damn him and his dry sense of humor.

'Not funny,' I say, putting out my lower lip and pouting.

'Did you honestly think I'd arrest you, Di? After all we've been through together. Come on. I couldn't do that.' His smile is gorgeous, and just for a moment, I'm taken back to a happy place, a place where I'm not worried about everything in my life.

'I thought you might.'

He gives me a piercing look. His cool blue eyes connect with mine. I study his face, notice the tiny scar above his lip, the slight crooked line of his nose. He's a fighter, alright.

'I brought you something. Can I come in?'

I nod.

I take him through. My place is a mess. After my folks died, I sold their old house and bought this tiny studio apartment. I couldn't face staying in that old house, with all those memories. Truth is though, I don't care about this place at all. Clothes are strewn all over the floor, and a couple meals' worth of crockery are strewn about the table.

'Damn Di, do you have any windows?'

'Yeah,' I say. 'Not much point in opening them, though.'

'Would you mind, just for me? I like a little sunlight.'

It's late in the day, and the sun's about to set, but I do as Carl asks anyway. I draw the heavy curtains and let a wash of weak orange light into the place.

'Looks worse in the light,' I say. I feel deeply embarrassed. There's nothing as humiliating as an old friend seeing how out of control my life has gotten.

'Don't worry,' he says. 'I'm not here to judge.'

He's got a hip bag with him and opens it up. Then, he takes something out. Looks like a shrub in a little pot.

'You brought me a plant?'

'Not just a plant,' he says, carefully putting it down on a windowsill. 'This is a bonsai tree. A Chinese Elm.'

I take a closer look at the plant. It does look like a tiny tree, with a twisted trunk and bushy little leaves.

'Uh, thanks, I guess.'

'This tree takes a lot of care. You'll need to learn about the way they grow, about how to support it without stifling it. This thing is ten years old. I've been looking after it for two of those years, but I wanted to pass it on to you because I know you'll do a better job of it than me.'

So it's not just a plant he's given me, it's almost like he's given me an entire hobby.

'I'll just kill it.'

'Maybe,' he says, walking around the space. 'But I believe in you.' He pauses for a moment. 'Say, where do you do your dance practice?'

'I don't.' I haven't danced for months.

'So you're not auditioning anymore? You don't want to be a dancer?'

'It's not that. I just... I can't face it anymore, alright? I'm just going to work at Tracy's forever.'

'Diana,' he says, putting a hand on my shoulder, 'you must never give up on your dreams. Even if you never make it, you'll get so much from trying. I really do believe in you.'

I can't meet his gaze. 'Well, I don't. Believe in myself, that is.'

'I can see that.'

He gently strokes my shoulder. It's a tiny, platonic gesture, but it gives me warmth, and just a tiny bit of strength.

'Look, Di, you need help. I can see that. Hell, a blind person could see that. This isn't you. I know you. I know that you're a talented, sensitive woman. You don't need to live like this. That thing with Liv, in Cartwright's, doesn't mean anything, not really. Liv's bad news, and I get that you're her friend, and you're loyal. But at the same time, you deserve so much more.'

It's the first time anyone's been straight with me since the accident. And I love the fact that he's not judging me.

'I want to help you,' he says, a hand on each of my shoulders. 'I want to give you support and structure, the same way that you'll be helping that little tree. With the right guidance and support, you'll blossom and bloom. I can see it.'

'Got a messiah complex, huh?' It's not me talking. It's my anger. But right now, my anger's in control. All my bad impulses are in control.

'I dunno,' he says, taking his hands away, wryly smiling, scratching his head. 'Maybe I do.'

'So,' I say, narrowing my eyes. 'Let's say I do want to accept your help. What exactly do you want me to do? How are you gonna help this little lost soul?'

The smile's gone. It's serious Carl again. 'Diana, have you ever heard of regression?'

\*

'Let me get this straight.' I'm still reeling, sitting at my dining table. There's an untouched cup of water in front of me, and Carl is sitting across from me, with a neutral expression on his face. 'You want me to act like a kid? A baby? And then you want to run my life, to help me?'

'I mean, it sounds weird when you put it like that, but...'

'You're not my father, Carl.' I don't even know if I'm angry anymore, but I find myself lashing out. As soon as I've said the words, though, I regret saying them. However outlandish his suggestion, I can tell from the earnest way he's talking that he really does want to help me.

'Of course I'm not your father,' he replies. 'I'd never try to replace Chris. That's not what I'm suggesting. I'd be more like a caregiver. I want to provide your life with structure and focus, so that you spend less time self-destructing, and more time pursuing your dream.'

'But why?' I ask. 'Why do you even care about me?'

He sighs. 'The answer's in the question. I *care* about you. You've always been important to me. I hate that we've grown apart these last few years. Seeing you almost get into trouble at Cartwright's was a wake-up call for me.'

I know he's telling the truth. I can sense it.

'What happens if it doesn't work? This regression stuff? What happens if I don't like it, or I'm no good at it?'

'That's the beauty of it. All that stuff — it's my responsibility. You'll be my Little, and I'll be your Big. You've got nothing to worry about apart from following the guidelines we agree on together, and being yourself.'

'And, I don't have to like, dress up or anything? You're not going to be checking me out in a skimpy outfit? It's not like a BDSM thing, is it?' As I ask this, I realize that I *do* want him to be attracted to me. There's something so calming and reassuring about the way he's talking to me. About the fact that he seems to know exactly what I need. But when I ask the question, he almost starts to blush.

He pauses a moment, looks up, as though collecting his thoughts. Then, he looks at me.

'The truth is, Diana, that some people *do* indulge in Age Play as part of an... intimate relationship.'

I'm stunned. Does he... like me? Is that what this is all about?

'Is that why you're here?' I ask, withdrawing slightly. 'You want to be intimate with me?'

Carl looks awkward, stifled. 'I'm here to help you,' he says, bristling slightly.

'I think you should leave,' I say, my voice trembling.

'I understand,' he says, 'but, think about what I'm offering. Nothing weird has to happen between us.'

'This is already weird,' I say.

Carl nods. 'I get it. Just remember, my offer still stands. I'd come stay with you. Help you sort this place out. Give you the time you need to thrive.'

'And in return, you just want my body?'

It's a cruel thing to say, but I'm not thinking rationally. This is exactly like me, lashing out at people who try to help. The worst thing: I'm crushing so hard on Carl right now I'm practically trembling.

'Well, I think I better go.' He stands up, puts his hands in his pockets.

I want to apologize, want to say anything to him. But I can't.

After he's gone, I look at the little tree he left for me. It's beautiful.

I sit there, in front of the tree for half an hour, thinking things through. And the more I stare at that vulnerable, twisted little tree, the more I see myself in it. And I realize that I do need help.

Something needs to change.

# CARL

S NOW'S COMING, I CAN sense it. My breath hangs in the air, and my fingers tingle as I cut my way through the park.

'It's cold enough to freeze my fucking nuts off.'

That's Atlas, a good friend of mine. We meet once a week for a ten-mile run. We snake our way through a local park and then dip up into the Rockies for a little uphill challenge towards the end.

'I thought you already burned those suckers off years ago.'

Atlas lets out a deep, gruff peal of laughter. His throat has been ravaged over the years. He's a firefighter, and Chief of the local unit. When he speaks, it sounds like a bunch of gravel being thrown around inside a cast iron skillet.

'You can't burn a firefighter's balls off,' he says. 'Asbestos ballsacks.' He winks. Atlas's a little more coarse than I am, but the two of us still get on really well. He's a softy at heart, even though he acts super tough. I mean, obviously, he *is* a tough guy. He saves lives for his job, for goodness' sake.

We head out of the park and uphill. The snowy peaks of the Rocky Mountains jab at the sky in front of us. Prince is with us, on a leash out in front of me. He knows this route so well that he's basically dragging me along.

'How's your love life?' I ask Atlas. 'Things still rough with Fern?'

He shakes his head. Sweat beads his forehead, and his cheeks are bright red. 'That's history,' he says. 'Real shame. I thought she was the one. Plus, you know how hard it is to find a good Little in a small town.'

Unlike me, Atlas has had lots of experience with partners who are into our lifestyle. He's left a trail of broken hearts around the state. Something tells me that this time it wasn't him who did the dumping.

'Speaking of which, how are you doing?'

How am I doing? Bad is the truth. My chat with Diana didn't go well yesterday. In fact, it went badly.

'I'm OK,' I reply. I find it hard to open up and talk about feelings with guy friends. It's something I'm trying to work on.

'You're not,' he pants, 'I can tell.'

For a few minutes, as we ascend a steep trail up the side of a mountain, talk is difficult. We never talk about it, but Atlas and I are deeply competitive. I think it's because we're both servicemen, both physical by nature. So while we climb, we dig in, we keep our mouths shut. But as we reach the peak of the hill and I see the countryside stretch out ahead of us, I feel the urge to come clean.

'You're right, of course,' I say. 'I'm not OK.' I explain the situation with Di as succinctly as I can, but I find myself stumbling, holding back information.

Eventually, Atlas stops me. 'I know the problem,' he says. 'You weren't honest with her.'

I bristle a little. I *was* honest, wasn't I? I told her about regression, I told her that for some people, Age Play is a sexual thing.

'I was,' I say.

'Nope. Because it's obvious to me — you like her. I bet you didn't tell her that. I bet you said that you were just there to help her, that while other people might be into this stuff as a basis for a relationship, that doesn't apply to you.'

Huh. He's right. I was so dishonest I even managed to deceive myself.

'You might have a point,' I concede.

We loop around the base of the mountain.

'You know, a lot of the training I went through when I became a firefighter was bullshit. Especially compared to what I went through when I became a Navy SEAL. But anyway, one thing they told me really stuck with me. We were told that the more dangerous a situation, the more entirely you have to commit to it.'

'Good advice,' I say.

'Sure. And I think it applies here. Because telling someone that you want to be her Daddy? That's about as dangerous a situation as you can get.'

I laugh. 'I guess you're right.'

'And in this instance, commitment means honesty.'

'Should I really be taking relationship advice from you?'

Atlas lets out a guffaw, looking around at me. His short beard is damp from sweat, and he almost looks like a wild man. 'I dunno, but I'm sure as fuck not gonna be taking it from you.'

Prince lets out a bark, as though he's agreeing with Atlas.

'Hey, boy, you're meant to be on my side.'

Prince barks again, so happy to be out in the real world.

'You know,' Atlas says, 'being totally serious for a second.'

'Whoa, that sounds risky. You sure you're capable of that?'

'Very funny. Not something I realized *you* were capable of. Look, the thing with Fern, she slipped through my fingertips. I thought she was my Forever Girl. But I made the mistake of not being totally honest with her. Tore us apart. Don't make the same mistake I did.'

We end our run by Atlas's place. It's an old gothic-style mansion on the edge of town. I don't even know how he came to occupy this place, but it suits his brash, in-your-face personality perfectly.

'So, what you gonna do about Di?'

'I think I'm gonna take your advice. I'm gonna commit.'

He reaches out and grasps my hand. 'Great workout today, man. Can't believe you kept up with me.'

'Soon, you'll be the one trying to keep up with me.'

As I walk across town, I see Tracy's Diner. Most likely, Diana is in there right now. I've decided that I'm gonna meet up with her as soon as I can, and come clean. I always felt like there was something between us: an energy, a connection.

Maybe I need to come clean with myself. Maybe the reason that I watch her, that I want to make sure she's doing well, that she's not miserable, is that I'm fucking in love with her. It's painful to even think it, but as soon as I do, I feel a weight lift from me.

I probably shouldn't drop that piece of information on her straight away. I've been in denial about my feelings for her for years. Probably safer just to say: you're right, I like you.

So I'm going to go home, shower, and then I'm going to find her and tell her how I feel.

I live on the outskirts of town. That's a little misleading, though, because all of Little Creek is kinda the outskirt. There's the main street, a couple little roads leading off, and that's about it.

When I turn the corner onto my street, I'm surprised to see that there's a figure waiting outside my door. It's Diana. And she's holding something in her hand. Looks like a stuffie.

As I approach, I try to work out what expression she's pulling. Is she here to fight? Or for some other reason?

She raises a hand and waves at me.

'Hullo.' She sounds tired. Like she's given up.

'Good to see you. I was about to come find you. Hang on,' I hold up a hand, 'shouldn't you be at work?'

'I took some time off,' she says. 'Someone convinced me that I had to make some changes in my life. So I've taken a week to look after myself.'

'Glad to hear it,' I say.

Diana leans over and pats Prince on the side of the muzzle. 'Good boy,' she says. 'I wish I had a treat to give you.'

At the word treat, Prince's ears perk up.

'So, you want to come in?' I ask. 'I need a shower.'

'Yeah, you look pretty sweaty.' There's something about the way she says that word that sends shivers up and down my spine.

'Who's this?' I say, pointing down at the plush toy, dangling by her side.

'Rabbit,' she says.

'Makes sense. Cute stuffie.'

'Look,' she says, 'I think I need your help. I find it hard with you because you were so close to my dad. It's almost like my parents are here, judging me.'

'I get that,' I say. 'But I'm not here to judge.'

'I know, I know. Plus, look, this is hard to admit, but I kinda used to have a crush on you. So that makes it even harder. I'm not really happy with who I am right now, with the life I'm living. And having you know that? It's hard.'

'You had a crush on me?'

She holds up a hand, her finger and thumb held close together. 'Just a tiny little one.'

My heart starts to pound, my mouth goes dry. Am I really about to do this?

'I need to come clean,' I say. 'Come in with me. I'm going to tell you a few things. Then, if you're still interested, we can talk about a contract.'

'A contract?'

'Trust me,' I say, 'we'll need one.'

She pulls Rabbit up to her mouth and follows me into my house.

# DIANA

'**O**H MY GOD, IT'S like a freaking forest in here!'

Carl smiles. 'I guess I kinda like to bring the outside inside.'

That's the understatement of the decade.

His place is beautiful. Couldn't be more of a contrast with my house. Everywhere I look, there are shelves full of houseplants. Tendrils full of bright-green leaves trail down, making a lush, crazy effect. It's like the whole place is alive.

'Do you own anything that's not a plant?' I ask.

'Prince. He just likes to eat the plants.'

We find a place to sit among the foliage.

'So, what did you want to say to me?'

'You told me that you used to have a crush on me. Diana, I *still* have a crush on you.'

He says it so simply, so straightforwardly, that he completely takes me off guard.

'You what?'

'Ever since I saw what a fine young woman you've grown into, I've felt something for you. I was plucking up the courage to ask you out, before the accident.'

I feel like I've been punched in the gut. There have been so many times that I've tried to imagine what my life might be like if my parents had never got into the car that day, if they'd left twenty minutes later.

But I've never once considered that Carl and I might be together.

'Plucking up the courage?' I ask. 'Why didn't you just ask me?'

'Two reasons. One, I respected your dad a lot. I didn't know if he'd have thought I was good enough for you.'

'Are you kidding me? Dad worshiped the ground you walked on.'

Carl smiles. 'Thanks for saying that. Anyway, reason two is a little more serious. Thing is, you were right about me. I am into BDSM. I'm a Daddy Dom, and I'm only interested in a relationship with someone who's submissive, and into Age Play, like I am. And believe me, that's a hard thing for me to admit.'

I can't believe how honest he's being. It's like he's baring his heart to me. He must feel so vulnerable right now.

'But Diana, you've got to know, that's not why I want to help you. I don't have some creepy grand plan to seduce you. I want to help you. Kinky sex doesn't come into it.'

My mind's reeling. Half the stuff he's said doesn't mean much to me. Words like Daddy Dom and submissive. Even Age Play is confusing.

But I don't just feel confused. When I think about Carl saying *kinky sex* it gives me a strange, fluttery sensation inside. A nice feeling.

'Thank you for telling me all this stuff,' I say. I feel so safe, so at ease with him.

'It actually feels really good to tell you. Feels like I've been wanting to say it for years. But my feelings for you, they're why it's so important that we have a contract. So that you feel protected and safe with me. And so that you know my intentions are pure.'

*What if my intentions aren't pure?*

I toy with the idea of telling Carl that I still have feelings for him, but for some reason, it feels wrong. He's being so adamant that he's not interested in seducing me. I guess he just wants to help me out.

'OK, I guess that makes sense,' I say, trying to be as positive as I can.

'Great,' he says. 'And you're OK to go ahead with my idea, even though I have feelings for you?'

'I think so,' I say.

'Great. I'm gonna put on a pot of coffee, and we can work through the contract.'

'I thought you said no sexy stuff.'

He grins.

*

'You don't *have* to call me Daddy,' he says, 'but it definitely would help. Our relationship is all about playing a role. And part of being a good Little is having respect and love for your Daddy.'

'It feels a bit weird.'

'I get that.' Papers are spread out on the table in front of us, and we're both looking at the words very carefully. 'But you've got to remember that it's a Daddy Dom, not a father figure. There's a big difference.'

'OK. Daddy.' It feels kinda weird to say it, but also, kind of exciting, too.

'Thanks, sweetie,' he says, grinning wide, showing me his bright white teeth. 'Now, I can't help but notice that you've lost quite a bit of weight in the past couple years.'

It's weird to hear him say that, and I'm not quite sure how I feel about it. He's right, of course. I've been eating badly. I normally skip breakfast and rarely eat much nutritious stuff.

'Bit of a weird thing to say,' I reply.

'Well, while you're my Little Girl, you're gonna have to eat three times a day, whether you like it or not. Good nutrition is so important for happiness. It's been proven that a healthy gut biome has a direct, positive influence on mental health.'

'Uh, so, you mean the little bugs in my tummy can make me sad?'

'Exactly. You need regular, healthy meals to keep you feeling good. It's not a cure-all, but I promise you that it'll help. So you're to follow the menu plan that I'm going to create for you. Breakfast and dinner we'll eat together every day, but I'll have to trust you to eat your lunch. Does that sound reasonable?'

This is not what I'd been expecting. Not at all. He's putting me on some kinda weird diet? I guess it might be useful. To be honest, there have been times in my life when I've wished that I didn't have any choice but to be good. And maybe that's what's on offer here.

'I don't know about reasonable. But I'm willing to give it a try.'

'That's fantastic,' he says. 'Discipline is so important.'

Discipline. The word makes me shiver.

'Now, when was the last time you did any dance practice?'

I knew this would come up. Ugh. I feel so ashamed of myself.

'A year and a half ago. I'm so dumb.'

'You're not dumb.' His voice is certain and quick. 'You've been through hell. Doesn't mean you're stupid and it doesn't mean that you're hopeless. You're a talented, bright woman, Diana. I don't want to hear you say anything bad about yourself from now on. In fact, I might just put that in the contract. No self-criticism.'

'But it's how I feel.'

'I understand that. But just for now, let's try redirecting those negative thoughts. You can express yourself in other ways. Deep breaths. Counting to ten. I know this stuff sounds kinda lame, but honestly, the more you talk yourself down, the more you'll believe your own bad press.'

I don't know if I completely agree with what he's asking, but for now, I'm going to do as he asks.

'OK,' I say, nodding.

'Back to the dancing. You're gonna start practicing again. Every day. For half an hour a day. If you do more, you'll get treats. If you do less... well, we'll worry about that if it happens, eh?'

I wonder what *would* happen if I don't do my daily practice.

I'm kinda excited to get stuck into this new routine, though. Starting exercise is always the worst part. This is exactly the kind of kick up the backside I've needed to get going with it again. Maybe this is gonna work out.

'That sounds good,' I say. 'But what about the regression stuff?' I've been curious to find out what he means by this. I did some research online, and it seems like there's a really wide spectrum of things that people can be into.

'Well, every day, after you've done your practice and some basic chores I set for you, you can have playtime. I'll provide a bunch of toys and activities, and you can just let go. I want you to try to get into a mindset called Little Space. A state of mind in which you don't have any inhibitions, in which you're free and happy, and you do whatever you feel like. I'm sure that if you spend a part of each day in Little Space, the rest of your life will get better and better.'

'That sounds... kinda nice.' I say. To get into the spirit of things, I pick up Rabbit and squeeze him tight. 'Maybe this is gonna help me.'

'I'm glad you feel that way. I'm going to be looking out for dance auditions for you. Maybe not straight away, I'm sure you'll need a couple weeks to get back int—'

'More like a couple years.'

'Hey, no putting yourself down.'

'I was just kidding,' I say, grinning. It's kinda nice to have him stick up for me like that. Also felt almost good to have him tell me off.

'Good.'

'Um... what about diapers?'

While I was looking online, I found out about grown men and women who like to wear diapers. I kind of assumed that Carl would be into that element of Age Play, I'm not sure why.

'I thought this might come up. Not everyone who is into Age Play likes to wear diapers. Some do. Some don't. I'll leave it up to you. If you want to try experimenting with diapers, I'd be cool with that. The idea is that people find wearing diapers relaxing and comforting. There's no pressure from me, though. If you get into it and want to try, then great. If not, that's also great.'

I wonder what it would feel like to wear a diaper. Never mind wearing one, I wonder how weird it would feel to, you know, *go* in the thing. The thought of it feels so taboo to me. In fact, just thinking about it is making me feel all tingling and weird. In a good way.

'OK, I think I can deal with that.'

We go through a few more things. His responsibilities to me. My rights as a Little. Everything seems above board and exciting. The more I listen, the more curious I am about this setup. I just hope my feelings for Carl won't get in the way.

'So,' he says, eventually, 'are you prepared to sign the contract?'

I nod, trying not to seem apprehensive.

'I want to just reiterate, this isn't about taking control away from you. I want to free you up from all the bullshit of life, to give you the chance to reconnect with your inner child, to let you remember who you are.'

'That sounds good, Daddy.'

As I reach for the pen, my hand touches his finger, just for a moment. There's something between us, and for a moment, I want to reach out and grab him. But I don't. I take the pen and sign my name on the dotted line.

'That took a lot of bravery. I'm proud of you,' he says. It's the first time anyone's said that to me in a very long time. It makes me tingle.

As he takes the contract from me and signs his own name, I can't help but think, again, about what might happen if I break one of the rules. I can't help but feel as though I might *enjoy* the punishment.

# CARL

I T'S BEEN A LONG day. Sometimes, the job of a Sheriff in a small town is a bit like being a therapist. You get to know all the characters of the place, all their little problems and neuroses. Some days, all I do is talk to the citizens of Little Creek, help them come to terms with problems they can't change, and think of ways to solve problems they can.

'Every day, she's there.'

Geraldine manages the dry cleaners. Squeaky Kleen, it's called. She's a good woman, but worries a lot about the youth of the town. Apparently, there's a young lady who keeps loitering across the street from Squeaky Kleen.

'She's not breaking any laws, Geraldine, but I can have a word with her next time I see her if you like?'

'Loitering with intent? That's illegal, isn't it?'

'What's her intent?' I ask. I'm desperate to check my watch. I'm due back home any minute. It's been two days since Diana started her new regime of regression and coddling. I need to make sure I can maintain her structure, and set a good example by being punctual all the time.

'Theft!' Geraldine crosses her arms, then brushes a stray hair away from her cheek. It's an awkward movement, and I can tell she doesn't really believe that the 'loiterer' is really out to steal anything.

'Look, you get any kind of real evidence that she's up to no good, you let me know. I'll be back here quicker than you can say... loitering with intent.'

A few more reassuring statements allow me to make my way back home, at the right time, thankfully.

As I approach Diana's front door, I wonder what kind of greeting I'm going to get.

I knock, and immediately, there's the sound of excited feet, scampering toward the door. She unlocks it and peers around the frame. Diana looks gorgeous, her emerald green eyes peeping at me.

'Password?'

'Confidence.'

It's a little idea I had. Almost like an affirmation. I want to hear Diana hear that word every now and then. Plus, she seems to find the idea of a password to be pretty fun.

'It's an older code, but it checks out,' she says.

I laugh. 'Time to see what my Little Girl has been up to. I wonder if you've done your chores?'

She opens the door wider. She looks absolutely gorgeous, and cute as a button too. I see that she's wearing a short green and white striped dress. I try not to let my eyes linger on the soft shapes of her body, on her slender legs and generous bust. Instead, I cast my gaze around her apartment.

'Hey, this actually looks better!'

Her chore for the day — aside from her dance training and eating right — was to get this place in some order.

'I've been a good girl,' she says, leading me in. There are no piles of dirty plates, and the curtains are open. It's light in here, and airy.

'Hey, is that detergent I can smell?' I ask.

'Uh-huh,' she says. 'I did a little extra.'

We walk in together. Looks like the bonsai tree has had a little attention, too. 'You trimmed your tree?'

'I googled it. Tried to figure out the best way to keep it healthy. Only snipped a couple of leaves. Thought you might like to check it.' Her voice is little, and she's looking up at me with big, hopeful eyes.

'Sure,' I say. I sit down in front of the tree. I can see, just from the way she's chosen certain leaves to remove, that she's seen the natural shape that's hidden in the tree. 'This is wonderful. You're trying to help it grow into itself, aren't you?'

She nods. I walk over to a little wall chart that I put up when we first agreed on the contract. There's a pack of shiny bright star stickers above the chart. I open the pack.

'So, it's one star sticker for tidying your apartment. Do you want to stick it on?'

'Uh-huh, uh-huh!' she nods ferociously and grabs the star from my hand. She's close to me, and I can smell jasmine on her hair. She smells wonderful.

Diana pushes the sticker messily onto the chart, beaming as she does so. I'm so happy with how she's acting. It already feels as though a weight has been lifted from her shoulders. As though she's really starting to blossom.

'Now, did you do your dance practice today?'

'Yep.' She twirls around, her pig-tailed hair swirling around her as she does. 'I loved it!'

'Feeling more confident.'

'I'm all achy.' She leans down and rubs her calf. As she does, it's hard not to notice just how flexible she is. There's no way I'd be able to bend at the waist in the way she does. 'My legs are hurty and my shoulders are sore.'

'That'll get easier for you as time goes on. You too sore to put on another star?'

'No way!' This time, she takes the sticker before I have a chance to peel it off, and then sticks it — more carefully this time — onto her achievement chart.

'OK, so, finally, I take it that you ate your lunch today?'

She looks up at me, shock and horror on her face. 'Oh no. I forgot.' She holds her hand up to her mouth. For a moment, just the briefest moment, it looks as though she's going to grin or laugh. Is she being deliberately naughty? Is she trying to push her limits?

'You forgot?'

'I was watching Netflix,' she says, 'after cleaning up. I just forgot to eat lunch.'

I put on a stern expression. 'Diana, you remember me saying that nutrition is a vital pillar of this regression?'

She nods. She's looking down at the ground, but I notice that she's not wringing her hands. She's not overly stressed. Good.

'I'm going to ask you whether you think you deserve some discipline.'

She looks a little surprised, but then her sweet face relaxes. She doesn't argue, doesn't try to disrespect me. She just says. 'Yes, Daddy. I think I do.'

'Well,' I say, 'I'm glad you think that. That's a very good attitude to have. Now, I'm going to give you a choice about what kind of punishment you get, seeing as it's the first time you've ever broken the rules.'

'Thank you.'

'Option one: a time out. That's twenty minutes, standing in the corner, thinking about why nutrition is so important.' I feel my heart rate spike. 'Or, there's option two: a spanking. With your clothes on. Right on the butt. The quicker option, but it won't be pleasant.'

As I say the word *spanking* her eyes widen. She bites her lip, and I see a little flush of blood in her cheeks.

Then, quickly, almost the instant I stop speaking, she says, 'I want that. Spanking. Please. I don't want time out.'

I feel my excitement rising. Obviously, I've been thinking about discipline, about how I'll help to correct bad behavior, but now that I'm going to have to go through with it, I feel apprehensive. I hate the thought of hurting this sweet Little Girl. But I know discipline is the single most important thing that will help her get her life back on track. And she *chose* to have her butt smacked. She actively wants this.

For a moment, I wish I could call Joel, to ask for his advice on the whole discipline situation. But I can't. I need to just trust my instincts and go with what feels right.

'OK young lady, let's get this over with.' I sit down on her couch and pat my lap. 'Come and lie down on my lap, please.'

She does as I ask, pressing her body down on me. She feels good against me. I do what I can to focus on the task at hand.

'Is it going to hurt, Daddy?' she asks, in a tiny Little voice.

'It will hurt a little bit,' I say, 'but it won't be too bad.'

I lift my hand and then bring it down onto Diana's butt. As it hits her dress, there's a low, smacking sound, and she lets out a little whimper of surprise. I hope I'm not hurting her too much. I only want to help her understand how important the rules between us are.

What she says next takes me by surprise.

'Harder. Please, Daddy.' She almost pants it. 'I need to learn.'

I lift my hand again, and bring it down, cracking harder against her. She yelps again, this time with a hint of pleasure in her voice.

'Lift my dress,' she says, whispering to me. 'I need to feel you against my skin.'

I'm starting to pant now, and I feel something beneath Diana start to stir in my pants.

'I don't know if that's such a good idea,' I say.

'Please,' she says. 'I'm sure.'

I start to lift her dress. Painfully slowly. I'm desperate to see more of her pale, creamy flesh. Beneath the dress, she's wearing a tiny, black thong. It parts her soft, pert buttocks, a striking contrast against her skin. I'm desperate to let my hand stray onto her, to feel her underneath me. But I don't. I can hear her breathing, hear it get deeper, more intense. The atmosphere in the room is crackling with anticipation.

This smack sounds different. The slap of skin against skin is sharp and sudden. This time, she doesn't make a sound, but I see her hands form little fists under her body.

Again I smack her, on the other buttock. Her skin is pink under my open palm. She shivers, her body tensing.

'I'm sorry, Daddy,' she says. 'I'll never forget again. Just, one more time, please. Then I'll know.'

With the final strike, she lets out a low, long moan, relaxing into me. I let my hand rest on the perfect skin of her ass, just for a moment, and I feel blood surge through my body. I'm more hungry for her than I've ever been for anything in my life.

Then, regardless of how difficult it is not to let my hand stay on there for longer, I pull her dress down again, covering her up.

'Good girl, Di. You've been very brave. Time for some aftercare.'

*

As she soaks in the tub, I read her *Harry Potter*. She's never read it before, and she laughs and gasps at the twists and turns, even in the first chapter. She's covered with suds, so her modesty is concealed. It's a dreamy time, and I'm in such a good mood that it feels as though something special is happening.

When she's finished and she's wrapped her towel around her chest, drying off in the living room, she looks at me with these big, expectant eyes.

'Daddy, could you stay over tonight?'

'I could sleep on the couch, sure.'

'No. I want you to sleep in the bed with me. To look after me. I want to be close to you. Nothing naughty, Daddy. Just a cuddle.'

How am I meant to say no to that?

'Of course,' I say.

I haven't brought any pajamas, so I sleep in my Sheriff's uniform. In truth, it's not a great night of sleep for me. But Diana sleeps like a baby, in my arms. I can't stop looking at her. I can't believe I'm so close to her.

When I finally do drift off, my sleep is full of warm dreams, of shards of hope. Of pride.

# DIANA

I T'S BEEN THE BEST week I've had for two weeks. Carl is amazing. He's slept over at my tiny apartment every single day since that first. I've been a good girl ever since I got my butt spanked, though. I want Daddy to be proud of me.

Today is a special day. It's Saturday, and Daddy's not at work. He's taking me out on a long walk, because we're going to talk about the future of our arrangement. I initially agreed to be regressed for a week, and then, to possibly extend it, if I felt as though it was helping.

It's *definitely* helping. I feel fitter, healthier and happier. Feels like, over the years, I'd really forgotten how to play, how to be carefree. There have been times this week, while I've been playing with simple things — blocks and paints and crayons and jigsaw puzzles — that I reconnected with feelings I've been keeping hidden for my entire adult life.

It's amazing. It feels like I'm rediscovering myself.

And then there's Carl.

My feelings for him have grown so much over the past few days that it's difficult to express. He's so kind and supportive, so firm and instructive. He's helped me so much. And being with him, knowing that he's gonna come home every day after work to spend time with me, it's given me confidence and stability that I haven't known for a long time.

'I can't believe that you've lived in Little Creek your whole life, and you've never been up into the Rockies.'

'I know, I know, it's shameful.'

We're walking down main street, and there's a bite in the air. Clouds up above are dark and thick, but there's not an atmosphere of foreboding. It's something else. Like the world's about to open up to us. Snow is coming, we can both feel it. It's a matter of when, not if.

'I've been thinking about your dancing,' says Carl. 'Ever since last night, I can't get it out of my head.'

Yesterday, I showed Carl a dance routine I've been working on. It's nothing like as complicated as the type of stuff I used to do before, but it's something. I loved showing Carl. Loved knowing that his eyes were playing over my body as I moved, as I expressed my feelings of growing joy to him.

'Have you?'

'Mmmhmm. I thought that maybe, you might like to set up some kind of dance school. You know, if you're not keen on auditioning for shows.'

It's a great idea. To be honest, I know that it's going to be difficult to get work in a show or even in music videos. I don't have connections, and I've been out of the game for too long. But maybe I *could* teach others. Up until now, I didn't think I was good enough, didn't think anyone would listen to me.

'You think I'd be a good teacher?'

'I know it.'

We walk in silence for a few minutes, until the streets of the town are behind us. I keep stealing glances at Carl, so proud to be walking with such a handsome, well-respected man.

'We don't have far to go,' he says. 'Which is good, 'cause I'm hungry as a hippo. I brought us some lunch.' He pats his rucksack. 'Can't have you missing a meal, Young Lady.'

Shortly, after a little walk uphill, we find a picnic table at the side of a trail. There's a view over a distant lake here. It's incredibly beautiful, and as I sit down, I feel peace wash over me.

'So,' he says, opening up his rucksack, 'I'm gonna admit, I'm really damn nervous about this.'

'Nervous?' I say. '*You* get nervous?'

His smile never fails to melt my heart.

'Of course I do. This is about as nervous as I've ever been. This is important to me. You're important to me.'

I can't help it. I stretch out across the table and take his hand.

'You're important to me, too.'

'Di, you've impressed me so much this week. It's been a pleasure to spend time with you. I hope that it's been useful for you.'

'Of course it has.'

'I know that we said that after a week, we'd talk about whether you want to continue. I hope that you do. But if you've got any questions for me, any concerns at all, now's the time to raise them.'

This is it. I've been waiting days for this. I feel my own nerves start to build. And then, just when I'm about to open my mouth and speak, I see a single flake of snow, falling slowly from the heavens. It lands on our hands, and a second later, melts.

'The thing is,' I say, 'I know I'm not meant to lie to you. I know you want me to be honest at all times. The problem is, right at the start, before we even signed the contract, I lied to you.'

He looks serious. Tender, but serious.

'You can tell me,' he says. 'You can always tell me anything.'

'I know.' I nod, looking down at the table. 'OK, here goes. I told you that I used to have a crush on you. Years ago. That was a lie. Because, you see, the thing is, I still like you. Always have.' His eyes soften, and he puts another hand over mine. Snow is falling faster now, settling and melting, settling and melting. 'This week, being closer to you, my feelings have grown even stronger. That night, the night you spanked me, it felt better than anything. Better than any sex I've ever had. Because I knew you were doing it for my own good. And since then, I've felt — I've *known* — that I want you to be my Daddy. In every way imaginable. For always.'

He's looking at me intensely, snowflakes falling between us.

'You know, it's really not why I did this whole thing. I always felt something between us, but I just wanted to help you.'

'And you have,' I say. 'I don't feel tricked, I don't feel anything but happiness for the way you've looked after me.'

'I'm glad.'

I squeeze his hand.

'Every night, when you curl up next to me in bed, so strong, so warm, so big, you make me feel safe. Safer than I've ever been.' I bite my lip. 'But you make me feel something else, too. Something in the pit of my stomach. Even lower than that.'

There's hunger in his eyes now. I can see it, can sense his desire for me.

'I want you, Diana,' he says. 'I've been trying to fight it, but I need you to know that I'm desperate to taste you. I want to make you mine.'

'I want it too,' I pant, moving my hand up his arm.

'Tomorrow,' he says, 'I'm going to take you somewhere very special. Somewhere we can be alone, and you can fully express yourself. I've been planning it all week. And now I know you want to commit to this life with me, I'm ready to show you.'

Excitement builds in my breast.

'There's something I've been wanting to tell you, too,' I say. 'Something to show you just how committed I am. Tonight I want to wear a diaper. I want you to put it on for me.'

'Are you sure?'

I nod. 'I want you to be my Daddy Dom. And I'm gonna be your Little Girl. I think I'm gonna like it. And if I don't... well, you can just take it off me again.'

He looks like he's going to say something, but he doesn't. Instead, he leans over the table and kisses me. His lips are soft, but the way he kisses is hard, voracious, like a beast. It's so instantly intoxicating, I forget everything. Forget the snow, the clouds, the towering mountains. And all I can think about, all I can perceive, is Carl; his mouth, his tongue, his hands on my skin.

And then, I smile. And he smiles. I can feel it.

*

Low light. Just a couple candles. Pillows underneath me, holding my body. Up above, my Daddy, Carl. I'm feeling dreamy and Little. We got back home and I played for hours, sitting innocently in the middle of the lounge while Daddy did important Daddy things. It's like I'm under a spell. Deeply regressed, lost in the moment.

'Will it hurt, Daddy?'

'Your diaper?' he shakes his head, grinning. 'Only if I do something terribly wrong.'

'Daddy, I like the way you look at me.'

'I like the way you look.'

I'm just wearing my underwear. It's like we're doing some ritual together. It's intimate and deeply sexy, but at the same time, there's an innocence and trust to this that I've never experienced before.

'Are you gonna take my panties off?'

'I kinda have to. How am I gonna put the diaper on you otherwise?'

'I'm nervous.' My voice trembles.

'Course you are, sweetheart. First time you do anything makes you nervous. Nothing wrong with nerves. It's your body, reminding you you're alive, getting you ready for the new experience.'

I look at the diaper nearby. It's big, bigger than I expected. I wonder what it's gonna feel like to have it against my skin.

'OK, you ready?'

I nod.

Carl slips his fingers under the waistband of my panties, then slowly, gently pulls them down. Even that sensation is too much for me. I feel a tingling sensation in my private parts, and it's so tickly that I flinch.

'Sorry, can't help it. I'm excited.'

I look down at his hands and see the light from the candles flickering over my smooth skin.

'Don't worry, sugar, you do what you need to do.'

He moves again, quicker this time, pulling my panties all the way down. I'm bare in front of him now, nude and vulnerable. He looks down at me.

'You're so beautiful,' he says. 'Always have been. Thank you for letting me into your life.'

He reaches for the diaper, and as he does, I find myself wishing that he was still looking at me.

'You can touch me if you like,' I say. The words come out quickly — a tumble of syllables that barely make sense.

He snaps around and locks eyes with me. 'You want me to clean you before I put the diaper on?'

I lick my lips. 'Mmmhmm.' I'm so wet for him. Just being this close to him, having him so clearly in control of the situation, it's making me squirm and moan.

'OK,' he grunts. It's an animal sound. Powerful, intense.

I feel his fingers first, on my thighs. Strong and confident. He pushes my legs apart. I yield to him.

'I've been dreaming about this,' I whisper. 'Dreaming about your hands.'

'Have you been dreaming about my tongue?'

He leans in quick, and before I have time to reply, I feel it, the trace of the tip of his tongue as it runs hungry up and down my pussy lips. The sensation is deep and overwhelming.

I reach down, touch his hair, and he dives in deeper. I know my wetness is engulfing him, too, because the more he licks, the wetter and wetter I get, like my body is opening up for him. He pushes into me now. He feels so good that I know it's not going to take much to push me over the edge.

I grip the cushions beneath me as his tongue vibrates slowly, working its way further in.

'Oh Daddy, oh my, oh fu—' I say. I'm about to say something I know I'll regret, but he stops me by slipping his tongue over my clit. And the moment he touches it, I explode, arching my back, tensing my muscles, pushing my pussy up into him as my pleasure focuses itself and I feel pure ecstasy.

The moments that follow are deep and slow. He leans in and kisses my forehead. And then, my legs turned to Jell-O, he lifts me and slips the diaper under me. It's soft and crinkly, and the minute he fastens it, I realize that I love it. I love the tightness. I love how secure it makes me feel. And there's something else I love too.

'Daddy,' I say, my voice dreamy and distant, 'I love... this.'

He gives me a knowing look.

'I feel the same way.'

# CARL

'ARE WE NEARLY THERE yet?'

I look back through the trees.

'You really know how to dress for a hike, don't you sweetie?'

She grins. 'I like snow-wear, OK?'

When I told Diana that we were going for a two-day break at a Daddy friend's Age Play cabin in the woods, she shrieked with delight.

She dug around in an old chest that was in her apartment, and finally emerged, triumphant, clutching the outrageous snowsuit she's wearing today.

Honestly, it kinda looks like a onesie. It's thick and plush, with a pale pink water-proof coating.

'I think I must have had a premonition that I'd become a Little when I bought this thing.' She catches up with me and tugs at my arm.

'I think, somehow, that you've always known. I always had a feeling about you, Di. You were always so cute and innocent. And I always felt like you were someone who didn't like the hardness of adult life.'

'Grown-ups are boring.'

'That's my girl,' I grin. 'And as for your question, yes, we're nearly there.'

I've never visited Joel in his Cabin before. We hang out in town from time to time. Last time I saw him in person was actually when

I helped him out with a little criminal issue he had to deal with. But for the most part, we drink at The Rocky Bar, and have coffee at Cartwright's.

See, the issue with visiting Joel is that there's literally no road. We had to park my car at Joel's garage and trek the final part of the journey through a thick pine forest, in driving snow.

It actually feels really damn romantic. As though we're losing ourselves, leaving civilization behind. And luckily, I've got a satellite GPS system (police issue, of course) so there's no real chance that we're gonna get lost.

'Hey, can you smell that?' Because of the cold, Diana's got really cute rosy cheeks today. The more time I spend with her, the more I pick up on the tiny details of her looks and personality. And there's nothing I don't like.

'No. What do you mean?'

'Smoke!' she says. 'Sniff again.'

I breathe in deeply, and sure enough, she's right. It's the warm, welcoming scent of woodsmoke, coming from — I presume — somewhere up ahead of us.

'We must be *really* close,' I say.

It's just a moment later that we catch sight of the smoke, billowing up, dark gray against the flecks of bright white that fall in front of it.

When we arrive at the cabin, Diana's eyes widen. I'm impressed too. Joel's built something really special here. The impressive thing is just how well the cabin blends into the surrounding environment. It's cozy and big, but because it's made from felled pine logs, it seems to belong here. In front of the place, there's a sign. Written in a cute, pastel peach chalk font are the words, 'Joel and Ella's Little Cabin.'

'This is so cool!' squeals Di. Joel must hear her, because a second later, the front door opens, and out he steps. It's good to see him. I always forget how massive he is. I guess all the outdoorsy work must have a good effect on his physique.

Then, another figure appears. She peeps out from behind her Daddy, eyes sparkling.

'Joel, Ella, so good to see you!' My voice sounds different now that the snow has settled — muffled, quiet, distant. Everything about today has an otherworldly quality.

Di's been slightly nervous about meeting another Little, so I look round to check on her. I'm happy to say that she actually looks excited to meet Ella, rather than anxious.

'Good to see you Carl, and great to meet you, Diana. I've heard a lot about you. Let me take that bag for you.' Joel helps Diana with her backpack and heads inside. 'Come on, let me show you around.'

As we walk through the front door, Ella says to Di, 'Is it true you're a dancer?'

'Uh-huh,' says Di, looking a little bit sheepish. 'But I'm not that good.'

'She's amazing,' I say. 'She's thinking of setting up a dance school in Little Creek. Working with children in the town.'

'That's so cool,' says Ella, beaming at us, her blue eyes full of admiration. 'I wish I could dance. Maybe you can teach me some moves?'

'OK,' says Di, smiling. I can feel my heart warming quicker than if I were in front of the open fire.

I knew that the two of them would get on, but there's a difference between hoping something and seeing it unfold before your eyes.

The cabin is amazing. Beautifully decorated with furs and antlers, with a roaring fire in the hearth. Smells like there's a pot of coffee on, and the view from the double windows across Purple Lake is wonderful. Joel ushers us into the playroom, which he seems very excited and proud to be able to show us around.

'So this is the nursery in the guest cabin,' Joel says. It's an amazing space, full of adult-sized baby furniture. Huge armchairs, a fully-stocked changing table, and lots of boxes full of toys. There's even an adult-sized crib, complete with wood bars. Next to the crib is a bookshelf, packed full of storybooks. 'It's been specially designed for couples just like you. Ella's stocked it with all her favorite toys—'

'There's Twister!' she cackles.

Joel gives her a stern look. 'I can see someone's a little overexcited today.'

'Sorry Daddy,' she says, 'it's just so cool to finally meet another Little.'

'I tell you what,' I say, 'why don't we let these two go play and we can catch up, Joel?'

'Dress up!' shrieks Ella, who's smiling so wide her lips barely fit her face. Diana giggles and runs over to her, before they start rifling through a box of outfits.

'Coffee?' Joel asks.

*

'Seems like things are going well between you two.'

Joel takes a sip from his cup. 'Yeah. I've never been happier. Ella seems happy, too. Getting away from the city has been good for her. And I think being able to be Little 24/7 — or at least for as long as she wants to every day — is wonderful for her. What about with Diana? I thought you said she was some kind of wild child? She seems sweet as candy to me.'

'A week ago, she was a different person,' I reply, sipping my brew for the first time. 'Damn, Joel, this coffee is so strong, you could use it as rocket fuel. I love it.'

'It's not coffee. Just ground-up charcoal. That's what us real moun-tain men drink.'

I snort. 'Says the city trader.'

'Not anymore.' He grins. 'You ever think of leaving Little Creek, coming out here? We could start a kind of commune for Littles and Bigs.'

It's an interesting idea. 'Problem is, I love my job. Little Creek's a special place, and I've gotta make sure that it's safe. Maybe when I retire.'

It's his turn to snort. 'What when you're eighty? I know men like you, Carl. You ain't the retiring type.'

'True enough.'

'Seriously though, how are things with Di? You two seem good together. I can tell you're having a good influence on her.'

'Honestly, feels like she's having a good influence on me, too. Before we started this little experiment, I was too focused on work. Now, it feels as though I've got something else in my life. Something good and pure and full of hope for the future.' I turn to look at the door, make sure that no-one's about to burst in. 'I'm falling for her, Joel.' I shake my head. 'No. That's bullshit. I fell for her years ago. I'm deep in love with her.'

'Have you told her?'

'You kidding me? After a week? She'd run away so quick I wouldn't even see the back of her.'

'I wouldn't be so sure,' he says. 'When you find your Forever Girl, you know. And if you feel it, I bet she feels it too.'

There's a peal of laughter, and then, a second later, a very seri-ous-sounding knock from the door.

'Here comes trouble,' Joel grunts.

Diana and Ella tumble through the door, both dressed in the cutest imaginable bear outfits. They look ridiculous, and they shriek with laughter.

'Raaarrrrr!' growls Ella, drawing her hands up like claws in front of her. Diana glances at her then does the same. It's so sweet to see her following her new Little friend's lead.

'There's bears on the loose,' I say, mock-serious. 'Quick Joel, get the hunting rifle!'

The girls scream and scamper from the door.

*

'So if you need anything, you've got my number.' Joel and Ella are all packed up, ready to head to his car. They're going to Denver to visit Ella's family for a couple days while we stay in the guest cabin, leaving us with the run of the place.

'Don't worry, we'll be fine,' I assure him. Ella and Diana share a brief cuddle, and I shake Joel's hand.

'Look after each other,' he says. Then the two of them turn and head into the woods. The snow has stopped, but there's a thick blanket of white all over the forest floor, and the trees bow under the weight of it all.

When the two of them are safely out of earshot, Diana turns to me. 'Ella is *so* cool! Did you know she makes jewelry? She said that she'd make me a ring or some earrings as a gift! I told her that I can show her some dance stuff in return if she wants. She agreed!'

'That's great, honey,' I say, giving her a cuddle. It's been nice to spend time with another couple like us. Joel and I have been close for a while, but I feel as though the four of us are going to become firm friends now. 'Now I guess we can just relax for a couple days. What do you want to do first?'

She pauses for a moment, then looks up at me with hopeful eyes.

'Twister?'

# DIANA

'**H**EY, THAT'S MY FOOT!'

Daddy laughs and shifts his body under mine. It feels so good to be this close to him, even if it is just a game. Even though we're not far from Little Creek, it kinda feels like we've come to a secret place, away from the daily grind of our lives.

'Sorry, baby,' he says. 'It's easier for you. You're so dang flexible.'

'But you're so strong,' I reply. My groin is pressed into his leg, as I struggle to reach for the spinner. It's strange to feel the crinkle of the diaper next to my skin, but it's also weirdly comforting.

I can't believe how lucky it is that there's another DDlg couple near Little Creek. Makes me feel a lot less isolated and weird in this brand-new lifestyle I've fallen into. And Ella seems so cool and, well, *normal*. I can't wait to get to know her better.

'Hand to green,' I say. We both twist and turn around, desperately trying to find a free green circle we can reach.

'Hnnnhhggg,' I groan, reaching out as far as I can. For a moment, it seems like I'm gonna be able to manage it, then, as I shift a tiny bit too far, I feel myself losing my footing, and then, with a comfortable bump, we both collapse down onto the floor, bodies intertwined, laughing and smiling with delight.

'I guess we both lose?' Carl says.

'Not how I see it.' I squeeze his arm. 'I feel like we both won.'

He puts his hand on mine, and then, before I have time to really take it in, his lips are on mine. This time, there's no hesitation from me, just instant submission to the mastery of his desire.

'Thank you,' I whisper, as his lips find their way onto my neck, kissing and gently biting. 'Thank you for everything.'

'Thank *you*,' he replies, pulling me in close to him. 'You're everything I ever wanted. And now, you belong to me.'

I close my eyes, yield to his kisses, find myself lost in this moment.

My hands grasp at him, feeling the hardness of his body beneath his t-shirt. I pick out his muscles, feeling them move as he shifts and grips me. It's a whirlwind of sensation, a blizzard of hot, tender feelings. My neck, my clavicle, and my chest all tingle as he slips my top up and over me. Then he carries on down, lifting and setting me on the mat, letting his lips and tongue trail their way down to my stomach.

I feel his hands on my pants, tugging at the band, unbuttoning me, and then, he grips the tabs of my diaper and he's ripping it, tearing it away. I gasp as I feel myself naked in front of him.

'I want to see you,' I say, hungry for him.

He separates himself from me and starts to unbutton his shirt. The wait is killing me. I watch him as he strips, feasting my eyes on his perfect body. All these years I've known him, this body's been waiting for me this whole time. I can see before he tugs his pants down that he's hard for me. Not just hard. Huge.

'I want to taste you, Daddy,' I say.

He pulls his pants off, and it springs up, his manhood, hungry for me. I gasp when I see it. How am I even going to fit that thing inside me?

'You want a taste, honey?' He grips the shaft of his manhood, pulling it gently back. The bulging tip is thick for me, and a sheen of wet glistens across it.

I lick my lips. 'Please,' I moan. 'I need it.'

He inches towards me, and when he's close enough, almost sitting on my chest, I grab his cock and pull it towards me. It's so big my hand can barely encircle it. But I stretch my lips and look straight up into my Daddy's eyes, then I plant a soft, wet kiss on the tip of his cock. He pushes the tip into me, widening my mouth even further, and I take it in, sucking and licking as best as I can. He reaches down, stroking my face.

'You can do it.' With his encouragement, I take him even further into me, widening myself for him. He starts to slip in and out of me, his cock slick with my spit. I feel my pussy blossom for him, tender and moist and ready. I'm trembling, yearning, desperate for him to split me apart.

I start to move in time with him, trying to let him know how good he's making me feel, how special. He starts to grunt and moan with each thrust. I reach down past him, touch myself, splitting my lips, rubbing my clit. He feels me squirm, looks back at me.

'You're hungry for it, aren't you? Open for me?'

I nod as I suck him. Then, a second later, he pulls back, and his cock bobs in front of me, level with my face.

'You're so big,' I say. 'Is it going to hurt?'

'No,' he says, cupping my face. 'I'll be gentle. I'll make it good for you.'

He slips down, lining his body up with mine. I can feel his heat, feel the intention behind his movement. I slip my hands up and over his back, feel the power and size of his shoulders. Then, the tip of his cock rests at my entrance.

'You ready, sweetheart?'

'I think so,' I say, my voice Little and impossibly hungry.

He nods. 'I know you are.'

Just the tip of his cock is enough to make my eyes widen with surprise. The pleasure of it, the tight, satisfying feeling of being filled up makes me feel completely delicious.

'More,' I whine. 'I want to feel you all the way inside me.'

'You're so wet,' he says, 'and so tight. You feel incredible, Diana.'

I shift down, pulling more of him into me, stretching myself wider and wider. 'I wanna gobble you all up,' I say. 'I belong to you, Daddy. I want you to do whatever you want to me.'

He slips in further, and I can feel every tiny part of him, every contour, every bulge of that masterful cock. He starts to move, dragging in and out, pushing down gently on me, so powerful, strong. I hook my leg up onto him, make myself wide and open, and let him do exactly what he wants. 'I'm gonna take it slow,' he says, panting, 'so slow you beg me to go faster, so slow you come on my cock just from desire.'

Sure enough, his movement is steady, but solid as rock. Unstoppable, his hands like iron vices on me, pinning me down into sweet submission as he starts to grind his powerful groin down and round. He's hitting every spot of me, and his hard body is rubbing into my clit as he moves. I don't know how he's doing it, but it's the most intense feeling I've ever experienced.

'Daddy,' I moan, 'please, do it faster. I need it, I want i—'

He keeps his pace, torturing me, making sure I know that he's in charge. 'You sure you could handle it if I go faster?'

I nod, desperately. 'I can take it, Daddy! Please!' I need release, I'm desperate for it.

'I want you to come for me first,' he says, moving closer to me. His fingers encircle my nipples, teasing, pulling, while his hot mouth slides over my neck, biting me, kissing up by my throat. It's so intense, it feels like my whole body is on fire for him, is burning up at his touch. I feel my pussy start to tighten, and my body starts to tremble and I know I'm close. He senses it too, because he grips me tighter, then looks me in the eye. 'Now,' he says, then he kisses me, biting my lip, tasting my tongue while his cock plunges into me with that slow, relentless pace.

My eyes roll back. I see bright white lights, and I grip him harder as I come, harder than ever before. More wetness spreads from my pussy.

'Good girl,' he says. Then, he starts to move. Fast. It's a new sensation — totally overwhelming. Deep and rough and unstoppable speed. So powerful I can barely cope, and so masterful that within seconds of my climax, I feel like I'm being dragged up to an even higher peak.

'Oh Da—'

But he stops me from speaking with a thirsty kiss, twisting his tongue around mine, then pummeling me with his cock, beating harder and harder into me.

I grab him and pull him further into me, digging my nails into his warm steel flesh. He grunts and groans with me and I reply with high-pitched whines of pleasure.

'I want you,' I say, 'I need you.'

'I belong to you.' And with that, he grips my shoulders and pushes his cock so far up into me that I feel like I'm gonna burst. But he's the one who bursts. And as he lengthens and stiffens inside me, I feel the warm electricity of a second orgasm surging through me. We kiss. We squeeze. We laugh. We collapse.

*

Our time in the cabin is so magical that I worry about leaving it. But in truth, our lives when we head back to Little Creek are even more magical.

Because they're ordinary. I head back to work. So does Carl. But in the evenings and weekends, when we're together, we're Daddy and Little together.

I don't break any more of Daddy's rules. I've been working hard, practicing every day, and eating super healthy, nutritious food. My figure has definitely improved, and I feel fitter and happier than I have for years.

After a month of our new life, buds start to appear on my little bonsai tree. I've been at home, cleaning my apartment, and when Carl comes home from his day at the Sheriff's office, he's super excited to see how my little tree is flourishing.

'I'm so proud of you,' he says, taking his hat off and looking intently at the little tree. 'And there's something I want to tell you.'

'What's up, Daddy?' I say.

He sits down on the couch and I head up to his lap, pushing my little diapered butt down into him.

'Well, I made a trip to the bank at lunchtime today. I thought that because you've been such a good girl recently, I might give you a little help setting up a dance school. So, I'm renting out premises for you.'

'Huh? Really?'

He nods. 'Yep. The old garage next to Cartwright's.'

Holy cow, that place is perfect.

'You're the best Daddy of all time,' I sigh. I think about my parents. I wish they were around to see me flourish like this. I can feel their pride, and I actually feel good for once.

'It's easy,' he says. '*You* make it easy. Because I love you. Always have. Always will.'

This time, when our lips meet, it feels different. It feels like home.

* * *

**Read on for Atlas and Mia's story: *Saved by Daddy*!**

# Chapter Three

## SAVED BY DADDY

# ATLAS

'**A**RE YOU KIDDING ME?' I ask the question with disbelief, but of course, I already know the answer.

'No, Karadinis, I'm not kidding you. I'm sending you out to rescue a cat from a tree.' I can see that the chief is struggling to stop himself from smiling.

I rub my temples. 'This is such a joke. The fire department is meant t—'

'The fire department is meant to provide a service when public safety is threatened.' His mustache curls with his lip as he gives in to the smile.

'Does a cat really count as *the public*?'

Even though I've been with the Little Creek Fire Service for coming up to four years, I'm still technically the new guy. I tend to get the weird jobs like this. Obviously, I've fought plenty of blazes in my time. We cover a wide, mostly rural area from our base in Little Creek, in the heart of Colorado. We mostly react to wildfires during fire season, but in springtime, it's mostly calls like this.

'It's not the cat I'm worried about. It's the very real possibility that the cat's owner climbs up the tree herself and falls out while she tries to coax that little bastard down.'

He's got a point, I guess.

'You want me to use the siren?' I ask, sarcastically.

He gives me a look. 'Just do your job, son.'

I decide, on balance, not to use the siren.

It wasn't like this when I used to live in Greece. I was a firefighter then, but my life was very different. You see, in Greece, in the summertime, there's almost no water. Except of course for the sea. So when there was a blaze in the countryside surrounding Athens, I used to strap into my trusty Canadair CL-415 aircraft and fly over the crystal clear Aegean sea. I'd dive down, scoop up gallons of water, then dump it over mountainside blazes.

Now I drive to get cats out of trees.

I came to Colorado for love. I fell out of love with the woman who brought me here, but fell in love with the country. The trees, the cold, the summer lightning. Everything about this majestic place. The people, too. So I stayed. Moved away from Denver and found a home in this tiny town: Little Creek. Now, the only thing that gives me away as not being a local Coloradan is my thick Greek accent.

The address is on the other side of town, but it only takes a few minutes for me to arrive. I'm in a small fire truck. I had to bring it, because no doubt I'll need a ladder to free this damn cat.

Ugh. Look, don't get me wrong — I love cats. It's just... they are assholes when they're up in trees. There's nothing that's less likely to get a cat to come down from a tree than the sight of a firefighter climbing up towards it.

But when I reach the house, I instantly get the feeling that something's wrong.

I park the truck and get out, heading towards the woman who's standing in front of her house, looking desperately up into a nearby fir.

'What seems to be the issue, ma'am?'

When she turns to face me, two things strike me. One: she's gorgeous. Like, drop-down-dead, burst-into-flames, throw-my-self-off-a-building, gorgeous. Like, the type of gorgeous that mere mortals like me only get the chance to experience once in our lifetimes. Transcendentally, life-alteringly, impossibly gorgeous. Green, almond-shaped eyes. Pastel pink, heart-shaped lips. High, delicate cheekbones. The kind of fiery auburn hair that does funny things to my insides.

The second thing that strikes me, though, is just how sad she looks. Not just sad. Terrified.

'It's my cat, Chuckles.' She points up into the tree. I follow her finger and look up, but I don't see a cat on a branch. Instead, I see something I've never seen in all my time rescuing felines from sticky situations.

A bag, dangling from a branch. A rucksack. It swings in the breeze, as though it could fall any second. From the way it moves, there's obviously something inside it.

'He's in the bag?'

She nods and looks down at the ground. She's clutching her left arm with her right hand, as though trying to protect herself from something. Instantly I get the strongest urge to look after this sweetheart. It's like my Daddy instincts are fizzing away in overdrive. This Little Girl needs looking after.

'What happened?'

'Bad people,' she says. 'They came. Put him up there.' She's still looking down, sobbing, her breath ragged and harsh.

I lean in, then touch her shoulder with my hand as softly as I can manage. I don't want her to feel threatened, just reassured. 'I'm gonna get Chuckles down. Then you and I are going to have a little chat, OK, darling?'

I know some women don't like to be called 'darling' by strangers, but it's an old habit of mine that I find hard to break, especially with a woman as sweet as this. Us Greeks tend to be more affectionate than Americans. I hope she doesn't mind.

She looks at me and smiles for the first time. It transforms her face, and even though there are still tears rolling down her cheeks, I feel hopeful that I can salvage this situation.

'Please, just make sure Chuckles is safe.'

I maneuver the truck so that it's under the tall fir, and extend the ladder. Then I climb up, quick and safe as I can. As I near the bag, I hear the poor cat, terrified, meowing like mad, non-stop. My blood starts to boil. Who would do something like this to a defenseless animal?

Luckily, the bag's hung on a branch that's easily accessible. How did they get it up here? Did they just throw it, hoping it would catch on something? It sure seems that way. I unhook the bag, but I don't open it. I want to make sure that this little creature sees a familiar face when we let him out.

'Is he alright?' Her voice is desperate.

'I think so,' I reply, glancing down. 'He's making a hell of a racket.'

I descend the ladder and step over to her.

'Thank you so much,' she says, taking the bag from me and un-zipping the top. The meowing stops and a tiny, ginger face appears at the bag's opening. 'Mr. Chuckles.' Tears are streaming down her face again. 'It's all my fault. I'm sorry, baby.' She kisses the cat's face. The cat doesn't look impressed. A second later, he shoots from the bag, and like an orange streak, zooms into the open door of the house.

'He seems OK,' I say.

'Poor thing.'

'How'd he get up there?' I remove my gloves, holding them at my side.

'They threw him.'

'Who?'

The instant I ask this question, it's like she freezes up. That pretty face becomes a stone, closed off entirely. 'I don't know. Just... thugs.'

Before I can stop myself, I say, 'I don't believe you.'

I'm expecting her to be angry or surprised, but instead, it seems like my honesty has had a positive effect on her. Her expression softens. 'Look, have you got time for a cup of tea?'

I don't, but that's not gonna stop me. Something's going on here.

'No. But I'll take a coffee.'

*

I'm surprised by how bare her place is. Almost nothing superfluous in here, no decoration. The most basic furnishing you could imagine. The only thing of any note is a poster that spans one of the walls. It's a huge picture of a grizzly bear, silhouetted against the moon, growling.

'You a bear fan?' I ask as she boils a kettle.

She turns around. 'What gave it away?'

Chuckles is getting busy with a tray of cat food while I wait for my drink.

'I'm Mia,' she says, 'and I'm a bear fan.'

She sets down a steaming cup in front of me.

'I'm Atlas,' I say. 'And I guess I don't have much of an opinion on bears, one way or another.'

She laughs. It's a beautiful sound. 'Where you from, Atlas? You've got an interesting accent.'

'Greece, originally. Athens. But I'm a Coloradan now.'

'Wow! What's Athens like?'

'Hot and old.' I'm keen to get the discussion back to her. 'Look, I know I'm a stranger, but if you're in trouble, I'd like to help.'

She looks genuinely stunned. Then, that stony expression from before returns. 'I'm OK.'

I scoff. 'Someone threw your cat in a tree. Doesn't sound very OK to me.'

For a moment, it looks like she's going to say something. Then, instead, she says, 'I don't need help. I can sort it out myself. I don't want anyone else to get hurt.'

'Anyone else? You mean you're OK with getting hurt yourself?'

She doesn't nod, doesn't shake her head. She just takes a sip from her tea in silence.

'Someone did this to scare you, didn't they?'

She flinches but stays quiet. 'Honestly, I'm fine.'

'Honesty has nothing to do with this.' I'm being harsh, but I don't know how else to get her to open up. I know something weird is going on here.

She puts her cup down. 'Maybe you should get going. I'm grateful for your help with Chuckles, but I'm feeling a little—'

'Intimidated into silence by someone?'

Her eyes meet mine, and her lip quivers. For a moment, it looks as though she's going to burst into tears again. And in that moment, I know I'm lost. I need to save this poor woman, whether she knows about it or not. 'Look, I'm sorry, I know I'm being pushy. I just hate to see someone in trouble. It's why I joined the fire service.'

'Seems like you're a natural-born hero.' Is that a hint of sass?

We have a relaxed conversation after that, full of small-talk but not much else. Any time I try to probe into the trouble she's in, she clams up. I do find out, however, that she's an aspiring naturalist, with a particular interest in bear habitats.

'It's why I moved to Little Creek,' she says. 'I'm from Colorado Springs, originally, but I wanted to do some research on the local ursine population. How about you? Have you always been a firefighter?'

'No, but I have been one for a long time. Nearly eight years. But before that, I was in the Greek army.'

'So you always wanted to help people, huh?'

'It's nice that you see it that way,' I say. 'In Greece, a lot of my friends were surprised when I joined the army. It's got a bit of a reputation for being — how do I put this? — just boys playing with toys.'

'Nothing wrong with that.' She gives me a mysterious look.

'I guess not.'

'I've always kinda found Greek guys to be—'

'Sexy?'

She laughs. 'I was gonna say arrogant.'

I join her laugh. 'Well obviously, I'm anything but arrogant.' I say, sarcastically. 'I'm too perfect to be anything like arrogant.'

'That's clear.'

'Look,' I finally say, sensing that there might be something between us, 'if I can't help with your problem, could I at least take you out for a drink?'

Stony face again. 'Uh,' she says. 'It's jus—'

I hold up my hands. 'Forget I asked. It was very unprofessional of me.' The atmosphere instantly changes. I look at my watch. 'I'd better go. The chief's gonna be furious. I'm gonna have to make up some story about Mr. Chuckles refusing to come down for ages.'

As I walk back to the truck, I feel the rage returning. That poor cat, and this poor woman. So I look back at her, and I say, 'I'm going to look after you, Mia. No-one's going to harm you while I'm working in this town.' Then I turn and climb aboard.

What I didn't tell Mia is that I was in the Greek Special Forces. I might be rusty, but that's training you don't forget. These thugs aren't gonna know what hit them.

# MIA

I FEEL HIM PUSH himself up against me in bed. It's such a warm, reassuring feeling, that it almost makes me melt.

'Mr. Chuckles, you know that technically you're not meant to be in here with me.'

I'm allergic to cats. I know, I know, I'm an idiot for keeping one, but I just can't help it. I love Mr. Chuckles too much.

As if on cue, I sneeze. Mr. Chuckles barely registers the sound — he must be so used to my sniffles and sneezes by now. He probably just thinks that's how I say hello.

I've overslept, but it's not my fault. It took me hours to get to sleep last night. How was I meant to relax after the day I had yesterday?

I don't know what I'm gonna do. I can't believe the Russian mob has tracked me down to Little Creek. I tried to be careful, tried to cover my tracks. But it seems like I'm gonna have to run, again. I've barely been in town for two months. I'm not gonna get the chance to study any bears, that's for sure.

I get out of bed, then start to pack my bag. I've become depressingly quick at packing it recently. Must be all the practice.

Diana's gonna be sad. I'm meant to be going to her new studio for a dance lesson. I met Diana online, on an ABDL forum. She's the real reason I thought that Little Creek might be a good place for me to lay

low. She described it as the smallest small town you could ever visit. I
was sold.

She's become a great friend since I first moved here. She even let me
stay on her floor for a couple nights while I got an apartment orga-
nized. Her Daddy is the local Sheriff. Seems like the logical thing to do
in my situation would be to go to him, and tell him my problems. But
the fact is the people who are out to get me eat local law enforcement
like Carl for breakfast. I know. I've seen it happen before.

Now there's another reason why leaving Little Creek is even more
shitty. Atlas.

I barely had time to get to know him. And he didn't have any chance
to get to know me. He must think I'm a maniac. But I couldn't tell
him about my situation. Because everyone I tell ends up getting hurt.

I can't stop thinking about what he said to me. *I'm going to look
after you, Mia. No-one's going to harm you while I'm working in this
town.*

I wish I could believe him. There was something about him. He was
so confident and sure of himself. I mean, his name is ridiculous, but
he somehow manages to live up to it.

He looks like a Titan, that's for sure. Big and strong enough to hold
the globe on those bulging shoulders. I even liked his beard, too. I'm
not usually one for beards, but on him, it looked so masculine, so
powerful. I think it's because he had such a boyish glint in his eye. He's
clearly a mature, dominant man, but with a streak of mischief. And I
seriously like that.

Those eyes — those deep hazel pools, thickly lashed and round, so
big and expressive. They were so full of concern and care, like he really
did want to look after me.

He asked me out, and I said no.

I let that thought sink in. The most gorgeous man I ever met asked me to go for a drink with him, and I turned him down. Maybe I am going mad.

Truth is, it's not just the mob. I'm a Little. Most men turn and run when they hear that I like to play like a baby and wear diapers as much as I can. I've given up on finding love. My life's just too complicated for that.

And now, the complications have found me in Little Creek.

'I thought we'd left all that trouble behind,' I say to Mr. Chuckles, who's stretching out on my bed as I pack my rucksack, clearly unsympathetic toward my allergies.

I shudder when I think that just yesterday it was Mr. Chuckles in this rucksack.

I'm gonna pack light, of course. I'll need to get the bus out of town. I wonder where I can go. I don't have time to do any research. I guess this means I'm gonna be homeless for a while. It's not the first time. Luckily I've got some money stashed away. In a way, though, the money is the source of all my problems. I've thought about giving it all away to the mob, but I can't. I can't let Mom and Dad down like that.

The traveling is always hardest on Mr. Chuckles. I'll technically be homeless, but I'll be able to book into Motels that allow cats, and I have my carrier, so there's no chance he'll get into any kind of real trouble.

The thought of Mr. Chuckles getting hurt, being confused and scared, wells up in me, and before I know what's going on, I feel hot tears pricking my cheeks again.

Who am I kidding? A cat needs a stable home. That's what Little Creek was meant to be. I should find a new home for Mr. Chuckles. It's not fair to keep dragging him around like this.

As I sit on my desk, crying heavily now, he comes up to me and rubs his lovely side against mine.

It's like he's telling me to cheer up, like he's telling me everything's going to be OK.

But I know it's not.

There's a bang at the door. And it doesn't sound like a nice bang. Sounds an awful lot like the way the mobsters said hello yesterday.

'Open up.' The voice is deep and thickly accented. It's not Greek, though; this is a Russian voice.

For a crazy moment, I think about running away. I didn't think they'd be back so quickly. Just yesterday they were asking that I transfer all the money I have. I asked for a week, and they threw Mr. Chuckles up into the tree.

'Time's up, Bitch. You've had a Russian week already. Open the door before I bust it down.'

I'm going to have to open it. 'Please don't hurt my cat,' I say.

It's the two guys from yesterday. A short, stocky bald guy, in his forties, and a younger, thinner blond thug. He's the one that does the talking.

'Don't worry, pretty thing, I've been told not to touch your pussy today.' He makes my skin crawl.

'I've started the bank transfer,' I say. 'Every penny my family owes.'

It's my brother Dan's fault. He's the one who borrowed money from the Bratva. He's the one who wasted all that money on gambling. And now, I have to pay all the money Mom and Dad left me in their will because the Mob don't care who pays, so long as someone pays. I haven't seen or heard from my brother in years. He's obviously in hiding, too, and he's doing a much better job of staying hidden than I am.

The thin man looks at his fingernails. They are weirdly neat. 'Why is it I don't believe you?'

The stocky guy grunts something in Russian and barges past me into the apartment.

'What are you doing?' I ask, my voice trembling.

'Taking our stuff.'

'That's not your stuff, that's my stuff.'

Blondie shakes his head. 'Nope. Everything in this apartment is now the property of Boris Karkov.'

Karkov. The crime boss my brother borrowed from. I've never seen him, but every time the thugs catch up to me, they spray his name around like tomcats marking their turf.

I feel so small, so helpless. There's nothing I can do when the short guy rips my television from the wall and carries it out of the place. I wasn't going to take this stuff with me anyway, but it's what it symbolizes that hurts. They're stealing my chance of a normal life. And when I do transfer the money — it's not like I'm gonna have a choice — I really will be homeless. No job. No possessions. No hope.

My hands tremble as I dig my fingernails deep into my palms, doing everything I can not to cry. There's no way I'm giving these assholes the satisfaction.

'I'm going to call the police,' I say. I don't know if I mean it. I called the police in Colorado Springs. It did *not* help.

'Oh shit fuck,' says the short guy, stopping for a moment. 'She's gonna call the cops, Vlad.' His English is terrible, and his voice is guttural. 'What we do?'

'Maybe we should commit a crime, Dimitri,' Vlad says. 'We don't want to waste their time.'

The short guy smiles a cruel smile and deliberately rams my chest of drawers. The whole thing comes crashing down, smashing into my table. Items spill from it. It takes me a moment to realize what those items are. Oh no.

It's my diapers. Tens of them splayed out on the floor. My dirty little secret, out in the open.

Vlad looks at the diapers, looks at me, then looks at his short companion.

'What is this?' he says, his eyes wide with mirth. 'Are you incontinent? You poop your panties because you're scared we gonna find you?'

Dimitri bends down and picks up an oversize pacifier that's spilled out too. There's all my AB stuff here. My storybooks, my stuffies, everything that helps me to relax and be myself. And they're just laughing at it all.

'She a little baby,' he snorts, between long, ragged chuckles. 'Fuck man, I thought she was hot. She's mentally ill.'

I can't handle it anymore. I'm crying. Again. And this is the worst yet. So many years, I've spent on the run, and this is how it ends. In ultimate humiliation.

Only it's about to get worse.

'What the fuck is going on here?' This time, the voice *is* Greek.

Atlas is standing in the doorway, his huge body blocking the light from outside.

He looks at each of the mobsters in turn, then cracks his knuckles. Then, his eyes fix on the pile of diapers and baby stuff that's strewn around the floor. His eyes widen. He looks at me. Then, he steps inside.

# ATLAS

T HERE ARE DIAPERS ALL over the floor and Russian gangsters ransacking the place. It's like a scene from an experimental French movie, except this is real life.

I'll deal with the diapers later. First, I need to get control of the situation.

Luckily, there are only two of them, and from the way that they're standing, I can tell that neither is trained in combat.

The short guy has a leg injury, and the taller guy looks like he's got the constitution of a child.

'I said what the fuck is going on in here? I don't like repeating myself.'

'Fuck off, pretty boy,' the blond guy says. 'This is none of your business.'

I had a feeling I wouldn't need to watch Mia's house for long before some bad stuff went down. Didn't expect it to be quite this quick, though. Less than twenty-four hours.

'Of course it's my business.' I glance at Mia. She looks terrified, poor thing. Something else, too. Ashamed.

Oh, I'm gonna make these fuckers pay.

'Well you should change career,' the little rat-looking one says with a snide expression.

'Look,' I say, ignoring his comment, 'I'm gonna give you guys a way out right now. I'm friends with the sheriff in town. He'll be here in a minute if I call him.'

'Why would the sheriff be interested in something like this? This is all legal. We're here liberating these items for our employer. All perfectly legal.'

His accent is strong. Russian. We had problems with the Russian Mob in Athens. Gangs of criminals who moved in from Eastern Europe, exploiting people in every way you can imagine. Bad news.

'Why is it,' I say, 'that I'm finding that hard to believe?'

The shorter guys steps up to me. 'Look, stupid fuck, piss off now or we hurt you. Not just you — the girl, too.'

I can't help but notice that he's got a scar across his face, right next to his eye. I don't *want* to give this guy another scar. Ideally, I wouldn't want to fight at all. But I've got a feeling that these fools aren't going to give me much choice.

'Like I say, I know the sheriff. This is your last chance to leave this poor woman alone and turn tail. I'm gonna start counting, and if I get to ten and you're still here, I'm calling the cops.'

They look at each other, and then burst out laughing.

But I know they're not going to be laughing for long.

The little guy turns away. I know he's about to attack me. I can tell by the way he's making himself vulnerable. I should move now, but I can't, not until I'm absolutely sure of his intentions.

'You know—' he starts, but it's a feint, because halfway through the second word, he starts to twist back towards me. Steel flashes in his hand. A knife.

My military training kicks in. Up close, knives are more dangerous than guns, and I'm very aware of that as his arm flails toward me. Luckily, I'm quicker than this guy could ever hope to be.

Mia lets out a scream of terror, but I don't look around. I don't lose focus for even a split second.

I don't think, I don't worry, I just act.

My body twists and stoops, and I bring my arm up to slap hard into the thug's hand. The knife flies from his grip and shoots across the room, landing in the pile of diapers lying on the ground.

'You guys are in trouble,' I say. 'You picked the wrong guy to attack, *malaka*!' I find his gut with my knee, hitting him hard, forcing the wind from his lungs. He makes a shocked gasping sound. My senses are on hyper-alert, waiting for his friend to join the attack, but to my surprise, when I look up, I see that the tall guy is running.

'Coward!' I shout after him, then I turn my attention back to the stocky guy. He's down on the ground, curled up in the fetal position, holding his stomach.

'Mia,' I say, 'I'll be with you in a second. You OK, honey?'

She nods, still in a state of shock. She keeps looking at the stack of diapers, as though that's the most important thing going on here. Can it be that she's really more worried about me discovering she's a Little than the fact that armed men were just stealing her stuff?

Hang on, *is* she a Little?

I stand over the thug, leg on either side, ready to react if he moves. 'Don't do anything stupid,' I grunt. 'I'm calling the sheriff now. You can either wait comfortably, just as you are, or you can make things difficult for yourself and try something tricky. And if you do that, I'll have to get physical.'

He shakes his head. I must have caught him harder than I realized because he's still doubled up in agony. It's been a long time since my life was put in danger. Not the greatest feeling. My heart rate is slowly coming down. I wipe my brow, then I take out my phone and put in a call.

*

While we wait for Carl — the sheriff — to show up, Mia furtively clears away the diapers. Now, I happen to know that Carl is a Big, but I don't mention that to Mia. In fact, we don't talk about the diapers at all. Now that I've seen them, everything about her demeanor makes sense to me. The shyness, the natural cuteness I saw the first time I met her, the strange vulnerability. It's clear now — she's a Little. Even if she hasn't admitted it to me.

I also understand why she seemed so cagey when I asked her out. I'd be nervous if I was in her situation too. Seems unfair that I know she's a Little but she doesn't know my secret. But now is not the time to talk to her about it.

Not with a Russian Gangster hanging around.

'There's no point in any of this,' he says, after a couple minutes. 'I'll be out in no time. I've got friends in the force.'

'Who sent you, asshole?' I ask.

Before the guy has time to reply, Mia butts in. 'Karkov,' she says, surprising me. 'That's the name of the man behind all this.' Her voice is delicate, vulnerable. I can tell that she's being super brave just talking right now.

I get a sudden urge to head right over to Mia and wrap my arms around her. I can only imagine what's going on in her head right now, poor thing. I'm desperate to find out what all this is about. She obviously needs someone to look after her, and I want to be that person.

I don't push her for more information. We can talk later, when this guy isn't around.

We don't have long to wait, thankfully.

Carl is a total professional. We're good friends, but it's obvious he's treating this like any other case.

The first thing he does, though, is to reassure Mia that she's safe and that everything's OK. He's got a lovely, calming manner to him, and he puts us at rest very quickly. Carl and I couldn't be much more different. He comes across as super-focused and by the book, and probably I seem a little like a loose cannon.

'He assaulted me,' says the thug, as Carl slaps a pair of cuffs on him.

'I don't even need to ask to know that it was self-defense. You bring a knife into someone's house, you better damn prepare to get assaulted.' And with that, he bundles the criminal into the car.

Finally, the two of us are alone.

'You OK?' I ask. I want to reach out and hug her, but I hold back.

'How did you know they were here?' she asks.

It's a good question. Truth is, there's a diner across the street from Mia's house that I've been basically living in since the incident yesterday.

'I've been keeping an eye out. I told you I'd look after you, and I always keep my word.'

'The diapers,' she says, 'I can explain. I'm not weird, I mean, I am weird, bu—'

'You're seriously worried about the diapers?' I ask. I hope I don't look too shocked, but I'm honestly gob-smacked.

She nods.

'Look,' I say, holding her shoulders, 'you don't need to worry about that. Just, what's going on with these gangsters? Let me help you.'

'I don't want to drag you into this,' she says. 'I'm just gonna do what I always do.'

'And what's that?'

'Leave town.' Her green eyes are welling with emotion, and her top lip is trembling.

'Out of the question,' I say, crossing my arms. 'I'm not gonna let that happen.'

'Why do you care?' she asks, flicking her eyes down.

'I can tell you're a good person, and I can tell that you need some luck. I'm gonna be that luck.'

She smiles — the faintest trace of happiness breaking across her face. It's addictive. I want to see that again.

'I'm not a good person, I'm just nothing.'

I decide to take a risk. 'Hey, I don't want to hear you talking like that, young lady. When we're together, no-one's allowed to say anything bad about you.'

She holds my gaze for a moment, then she nods. My hunch was right: she's responding to my Daddy voice.

'Now tell me all about your problems. We're gonna work out how to get you out of this situation.'

So she does. She tells me about the way she's been running across the country, trying to escape a gang of dangerous criminals desperate to recover money. She tells me about her brother, about his gambling debts. The more I hear, the more tender and protective of her I feel.

'Look,' I say when I've taken it all in. 'I'm not gonna sugar coat this. You're in a tricky situation. But I promise you that I'm gonna get you out. There's no way I could live with myself if I didn't help. I understand about not wanting to go to the cops, but I think we *should* work with Carl. He's not a regular sheriff's deputy. And there's someone else I know who can help, too.'

'You really think you can help?'

'I know it.'

'How am I ever going to repay you for all this?' she blurts out.

'I don't need repayment. Helping people who deserve it is reward in itself. Having said that, I'd still like to take you on a date. I know the perfect place too.'

'You still want to date me? Even with all this madness? And with the whole diaper issue?'

'Mia, can I ask you a question?'

She nods.

'You're a Little, aren't you?'

'You know about Littles?'

'Course I do. I'm a Big.'

The look of relief on her face is incredible. Then, she throws herself at me, reaching her arms around my thick body and squeezing me tight. 'Oh my god, oh my god, I'm so glad. It's a miracle.' Then the sobs start; a huge, cathartic release. I can feel the emotions, spilling out of her.

'It's OK, baby, let it out.

I let her hug me, feeling her tears soak into my shirt. And I start to formulate a plan.

# MIA

Dating. It's been something I've not even thought about for years. Something so far from what's important that I've kinda been pretending that the whole world of romance and love just doesn't exist.

And yet, right now, in the middle of all this nonsense, at a time when all my instincts are telling me to run, I'm about to go on a freaking date.

Is it weird that I'm excited?

Atlas isn't just any guy. He's a Big. That's what he said, at least. And he wasn't freaked out by the explosion of diapers in my apartment. And the way he speaks to me is just so yummy it makes me feel like I've eaten a rainbow.

Technically, it's not a good time for me to be dating. But honestly, is there ever a good time?

I look at myself in the mirror, and Mr. Chuckles threads his way through my legs, rubbing his tummy against me.

'You think Mommy looks pretty?' I ask him. He stops dead still, then lets out a tiny meow. 'Thank you!' I say.

I'm wearing a retro-print red and white mini dress — not too short as I always wear clothes that can comfortably cover my diaper — and some white pumps. I've put some effort into makeup this morning, which isn't normally my strong suit. It's amazing, though, that when I really try hard at something, the results tend to be OK.

A hint of lip gloss. Mascara. A lick of eye-liner.

I look pretty good.

Huh, that's weird. I normally never feel confident in my looks.

*What's wrong with you, Mia Andrews?*

Just when I feel as though I'm finally ready, there's a knock at my door. I don't think I'm ever going to be able to have the door knocked without freaking out just a little bit, but this knock is about as non-threatening as a knock can be.

'Coming,' I say, slipping a bag over my shoulder. I feel a fizz of excitement in my tummy. None of this feels like real life. But when I open the door and see Atlas waiting there, everything suddenly seems super real.

He looks amazing.

There's something about the way he's standing, so confident, that makes it seem as though he owns the place.

'Mia,' he says, taking his sunglasses off, revealing those deep brown eyes, 'you look incredible.'

*Don't blush. Don't blush. Don't blush!*

I blush.

'Thank you,' I say. 'It's the first time I've tried to dress nice for years.' I hope I don't sound too pathetic. I'm amazed that Atlas is interested in me at all. I must just seem like a lost little girl.

'Well, I wouldn't know.'

He looks so good I wanna reach out and bite him. A thick plaid shirt, red and black, pulled up at the sleeve to reveal his thick, tattooed forearms. There are letters in a language I don't understand — Greek I guess — and there's an angular dragon snaking its way up his arm. His jeans are tight around his thick legs, and he's wearing a pair of those workmen's boots. He's about the most masculine thing I've ever seen.

'So, you ready to have some fun?'

Fun. It's a word I've barely thought about lately.

'I guess so.'

'That's the spirit.'

'So, where are we going?'

'Aha, that's a secret. I brought my pick-up. We're heading out of town. Not too far though, you'll be pleased to hear.'

His pickup looks just like he does. Rough around the edges, a little beat up, but as tough and reliable as you can imagine.

Spring in Colorado is glorious. The sun is shining and it's a perfect temperature — just warm enough for light clothes. As we drive from Little Creek, the roadside verges are full of blooming flowers, reds and blues, tiny smears of yellow, and the delicate, nodding heads of daisies.

For a moment, I manage to forget about my problems.

'You know what?' Atlas says. 'I'm starting to feel as though Little Creek is at the center of the DDlg subculture.'

I laugh. 'That's why it's called Little Creek, dummy.'

'You think?' He's looking at me with honest curiosity. That's the moment it hits me. Atlas is super-trusting and good-hearted.

'I think it's just a coincidence,' I say, not wanting him to know I was just kidding. 'I came here because of a Little friend, though. Diana.'

'You know Diana?' He glances around at me, so shocked that he takes his eyes off the road just for a second.

'Only through the Internet. But I know that was her Daddy yesterday: Carl.'

'You kept that quiet.'

'I didn't want to make him feel uncomfortable.'

He scoffs. 'It's impossible to make Carl uncomfortable. He's as cool as ice.'

Not like you, I think, you're as hot as fire.

We make our way down winding mountain roads, round slinking bends. To be honest, I wouldn't even mind if this was the entire date — just the two of us comfortably chatting in the pick-up. Eventually, though, we arrive at our destination. I hear where we are first. There are excited screams in the air, as well as the ratcheting clunk of heavy machinery.

'Oh my god!' I say, my excitement spiking. 'Grand Park!'

I haven't been to a theme park since I was a little girl. I can't believe that Atlas has brought me here.

He smiles. 'I'm glad you're excited. I wanted to give you a break from your life, to remind you that there's happiness and excitement out there for you. The future doesn't have to be bleak, sweetie.'

'Can I go on all the rides?' I ask, my voice suddenly Little.

'So long as you're tall enough,' he teases.

We walk towards the entrance turnstile, and without thinking, I grip his hand in mine. I wish I could grab his whole body. In fact, I'm so quickly dipping into Little Space that I kind wanna climb up onto him and get a piggyback ride around the park. But I restrain myself.

He pays for our entry, and then, we're in the park. There are smiling faces all around, families and couples enjoying all the thrills and spills of the park.

'So, what do you want to go on first?' he asks, unfolding a map of the place.

'I want to find the biggest, fastest, scariest ride. And then I want to go on it over and over again until I puke.'

He shakes his head, laughing. 'Well, I guess we better go get in line for The Dominator, then.'

I gulp. 'It's called The Dominator?'

He points up into the sky, and in the distance, I see the giant loop of a huge roller-coaster. A cart shoots around the loop, and I hear the ecstatic screams of the riders.

I gulp again.

*

The line for The Dominator isn't as long as I expected. The closer we get, the more that knot of excitement and anxiety builds in my stomach. Atlas, on the other hand, seems totally calm.

'I guess being a firefighter must prepare you for thrill rides like this, huh?' I ask.

He shakes his head. 'No way, I'm just as nervous as you. Thrill rides are super scary!'

The idea of Atlas being scared of anything is just crazy to me. 'No way!'

'*Yes* way! This is the highest rollercoaster in the state, and it's got the most inversions, too.'

'You seem to know a lot about this place.'

'Well, I've been wanting to come to a real, American theme park ever since I arrived. We don't really have theme parks in Greece. Well, we have tiny little ones called Lunar Parks, but they're normally desperately unsafe and the rides are nothing compared to this type of thing. This is the first time I've had a real excuse to come to a big one.'

I look at him. 'So you've never been on a roller-coaster?'

'Never.'

I laugh an evil laugh. 'I can't wait!'

We don't have long to wait at all.

Soon, we're being strapped into the monstrous cart. It's shaped like a bullet and looks like it could do just as much damage. When we're safely strapped in, a countdown begins. I can feel the fizz of anticipation in my tummy, and without thinking I grab hold of Atlas' hand. He squeezes tight.

'Ready to be dominated?' he whispers into my ear, a wicked glint in his eye. Before I have the chance to reply, the cart lurches forward. I let out a tiny shriek of surprise, then burst out laughing.

As we head up the first hill towards that impossibly high drop, I think about all the things I've faced over the few years. I've always thought of myself as a scaredy-cat, but for some reason, right now, as I'm sitting on this roller-coaster, next to Atlas, I feel as though I could take on the world.

Then we reach the top. I look at Atlas. Atlas looks at me. Then, the world falls away, and all that's left are our screams, hanging in the air.

*

'I do *not* look scared.' Atlas holds up the photograph pointing at the little, terrified version of himself. 'Plus, look at you, your cheeks are a more vivid shade of green than your eyes are. And that's saying something.'

'But I'm not the big strong Daddy,' I say, letting my hand rest on his arm. 'I'm just a poor Little Girl scared of fast rides.'

'Yeah, right,' he says.

We've been on a load more rides since the roller-coaster, and now we're in a café in the theme park. I'm eagerly sucking a chocolate milkshake, and Daddy's got a grown-up drink: coffee.

'Thanks for buying the picture for us,' I say, snuggling up to him a little. I feel so safe when I'm close to him. It's the first time I've felt protected for ages.

'That's OK. I wanted to remember our first date.'

'Are there gonna be more dates?' I ask, looking up at him.

'I hope so.'

'I've never dated a Daddy before,' I say. I've got a feeling that he's way more experienced in DDlg relationships than I am.

'I've dated a couple Littles,' he admits. But nothing serious, really.'

'What's it like? A DDlg relationship?'

'You can find out if you want.'

My heart starts to beat even faster. 'You want to be my boyfriend?'

'More than that. I want to be your Daddy,' he says, squeezing my hand.

There's a moment between us. Feels like two souls, coming together for the first meaningful time.

I feel his big hand hold mine tight. He looks at me, tenderness in his eyes.

Then I close my eyes and push my lips to his.

He tastes of coffee. A strong, bitter taste that's intoxicating. His lips first — softer than I was expecting — then his tongue, stronger and more forceful than mine. He's talking to me with his kiss, letting me know just how much he wants me. I'm lost in the sensation, swept up in the feeling of overwhelming lust.

I cup his chin, feel the sharp hardness of his long stubble, and run my hands up and down his neck. His hands are on my dress, pulling me close to him, forcing my body into his. We're connected by a hot strip of flesh, as we push into each other, my breasts squashing into his hard chest, his arms squeezing around me now. I feel soft and pliant as I give in to his hungry kisses, and then we pull apart.

We look at each other, hungry, panting.

'You wanna get out of here?' he asks. The sounds and smells of the café slowly come back into focus for me. While we were kissing, I completely forgot where I was.

'Uh-huh,' I say. 'Let's go back to yours, Daddy. I wanna see where you live.'

He smiles. I'm still reeling from the kiss. I almost feel dizzy. Is this what love feels like?

# ATLAS

W HAT A FUCKING KISS. I'm still recovering from it. I'm a guy who likes to be in control. And when I tasted Mia for the first time, it felt like I was losing it.

I can't explain it. It's like there was a chemical reaction going on between us — like we were exchanging electrons and becoming charged with each other.

Right now, as I'm leading this heavenly creature up the path to my place, I can feel a force tugging me towards her, like I'm trapped in her orbit.

We can't keep our hands off each other. I had to keep telling her off in the car, because her hands kept straying onto my legs as I drove, threatening to distract me. A couple times, I let her fingers stray close to my cock, and I felt the swell of arousal.

I'll admit it, I should have told her off sooner, but feeling her touch me like that was intoxicating.

'You feel so strong,' she says, as her hands dig into my arm. I keep getting lost in her eyes, keep getting distracted by her transcendental beauty.

'You feel so soft,' I reply, letting my finger stray up and down her arm.

'Come on,' she says, her eyes flashing wide, 'let's go inside. I wanna see your place.'

I live in a tiny condo on the outskirts of town. It's a simple place, but I've decorated it in a way that reminds me of home. I'm something of a painter. It's how I like to unwind and relax. Oil paintings, mostly, landscapes of scenes that inspire me. Quite a few of my canvasses hang from the walls in my place. I don't think they're particularly good, but I've got nowhere else to put them.

It's the first time I've shown anyone my work, and it's dumb, but I'm really fucking nervous.

'Holy cow,' Mia says, as she steps inside, 'this place is amazing.'

I've painted all the walls white in here, just like we do in Greece, and all the detailing is in sea blue. The one thing I miss about Greece more than any other is the sea. The lakes here give me a feeling of being by the sea, but it's not quite the same.

I've got a few other things to remind me of home. A painting of the Acropolis that I brought from Athens, and my grandfather's old Bouzouki — a stringed instrument that makes an iconic twanging sound. My grandfather was a performer in the nightclubs of Athens, quite famous in his own way. I had a complicated relationship with the man. He was strict but loving.

There's a portrait of my grandfather, hanging over the hearth. A stern-looking man, with a traditional, thick, mustache, and a scowl in his eye.

'This painting is amazing!' she says. 'Is it of someone famous?'

'No,' I laugh, shaking my head. 'That's my grandfather.'

'Hang on, did *you* paint it?'

I nod.

'You're so talented! Wow. Can you teach me?'

'Sure, but, I don't know much about painting. I'm self-taught. You'd be better learning from a book.'

She shakes her head. 'No way. You're definitely better than a book.'

I smile at her. 'So, you like the way I've got the place?'

'I like you. And this place is like a reflection of you. So I like it.'

'You like me, huh?' I say.

She nods and bites her lip. I've never seen anything sexier in my entire life.

'I like you, too,' I say. 'A lot.'

She keeps her eyes on me as she reaches back and undoes her dress. With each twist of her fingers, the fabric becomes looser, more revealing. I marvel at the shape of her, and then, when the dress drops fully down to the ground, my eyes widen in stark surprise.

I'd known she was probably wearing a diaper, but I hadn't really thought about it all day. Now, though, that she's standing so vulnerable in front of me, in just a bright white bra and her padded diaper, she seems so innocent and cute that I can barely handle it.

'Do you miss Greek girls?' she asks coyly.

'Not a chance,' I say.

I undo my shirt and she licks her lips, then I lunge forward and lift her up and carry her through my condo, into the bedroom. There are big windows in here, looking out over my little green yard. It's a peaceful view, and the light is beautiful. I lay her down on the bed, planting kisses on her stomach.

'You lie down there, sweet girl,' I say. 'I wanna look after you.'

She does as I ask, resting her lithe body down on my bed. 'I feel like a Little Princess,' she sighs. 'So nice to be treated so well.'

'I want to give you so much more, darling,' I say. I let my hands play over her body, gently stroking up and down her smooth skin, sending shivers up and down her spine. I see her tingle and shake. I bring my hands to her diaper. I know just how much trust it must be taking for her to let me touch her like this. There's no way I'm going to let her down.

I open up the tabs of the diaper and with each tiny ripping sound, she lets out a gasp. I feel a burden of responsibility, and that responsibility makes me excited. Because it means that I care. I really care.

A moment later, as I pull the diaper away, I'm faced with the most incredible sight.

'Thank you for sharing yourself with me,' I say. She smiles up at me.

'Thank you for being you,' she says.

I lean in, close to her skin. I can smell coconut, vanilla, and a hint of cinnamon.

When my lips brush over her, she lets out a moan of pleasure, of anticipation.

'Do you trust me?' I ask, whispering into her skin.

'I do,' she says.

'I'm gonna make you mine,' I whisper. 'By the end of this, you're going to be calling me Daddy.'

Then, I kiss her, inches above her pussy. I trail down, letting my tongue brush over her. She grinds her butt down into the bed beneath, letting out a soft, low moan.

I taste her, running my tongue up and down her entrance. Her fingers run through my hair, then she tugs a little as I slip my tongue into her, pushing far inside. She tastes so sweet, I can't help licking faster, and I grip her hips with my hands as I explore her.

'Atlas,' she says, groaning with pleasure.

'You know what I want you to say,' I grunt, pulling her ass up, pushing her pussy right into my mouth. I flick my tongue over her soft little clit and she yelps with surprise, then melts underneath me.

'I'm close,' she says, and I can tell from how wet she's getting. I don't stop licking, tracing little circles around the nub of her pleasure, making her squirm, forcing her to submit to me. She breathes more heavily, and pushes into me in time with my movements — then, in a moment of pure submission, her hands fall away from my hair and she lets out a slowly growing moan until I know she's reached the peak.

Seeing her like this, spread out on my bed has made me so damn hard that I can't contain myself anymore.

'You want me, don't you?' I ask, as she finally opens her eyes.

'I need you,' she whispers. Her lips are moist, her eyes starry.

I slowly slip my pants down, letting my hard cock spring up to my waist.

'You're so big,' she says. And then, a moment later, 'Daddy.'

It's all I need to hear. I lean in, resting the tip of my cock on her entrance. She's ready for me, and she pushes her hand onto my chest, running her fingers over my body. Her touch is wonderful — so light and lustful.

'Please,' she says, 'I want to feel you inside me. Don't make me wait anymore.'

She feels so good as I move into her. I hold back, taking my time, making sure that she's comfortable with my size.

'Oh my god,' she says, pushing her hand hard into my abs. 'Don't stop.'

So I don't. I push all the way in, engulfing myself in pleasure. It's hard not to get lost in the moment. I want to tear into her, to fuck her rough and deep, to show her just how much I need her. But I don't. I take my time, exercising all my willpower to savor this moment.

I reach down, holding her hands, and I kiss her with passion as I slip slowly in and out of her. 'You belong to me now, and I'm gonna look after you.' I kiss her forehead, pushing into her again, grinding my cock into her, then, as she moves with me, I speed up, moving faster and with more power, taking exactly what I need from her, plundering her body.

I lace my fingers between hers, and soon it feels like we're one body, bucking and grinding together. With each push, I feel closer to her, and closer to the edge. Her hands are everywhere, gripping my back, slipping down to my butt, over my hips, my hair. I push my fingers into her mouth and she sucks as I shift her around, hitting a deeper spot inside her, and rubbing my fingers over her clit. The effect is instant, electric. I feel her pussy tighten around me as she comes again. I'm lost, deep inside her. My pleasure peaks and I see stars as my body tightens and I explode inside her, holding her close to me, kissing her deep and strong and fierce.

We lie there together, connected for a long time, silently stroking each other, then quietly whispering sweet nothings to each other, so close we feel like one.

*

'I wish I didn't have to go back home.'

'Well, you're not really *going back* going back. We just need to pick up your stuff, then we'll be heading out while I get everything sorted.'

After a heavenly evening and night together, Mia and I are getting ready to head back to her place. Carl has been looking into some leads for me and has managed to mobilize some assets to tackle the gangsters in their home.

*Mobilize assets* is police chat for 'we gonna bust some shit up.'

As we walk back across Little Creek, I feel like I'm walking on clouds.

'I'm having the best time with you,' I say, giving her hand a squeeze.

'Me too, Daddy,' she replies. She happily swings our hands together. Mia's been in Little Space ever since we had sex. It's exciting to get to know that side of her. So sweet and innocent, so full of wonder. I've been shocked by the change in her, ever since she's felt a little more secure and safe, now that I'm around.

'Daddy, what's that?'

Suddenly, there's fear in her eyes. I look out across the sunny Little Creek street, and in the distance, I see a pillar of gray smoke. It's coming straight from Mia's home.

# MIA

S UDDENLY, DADDY ISN'T CONFIDENT and carefree. Suddenly, he's full of concern.

He leads me through the streets quickly, and I struggle to keep up with him, almost stumbling a couple times. When we get close to my house, the source of the smoke is obvious.

My place in on fire. Angry flames lick and spit from windows, smoke belches from every opening. But as terrifying as it is to see my former home being reduced to almost cinders, there's only one thing I can think of.

Mr. Chuckles.

Atlas looks at me, and as if he's psychic, he says, 'I've got to save your cat.' He says it in such a matter-of-fact way that I know he's serious.

'You can't — it's too dangerous.'

He doesn't answer. Without pausing for a second, he rips his shirt off, then tears a huge strip from it. I hear sirens coming from across the town — the fire department is coming, but they're still gonna be a couple minutes.

Atlas wraps the strip of his shirt around his face, and then, before I have time to even think about stopping him, he runs to the open front door.

I scream, I can't help it. I've never been in a situation quite like this, I've never seen someone risk their life before, and being confronted with it is making me sick to my stomach.

Every second that he's inside that blazing house feels like an hour. The longer he stays in there, the less chance there is of him coming out. A moment later, a fire truck pulls up at the side of the street. I'm panicking.

A gruff firefighter approaches me.

'Is there anyone inside?' he asks.

I nod. 'Atlas,' I say.

'Atlas? How long's he been in there?' He gestures to the other members of the crew, and they start unlooping a hose. Looks like one of them is suiting up, getting ready to head into the house.

'Just a minute or so. He went in after my cat.'

'Fucking idiot,' he says, shaking his head in disbelief.

'Hey, what did you just call me?'

I turn and to my insane relief, I see Atlas standing a few feet from my former home. Mr. Chuckles is cradled in his arms.

'You heard exactly what I called you, Karandinis.'

Atlas's face is covered in soot, and his torso is black too. As he walks closer to me, I see that his eyebrows have been singed off. Amazingly, he still looks stupidly handsome like this. In fact, as his body glistens with sweat and soot, he almost looks like a sexual fantasy come to life.

'I think Mr. Chuckles is gonna be just fine. Although he might need a little bath, which I guess he won't be that excited about.'

In the background, the fire crew is starting to douse the place in water, and the flames are starting to subside.

Atlas sees me looking concerned.

'You don't need to worry,' he says. 'I'm gonna take care of every-thing.'

'What are we going to do?'

'Well first,' he says, stroking Mr. Chuckles' head, 'we're gonna get a cat carrier. Then, I'm going to take you somewhere safe. And after that, we stop this harassment forever.'

*

I've never been out in the woods like this. After the crazy morning I've had, it almost feels as though I'm in a brand-new world. It's dangerous and thrilling and crazy.

I'm used to a nomadic lifestyle, but this feels different. The little snatches of happiness I have with Atlas, between all the madness, are making me long for a permanent home. And the more time I spend with him, the more sure I am that I want him to be a part of my life.

No. I want him to *be* my life.

'You doing OK sweetheart?' he asks, looking back at me. He's carrying Mr. Chuckles in a plastic cage. The poor cat is meowing. I wish I could stop and pet him, but I know that we shouldn't waste any time.

'I'm alright,' I say. 'I can't believe that I'm getting the chance to visit the Little Cabin.'

I've known that there's an ABDL sanctuary outside town somewhere for quite a while, but it's a really exclusive affair. There's always a massive waiting list, and the prices are pretty dang high too.

'I'm just sorry that it couldn't be under better circumstances. I'd been dreaming of bringing you here for a short break. I guess that it's more of a hideout now, though.'

The cabin is so far away from civilization that there's no road. We have to trek the final few miles through the forest. Before too long, I start to see the cutest thing: someone's drawn love hearts on the trees in bright pink chalk. There are arrows too, pointing in the direction of the cabin.

'I think we're close,' Atlas says, grinning at me. 'You getting excited, baby girl?'

I nod. 'Look at that!' This tree has a knitted, multicolored sleeve around it.

'I think Ella makes those for the trees,' Atlas says. 'Makes you feel welcome, doesn't it?'

Eventually, I see a sign. Joel and Ella's Little Cabin.

And waiting by the pretty Little Cabin we find nestled in the heart of the forest is a man I recognize.

'Good to see you, Carl!' Atlas says, holding out his hand.

'Glad to be here.'

On the way here, Atlas explained his plan to me. He's meeting Joel and Carl out here in the cabin, and together, the three are going to join a SWAT team and storm the hideout of the Russian Bratva. And then, hopefully, this nightmare will all be over.

I'm nervous, though, because there are two Littles here, and I'm gonna hang out with them while the boys head out on this ridiculously dangerous mission. At least I know Diana. I'm sure Ella's gonna be lovely, too.

Carl and Atlas shake hands.

'Everything good for our little task?'

Carl nods. He looks so serious. Hard to believe that he's a Daddy, too. I guess he must have a softer side to him.

'Everything is good to go. Why don't you take this Little cutie inside to hang out with the others? Then you, Joel, and me can go over the battle plan. You don't know this, but I've been trying to take down this particular gang for quite a while. I'm the sheriff of Little Creek, but I care for the whole of Colorado. And if this goes well, it'll help a lot of people.'

All this fuss, just for me. I can't believe all the trouble these guys are going to. It makes me feel a little better to know that this is just part of Carl's job, and that by chance I've given him information that will help him catch a dangerous criminal.

'Let's go meet the two terrors,' Atlas says, pointing to the smaller of the two cabins.

Another man steps out of the larger cabin. He's wearing a tight plaid shirt. His body is absolutely massive, a real bear of a man.

'They're in the playroom, of course.' This must be Joel. 'Good to meet you, pudding,' he says to me. Huh, it's the first time anyone's ever called me pudding. It's kinda cute.

'Good to meet you, too.' Being around all these Daddies is helping me to stay in Little Space. I feel so accepted and happy to be around my people.

There's a sudden screech of laughter from inside the smaller cabin, and a burble of high-pitched chatter that I can't quite make out.

'Can I?' I ask my Daddy, giving him big eyes.

'Sure you can.'

I head inside, tentatively. I'm met with a scene of absolute chaos.

They're painting, I guess. But this has more in common with the way Jackson Pollock paints than I'd normally expect.

Even though Ella and Diana both have blond hair, they couldn't look more different. Ella's got short hair in a bob, and these pretty, pale blue eyes. Di's wearing her hair in cute little pigtails, and her eyes are emerald green. They're both dressed in painting smocks, and I can see diapers peeping out from underneath the paint-splattered aprons.

Ella has red paint splattered in her blond hair, and Diana has a smear of blue across her face. I'm so shocked by the scene that's confronted me, that I barely take in the fact that we're in an amazing, adult-sized playroom. This would be an unbelievable place to play, and it looks like that's exactly what these two are doing. There are a couple easels set up in the middle of the playroom, and the papers laid out on them are splattered with thick splodges of paint.

The two girls look at me and then grin. They look really nice, super friendly.

'You must be Mia?' asks the girl with green eyes.

I nod.

'Hooray! I'm Ella, and I think you know Di. We're playing painting? You wanna join in?'

I bite my lip, and then, so excited that I feel like I could take off, I say, 'Please.'

*

'Do you think we're gonna get into trouble?' I've never been this messy. We've been painting, but most of the paint is on us, rather than on the paper. I've got streaks of black paint up and down my arms, and a splodge of white in my hair.

'Depends on your Daddy. Her Daddy is stricter than *my* Daddy,' Ella says.

'It's true,' Diana says. She's been sucking on a little pacifier, but takes it out to talk. Her voice is so cute-sounding and sweet. 'But he's kind too. It's good for me. Because I'm wilder than she is. So I need a stricter Daddy.'

'What about you, are you wild?' Ella asks.

I think for a moment. 'Honestly, I don't know. I've been on the run for so long, I don't really know who I am anymore.' It's the most honest I've been with strangers in as long as I can remember.

I feel a hand on my shoulder. Ella's touching me. 'You poor thing,' she says. 'Hopefully, all that's gonna finish soon.'

It's amazing, to feel so completely myself. Emotions are welling up inside me that I haven't felt since I was a kid.

'Thank you for being so kind,' I say. My voice cracks. Ella squeezes my shoulder.

'You're one of us, silly,' she says. Then, her eyes widen a little and she looks surprised. 'Oops. I need a diaper change! Do you need one?'

I haven't even noticed, but I *do* need my diaper changed. I nod, a little embarrassed, even though I don't need to be.

'Shall we get our Daddies?'

Just then, there's a knock at the window.

All three of us look up, and all three of us freeze.

Because there's a man out there, holding a gun.

Thing is, only I recognize the man. He holds his fingers up to his lips and shakes his head. He looks at me with a sick grin on his face.

It's my brother.

# ATLAS

'THE GIRLS ARE AWFULLY quiet.' Joel's looking across at the guest cabin, a look of concern on his face.

'I'm sure they're fine,' says Carl. He's poring over a set of reports, which break down everything we know about the Bratva operation in Denver. 'Probably just up to something naughty. Planning to throw paint bombs at the cabin.'

The cabin here is wonderful. Joel's done an amazing job of making it comfortable and homey, while at the same time not sacrificing any of the wild outdoor vibe that living in the middle of a forest provides.

'Oh, I'll have to tan Ella's hide if she does something like that.' Joel says, looking over at us.

'What's your stance on discipline, Atlas?' Carl asks.

'Hmm, well, it kinda depends on the girl. In my experience, all Littles need some discipline, but as long as it comes from a place of love, it's all good.'

'A man after my own heart,' Joel says.

I know Joel less well than Carl. I think that's because he mainly stays out here most of the time, and doesn't come to Little Creek so often, only to get supplies every few weeks. He seems soft-spoken, a real gentle giant.

'I wish I'd met Mia earlier,' I say, letting my thoughts wander. 'I wonder if I might have helped her avoid some of her problems. Somehow, it makes me feel guilty.'

'I totally get that,' Carl says. 'With me, it's even worse. Because I've known Diana for years. I was always just too nervous to ask her out. Her father was a good friend of mine.'

'The guilt means you care,' I say, realizing it's true about myself, too.

'Hate to break this chat up,' Joel says, his voice suddenly serious, 'but the girls aren't planning mischief. They're in trouble.'

I spring up, looking through the window, and so does Carl.

What I see chills me to the bone.

All three Little Girls, lined up, and next to them is a man holding a gun loosely in his hand. The Littles look terrified. Another guy stands off to the side, twitchy, dressed in a dirty business suit and crumpled white shirt.

The man with the gun opens his mouth. 'Come out! All of you! No stupid stuff or I start shooting.'

Carl hisses under his breath, 'Do what they say. We can get out of this.'

It's not super-reassuring, but it gives me a touch of courage at least. Can Carl really have a plan for a situation like this?

The three of us head out of the cabin. We stand in a little courtyard. Everything is silent, except for the sound of the wind in the trees. Then, the guy breaks the silence.

'Vasily, tie these men up for me.' Huh, that's strange. I woulda bet money on this guy having a Russian accent. But no. He's a local.

The second man takes a rope from his rucksack and starts to tie up Joel, forcing his hands behind his back. I can't believe this is happening. The thugs must have followed us from Little Creek. We've been planning to move quickly, but they were still too quick for us. I don't get it, though — all this hassle just to retrieve old gambling debts. It feels like there must be something else going on here. Something personal.

'How could you do this, Dan?' Mia's voice is strained and desperate. How does she know this guy's name?

'How could I do this? How could I *do* this?' There's venom in his voice. True hatred. 'I don't know, Mia, maybe it's because Mom and Dad left *all* their fucking money to you. Maybe it's because I hate you because they loved you.' He shrugs. 'Maybe it's none of that, though. Maybe it's just because I want your money and I want you to suffer.'

'I thought you were dead.'

'I might as well have been. I couldn't pay Karkov back, so I did the only thing I could. I agreed to work for him.'

'Wait,' I say, butting in as I finally wrap my head around what's going on here. 'You're her brother?'

'Not anymore,' he spits. 'Now I'm her enemy.'

He's got a crazed, manic energy to him. His eyes are wide, and there's a thin sheen of sweat across his brow, even though it's perfectly cool here in the shade.

'Why is Karkov so obsessed with her?' I ask. The second, twitchy man is tying up Carl now, forcing his hands behind his back. Carl grunts with annoyance. I wonder what's going on in his head.

'Obsessed? He's not obsessed. He barely knows her name.' Mia's brother is laughing now. 'This is all my doing, idiot.' He pauses for a second, then he walks right up to Mia and looks her in the eye. 'You know, if Mom and Pop had just given me their share of the inheritance when they died — like they were meant to — none of this would have happened. I could have paid Karkov off, and things would have been just fine. But no. They had to give it all to you.'

A sickening thought crosses my mind.

'You killed them, didn't you?' Mia hasn't told me much about her parents' death, but I know enough. An accident, mechanical failure in their car. Mia's brother's face twitches at my question. Then he walks over to me, pauses a moment, then brings the butt of the gun into the side of my face, hard. I taste blood. The pain is intense but manageable.

Somewhere nearby, Mia sobs. 'I wish you were still lost,' she says. 'I wish I didn't know any of this stuff about you.'

'Oh yeah?' he says, snapping back to look at her. 'Well, I wish there was stuff I didn't know about you. I wish I didn't know you dressed up like a fucking baby and hang out with perverts in the woods.'

Fury is building in me as he tears into my Little Girl. Each of his words is like a dagger in my heart. My blood is starting to boil — thick and furious — like the heart of a bear.

He keeps talking, spit spraying out from his mouth. 'I'm ashamed of being related to you. You're just like our parents were. Weak. Pathetic!'

I can't take it anymore. With a low, resonant grunt, I surge up from the ground as he's looking away from me, and I punch him hard in the gut. He yelps out in surprise and brings the gun round again, but I block his arm. I hear screams from the Littles, and shouts from Joel and Carl, but I'm lost in the moment. I grab his wrist, and I'm about to wrench the gun away from him when I feel the sickening pain of a punch to my kidney from behind. The pain of a kidney shot is like nothing else. It feels like I've been stabbed. When I look back though, I see that I haven't, it's just the lanky guy standing there with a clenched fist.

Dan pushes me down and I tumble onto the ground. How could I have been so stupid? I've risked everything, just because of my anger.

'Stupid fucker,' Dan says, a wicked grin on his face. 'I wasn't gonna kill any of you, but I think I've got other plans now.'

'No!' cries out Mia.

I can't believe I've let her down like this. I'm on my back, my side still throbbing from the punch. Dan is looking down at me, along the barrel of his gun.

'Sorry about this, but it's just business.'

I hear something strange. A sharp, high-pitched whistle, shrill and almost painfully loud. It's Carl.

Dan stops, distracted by the whistle, and looks at Carl. 'What th—'

Before he can finish his question, there's a snarl and the sound of foliage being crushed under something heavy. Then, Dan is smashed aside by something furious and furry. It's Prince — Carl's German Shepherd. Dan screams and there's the hollow crack of a gunshot. Now's my chance.

I spring up to my feet, then fall onto the second gangster. I rain my fists into him, connecting with any part of him I can find — the chest, the head, the gut. He yelps as I push him down on the ground, then, when I'm confident he's incapacitated, I look back at Dan. There's a dog on him.

I've always known Prince as a super-docile good boy, but right now, he's entirely incapacitated Dan. His jaws are round his wrist, and he's pinned him down on the ground at an ugly angle. Dan's crying out, 'Get it off! Get it off!'

I move fast, untying Carl first, then Joel. Carl rushes over to Prince and Dan, gets his dog off the wretched man, and claps handcuffs around his wrists. I move to my Little Girl, throw my arms around her, then stroke her hair, planting kisses on her forehead. 'You OK, baby?' I ask, my voice as soft as I can manage, even with all the adrenaline pumping around my body.

'I thought I was gonna lose you,' she replies, pushing her head against my chest. 'And I've only just found you.'

'Don't worry, sweetheart, I'm not going anywhere. I told you, you're safe with me.'

We kiss, and it's like nothing else. A communication of love, a sharing of reassurance, a desperate, painful need.

'You're bleeding,' she says, holding her tiny hand to the side of my head.

'It's OK,' I reply. 'Means I'm alive.'

She smiles.

# MIA
## TWO MONTHS LATER

A LOT CAN CHANGE in two months. And I mean *a lot*.

I'm trekking back to the Cabin, with a special piece of paper in my hand. I can't wait to show my Daddy — I've got a feeling that he's going to be seriously proud of me. I've gotten very familiar with the walk through the woods back to the Little Cabin recently. We've been spending a lot of time out here.

Diana is walking with me — there's no way our Daddies would let us trek through the forest on our own, and she's in a dreamy mood, looking up at the tree canopy.

'A bald eagle!' She points up, and I follow her gaze. She's right — there's the iconic white and yellow of an eagle, perched on a branch, looking down at us, sharp eyes fixed on the strange creatures moving through its domain.

'Wow,' I say, as I stare up. 'Did you know that female bald eagles are way bigger than male bald eagles?'

'Seriously?' Diana asks, giving me a disbelieving look.

'Uh-huh.'

'I forget that you're like a serious nature nerd sometimes.'

I hold up the piece of paper. 'That's right, and I've got the paper-work to prove it.'

She giggles, then, looks thoughtful for a second. 'Hey, sorry the stuff with Liv took so long.'

While we were in town, Diana met with an old friend of hers, Liv. She's just got out of jail, where she was for a few months. Diana was vouching for Liv so that she can get a job at Tracy's, the diner in town.

'Don't worry about it. Everyone deserves a second chance.'

'Yeah, but I'm worried that she might need more than one second chance, if you know what I mean.'

'With you as a friend, I bet she'll be fine.'

She smiles, then reaches out for a hug.

*

When we arrive back at the cabin, we're confronted by a welcome, if slightly unexpected, sight. Atlas, topless, carrying a log.

'Hey there,' he says happily, before dropping the log down onto the floor and coming over to embrace me. 'Glad that you made it back OK.'

I give him a long, tender kiss. I hate being away from Daddy, but he's so busy at the moment that I didn't have a choice.

'Yuck!' says Diana, her voice little. 'You two need to get a room!'

'What do you think I'm carrying this log for?' Atlas grins.

Things are changing at the Little Cabin. Atlas and I are building a permanent lodge out here. After what happened with my brother and the Russian Mob, we figured it'd be good to have a home away from the hustle and bustle of Little Creek. Plus, Mr. Chuckles seems very happy out here. He's been staying in our guest cabin ever since the fire in Little Creek, and I can't wait to move him into our new permanent address once it's finished. It's so cute to see how much he loves being surrounded by nature out here. He spends whole days just sitting at the window watching the wind in the trees. I think he's happy to finally have some peace.

'OK, I'm gonna go check on my Daddy,' Diana says, giving us a smile. 'I'm looking forward to our swim later!'

We wave her off, and head to the site of our new cabin.

It's not finished — nowhere near — but it's definitely starting to come together now. Atlas has been working so hard, and Joel's been helping him out loads. I'm proud of my Daddy and what he's doing.

'So, did the letter come?' he finally asks as he puts the log he's been carrying into place, forming one of our walls. The skeleton of the cabin is done, and Atlas is just completing the roof. It's not quite as grand as the guest cabin, but it should be enough for our needs.

I nod. 'This is it,' I say, holding it up to him.

'You got it?'

I nod. 'I got the funding!'

As soon as I decided that I was going to stay in Little Creek, I knew that I was gonna have to earn some cash. So I applied for funding at my old college, Denver University, for a research grant. I want to study the habitats and ecology of grizzly bears near Little Creek. Thankfully, my old professor liked my application, so for the next twelve months at least, I've got enough money to live.

'You clever thing!' Atlas grabs me and lifts me up high. It's a thrill to feel him holding me like this. It's so easy for him to move me around. I squeeze my thighs around him, feeling the bulk of him.

I instantly feel a wetness spread through my diaper. This happens every time I'm near my Daddy — it's like he's got some kind of hypnotic power over me.

'I'm so proud of you,' he says, his voice snarly and guttural. I can tell by the way that he's talking that pride isn't the only thing he's feeling.

'Daddy,' I say, whining a little bit. 'I've got this funny feeling.'

'Oh?' He knows exactly what I'm talking about.

I whisper. 'Between my legs.'

There's a sudden shout from the other cabin. 'Hey, guys!' It's Joel. I feel all hot and flustered, but luckily Joel doesn't come see us. 'We're just heading down to the lake for our swim. Come join us when you're ready.'

'Will do,' shouts Atlas, giving me a wicked look. The next time he speaks, his voice is quiet, full of purpose. 'I guess that means we're all alone then...'

'I guess so.'

He growls. 'I'm gonna destroy you, you sexy little research student.'

'Oh Daddy, be gentle,' I moan as he bites my ear gently. His hot, hungry lips work their way down my neck. I feel like I'm melting in his arms, just like always.

We've had sex so many times this past month, but every time feels fresh, feels new. He's a generous, passionate lover, and I love how dominant and demanding he is of me.

'I don't know what gentle means,' he growls, his sexy accent driving me totally wild.

'Please...' I say, as he squeezes my nipples through my top, 'not too rough.'

He grunts, pulling my shirt open. My breasts relax down as he frees them, and he hungrily laps at my flesh, making me tremble with delight.

He moves his hands so that they are just under each of my breasts, and then he touches me, trailing lines over me. The pleasure is intense, almost impossible to take. He's so warm and his hands always surprise me with how soft they are. I feel a great wave of pleasure start to radiate out from each of my breasts as he starts to stroke them. I let my ass sit gently down on his lap and feel the hard, upward bulge of his cock straining against my body.

'You feel so big,' I say.

He snarls — a bestial, animalistic sound — and then moves his head up to my chest, fully taking my left nipple into his mouth. He sucks gently and then, with a mischievous look, he bites down tenderly on my flesh. I shudder — it's pleasure unlike any other. He closes his teeth even harder on me, making me squirm. There's a tiny hint of pain, and it feels totally delicious.

'You know just how to touch me, Daddy,' I say.

He hooks his hand around my body and grabs my ass. He is so ridiculously strong that it's almost scary. He rubs his hands all over me, taking huge handfuls of me, squeezing my flesh, making me feel desperate for more.

'I want to eat all of you,' he says, and without waiting for a response, he yanks my dress to the side, and tugs my diaper down. The fabric tears away and he flings it across the floor of the half-built cabin like garbage. Then, with a grunt, he lifts me up and pushes me down onto the ground. I feel my naked back against the hard floor and the rough wood against my soft buttocks. A moment later, his head is between my legs and his tongue is hungrily lapping. His tongue feels so warm and strong and slick, like it's been specially designed to give me pleasure. It slithers over my clit and I groan.

'You're so wet!' he growls, then gets back to his work. It's like he's totally in control of my body, of my pleasure, like he's a puppeteer, pulling my strings, making me dance to his tune. He laps up, down, around and around, flicking playfully over my entrance and then I feel something at my entrance, a finger, then two as they push their way into my pussy, forcing my lips apart and making me shake.

'Please Daddy, I need you inside me,' I whimper. I find his hardness with my hand and feel him through his jeans. 'I want this in me, I want to swallow it up — I want your skin, I want your flesh, I want all of you.'

He straightens up, kneels on the floor, and looks down at me.

'I'm gonna give it to you,' he says. I marvel at the chiseled shape of his ripped torso, watching as his muscles ripple under his skin. He is a machine, built for fucking. While I watch him, my fingers crawl to my pussy. I can't stop touching myself. I push my fingers into myself as he undoes the buttons of his pants.

'You're an excited Little Girl, aren't you?' he says.

When he pulls the waist of his jeans down, his cock springs up like an iron rod from inside. Before he has time to do anything, I bend up to meet it and start to kiss and lick his manhood.

'I want you so much,' I say, 'I belong to you. You can fuck me however you want.' I take the tip of his meat into my mouth and start to suck. I'm salivating so much that my spit is pouring down his shaft. He moans with pleasure and then he grabs me.

'I'm gonna destroy you,' he says, then lifts and bends me over so that I'm on all fours. My pussy is seeping, and when I feel the tip of his cock push slowly into me, I hear a slick, moist slurp as my body accepts him into me.

'So fucking wet,' he moans, 'so fucking warm and wet and good. Your pussy is incredible.' His dick feels strong and thick and like it's pushing my insides apart and he slides in deeper and then he's fucking me, pounding over and over into my body. I shake with each thrust and feel my tits swing beneath my chest. I move my legs further apart and wriggle back against him. I want him further in, and then, he reaches over and grabs my tits and pulls me back and his dick *is* further in me. I'm kneeling up with him jammed inside me and he just fucks me and fucks me, now holding my hands back behind me and angling himself so that he hits some secret spot inside my body. I feel his other hand snaking around my torso and with a single, feather-light touch on my clit I feel the beginnings of a powerful orgasm. My body is wracked with it — I squeal and feel my muscles contract, and then he begins to unload in me, his seed mixing with my fluids, and I know that this pleasure is all I want from life.

# ATLAS

THE SUNSET OVER THE lake is incredible. Salmon pink sky, flecked with purple and peach, underlined by the shimmering, crystal-clear water of the lake. It's been an incredible day and an amazing few months.

Mia and Diana are frolicking in the water together, and Joel is heading in to meet them. Carl and Ella are chatting about something or other on the shore nearby. I've finished setting up my easel, trying to catch the light before the end of the day.

I feel as though I've finally found a little home here in Colorado. I'll always remember my roots in Greece, but my heart beats red, white and blue.

Mia's changed so much in the past couple months. Her brother caved under pressure in jail, giving up crucial evidence against Karkov. Carl and the state prosecutor managed to bring down the entire criminal organization. For the first time in her adult life, Mia is totally safe.

She's blossomed, becoming more confident and much happier. Helping her is the thing I feel proudest of in my life.

I block out the shapes of the mountains and lake with thin washes of paint, moving as quick as I can to capture the scene. It's not long before the sun dips behind the peak of a nearby hill and everything starts to change.

My Baby Girl comes running out the lake, and her little swim diaper crinkles as she walks up to me. I take out a towel and wrap it around her before she has the chance to feel cold. Joel and Diana are still in the lake, slowly swimming, then splashing each other.

Mia kisses me softly. 'I missed you in there,' she says.

'I know sweetie, but I just needed to paint the scene.'

She comes round to look at the easel. 'It's beautiful,' she whispers. 'Look at the light, it's amazing.' Her eyes widen. 'Oh my god, is that me?' She points to a figure by the lake.

'How could you tell?' I ask.

'You painted my swim diaper! It's bright orange.'

I laugh. 'I thought that might give the game away.'

'Why d'you paint the swim diaper? You can't display this at any galleries with a diaper in it!'

'Why not? I'm not ashamed of who you are. Who we are. I want to paint our lives together, to let the world know about our love.'

She looks at me, and her lower lip starts to tremble. 'I never thought I'd find someone like you, Daddy,' she says, lacing her fingers into mine.

I say the only thing that seems right. 'I love you, Mia. Feels like I always have.'

'I love you too.'

Then, by the fast-fading light, her lips find mine and we melt into each other, and I feel saved.

\* \* \*

**Read on for Gabriel and Bailey's story: *Stuck with Daddy*!**

Chapter Four

---

# STUCK WITH DADDY

# GABRIEL

THE SCREAM CUTS THROUGH the calm of the evening like a knife through flesh.

I clap my book shut, uncross my legs, and stand to attention. There's adrenaline in my veins and sweat on my brow.

That sounded close. Really damn close. Had to be someone in Hiker's Foe canyon. Maybe they've fallen. Maybe they're being mauled by a bear. Maybe one of a thousand other terrifying scenarios is unfolding right now.

There's the rhythmic sound of paws, scraping on the hardwood floor, and moments later, Brandy careens through the living space of the cabin, coming to a stop just a few feet away from me. Her tongue's out and she's looking at me like she knows exactly what's going on: expectant, dutiful, ready for action.

'Alright girl, let's get going.'

With an excited yelp, Brandy heads out of the cabin. I grab my go-bag and follow her into the cold November night.

*

It's dark, and hard to keep up with Brandy. Even though she's a bulky dog — 220lbs of lovable St. Bernard — she's nimble through the trees. She knows the way down to the bottom of Hiker's Foe even better than I do, plus she's got that amazing nose to help her find her way.

She might be called Brandy, but instead of a tiny keg of liquor, I've attached a bell to her collar so I can keep track of where she is when I can't see her. Kind of. She's darting in and out of the dark firs right now, finding her own path parallel to the track I'm making a meal of following.

'Slow down, girl,' I call out. She pauses — just for a second, bless her — then she bounds on again. But luckily, that second is all I need to find her with my torch beam.

She's surging ahead, downhill, toward the bottom of the canyon.

It's called Hiker's Foe for good reason. We're in the foothills of the Rockies here, and the trail down to Little Creek River gets notoriously steep. It's not just the incline that causes people trouble, either. The trail is stupidly narrow — at times there's barely enough width for a single foot. It's uneven too, with crumbling rock giving way at inopportune moments. If it weren't for the spectacular views at the northern end of the canyon, the trail would have for sure been shut by now.

But people keep coming, and people keep getting into trouble.

Since I built my cabin here three years ago, I've rescued five hikers from varying points of Hiker's foe. No one pays me to do it. Heck, I don't think that the national parks service particularly wants me here. But I'm glad I picked this spot for my mission. It's all I can do to try to buy redemption for myself after what happened to Pete.

Brandy's bark pulls me out of my grim thoughts, focusing my mind on the task at hand: finding whoever made that scream.

Although I've walked this path countless times, I still need to keep my eyes down. Each footstep is a potential accident.

I met Brandy when I used to work at Mountain Rescue. She was my partner back then — well, my canine partner, that is. She's been trained since she was a tiny pup to seek out those in need of rescue. She retired at the same time I quit, so I decided to take her in. Seemed like a good idea to have a friend in my self-imposed isolation, and it was one of the best decisions I ever made.

We're nearing the bottom of the crevice now, and I can sense the slopes of the mountains on either side hemming us in. I can't hear any moans, can't see anyone. I get the feeling, though, that Brandy knows exactly where to go.

'Please don't be in the water, please don't be in the water.' My voice is quiet and desperate.

To my dismay though, Brandy's heading straight for the creek.

I sweep my torch beam left and right over the fast-flowing surface of the water. Under normal circumstances, I'd be stopping to take in the peace and majesty of Little Creek River after dark. It's a truly gorgeous part of the world. Seems crazy that somewhere so awe-inspiring can be so deadly too.

Finally, I find Brandy with the light. She's on the riverbank, looking into the current, she looks back at me, and the backs of her eyes flash red as the light picks them out. Then, when I move the beam of the light to the water, I see her.

Stretched out, lying awkwardly on her back, up to her waist in the water.

I forget about looking down. I hit the track with ferocious speed, closing the gap to the stranded woman in seconds. Because in this cold, seconds could be the difference between life and death. I put the flashlight in my mouth, gripping the end with my teeth so that I can use both my hands to help the poor woman. It's hard to see in this low light, but she looks pale. I put my ear to her mouth. Thank god — she's breathing. Her breath is soft and slow, but definitely there.

I quickly think back to my Mountain rescue training. It's been years since I've had to treat someone with hypothermia. It's only been ten minutes or so since I first heard the scream, so I'm hopeful that things haven't progressed too far. The first and most important thing is that I've got to be super gentle. Sudden, harsh movements can trigger dangerous heart rhythms when a body is this cold.

I'm grateful that Brandy's being such a good girl — she knows how important it is to stand back and let me do my thing here. I move my hands slowly and purposefully underneath the body in the creek, and gently, as steadily as I can, I pull her up and out of the flow of the water. Her clothes are soaked. This is not good.

The temptation is to try to rapidly heat her up, but I know that's almost as dangerous as leaving her in the stream. That's the agony of treating hypothermia: move too fast and it can be fatal, move too slow and it can be fatal.

'No mistakes, Gabe,' I say to myself.

The woman's eyes flicker — a good sign. Maybe she's almost conscious. Maybe it's just her body, working to warm itself.

Now that she's out of the water, I'm gonna have to get her out of these wet clothes. There's a time and a place for modesty, and now isn't it. I take a couple things out of my go-bag — a blanket to lie her on, and a knife to cut her free of her clothes. I lay the blanket down to insulate her from the cold ground, then I start to strip. I don't have any spare clothes, so she's gonna have to make do with mine. When I've got everything ready, I work as fast and precise as I can, cutting her out of her soaking wet blue jeans and hiking top. Right now I'm in medic mode, and I barely take in her body — all I see is a desperately sick woman who needs my help.

There's a nasty bruise on her ankle. I hope she hasn't broken it. There's only so much I can do for her in my cabin, and it's a long trek to the town of Little Creek, where the nearest doctor is, never mind getting her to a hospital.

I dry her with a towel, then lay her on the blanket, before wrapping it around her. Then, to give her even more chance at warming up, I lay my clothes on top of her. I hope with all my heart that it's enough to bring her back from the brink.

Her breathing seems a little stronger, a little less labored. Brandy's standing guard, looking this way and that. 'Good girl,' I say, reaching over to her and patting her muzzle. 'Sorry you have to see Daddy with his clothes off,' I say. She whines sympathetically.

It looks as though the hiker is starting to warm up. Color is slowly returning to her cheeks, and her breathing is definitely stronger now. I'm going to have to get her back to my place though, sooner rather than later. If I leave it too long, I might even be at risk of hypothermia. I can already feel my body temperature start to fall. We haven't had the first snowfall of the year yet, but it's close, you can tell by the bite in the air.

'Two more minutes,' I say, watching my breath hang in the air, a cloud of warmth, leaving my body. Within a minute, I'm starting to shiver, but there's no way I'm taking my big jacket off that poor girl.

When I'm convinced that she's over the worst of it, I lean over her and get ready to scoop her up.

Now that she's looking more healthy, and I'm so close, I can't help but notice how pretty she is. She's got this gorgeous little mouth. Her upper lip looks like the bumpy top of a love heart, and the lashes on her closed eyes are long and delicate. 'Now's not the time for distractions, Gabriel, no matter how much of a cutie she is.'

To my horror, as the final words of that sentence leave my mouth, her eyes flicker open. The clearest, brightest blue, looking straight at me. I've never felt so embarrassed in my life. For a moment, it looks as though she's trying to understand what on earth is going on. Why is a huge, near-naked man leaning over me? Why am I wrapped up in a blanket? Am I being saved, or murdered?

Her mouth opens, then, before she can say a word, her eyes roll back and close. For a moment I'm worried she's having a heart attack, but it's soon clear that she's just passed out again.

'Why is it that I always bore women to sleep?' I ask Brandy as I lean down to scoop the hiker up. She's lighter than I expect. I keep her wrapped up tight in the blankets, holding her close to me — partly for her benefit, partly for mine.

As soon as I'm holding her, Brandy knows we're heading back. She darts ahead, up the path, into the dark.

The trek up is more treacherous than the trek down. I've never done this walk while carrying someone at night before, and it's not an experience I ever want to repeat. Every single footstep is difficult to judge, and a couple of times I flay out wildly to the side to keep my balance. At times I'm grateful for the dark — it means I can't see how far down I might fall. Eventually, though, I see the glow of my cabin in the distance, then I smell the smoke from the chimney.

As I approach, I feel a few delicate flakes of snow on my bare skin — resting for a second before melting away to nothing.

'Just in time,' I say, then I kick my front door open, and feel the warmth of the inside envelop me like a soft, downy quilt. Walking through to the bedroom, I carefully lay down the hiker, being as gentle as I can.

That's when I really see her for the first time.

My jaw drops. She's perfect. So much more beautiful than I realized out in the creek. Not just beautiful — there's something else about her.

This is crazy, but I feel something big, something powerful in my heart. That she and I were meant to meet. That she's a Little.

That she could be my Forever Girl.

# BAILEY

I 'VE NEVER HAD A nightmare like it before. So cold and dark and lonely, like I was at the edge of the world. Faces flashed up — some I recognized, some I didn't. My boyfriend (or should that be my ex-boyfriend?) Dougal. My mom, my pop. But a stranger too. A hulking brute of a man, with a bare chest. Skin stitched with dark black ink, eyes burning with the intensity of wildfire.

When I finally wake up, I pant and feel moisture on my brow. I'm sweating, and I don't know where I am.

It's warm in here, thank God. The last thing I remember is icy coldness surrounding my body, my strength slowly sapping away. I don't ever want to go back to that feeling, so weak and vulnerable.

I look around, trying to get my bearings. Where the hell am I? I swear I've never been anywhere like this before. I'm in a four-poster bed, but like everything else in here, it doesn't look like the kind of bed you could just pick up from Sears. All the posts have a hand-whittled feel, just like the uneven ceiling panels.

The windows have old plaid curtains drawn across them, and the only light comes from a flickering candle in the corner of the room. I could be anywhere.

I'm torn between wanting to find out where I am, and loving the comfort of being in bed.

When I shift my weight up, pulling myself onto my elbows, there's a spasm of pain in my ankle, and suddenly, memories flood back.

The argument with Dougal. The treacherous trail. My terrifying fall.

My scream — a sound I didn't even know I could make.

Then a memory hits me like a sledgehammer, and it feels like all the breath has been forced out of my lungs.

Two hands pushing against my chest, forcing me back off the path and down to my doom.

I look around desperately, trying to find Charlie — my stuffie. But he's nowhere to be seen.

Before I can think any more deeply about the implications of my realization, I'm brought out of my thoughts with a bump.

'Did I hear something? Is our guest finally awake, Brandy?'

I don't recognize the voice. It's a man — there's no mistaking that. Super deep and resonant, like it's bouncing around a rib cage the size of a small country. I look over at the door. It slowly creaks open, and a figure steps into the room. It's so murky in here it takes me a moment to make him out.

His voice was enough to scare me, but now that I can see him, so much adrenaline is released into my system it feels like my heart is gonna explode.

Tall. Dark. Broad.

His jaw is covered in jet-black stubble, and his eyes are a deep brown. I can't tell if he's scowling or smiling. He's got the muscular, confident stance of a prize fighter or a rockstar, and there's power behind every step. I can see the tip of a tattoo snaking up from his chest, although I can't make out the picture.

Damn. I don't think I've ever seen anyone wear a simple white t-shirt as well as this guy does. His body underneath the cotton is impossibly taut, like a collection of thick, coiled ropes, ready to snap straight.

That's when I realize that I do recognize him. He's the man from my nightmares. That strange, angry face, and those burning, intense eyes.

Then I hear another voice. To my surprise, it's me. 'Don't hurt me.' It comes out hoarse and strained, like I haven't spoken for days.

He looks puzzled for a moment, then holds up his hands. To my surprise, I see that even his palms are tattooed. 'Don't worry,' he says, in that slow, deep voice, 'after what I did to save you, the last thing I'm gonna do is hurt you, sweetheart.'

I pull the cover up to my chin, and the mystery man walks over to the candle. He reaches down to a cabinet and grabs what looks like an old-fashioned oil lamp, then he holds the wick to the flame. 'That's better,' he says, as the light in the room starts to grow. 'Now we can see each other a little more clearly.'

'Where am I?' I say. My voice is still shaky, although I'm doing everything I can to sound brave.

'You're about fifteen minutes trek from where I found you, at the bottom of Hiker's Foe canyon.'

I feel my brows knit together. It's like I'm not in control of my body, like I can't help but react with emotion to every new piece of information. 'You found me?'

'Damn right,' he says, putting the lamp down on a bedside table right next to me. 'When I picked you out of the creek, you were in a bad way. Hypothermia.'

'I don't remember,' I say, pathetically.

'Course you don't. The brain protects itself from trauma. It can take years for suppressed memories to emerge.' There's something about the way he says that that makes me wonder whether he's speaking from experience. 'So how did you get to be at the bottom of that canyon?'

'I slipped,' I lie. I'm the world's worst liar. Always have been. Ever since my pop caught me cutting my little sister's doll's hair. I told him she wanted me to give her a new haircut. Bless my dad — he humored me, went to ask my sister about it. But he knew I wasn't telling the truth.

'I see,' he says, nodding. 'Well, the path can be treacherous. But at least your traveling companion made it out.'

This takes me off guard. 'How do you know about Dougal?'

'Dougal huh? I found his tracks. Went out today to scout. There were tracks, around an hour's trek from the top of the canyon, heading back to Little Creek.'

The full enormity of the situation hits me. So Dougal just left me? For a moment, I think I'm gonna cry then I pull myself together. I have to be stronger than this. He's got no power over me anymore.

He seems to pick up on my energy.

'Don't worry, I'm sure they're fine. Probably got picked up by the official mountain rescue farther down the trail.'

'Probably,' I say. My voice comes out super-quiet. I've always acted Little around new people, especially stern-seeming men. Makes me feel more comfortable to take the backseat, to do as I'm told.

'Sweetheart, what's your name?'

'Bailey,' I say, quietly.

'I'm Gabriel,' he says. He smiles for the first time, and as he does, it's like his whole face changes, his whole persona. That tough, gruff exterior just seems to melt away. 'And it's good to meet you, Bailey, even in this crazy situation. Now, let me ask you a question. Are you hungry?'

And at that exact moment, my stomach growls louder than a crack of thunder.

'Can I have my phone?'

He inhales sharply. 'Got some bad news on that front, I'm afraid to say. It got busted up pretty bad in the fall. Couldn't find it in your clothes yesterday, so I went back to the creek to see if it was around.' He reaches into his pocket and takes out a handset. 'Found it about ten feet from where I found you. It's trashed. Dunno if it was the water that did it, or the fall, or both, but this thing ain't coming on.'

As he hands me my phone, just for a moment, his fingertips brush mine. I catch his eye, then look down bashfully at my phone.

'Hang on,' I say, looking up at him, 'what do you mean, you couldn't find it in my clothes?'

He grimaces, then scratches the top of his head awkwardly. 'Ah, yeah, I kinda had to strip your clothes off you.'

I look down under the covers. I'm wearing a t-shirt that's way too big for me, and a pair of sweatpants I don't recognize either. My cheeks burn red. 'Uhhh...' I can't think of what to say. This stranger has seen me naked. But for some reason, it's not making me feel yucky. No. It's kind of exciting.

'I had to get your wet clothes off quickly. It's the most important thing to do when someone's suffering from hypothermia.' He sees my embarrassment. 'I can show you my medical training certificate if you want. I worked in mountain rescue for ten years. It was my job.'

Something about the way he says that puts me on edge. 'But you don't work in mountain rescue anymore?'

He purses his lips and narrows his eyes. 'It's complicated.'

Finally, I look down at my phone's screen. There's a bunch of ugly cracks along it — the glass is practically crushed in the center. I try the power button, but he's right, there's no way it's coming on.

A nasty thought crosses my mind. What if he's lying to me? What if he smashed the glass and broke the phone so badly that it won't power on? What if he wants to keep me here?

'You can use my phone if you want,' he says as if reading my mind. 'Call anyone you like, let them know you're safe, that you'll be back with 'em in a couple of days.'

I don't actually know Dougal's number, but the truth is, after what he did, I don't even know if I want him to know where I am. 'It's OK,' I say, 'I don't really have anyone to tell.'

He raises an eyebrow. 'I find that hard to believe.'

'Well, my parents both passed away a couple years ago and... well, I don't have a boyfriend anymore.'

'I'm sorry to hear about your parents.' There's a look of genuine sympathy on his face.'

'It's OK, they died doing what they loved most — cruising on Pop's yacht.'

'Well, I don't really know what to say to that.'

I smile. 'It's OK. What can you say?'

An icy thought lodges its way into my brain. I'm all alone with this guy, and I literally just told him that no one would care if I went missing.

'Look,' I say, my voice suddenly nervous, 'thanks for all the help, but I really think I should get going.'

'I don't know if that's such a good idea,' he counters. 'You're sure to be really weak fro-'

'I really want to just leave.' My voice sounds desperate now — I don't even bother to try to hide it.

To my surprise, he puts his hands on his hips. 'I'm afraid there's no way that you can leave right now. I won't allow it.'

I swallow, my throat suddenly dry.

'What do you mean?'

'Come through here. I'll show you.'

*

The instant he opens the front door, it's like I'm staring into a white sheet. The snow is so thick and heavy that I can't even see a foot out of the cabin. There's a drift already piled up against the walls that's four-foot thick. Outside, the air is bitterly cold. It cuts straight to the bone, even though I'm safely inside.

'It's the heaviest November snowfall I can ever remember,' he explains, pulling the door shut. 'There's no way I can get you to Little Creek today. Probably no way I'll be able to get you there tomorrow either.' He gives me a sincere look. 'I don't want to keep you here. You're not a prisoner — far from it. But I'm afraid to say that there's no way I'm going to put someone like you in harm's way. No chance. And I'm putting my foot down on that. When the time is right, you'll get back to civilization, but until it's safe, you're stuck here. Stuck with me.'

One of his phrases stuck in my mind. 'What do you mean *someone like you*?'

He looks slightly sheepish. 'Did I say that? Must have been a slip of the tongue.'

Now I thought *I* was the bad liar.

Even though he clearly does know what he said, I'm not getting any kind of bad vibes from this guy. Maybe I'm dumb and confused because of how hot he is, but I'm finding how possessive and protective he's getting to be a real turn-on. It's like he's acting exactly as a Daddy would act.

'Now,' he says, 'let's get some food inside you.'

Five minutes later, I'm tucking into one of the most incredible plates of food I've ever eaten.

'This is the best chili I've ever eaten, bar none.' There is so much flavor going on. Chilies, garlic, black pepper — sure. But there are other, subtle hints going on too. Cinnamon, ginger... mace? It feels like I haven't eaten for a week. Every single mouthful of the delicious, nourishing, spicy stew is making my tongue dance with delight.

'I'm sure the fact you haven't had a morsel to eat for two days might be helping it go down, young lady.'

'I dunno,' I say, chowing down another forkful. 'This is pretty dang special.'

'There's not much to do out here,' he says, raising his eyebrows, 'so I like to cook. Long and slow.'

Suddenly, there's a frenzied panting from somewhere else in the cabin.

'Oh,' Gabriel says, 'here comes trouble.'

A moment later, a huge — and I mean enormous — dog comes bounding through the space, right up to the table. 'Brandy!' says Gabriel, sharply, 'Have some manners. No paws on the table, girl.'

The dog is a mass of brown and white fur. Her tongue is long and lolling out, and her bright, dark eyes look straight at my plate.

'Ooohhh,' I say, 'she's so cute!' I've always had a thing for big dogs. Mom had a Doberman called Sergeant who I absolutely adored growing up. I've always been impulsive. It's what gets me into so much trouble. Before I have time to properly think about what I'm doing, I lift a spoonful of chili to Brandy's mouth. She eagerly licks it all up.

'Hey!' says Gabriel, 'That's against the rules! Read number five.'

He points up at a wall. Sure enough, on a blackboard I hadn't noticed up until now, there's a list of rules, written in white chalk. 'Number five: Human food is for humans. Dog food is for dogs. No exceptions. Sorry. I didn't see. Didn't think there would be rules up on the wall.'

He nods, 'It's OK, you didn't know. Anyway, the rules are just suggestions. But if you follow them, you'll get treats. While you're here, I'm going to look after you in a special way, to make sure you're protected and safe. The rules are part of that.'

He wants me to follow a set of rules? I mean, I love rules, but this is starting to get really weird. I'm just trying to work out whether this is good-weird or bad-weird.

'It's your house, so I'm happy to follow whatever rules you like,' I say. All this feels like it's piling up on me, making me feel vulnerable. 'Could I ask you a favor? I'm kinda missing something. I've got this dumb old teddy bear, and—'

'Of course,' he says, hitting his forehead with his palm, 'let me get him for you. I should have known you'd need your stuffie in a strange situation like this.'

While he's away, I stroke Brandy. She's a really good girl, not begging or whining, just pushing her warm body up against mine.

He comes back, holding Charlie. He looks a little scuffed, but still in good condition.

'I know it's dumb for a fully grown woman to need a teddy.' I know I shouldn't but I don't want him to be weirded out. But why do I care so much about what this guy thinks of me?

'It's not dumb,' he says, 'and I don't want to hear you criticize yourself like that, OK, miss? I think it's wonderful. Means you're free enough to be yourself. It's great.'

As I sit at the table, eating the chili and cuddling Charlie, I feel a wave of happiness wash over me. And I don't even think about Dougal once.

The fact that I'm sitting across from the hottest guy on the planet definitely helps with that.

# GABRIEL

I CAN'T GET HER out of my head. No matter how much I toss and turn, no matter how carefully I try to focus on literally anything *but* her, I can't stop.

She's asleep now just a few feet from me. I mean, granted, she's on the other side of a timber wall, but if it weren't there I'd be able to see her beautiful smile. Her sexy dimples.

I know, she's got dimples, for fuck's sake. I'm such a sucker for them — there's nothing cuter, in my opinion. I can't remember the last time I saw an adult woman with actual dimples. Gives me an extra incentive to make her smile — as if I even needed it.

My Daddy instincts have been going berserk, ever since I saw her lying down in my house. It's like she's been specially designed to make me crazy. She's so vulnerable, and clearly, something's going on with her that she's not sharing with me right now. Besides that, she's got a stuffie for heck's sake. Even if she doesn't know she's a Little, there's a good fucking chance she is one. Or she could be, with some coaxing.

I've got a feeling that the Dougal guy is her boyfriend, but I have no idea why she won't tell me that. This Little Girl is a mystery wrapped in an enigma, tied up in a puzzle.

I pull my blanket down a touch. I piled the logs on the fire tonight, trying to get it extra warm in here. I figure Bailey's had enough cold to last her a lifetime in the past few days. I tend to run hot though, so normally I'd never have the place as warm as this.

Since I built this cabin and decided to live away from society, I gave up on the idea of ever finding love. My plan was to dedicate myself to saving lives, and I guess I started to see myself almost like a monk — celibate for a higher purpose. It was easy to give up, in a way, because I've only ever been interested in forging a DDlg relationship, and finding Littles in rural Colorado just never seemed to happen for me.

But having Bailey in the house with me is giving me feelings I haven't felt in... well, forever.

I think the thing that threw me the most was just how naturally she responded to my rules. It had been a crazy risk, to write up house rules on my chalkboard — I just had this weird hunch she'd go for them. After we finished dinner, I talked her through them. They're simple things for the most part, and honestly, there's a few more *interesting* rules I'd really love to suggest to her, but I don't want to freak her out.

Not yet at least.

'Dammit, Gabe,' I whisper to myself, 'you've got to stop thinking about her like this. She's not into you, she's practically half your age, for fuck's sake. She needs your protection, not your cock.'

I sound convinced, but it's just an act. There's no way I can stop myself thinking about what it might be like to kiss those soft lips, to feel her smooth skin against mine, to move with her, deep in the night, all the way through to morning.

Eventually, I do get to sleep, but my rest is shallow and disturbed, as the blizzard blows against my tiny cabin, trapping us more firmly together.

I get up early — same as every morning — to check the weather and conditions for the day. I take my responsibility to safeguard Hiker's

Foe seriously, and even though Bailey's here, I plan to patrol later on today.

Soon as I woke this morning, I knew that the snow was thick and heavy. You can always tell by the light. It's got this silvery, luminescent quality, like it's been filtered through an angel's halo or something. Shit, having Bailey here has got me feeling all poetic.

We're due another heavy snowfall today, so my plan is to wait that out, then maybe tomorrow, I'll make my way with Bailey to a friend's cabin. Joel's a former investment banker who runs a kind of 'getaway' for Littles in the Colorado wilderness. He's not been here that long, but he and I get on like a house on fire. His place is about halfway to the town of Little Creek, so I figure Bailey and I can stay there overnight before we finish our journey back to civilization.

I pour a handful of coffee beans into my grinder and blast them for a few seconds. When that scent hits my nostrils I practically snap to attention. I'm a real coffee nerd. Gotta make sure that the roast on my beans is just right, gotta make sure the grind is the perfect coarseness for my pour-over filter. I don't have many creature comforts out here in the wilderness, but good coffee is the one thing I don't think I could live without.

'Eeek!' A little shriek comes from the direction of the second bedroom, where Bailey is staying.

I look over and see her standing by the door. She's wearing an old pair of my pajamas, with the waist cinched in super-tight, and a Minnie Mouse t-shirt. That one's hers. She rubs her eyes and yawns.

'Everything OK?'

'Just got a bit scared by the loud noise.'

For a moment I'm confused. 'Oh, you mean the coffee grinder? Don't even think of that as loud.'

'Maybe to you it's not,' she says, walking across the room and parking her butt on a chair at the breakfast table. 'But I'm not brave like you. I'm a wuss.'

Perhaps I'm imagining this, but she seems more relaxed this morning. It occurs to me that up til now, she's probably been in survival mode. Maybe I barely know what she's like.

'I'm sure that's not true,' I say, tipping the ground coffee into the filter. 'How do you take your coffee?'

'Sweet and milky!'

'I should have known.'

I pour hot water over the ground coffee and wait patiently as the warm black liquid seeps through the filter.

'No coffee machine?'

I grin. 'I try to keep electricity use down. I'm off-grid here. It's camping gas for cooking and a generator for electricity I absolutely can't do without.'

'Off-grid,' she says, then sighs. 'Wish I could go off-grid for a while.'

'Oh? Why's that?'

She gives me a long look. 'Well, I've kind of got this issue with my ex-boyfriend.'

I knew it was coming sooner or later. Still, it's nice she feels comfortable enough to share personal information with me.

'What kind of an issue?'

'He's a stinky old jerk.'

A chuckle leaves my mouth. 'You know, it's very common for exes to be stinky old jerks, in my experience.'

'Yeah but this is different,' she says. 'Dougal is *really* stinky.'

'Wasn't Dougal the name of the guy you were hiking with?'

She nods.

'Didn't realize he was your boyfriend.'

'*Ex*-boyfriend,' she corrects me. 'Emphasis on the ex part.'

'How come you went hiking with your ex-boyfriend? Doesn't sound as though you two get on so well.' I pour the coffee into two small mugs and add milk and sugar to Bailey's. I stir it a couple times then hand it over.

'It's kinda complicated,' she says, giving the coffee a sniff. Her face lights up. 'This smells insanely delicious! What is it?'

'Just coffee. Made with love.'

She blows on it, exactly the way a little kid would, eyes full of wonder and excitement, then she takes a tentative sip. 'Mmmmm,' she says, 'your love tastes good.' She realizes what she's just said, and her cheeks go bright red. 'Ummm, I mean... damn it.'

'Hey,' I say, 'what's rule number three?'

She looks up at the chalkboard. 'No cussing.' Her voice is little, her face fragile.

'That's right. No punishment though, not for your first mistake.'

'I'm sorry,' she says. 'You can forgive me, right?'

'Course I can.' She sounds so tender, so desperate for approval. What has this guy Dougal done to this poor girl?

'So anyway, I've been going out with Dougal for like, ever.'

'That's a long time,' I tease.

'Six years. Since high-school. Since before I lost my parents.'

'That is a long time,' I concede.

'Thing is, I've known deep down that it wasn't gonna work between us right from the start. I need something that he can't give me. Something he doesn't *want* to give me.' She's being purposefully vague now. I respect the fact there's stuff she doesn't want to share.

'Sounds tough.'

'I've been wanting to end it with him for years, but I'm not very good at confrontation, so I've kind of been putting it off.'

'Ending a relationship is always hard.'

'Yeah,' she says, 'and I think it was doubly hard because, you know, he knew my parents. So it's kind of like he's been a link to them, if that makes sense.'

'Sure it does,' I nod.

'So I finally plucked up the courage to tell him that it was over, and on the day I was gonna do it, he sprung this vacation on me. He'd already spent all the money, booked the flights, Airbnb.' She sighs. 'I shoulda never agreed to come on the trip with him, but I just couldn't break up with him when he'd booked a da...' she glances up at the chalkboard, 'dang vacation. I'm a bad person, aren't I?'

'I don't think so. This stuff is complicated. So, he still doesn't know he's your ex?'

'Oh no,' she laughs a wry laugh, 'he knows. We were slowly heading up Hiker's Foe, and he was talking about all his plans for our future, how he wants me to sell my family home and buy a place in Florida, and I felt so guilty that it was like I was gonna explode. Then, he reached for his pocket and I just *knew* he was gonna pull out a ring. So I stopped him and told him that I couldn't be with him anymore.'

'Then you slipped and fell?'

She looks down, suddenly sheepish. 'Yeah.' Another sip of her coffee. 'Um, well, I guess I don't really remember how that happened.'

That look tells me everything I need to know.

'Was Dougal ever violent with you?' I ask. I can barely contain my rage. I hope it's not freaking Bailey out. I take a sip from my coffee cup, hoping to cover up my disgust.

She can't bring herself to say anything. She looks at me, the lower rim of her eyes watery. Then she nods. One tiny movement.

'That fucking piece of trash,' I say, losing control.

'Hey, rule three,' she smiles, through her tears.

'When it comes to men hitting women, I think the normal rules don't apply.' I pause for a moment. 'I won't tolerate violence against women. No way. I'm sorry you had to go through that. Even thinking about someone hurting you makes me feel sick. It's not going to happen again.'

'You gonna look after me?' I can't tell if she's teasing, or serious.

'If you'll let me.' My reply is serious as the grave.

She looks shaken. 'Thank you. I'll definitely take you up on that while I'm here.'

'I mean it,' I say. 'If you need to lie low, to get off-grid for a while, let that a-hole cool down, you're welcome to stay here for as long as you like. You can trust me, Bailey. I won't let anything bad happen to you.'

She smiles. 'I know I can trust you. I can feel it somehow. You're a good man.'

'I'm a nobody,' I say.

A paw shoots up and lands on my lap. 'Hey girl, I didn't see you there.'

'Brandy knows,' says Bailey, rubbing the dog's head.

'She knows that it's time for me to get scouting.' I look up at the clock on the wall. 'I'm gonna head down to Hiker's Foe and make sure there are no poor saps hurt or stuck in the snow. It'll take me a little longer than usual because of the weather, but I'll be back. I'll leave a walkie-talkie, so if you need me, you can call.'

'OK,' she says.

'I got plenty of books if you like to read. Plus I'm gonna leave Brandy with you to look after you. She's always fun to play with.'

'You're a reader?'

'Ohh yeah. Sci-fi mostly, but I've got a pretty decent library, feel free to look through any of them.' I point to the bookshelves in the corner of the living space.

'Thanks, Gabriel,' she says.

'Oh, just one thing, I'd prefer it if you didn't head through that door there.' I point over at the door in question. 'That part of the cabin is kind of a work in progress, and I wouldn't want you hurting yourself on building equipment.' It's a white lie, but one worth telling.

She nods. 'Sure.'

As I strap on my snow boots and head out into the freezing cold, I get this nagging feeling, like I shouldn't be leaving Bailey alone in the cabin. But it doesn't stop me, because I'm gonna check that canyon every day until the day I die. It's the only way I can make peace with the past.

# BAILEY

I LOVE EXPLORING OTHER people's stuff. I know, I know, it's kinda naughty, but I can't help myself. I find other people fascinating, and the best way to learn what someone's like is to have a good old rummage through their possessions! And Gabe isn't just fascinating, he practically makes me salivate, so there's no way I'm not gonna have a little poke around.

I wait five minutes or so after Gabriel's gone, then start to look through his bookshelves.

Huh.

There's lots of stuff here I don't recognize, but a couple names I do. My Pop was a big reader, and he quite liked sci-fi and fantasy, so I know Isaac Asimov and Iain M. Banks. There's a lot of obscure stuff too though. Then, to my surprise, on the bottom shelf, right next to the fire poker, I find a secret stash.

'Brandy, looks like your daddy has a soft spot for romance!'

I pick my way through the novels. They're not names I recognize, but some of them look kinda *kinky*. And when I leaf through a few pages of one particularly racy-looking book, I find myself blushing. Brandy comes right up next to me and looks at the book.

'You're too young to be reading this stuff,' I say, giving her a stroke.

I'm kinda surprised by how much I opened up to Gabriel. Talking to him felt so natural, and he wasn't judgmental or annoying. It was like he was actually interested in what I had to say. I've been kinda worried that he just views me as this silly little girl, but I'm glad he took the time to listen about my past and my troubles with Dougal — even if I left out the most shocking detail. Gabe looked so angry when I admitted that Dougal has been physical with me in the past. I wonder what he'd have done if I told him that Dougal pushed me down the slope.

My relationship with Dougal has always been complicated. It's easy to think that leaving someone who's been physical with you is an obvious decision, but it's not that straightforward. Even though when I told Dougal that I wanted to explore my Little side he snorted and laughed, I did come to rely on him for a lot. It's only now that I'm not with him that the trap I was in has become obvious to see.

It's been hard to admit to myself, but I think I've been the victim of carefully planned, emotional abuse. Hard to admit because I don't want to be a victim. I don't want to be the weak person he made me.

'That's all in the past now, Brandy,' I say.

Gabe doesn't really strike me as a homebody, but he's done an amazing job decorating this place. All the objects in here are practical. There are no paintings or sculptures. But I think the fact it's all practical makes it beautiful. Simple, humble bookshelves. A solid oak table. Exposed wooden beams. His personality is on display here; humble, solid, strong.

Next to the bookshelves is a small musical instrument in a stand. Looks kinda like a Ukulele, but it's bigger than that. I wonder what it is. I wonder if he plays it. I put down the romance books, carefully recreating the order they were in before (alphabetical, of course), and take a closer look at the instrument. It's got eight strings, strung in pairs, and the face is inlaid with gorgeous, polished wood.

I lean in and pluck one of the pairs of strings. The sound is clear, high, and sweet.

Just thinking of Gabe's strong fingers plucking these strings is making me feel kinda funny.

Dougal never made me feel the way I do about Gabriel. He's a real man, someone who could sweep me off my feet and sling me over his shoulders easy as pie. When I think about what those strong fingers could do to me... well let's just say I'm thinking about it *a lot*.

My eyes flick up to the list of rules.

1. Gabe makes all the food.

2. Ten O'clock is bedtime.

3. No cussing.

4. Tell Gabe any worries you might have.

5. Human food is for humans. Dog food is for dogs. No exceptions.

6. Don't go anywhere Gabe says not to go.

7. If Bailey wants more rules, she should ask.

I've been thinking about number six ever since I got here. Gabe said that he finds rules helpful in situations when he has people staying with him so that boundaries can be respected. I love rules for a couple reasons. Number one: I tend to get forgetful, and rules give me structure. Number two: I *love* breaking rules.

I asked Dougal to write some rules up for me once. It was at a time I was looking for a job, and I needed someone to help me stay motivated. I know it sounds dumb, but I'm *so* much better at doing things for other people than for myself. Dougal never got that about me. Just teased me for even asking about it. I did get a job in the end — at a Build-A-Bear Workshop (I *love* it, by the way) — but it took me nearly a year.

What rule would I ask Gabe to write up on that board?

About a million naughty thoughts flash through my head.

*Gabe always chooses Bailey's panties.*

*Gabe always inspects Bailey's panties to make sure they're on right.*

*Gabe always helps Bailey put on her bra.*

*Gabe kisses Bailey's princess garden whenever Bailey wants.*

'Brandy, don't tell Daddy, but I'm breaking rule three in my head. Repeatedly.' I wonder what Gabe would do if I *did* break some of these rules. I guess there's only one way to find out.

The more I think about it, the more I have a sneaking suspicion that Gabriel would be a *phenomenal* Daddy. He's so caring, so certain in his protection, so tender and dominant at the same time.

I'll probably never get the chance to find out. He told me we'd be heading back to Little Creek tomorrow. No doubt Dougal has already left our Airbnb. I'll just get back to Denver and then head back to work.

For a moment, I fantasize about what life could be like in a place like this. Without cars and pollution, without screaming crowds and angry customers. Peace, quiet, tranquility.

And a bad-ass Daddy to spank my butt from time to time when I step out of line.

It would sure beat living in a huge house by myself and trudging to Build-A-Bear every day. Heck, maybe I could even learn to build Teddy Bears for real. You know, as a hobby.

I pluck the strings of the instrument again, absentmindedly. Gabe did say he'd look after me if I wanted him to, but no doubt he didn't *really* mean it in the way I'd want him to mean it.

'What do you think, Brandy, should I stay here with you guys?'

Brandy seems suddenly excited. She springs up and starts panting, and then, a moment later, she speeds off across the room. She ducks underneath a coffee table and stops right outside the door to the building site. The only part of the cabin I've been forbidden from exploring.

'Come here, silly,' I say.

She stands still, then surprises me by letting out a sharp bark. I've not heard her bark before. She's always so well-behaved. It's like she doesn't do anything silly or thoughtless. I know this is crazy, but I instinctively feel like she *wants* me to open the door.

I stand up. 'This is naughty,' I say. 'Very naughty.'

I'm only going to have a peek. Just for a second. It's not like it would actually be dangerous just to open the door and see what's inside, would it? How could it be?

The door handle feels cool in my hand, and as I start to turn it, I feel this incredible build-up of nerves in my tummy. Then, I hear the click and I push the handle down, and open the door.

When I see what's in here, my jaw hits the floor.

It's a workshop, that much is clear. There's a workbench and tons of tools attached to a wall behind the bench. But it's what's on the bench that makes me so excited.

Toys. Loads of them. All carved from wood. Little bears and tiny soldiers. Dolls and dogs and funny little horses. Some of them are painted, some of them are bare wood, but all of them are gorgeous.

Lost in my excitement, I run into the shop and look around, before letting out a tiny squeal of delight.

'This. Is. So. Cool!'

I pick up a little horse and sit down in the middle of the space. I start to play with the horse. Gabe has even threaded through a loop of twine so that it looks like the horse has a tiny mane. It's the cutest thing ever.

It's only while I'm playing with the horse that I start to notice some other more... interesting stuff. There are piles of wooden items in the corner of the space, projects that he's obviously recently completed. It takes me a moment to realize what I'm looking at.

The horse falls out of my hand and lands on the floor with a muted thunk. My mouth opens wide and my eyes are practically bulging out of their sockets.

It's a crib. But not for a baby. This is adult-sized.

Behind the crib, there's what can only be described as a changing station. It's made from wood, and it's full of all kinds of things. Adult diapers, diaper cream, wet wipes, tiny little towels.

Is Gabriel some kind of... *adult baby* carpenter?

My head's reeling from this revelation when I hear something from the other room. The wind howls like crazy, and then I hear the front door swing open. Like a shot, Brandy leaves the door of the workshop and heads outside.

'No, Brandy!' I call after, but she doesn't listen. Not thinking, I rush after her, through the cabin living space, and then straight into the cold white of the snow-covered mountainside.

# GABRIEL

T HE TREK DOWN TO the bottom of Hiker's Foe takes longer than usual, but it's the climb back up to my cabin that really makes me late.

It's beautiful out. The trees have this serene calmness today, and the light gusts of wind which occasionally disturb the snow-laden boughs only add to the eerie calm. It's weird not being out with Brandy too. Normally, she'd be surging up ahead, sniffing the breeze, guiding me to my destination. I'm glad she's back at the cabin with Bailey, though. Brandy's a gentle dog, but she's been trained to be super-protective.

Obviously, I thought about my guest the whole time I was out today. Thinking about her scumbag ex, imagining what it might be like to have her stay with me for more than just a couple days. She seemed to be into the idea of off-grid life, but I'm sure she was just saying that to humor me.

I've probably been so starved of social contact for such a long time that I'm clinging onto these scraps of affection like a dog with a dried-out bone. The only people I ever really see are Joel, Ella, and whoever might be staying at their Little Cabin. They're good people, and obviously, it's nice to be able to talk to a like-minded community from time to time. I make toys for them, and bespoke furniture. Also, when the season's right, I trade them some home-grown veggies for stuff like milk and cheese.

Sometimes Joel says that I should stay with them and be the live-in farmer for the Little Cabin. He says he'd work with me to build a cabin, a few hundred meters from the main compound, and he'd build a big kennel for Brandy. As tempting as it might be to be offered a little slice of something more homely, there's no way I can take him up on the offer. With local budgets being squeezed tight by the recession, there's almost no mountain rescue left covering the Little Creek area. So if I don't watch Hiker's Foe, no-one will.

When I finally arrive back at the cabin, I'm surprised to see that the front door is open.

'Bailey?' I call out, cupping my mouth with my hands.

No response.

I unclasp the walkie-talkie from my waistband and hold it up to my mouth. 'Bailey, are you there?' I hear a crackly echo of the sound of my voice coming from inside the cabin. 'Dammit, Bailey,' I hiss, and I step through the front door. The other walkie-talkie lies on the coffee table in the living space.

Adrenaline spikes my veins.

I should never have left her. I'm the dumbest man in the world. As if I could ever be a Daddy to this girl. I've endangered her within three days of meeting her.

It's only then, at the height of my panic, that I see the door to my workshop standing ajar. 'Oh no,' I whisper. Things just went from bad to disastrous.

I surge forward, hoping that Bailey's still in the workshop, but she's not. There's one of my little toy horses sitting in the middle of the room, almost as though someone had been playing with it and dropped it on the floor. Fuck. I ruined it. Everything's on display. Not just toys, but the damn adult crib I'm building for Ella right now, and the diaper change station for Joel's guest cabin.

And the packs of adult diapers I'm using as a size reference. She must think I'm a pervert. Some maniac who's keeping her trapped in the woods for who-knows-what fucked-up reason. Why didn't I lock the damn door?

I stand there for a moment, trying to collect my thoughts. What am I gonna do? I found my forever girl, and three days later, I lost her.

*Think, Gabe, think. You can turn this around.*

But before I have a chance to come up with some grand plan, there's a sound from the front door. Footsteps, and the scrape of paws on a wooden floor. I snap my head around. 'Bailey! Brandy!' There's so much relief in my voice that it takes Bailey by surprise. She's wearing her hiking coat over the top of my old pajamas, and she's got her boots on. Next to her, Bailey's panting. She looks as happy as you could imagine. 'Where have you two been?' My voice sounds harsh, and Bailey cringes back.

'Just out for a little walk. Brandy kinda escaped.'

'Why didn't you take the walkie-talkie? I've been trying to contact you.'

'It all happened so fast,' she says, 'I thought Brandy was gonna run off, and I didn't want to lose her—'

'I don't want to lose *you*.' I'm almost shouting, I'm so shook up. I pause a moment, taking a deep breath. 'I'm sorry, Bailey, that came out wrong. I'm not angry with you. I'm just... well there's a few things you should know about me.'

She nods, looking down. 'I saw your workshop. I'm sorry I went in. I just couldn't help myself.'

'It's OK,' I say. 'I thought you'd left because of what you saw. I'd understand if you did. I understand if you still want to leave, right now.'

'Actually,' she says, smiling, 'I thought it was very cool.'

I snort. 'Cool? You're joking, right?'

'You make toys and furniture — seems pretty innocent to me.'

Of course. She doesn't understand what the workshop is all about. I got away with it. She probably just thinks I make toys for kiddies at Christmas. I mean, I *do* do that too, but that's another story. 'Right,' I say.

'So,' she asks, innocent eyes wide. 'What is it that I should know about you?'

'You know what?' I sigh. 'I think we should have some breakfast before we get into all that.'

*

'You know, Rule One is fast becoming my favorite rule of all.'

'Well, I like to cook, so it suits me too.'

I've never seen a girl eat as much breakfast as Bailey is eating right now. She's shoveling huge forkfuls of eggs and bacon into her cute mouth, barely stopping for breath between each mouthful.

'You should do like Airbnb here,' she says, taking a sip of her second cup of coffee of the morning.

'I've got a friend who used to do that,' I say. 'But he stopped a while ago. Turned his guest cabin into something a little more... niche.'

'Oh?'

'Yeah. He offers it up for free to people in trouble now. Anyone who needs a place to lie low for a while.'

'Sounds like a nice guy,' she says. I love watching her as she speaks. The way her little mouth moves, the left side always pulling slightly higher than the right. I love the almond shape of her eyes, her snub nose, all the tiny freckles under her eyes. I can't believe how lucky I am to even get to spend time with someone as beautiful as her.

'Yeah, he's nice,' I say, lost in my thoughts. I'm dodging the issue. I always find it so hard to talk about my past. But with how open she's been, and how angrily I reacted to her leaving the cabin, Bailey deserves an explanation. Time for me to man up.

'Bailey,' I say. 'I'm sorry I snapped at you before. There's no excuse for it.' I breathe in deep, then let out a slow, soft breath, trying to calm myself. 'The truth is, I'm broken.'

'Broken?' She looks concerned, her eyes suddenly sad, suddenly worried about me.

I nod. 'It's why I'm here by myself in this tiny cabin, with only Brandy for company.'

'How do you mean, broken?'

'Hiker's Foe is what did it to me. I worked in mountain rescue then. Four years ago. I still remember that day like it was yesterday. The cold, the clear blue sky. We'd had a report of a hiker trapped in a particularly dangerous spot. He'd fallen from the top of the canyon and had managed to get his leg stuck between two rocks. He was OK, but obviously, he needed help to get free.'

I thumb the handle of my coffee cup. The memory is so raw, so painful for me that I'm struggling to get my words out. I feel Bailey's hand on mine. Her tender fingers start to rub mine. She's warm. 'It's OK, Gabe, you can tell me.'

I nod. 'So we went out. It was just a job, like any other. I went out with my partner, Pete. We needed to abseil down to the rescue spot — there was no other way down. We had rock-cutting saws and other heavy equipment with us, so I tested and double-tested the safety ropes. I wish I'd triple-checked.'

Bailey smiles weakly and squeezes my hand in hers.

'The inquest said that Pete was killed by mechanical failure. A freak accident — two of his safety ropes snapped at the same time. Whatever the cause, I'll never forget the look on my brother's face as he fell down to the bottom of Hiker's Foe. The fear, the sadness, the hopeless brutality of a chance accident.'

'Pete was your brother.'

I nod. 'My big brother. We grew up in Little Creek. Both wanted to work in mountain rescue since we were little kids. Pete was the sociable one, always taking the lead in conversation, always looking after me, protecting me from bullies, and sticking up for me when I got into fights. I'll carry the shame of that day in my heart forever.'

'It's not your fault, Gabe,' she says.

'I know that, and it doesn't help.' I say. 'The only thing that helps is making sure that no-one ever dies in this stupid canyon ever again. That's why I can't lose you. There's no way I'm ever going to lose anyone I care about, ever again. That's why I exploded back there when I got back. I thought I'd lost you. I thought I'd ruined things with you.'

The next four words come out so little that I can barely hear them. 'You care about me?'

'Of course I do,' I say. 'You must have seen the way I look at you. Must know how wonderful I think you are.'

Her eyes are laser-sharp, fixed on mine with total focus.

'Gabe, there's something I want to tell you, too.'

# BAILEY

'**I** KNOW THAT YOU'RE making adult baby furniture in your workshop.'

The words hang like ice in the air for a moment. Gabriel looks so shocked that he's struggling to speak. The silence is deafening.

'How do you know about that?' he asks, finally.

'Can't you feel it?' I ask, my voice trembling. I can feel my heart in my chest, pounding away, making me feel emboldened and nervous at the same time. 'Can't you feel that there's something different about me?'

He pauses, nods. 'I can feel it.'

'The way I followed your rules without questioning? The fact I've got a stuffie?'

'The way you look at me.' His eyes are burning with intensity now. 'The way you talk to me. The fact you work in Build-A-Bear. I feel it, Bailey. You're a Little, aren't you?'

It feels like my heart rate doubles. I nod. 'The last person I told about this laughed in my face. So go easy on me, OK?'

'I'm sorry they laughed at you,' he says. 'It must take so much courage to come out to someone about being a Little. And they just laughed at you.' He shakes his head from side to side. 'That must have really hurt.'

I still remember how spiteful Dougal's stupid face looked as he mocked me. 'You want me to do what?' he said. 'Treat you like a baby? Make you suck a pacifier? I knew you were crazy, Bailey, but I didn't realize you were actually clinically insane.'

'It wasn't great,' I say. 'I buried the pain, forgot about it. I vowed to never tell anyone else about it. I've been trying to repress that side of me ever since.'

'Repress it?' he says, confused. 'Why would you want to repress something so wonderful?

I snort out a disbelieving chuckle. 'I don't think many people think that age play is wonderful.'

'Well who cares what they think?' he says. He starts to stroke my hand in long, soft movements. I love the way his hands feel against mine.

'You care,' I say. 'You tried to hide your workshop from me. I knew you were a Daddy. I've been going crazy, second-guessing myself the whole time I've been here. Now that I know for sure, everything makes sense.'

'You could honestly tell I'm a Big?'

'Of course. Who else puts rules up when they have a visitor? And the way you've been looking after me. It's been making me feel seriously yummy.' I can feel my cheeks reddening. 'Like, seriously yummy.'

'Yummy huh?' He gives me a dirty look.

'Mmmhmm,' I say.

'So how long have you known that you're a Little?'

'My whole life.' I reply, a touch of sadness in my voice. 'I just never grew up. All the other kids stopped playing with stuffies and dolls. I never did. My folks worried about me for years. I was always the family embarrassment. Like a dirty secret. The weirdo playing with dolls and doing coloring books in the attic. My parents were pretty wealthy, you see. I always felt like they were ashamed of me. One time, at the country club-'

'Country club?' His eyebrows arch playfully up.

'Hey, it was never *my* idea of a good time. Anyway, we were at this swanky dinner with all these mega-rich buttholes-'

'That's straying dangerously close to breaking rule three,' he says, half serious.

'But what could possibly be naughty about the word butt?' I ask, innocently as I can manage.

'Thin ice, young lady,' he deadpans.

'So it was this fundraiser for a new roof for the country club or something. And there were speeches and canapés and all that crud. And I was so bored and nervous, I took Charlie — my stuffie — out of my bag and put him right there in front of me.'

'That's not so bad,' he says.

'I was sixteen at the time. I got a real telling-off for that, believe me. My parents were not impressed.'

'Shame they weren't more understanding.'

'I don't know. At times they were good about it. I was lucky, in a lot of ways. I mean, they loved me, that's for sure. And I can imagine it's not the easiest thing, to have a Little as a daughter.'

'Sure,' Gabe says, thoughtfully, 'but there are good ways of dealing, and bad ones. Anyway, I'm glad that you and Charlie haven't parted company. I wanna get to know that bear a little better.'

'You do?'

'Course.' He smiles. 'Any friend of yours is a friend of mine.'

I bite my lip. 'I'm gonna go get him.' My heart's fluttering in my chest. I feel so vulnerable, and it's making me excited. I go through to the room I've been sleeping in and grab Charlie, then I walk slowly back to Gabriel, who's grinning his head off.

'Hey Charlie,' Gabe says.

'Hey Mr. Gabe,' I say in my Charlie voice. It's gruff and gravelly, just the way you'd expect a tough old bear to talk. 'So you're interested in dating Bailey, huh?' I feign shock, as though I can't control what Charlie's saying. 'Charlie!' I say, in my normal voice, sounding scandalized.

'What?' says Charlie. 'It's obvious he's into you.'

'Charlie,' Gabe says, 'you can read me like a book.'

'Like one of your sexy paperbacks.'

Gabe lets out a chuckle. 'Charlie, you're a bad dude.'

'The baddest,' Charlie says, and I burst out laughing, unable to keep the game going any longer. It feels so fun to be in Little Space with Gabe. So natural.

'So what's your story?' I say as me again. 'When did you know that you were a Daddy?'

He inhales sharply and his forehead wrinkles.

'That's a tough one. I don't think it's as straightforward as waking up one day and realizing I was a Daddy. I've been on a long journey of self-discovery. I've always known that I have an old-fashioned attitude when it comes to relationships. For me, it's important for my self-worth to feel as though I'm providing security and support to my partner. And it feels so good to be relied upon. Truth is though, I've never actually had a Caregiver/Little relationship, so I'm new to all this.'

This surprises me. Gabe always seems so confident and sure of himself. 'So I'm the first Little you've spent any time with?'

He nods.

'Poor Daddy,' I say. Immediately, my breath catches in my throat. I hadn't meant to call him Daddy, it had just slipped out. I'm half-expecting him to criticize me, or to say it's too soon, but to my surprise, he smiles warmly.

'I kinda like how that sounds.' He fiddles with his shirt sleeve. 'I mean, the Daddy part. Not the poor part.'

'I'm sorry, it just slipped out. I did—'

'Don't you dare say you didn't mean it.' There's an intensity in his eyes. 'In fact, if you don't mind, I'd kinda like to add a new rule to the list. If you'll let me?'

'OK.'

He stands and walks over to the chalkboard, deftly avoiding a napping Brandy. He picks up a piece of chalk from the shelf under the board, starts to write.

*8. Bailey must call Gabe Daddy when she's in Little Space.*

'I like that rule, Daddy,' I say, clasping my hands together.

'I'm glad to hear it.' I say. 'Are there any others that you want to add?'

'Um, there's one that I really want to add. It's something I've always dreamed about.' It feels like my senses are heightened, like I can hear all the tiny sounds Gabe is making, like I can smell his gorgeous scent, even though I'm far from him.

'Well you better add it yourself,' he says, giving me an encouraging smile.

So I walk all the way up to him and hold out my hand. He places the chalk in my palm, and slowly closes my fingers in, making a fist. I love the way he moves me, like he's filling me with tenderness.

I reach up to the chalkboard and write.

*9. Daddy chooses Baby's panties. Baby has to show Daddy.*

As I write, I feel myself get turned on. My cheeks flush, and there's a rush of blood to my loins. I can feel moisture down there too, because I just know that Daddy's thinking about my secret spot, the soft place between my legs that I'm desperate to give him.

'That sounds like a fair rule to me,' he says, in a strange, stifled voice.

'Good,' I say.

'So, what kind of panties are you wearing now?' he asks, his voice cracking slightly.

'You wanna see?'

'I think I kind of *have* to, according to the new rule. So go ahead and drop those pants, cutie.'

'OK, Daddy.' I'm trembling now, and my tummy feels funny. I hope I'm not so wet that my panties are soaking. I hope he likes the way my legs look. I slip my fingers under the waistband of my pants and slowly, carefully wriggle them down my legs.

I'm wearing a simple white thong, nothing special at all. But the way Gabriel, my new Daddy, is looking at me, it's as though I'd just revealed a pair of designer lingerie.

'You're so beautiful,' he says.

'Yeah,' I say, 'but are the panties OK?' I can feel the goofy grin spread across my face, and to my relief, he chuckles.

'Well you know, I haven't seen the back yet. You're gonna have to turn round for me.'

I swallow and start to turn on the spot. I resist the urge to stand on my tiptoes to try to make my butt look better.

'You know, it's taking all my power not to come over there and grab you right now.' Gabe's voice is so raw it's almost bestial. The thought of him grabbing me is pretty damn delicious right now.

'I'd like that,' I say, as I finally come round again. He looks so hot right now — the lust on his face is giving him this earthy, powerful quality, like he could just take me right here and now if he wanted.

For a moment, it looks as though he's considering it.

'No, Baby, that wouldn't be right. Not now. Not yet.' He breathes in deeply. 'I don't want to rush this. Don't want to rush anything. Pull up your pants, sweetheart. The panties are great for now.'

I'm equal parts disappointed and impressed. There's something so sweet about the fact he wants to wait. Dougal couldn't wait to get into my panties. Everything with Gabe is so fresh, so new. So right.

I think he can sense the disappointment though, because he says, 'I'd like a snuggle, though, if you're up for it?'

I nod, coyly, then run at him, wrapping my arms around that tree-like body.

'You smell good,' I say, burrowing my face into his shirt.

'So do you, my little coconut.'

'That's a nice name.'

'You're a nice girl.'

Something swells up in me, a bright, overwhelming wave of happiness. Without thinking, I stretch up, onto my tiptoes. There's a moment of anxiety, like I'm doing the wrong thing, then his lips meet mine, and I taste sunlight.

I spend the rest of the day playing with Daddy's hand-made toys, while he prepares a steaming pot of gumbo for the two of us. It's a blissful afternoon. It feels like we're in our own little world here, like nothing outside the cabin even matters. Maybe I could just stay here. Stop paying rent on my apartment in Denver, hand my notice in at the bear store.

We decide to sleep in the same bed tonight. Daddy brushes my teeth, reads me a story, then we curl up together. It feels so good to be next to his big, strong body, so warm, so safe. With his arms draped around me, I feel like I'm in my own Little cocoon, like I don't need anything else.

'Daddy,' I say, sleepily, 'you remember you said that you'd look after me if I want?'

'Sure,' he replies, kissing the back of my head.

'Do you think I can stay here for a few more days?'

'You can stay as long as you want. But there's somewhere I wanna take you tomorrow. It's time for you to make some friends.'

# GABRIEL

'SO THE TOYS AND furniture you make, they're all for this Little Cabin?' Bailey's looking gorgeous this morning. The sun is out, and the light as it bounces off the snow is making her look like an angel. We're weaving our way through the snow-buried trees, trying to stick to a trail that's normally easy for me to follow.

I can't believe that Bailey kissed me yesterday. Her lips were so soft, her tongue so warm, her body so close to mine. I can't stop thinking about it — about how lucky I am that a girl like her is interested in a gnarled old fella like me. I also can't stop thinking about the pale pink, lacy panties she's wearing today. The thought of them between her legs as she slips between the trees is driving me crazy.

'That's right,' I reply. 'It started out as a kind of hobby, now it's kinda like my job. I know Joel, who runs the place, as well as his Little, Ella through an old friend of mine, Atlas.'

'Atlas? That's a fancy name.'

I snort. 'He's not fancy. He's Greek. He'd laugh his head off at being called fancy. Heck, maybe you'll meet him later and you can tell him to his face. He's a fireman, and at Mountain Rescue, we used to work quite closely with the fire department. Atlas is a Big, and he's pretty open about his relationships. He was quite... promiscuous before he settled down with Mia.'

'Sounds spicy.' She raises her eyebrows.

'Yeah well, he's very monogamous now. Totally changed his ways. Think he gave up his work as a fireman, and now he lives at the Little Cabin with Joel and Ella.' I gesture toward the pack on my back. 'I've been meaning to drop these items off to them for a couple weeks now, so I thought it might be nice for you to meet some other Littles. I know you don't have much experience in that world. Also, I want to chat with Joel about an idea I've had.'

'Very mysterious,' she says, lowering her voice.

'That's right,' I say, smiling.

I'd like to be able to offer Bailey a real life out here in the wilderness. Thing is, a young woman needs things that an old curmudgeon like me doesn't. She needs friends, a community, contact with the outside world. I've got an idea I want to run past Joel, so that maybe I can convince Bailey that a life with me could work for her.

It's about a two-hour trek to Joel's cabin. Originally, I'd planned on it being a halfway spot on the way to Little Creek. But seeing as Bailey hasn't shown any interest in heading back to society just yet, I figure we'll just stay for lunch, then head back home. That way, I won't even miss out on my daily patrol of Hiker's Foe. We've brought Brandy along for the walk. She loves playing in the snow. She's off somewhere right now, probably chasing ground squirrels and gophers, but every few minutes she charges back to us to check-in.

'So do you get food for Brandy from Joel too?'

'Uh-huh,' I nod. 'I put an order in every time I visit. In summer and fall, I've got vegetables that I can trade, and for the rest of the year, I give 'em toys and whatever fixings they need for the place. Joel's a half-decent carpenter, but I've got years of wood-work experience. My dad was a carpenter.'

'Sounds like a good arrangement you've got going,' she says, sighing.

I'm about to say something, about the fact that sometimes I get lonely, when there's a strange sound. It comes from the right, and at first, I'm convinced it must a wild animal — although I've got no idea what could make a sound like this. A second later though, I get my answer. Footsteps and screeching, and then, from through the trees, a figure moving so fast that I don't have time to react.

If I hadn't been taken by such surprise, I probably could have stayed up. The man who barges into me isn't as big as me, and he's skinny as fuck, but before I know it he's on top of me, punching me with his left hand, waving a knife at me with the right.

'You fucking pervert!' he's screaming. 'You wife-stealer! You piece of shit!'

'Dougal!' Bailey's voice is shrill and full of terror. 'Don't hurt him! Please!'

His head snatches around. 'Bailey, babe, I'm so glad you're OK.'

The fucking liar. He pushed her. He's the reason she nearly died. There's no way I'm gonna let him get away with this.

'Get off him,' she cries.

I'm surprised by how scrawny this guy is. A girl like Bailey could have her pick of guys — no-one in their right mind would turn her down. And yet she settled for this ratty, scraggly-haired dude with a bad jacket and even worse teeth.

'Bailey,' he says in a high-pitched voice, 'did this ape try to hurt you?' He looks back down at me. 'You try anything, asshole and I'll tear you a new windpipe.' He's got a posh accent, and the words just sound plain wrong coming out of his mouth. In fact, they sound so bizarre that I can't help but laugh. 'You think this is funny?' he says, holding the sharp point of the knife straight at my Adam's apple.

'No. But I think the chode holding it is pretty fucking hilarious.' There's no way this guy is gonna hurt me. Maybe he can muster up the courage to push a girl down a hill, but there's no way he'd actually murder someone while looking into their eyes.

He clenches his teeth, then tries to growl and punches me in the face again. There's not much strength behind these blows, but the pain is starting to build up. I might not be able to take so much more of this.

It's time to make my move.

'So what's your play?' I say. I can taste the blood in my mouth. 'You gonna beat me senseless and then expect Bailey to take you back?'

His eyes dart back to Bailey then at me again.

'Bailey loves me,' he says.

'Does she? Interesting. Maybe you've just come back to kill her. Maybe you'll get some of her cash when she dies? That's why you asked her to marry you, isn't it?'

His rage is building, the whites of his eyes growing bigger and his teeth grinding together.

'You don't know me!' he shrieks. 'You don't know the shit I've had to put up with, dating this fucking freak baby.'

Good, get angry. Because when people get angry, they get stupid.

I feel his weight shift back. Maybe he's actually preparing to stab me. Maybe it's another punch. Whatever he was planning, I never find out.

I surge upward, concentrating all my strength, focusing all my power in a single, wrenching blow to his face. His nose explodes with blood. He screams, clutches his face, and I push him up and off me. He scrambles back, leaving a spray of crimson petals in the pure white of the snow.

'Fuck you!' he shouts, getting to his feet.

I don't say a word, I push my newly free fingers into my mouth and let out a single, high-pitched whistle.

'What th—' he starts. Then, 220lbs of St. Bernard slam into him and he's down, yelling, trying to twist out of the dog's firm but gentle bite.

'Good girl, Brandy,' I say, heading in, patting her on the back.

'Get her off me!' he shrieks.

'Are you gonna be a good boy?' I ask.

'Anything!'

I whistle again, and Brandy releases her grip. I untie one of the ropes I have wrapped around the pack on my back and start to tie Dougal's hands behind his back.

'Daddy?' Bailey's voice is shaken, but defiant.

'What is it, Princess?'

'What's a chode.'

I grin. Dumb but I can't help it. 'A chode is a cock that's wider than it is long.'

Bailey bursts out laughing. 'Rule three, Daddy!'

*

'Well, that's a detour I wasn't expecting to make.'

We're standing outside the sheriff's office in Little Creek. I haven't been to the town for what feels like ages, and it's got to be coming up to a year now. Of course, this place is still much the same. Still the same friendly faces, the same small, independent shops. Still Sheriff Carl, keeping the peace, thank goodness.

When we dropped Dougal off to him, he believed our story, one hundred percent. He locked Dougal up for processing, and now he's with us outside the Sheriff's office.

'Long way for you,' he says. 'But probably worth the trip, right?'

'Course,' I reply.

'Pleasure to meet you, miss,' he says to Bailey. She smiles.

'I know this is dumb,' she says, 'but whenever I'm near a cop, I always feel like I've done something wrong. I feel super guilty.'

'Hmmm,' says Carl, rubbing his chin. 'That's a very typical reaction among criminals.'

Bailey lets out a little gasp.

'Come on,' he says, 'fess up — what mischief have you been up to?'

There's a moment when I'm convinced that Carl really has tricked Bailey into believing he's serious.

'The look on your face,' I say, creasing up with laughter. A second later, Bailey's following my lead, then Carl joins in.

'You meanie!' she says, punching his arm. 'How could you do that?'

'I know, I know, I'm evil.'

'That's one word for it,' I chip in.

For a moment, Carl looks serious. 'Don't worry,' he says, 'I can tell you're a good person. It's obvious from the company you keep.'

Her cheeks darken, but really it feels like it should be me blushing right now.

'Your Daddy's a good man,' he says.

Bailey looks shocked.

'How do you know?'

'I told you,' I say, 'Carl's a Daddy too. He comes out to the Little Cabin from time to time, ain't that right?'

'Yup. Me and Di have a kind of "weekend room" there. Maybe we'll see you there sometime in the future?'

'Maybe,' says Bailey.

'You two take care of each other. I don't suppose I can convince you to stop that foolishness at Hiker's Foe, can I? You're doing a noble thing, Gabe, but it's dangerous. You're so far from help, from a hospital, and from other people. Maybe it's time for retirement. I spoke to your old boss at the Mountain Rescue. Trying to convince him to install a permanent ranger up there. You know, a paid job, with security.'

'I dunno,' I say. 'Not sure I can trust anyone else to do the job right.'

Carl reaches out, putting his hand on my arm. 'You've saved what, five lives now? Your debt is paid, Gabe. Not that you even ever had one.'

And with that, he turns and heads back into the Sheriff's office.

'He's really nice,' Bailey says.

'Oh sure,' I admit, 'he's a good guy.'

We start to head back to the edge of town.

'He's right, you know,' Bailey says, rubbing my arm, 'you've saved enough people now. It's time to save yourself.'

I look deep into her gorgeous blue eyes and put my hand on her cheek. The kiss, this time, is totally different to our first. But the strength of our connection is just the same. Two souls, one heart.

# BAILEY

'HAVING YOU AROUND SURE keeps things interesting.' Daddy's voice is full of tenderness. We're back at the cabin, and he's bent over the burner, arranging logs. I like watching him work. He's so methodical and careful in the way he works, placing each log just so. His big hands manipulate the chunks of wood, and soon he's got a stack built up. It's chilly in here, and I can't wait for the fire to warm the place up.

'I'm sorry about Dougal,' I say. 'He must have been waiting outside the cabin for us to leave together. Maybe he was watching us the whole time.' It's an eerie thought, and it sends shivers up and down my spine. Had Dougal really been planning to kill me? I can't even bring myself to think about it. I wonder what the police will dig up.

'Well, you don't have to worry about that jerk anymore,' Gabe grunts as he finally strikes a match.

The flame eagerly licks at the kindling, and soon, there's a hungry little fire growing in the hearth.

I hold out my hands, enjoying the warmth as it starts to spread through my body. Brandy steps up and takes her usual relaxed position in front of the fire.

'You've earned a real break today, girl,' I say, rubbing her back gently. She looks up at me with those big brown eyes, and I swear she smiles.

Daddy comes over to the couch and sits down next to me. His leg presses into mine slightly, and he lets his hand rest down on my thigh. Feeling his touch makes my head swim.

'You know, I thought a lot about what you said today on our way back.' The trek through the snow took us ages, and we haven't had time for anything else today. I was a little disappointed that we hadn't stopped into the Little Cabin, but Daddy promised me that soon, we'd visit.

'Did you?' I ask. I curl up on the couch, draping my head across Gabe's strong chest.

'Yep. And you know what, I'm starting to think that the two of you may be right.'

I feel my heart swell.

'That sounds good,' I say, letting my hand rest on his.

'Plus, if Carl's right when he says that Mountain Rescue might actually be able to cover this area, there's no reason for me to be here, anyway.'

'How do you feel about it, Daddy?'

He sighs. 'Mixed. Watching over Hiker's Foe has been my life these past few years. Feels like I'm gonna need to find new purpose. But that could be exciting. Especially now that I've met you.'

I feel suddenly warm, and it's not just the fire in the hearth. Feels like there's a fire in my heart too.

'Look,' he says, suddenly taking hold of my hand, 'I know we don't know each other so well, but I feel strongly about you. Really strongly.' His deep brown eyes are full of emotion, his furrowed brow full of concern. 'I want you to come live with me, if you like. I know you've got a house back in Denver, and you'll always have a life there if you want it. But right now, when you're finding yourself after breaking up with Dougal, when you've got the whole of your future ahead of you, maybe it wouldn't be such a bad idea to live out here with me. I was thinking about joining Joel's community. That way, I could start a little farm there, in among the trees. You could help, if you want.'

I can feel the excitement build in me as Gabe's speaking. Could I really do it? Leave my house in Denver, cut all my ties at work?

'You know,' I say, 'for years now, I've dreamed of learning to make my own stuffies. Not like the pre-made ones at Build-A-Bear. I'm talking hand-sewn, hand-stuffed, one-off items. I've got a lot to learn, but I think I could do it.'

'Course you could do it,' he says, squeezing my hand. 'You're super smart, and real determined. You want to share the love you've gotten from Charlie, don't you?'

I nod. For the first time, it feels like I've met someone who really gets me.

'I think you're really special, Daddy,' I say. I take his hand and slowly lift it up to my mouth. The fire is crackling away in the hearth, and I feel a closeness unlike anything else between the two of us. I'm about to kiss his skin when he swoops in and pushes his lips against my fingers. It's a sudden move, and it feels like he's taking control. I submit.

I close my eyes, concentrating on the sensation of his lips against me. How can something as simple as a kiss feel so complex? The tenderness, the firm force. Now he slips one of my fingers into his hot mouth, and I gasp as he gently sucks, before nibbling my flesh.

'Daddy,' I groan, 'no-one's ever done th—'

'By the time I'm finished with you,' he growls, 'you won't be able to remember that anyone else exists except me.'

My heart races as his kisses start to move down my bare arm. My skin puckers in anticipation, and my pussy starts to weep with desire.

'Rule ten,' he says, 'Daddy is always available to his Baby Girl.'

I open my eyes, glance down at his crotch, and see something huge in there, straining to get out.

'Rule eleven,' I whisper, 'Bailey's pussy only gets wet for Daddy.'

He lets out a low growl, and tugs my t-shirt up and over my head.

'I've wanted this since the first time I saw you,' I pant.

'And I'm gonna give it to you,' he says. He yanks my bra away, barely even registering it as an obstacle, then seconds later, that hot, hungry mouth is kissing my chest, planting wet splotches of moisture as he licks and sucks, flicking my nipples gently, making them hard for him, making me gasp with arousal as he plays my body like an instrument. 'Let me see those panties,' he says, pulling away. 'Daddy needs to see them, now.'

I nod, shaking, barely able to contain my excitement. As I stand up, facing him in front of the fire, he looks at me the way a starving man looks at steak.

Slowly, I pull down my pants. This time, there's no hiding how wet I am. There's a damp patch on the front of my pink panties — I can feel it. But Daddy doesn't seem disgusted. In fact, he seems quite the opposite.

'I've never seen anything as sexy in my whole damn life,' he says, rising from the couch. 'I think it's your turn for a little show.'

He reaches up to the top of his red plaid shirt and slowly lifts it off. I marvel at the shape of his body underneath, the way his muscles gleam in the firelight. His skin is covered with thick, dark tattoos — swirling shapes that are almost dizzying to look at. I've never wanted to touch anything as much in my whole life.

Now his hands dip down to his waist, and slowly — painfully slowly — he pulls down his jeans. He's wearing a sexy pair of tight briefs, and I can instantly see the curve of his cock inside as it fights to get free.

'Come here,' he says, in a low, guttural voice.

I walk to him, then press my body into his. Our lips meet, and our bodies kiss — my breasts into his chest, my wet pussy against his thick, hard cock. I moan as he claims me, pushing his tongue deep into my mouth, running his rough hands up and down the smooth skin of my ass. I clutch at him too, almost unable to believe just how solid he feels. He could tear me apart with this body, and as I think of that, I realize that's exactly what I want.

'I want you to destroy me, Daddy,' I whisper in his ear. 'I want to just be yours, and I want you to stretch me wide as I can go.'

'You've got a filthy mouth, don't you?' he says, gently biting my ear. 'So filthy I better fill it up.'

I feel a pulse of lust as I realize what he's asking of me. Then, before he can say another word, I'm down on my knees. I want Daddy to know what a good, obedient Little Girl I am. I eagerly hook my fingers under the waist of his briefs, then pull them down. His cock springs up like a rod, making my eyes wide with surprise.

'How am I going to put that all in my mouth?' I ask.

'I'm sure you'll work it out, sweetheart,' he grunts back.

But before I put it in my mouth, there's another thing I want to do. I kneel a little higher, then place his dick in between my big, soft breasts. I push my breasts together, sliding his dick up and down between them. It feels so good to finally have his cock against my body, it feels like I'm tingling up and down.

Daddy groans and I start to jiggle even faster, feeling his dick grow even harder and thicker between my tits. Then, before he has a chance to come, I kneel back down again and take him into my mouth.

Finally.

He tastes so good. Masculine and powerful, earthy and fresh. It's a struggle to fit much of him in, but I want to show him how accommodating I am, how completely I want him inside of me. So I push myself, taking more and more of his shaft into my tiny mouth, almost gagging on his size as I force his tip down my throat. I'm careful to flick my tongue ever so lightly over the tip every now and again, teasing him, reminding him how delicate and girlie I am.

'Good girl,' he says, stroking my hair. He looks down at me with admiration, and I look up at him with pure lust. I suck him faster and faster, and then, just when I feel that he's getting to where I want him to be, I start massaging his balls too, and gently rubbing his perineum.

I'm so damn wet now it feels like there's a waterfall between my legs. My panties are soaked through, and I can feel juice dripping down my leg. No man's ever done anything like this to me before.

He grabs onto a chair that's next to us and moans. 'Fuck it,' he says, 'I can't hold on for much longer. I want you, now.'

Before I can even answer, he grabs me and lifts me up. He eyes my panties, dark pink now, and then he slides his thick dick between my legs, slipping that hard shaft against the soaking fabric that's next to my pussy. He moves his cock back and forth slowly, making me groan with pleasure.

'Yes Daddy,' I moan, 'that feels so good.'

'I know,' he says, then, he plucks the pink fabric from the cleft of my buttocks and moves it to the side. There's a moment when the tip of his cock catches in the lips of my pussy, and then, he's in me. Slow and confident, full of hard intent.

'Now, you belong to me.'

With those words, I feel his dick stretching open my moist entrance. I'm so turned on that I welcome him into me easily. He slides in with a groan until his cock is pushing against my pussy walls — stretching me wide and tight. And then he begins to thrust.

I almost can't believe this is happening — finally. And it feels so good that I never want anything else, ever again. I moan and sigh, enjoying every moment of it. Every time he pulls out of me, I can't wait to feel him plunge back in again. And every time he plunges in, I can't wait for the next thrust.

'You're incredible,' Daddy pants, holding my hips tight so that he can thrust into me harder. I shout out in ecstasy as his surges become faster and faster. He's holding me up like I weigh nothing. I'm looking into his eyes, and he's looking into mine. There's a connection between us; heart to heart, mind to mind, pussy to cock. He fucks me rough and deep now, twisting and wrenching into me with such commanding force that it's almost scary. I couldn't stop him now — not that I'd ever want that. I can feel how close he is to coming now — his dick feels so big and I can feel his heartbeat in it, throbbing, pulsating with desire for me.

I reach between my thighs, under my pussy, and massage his balls as he fucks me, sending him into overdrive. He thrusts harder still, until suddenly, he cries out in pleasure, and holds his cock all the way inside me while it throbs and empties itself into my most intimate place.

Then, keeping his still-hard dick where it is, I feel his fingers on my clit, working me until I too am brought to orgasm, and I moan in euphoric joy as I look into the still-burning fire.

# GABRIEL

## FOUR MONTHS LATER

I T'S NOT SPRING YET, but there are signs in the air. The snow's starting to melt. Birds are starting to sing. There are even flowers, starting to push their way up through the banks of white, and some are threatening to blossom soon.

'It's looking pretty good.' Joel slaps a hand onto my back. 'Almost like you're a trained carpenter or something.'

He's grinning at me. Man, his beard has gotten long. I guess that's what living out in the wilderness does to you. I had been heading that way, but when Bailey and I decided that we were definitely gonna join the Little Cabin community, I felt like it was time for a trim. Plus, Baby says she likes the scratchy way my stubble feels against her skin.

'Especially the skin of my thighs,' she said to me. I'll never forget that moment.

*Damn it Gabe, stay present.*

'Yep,' I reply, 'the cabin's looking lovely. The view helps too.'

Joel's place overlooks Purple Lake, one of the most beautiful bodies of water in the United States. We're incredibly lucky to be able to call this place home now. There are three cabins here. The first is Joel's original lodge, where he lives with Ella. It's a modest building, but stunning in its own way. Next is what was the old guest lodge, which now is home to Atlas and Mia. It's a little smaller than the first lodge, but I guess Mia and Atlas like it that way.

Now, there's the Third Cabin. That's actually what we've called it. Atlas even painted a little sign for us to hang above the door. The cabin took months to design and build because I wanted it just perfect. We're a little farther away from the other two. I've been living by myself for so long, I don't want to feel overwhelmed. But it's only a five-minute walk back to the community.

I made the place from pine — huge planks of it, expertly sawed and hammered together. Big windows, high ceilings, the place is a palace.

'I'm glad you're happy with it,' Joel says. 'And I couldn't be happier that you decided to come live with us. We've been needing a farmer for a while. Hopefully, soon, we'll be self-sufficient. Food-wise at least.'

'Then, after that, I reckon it'll be about time for me to build a special place for all the Littles to play. Might need your help for that, Joel.'

'Be happy to give it.'

We stand in silent appreciation of the cabin, and for the first time in years, I really feel as though I've found a community of people I can be happy with. And it's the right time for me too. I contacted my old boss, who confirmed Carl's suspicion — he's setting up a ranger station near Hiker's Foe. Saving Bailey was the final piece in my personal story for redemption. But with our young relationship looking to stretch out into the future, it feels like I've got lots of work ahead of me. Now she's stuck with me, and I'm stuck with her.

'I'm gonna go grab Bailey,' I say. 'No doubt she'll be annoyed — she's loving her playtimes with the girls — but she's gonna be so happy to see this place finally finished. If I'm lucky, I'll catch the sunset too.'

'I'll head along. Wanna make sure Ella's not too hyped up before dinner, otherwise she'll be wired all night. I know the way that cutie gets.'

We walk back along the trail to the two cabins, enjoying the stillness of the day.

'So I wanted to ask you,' I say. 'How are the plans going? I know you wanted to turn this place into a kind of sanctuary for Littles and Bigs.'

He grins. 'Pretty damn well. In fact, I got a call today from a guy called Tanner. I don't know him, but he's some kind of artist — a sculptor — working out of Boulder. He used to be a kind of 'professional Daddy' if you can believe that. Worked in some kind of BDSM club in the big city. He's looking for a place to lie low. So he's coming by in a couple weeks. I've got a feeling that things are gonna get interesting around here.'

There's a loud whoop from up ahead.

I raise my eyebrows. 'Feels like it's already kinda interesting.'

'Bailey seems to be getting on with Ella and Mia pretty darn well.' Joel's voice is the epitome of understatement.

'You can say that again. And when Diana comes to visit it gets even more raucous.'

'You'd have thought Atlas would be calming them down right now.'

I scoff. 'Atlas positively encourages naughty behavior. Nothing he likes better than to see Mia acting up so that he can administer some *funishment* later on.'

Joel sniggers. 'You might be right there.'

The girls are in the nursery right now. It's an extension to the main cabin which Joel built shortly after this place was first put up.

'Do you want to go in first, or shall I?' Joel asks.

'I'll do it,' I say. 'I don't want your tender eyes to have to see whatever craziness is going on in there.

I grab hold of the door handle and twist it. There are shrieks of excitement from inside, and when I push open the door, I can see why.

Atlas is wearing his full firefighter gear, and the girls are taking turns to pelt him with water bombs. Thankfully, there are waterproof mats down on the floor, and anything which could be damaged by water has been moved right out of the space. Atlas looks round at me, grinning, his dark hair soaked through.

'I couldn't say no,' he offers, pathetically. I burst out laughing, but Joel's reaction isn't so benign.

'Who's gonna clear this all up?' he says.

The three Littles are doing everything they can to look innocent and sweet, but all of them know they're in trouble. 'I can't believe you were in on this,' I say to Bailey. She's got her hand to open mouth, pulling a shocked expression.

'But they *made* me do it, Daddy,' she says, rushing up to me. Her dress is soaked through, and when she pushes up against me, I feel my own clothes getting damp.

'You know what,' I whisper to her, 'you're so wet I wonder if you're gonna need something super-absorbent tonight.'

She looks up at me with mock horror on her face. Sometimes I put her in diapers when she's acting up. It's not really a punishment though, because she's gotten really into wearing them recently. I know she loves it.

Joel's having stern words with Ella right now, which leaves Mia to snuggle up to Atlas, whispering something in his ear.

'Don't worry guys,' Atlas says, 'I'll clear this mess up. It's my responsibility. Plus, I'm the only one of us who's had water training.'

'You're a pushover, Mr. Karandinis,' Joel says. But his voice is less stern now, more relaxed.

'He's a lovely Daddy,' says Mia. She's wearing Atlas' helmet now, and she's stroking his hair.

'I can't resist these cuties,' he says.

'I think that's a problem we all share,' I say.

\*

Later that night, I light the fire in our new cabin for the very first time. As the flames take and Brandy gets comfy in a new spot by this brand new hearth, Bailey and I whisper to each other. We talk about the future, about what plants she wants to grow on our little farm. I ask her what kind of materials I'm gonna need to pick up from the haberdasher's in Little Creek so that she can start building her bespoke stuffies. She tells me how happy she is with our new home, with the new view over the lake. As the sun finally dips down into the misty blue water. We curl up around each other, and I wonder how it is we managed to find each other, and what the future holds for us.

As we're both dropping into a quiet sleep, I hear her mumble something to me.

'What was that, darling?'

'I love you, Daddy,' she says. Then her sleepy lips find mine, and we dip into happiness together.

\* \* \*

**Read on for Tanner and Liv's story: *Trained by Daddy*!**

# Chapter Five

## TRAINED BY DADDY

# LIV

I'VE BEEN WAITING FOR this day for six months. But now it's actually time for me to get out of prison, the sense of anticlimax is overwhelming.

'Here are your things.'

I don't recognize the guard on reception. He's got a thick mustache and he's wearing aviators, even though we're inside. He can only be about twenty years old — might even be younger than me.

He thrusts my old rucksack toward me. I can barely remember what's in it. My wallet, I guess. Makeup? All the stuff that seemed essential before prison and totally irrelevant as soon as I got in. I grab it from him and sling it over my shoulder, then I'm about to make for the front door when the guard raises his hand.

'Not so fast,' he says, then points up at the big white-faced clock behind him. 'It's only 8:29. You've got one more minute of time before you're free, Miss Burton.'

I don't know why, but something about the way he says that really gets to me. I feel fire rising up in my stomach, and for a moment I don't know whether I'm gonna scream at him or cry. Then I do neither.

*Come on Liv, you're better than this. Just another minute and you'll be out of this nightmare forever.*

Yeah, out of this nightmare and then straight into another one. Regardless, I wait.

It's a minute, but it feels like a damn hour. Six months of jail time for attempted shoplifting. I mean, sure, it hadn't been the *first* time I'd done something naughty. I've been in and out of trouble with the law ever since I was a teenager. I remember the first time Sheriff Carl had a stern chat with me

'I know you have trouble with your parents,' he said, 'but that doesn't excuse your behavior. And believe me, when you're older, no-one's gonna care where you came from, only what you do.' At the time, I thought he was just a jumped-up, arrogant jerk. Now that I've had a little time to think about it, it turns out he was totally right.

I'm trying to think of this as a chance for a fresh start, but honestly, I've got no idea what I'm gonna do with my life now.

I'm not like other people. Other people have dreams. Other people know what they want to be when they're older. Other people want fame and success. Not me. All I've ever wanted is trouble. I'm addicted to it. I need it. And nothing else seems to scratch the itch in the same way.

'OK, time's up, get out.' He laughs as he tells me to leave.

'So I'm free?'

'Yup. You're mom's meeting you, right?'

I nod.

'Good luck, kid. I give it three months before we see you again.'

I resist the urge to swear at him, and instead, I just give him the most sarcastic smile I can manage. 'Whatever you say, mister.' I turn away, then whip back, as though I forgot something. 'Oh one thing,' I say, 'That mustache of yours is awesome.'

He looks confused for a second, then smiles weakly. 'Thanks.' His voice cracks.

'When puberty kicks in, it's gonna look incredible.' He sits there with his mouth open. Before he has a chance to say a word, I walk outside and smell the sunshine in the air.

Obviously, Mom isn't here. Why did I even think for a minute that she'd turn up to collect me? Only appointment she's ever kept is with her drug dealer. Ha. That makes me snort. As if my mom has just *one* drug dealer.

I've got nowhere to go, nothing to do, so I do the only thing I can think of. I slump to the curb around ten yards from the entrance to Denver Women's Correctional Facility, and I sit there.

I wonder where Mom is right now. It's later than 8 am, so she could be in a 7-11, buying booze. She could just be in a meth house. Maybe she's at her apartment, filthy and frazzled. Or maybe she's fallen foul of the law herself. Trouble does seem to run in the family.

I open my rucksack and look through the contents. As I half-remembered, it's a bunch of mostly useless trash. Still, there's a little compact mirror in here, with a lipstick and a crappy old mascara. Probably dry as heck by now. I look at myself in the tiny mirror. I look so much older than I did six months ago. I used to be cute. Now I'm just tired. I let out a long, drawn sigh.

There's twenty bucks in my wallet. At least I've got that. Enough for a hot meal somewhere, but that's about it. My phone's in here too, but it's dead as dubstep, and I don't even have a charger. I start to run through the options in my head, trying to work out just what I'm gonna do.

Someone new is in my old apartment, I know that much. My landlord sent me a message while I was in prison telling me that he had no choice but to accept a new tenant. I bet he was *mortified* to have to evict me.

I'm going to *have* to go back to Jackson, aren't I?

After I said I'd never go back to him.

After all he put me through.

And now he's my only option.

But how am I even gonna make it back to Little Creek? As I'm thinking, a clapped-out old Ford pickup sputters past me. The sun's beating down on me. I wonder what I must look like to the driver of that car. A skinny-looking girl with hotpants and a small pink top. I must look like a streetwalker.

I fish my hand back into my rucksack, and that's when I find him — a balding, super-soft little stuffie with two long ears and floppy arms and legs. It's Red Rabbit. The only thing I've got that I know for sure my Dad gave to me. I feel like there's more love in this little guy than I've experienced in the whole of the rest of my life. I take him out of my bag and hug him tight to my chest.

'I missed you, friend,' I say, on the verge of tears. At least when I go crawling back to that abuser, Jackson, I'll have Red Rabbit with me. Maybe this time he'll manage to keep me safe.

And then, as I'm hugging my little stuffie, I hear a voice I haven't heard in months. It's light and cute, and I recognize it instantly.

'Liv? Honey?'

It's Diana. My oldest friend. My only friend.

I look up and see her. She's hanging out the window of the old Ford pickup which I'd assumed had just driven straight past me. She's got a goofy grin on her face and her deep brown eyes are glinting in the Spring sunshine.

'Di? What are you doing here?'

'Are you kidding me? I heard you were out today. I'm just sorry that I'm so late. I wanted to be here when you got out.' She ducks back into the car and then, a second later, she opens the door and steps out. Then, from the driver's side, another figure emerges. Damn. It's Sheriff Carl.

'You here to arrest me again?' I ask, sarcastically.

Carl looks at Di. 'I told you, Diana, she doesn't want help. She just wants to be angry.'

I sit there for a moment, and I feel emotion bubbling up inside me. Diana's here to help me? She convinced *Carl* to come out and pick me up?

'Wait,' I say, my voice choking. 'I do want help. I *need* help.'

Diana's face brightens, and she crosses the street toward me. She holds out a hand. 'Come on, sweetheart, come with me. A new life awaits.'

\*

'Let me try to understand this.' I'm sitting in the back of the pickup with Di, while Sheriff Carl drives the bumpy thing along the rural Colorado road. 'You want me to stay with a bunch of strangers at a cabin in the middle of the woods?'

'That's pretty much the long and the short of it.' She's shouting over the sound of the engine and the wind.

We've been on the road for an hour or so now, and I still feel totally lost.

'I don't know,' I say. 'If you drop me off in Little Creek, I'll probably land on my feet. You know. Eventually.'

She shakes her head. 'I'm not gonna do that, Liv. I'm not letting Jackson get his hands on you again. I know he's the reason you ended up in prison. He was making you steal, and I know he was hurting you too.'

I bite my lip. She's right of course. For some reason, I'm not ready to give in yet. I've got a stubborn streak the size of the grand canyon.

'I just don't know if I should be joining some kind of kooky commune right now.'

'What other option do you have?' She looks different from the girl I remember. She's confident now, and there's a spark of happiness in her eyes that I don't recall ever seeing there before.

I'm quiet for a second. I watch the road stretch out behind the car. All the empty land, the endless swathes of nothingness. What other options *do* I have?

I sigh. 'So tell me again about these people.'

'Well,' she says, her face lit up by excitement, 'the place was set up by Joel. He used to be an investment banker, so he's really well off. His Little is Ella, an-'

'His Little?'

'Yeah, it's like,' she squints, trying to work out what to say, 'it's what he calls his girlfriend. Because of their type of relationship. He's a Big, so he's in charge, and she's his Little. Like, he looks after her.'

'Riiiiight,' I say, drawing out the word. This sounds weirder and weirder.

'Trust me,' she says, 'they're good people. And I know that you're gonna get on with them. There's Atlas and Mia too — he's a firefighter, and she's a conservationist. Then, recently, Gabe and Bai-'

'I don't think I'm gonna remember all these names,' I say. My head's buzzing right now. I feel like I'm an old rag that's been tossed up into a gale. Who the hell knows where this dirty shred of fabric is gonna land?

'Main thing is, they're gonna look after you.' She rubs my arm.

'There's gotta be a catch.'

She frowns, trying to think. 'Well, you will have to help out with chores, I'm sure of that. But you'll be able to stay there as long as you need.'

The drive is a long one, and we go straight past my hometown of Little Creek. As I see the outskirts, I get pangs of melancholic sadness. I'd love to eat a waffle at Tracy's. Heck, I'd even like to smell that old detergent smell at Squeaky Kleen.

But we don't stop. Soon, we're parking the pickup at a weird old lockup on the edge of the Rocky Mountains. There's trees all around. Where the heck are we?

Carl gets out of the front of the pickup and looks at me. 'Liv,' he says, 'what I said back at the prison — I only said it to get you angry. I was so happy to see that you fought back. I believe in you.'

It's a simple thing, but it makes me smile.

Then, the three of us duck between the dark fir trees and step into the unknown.

If I knew what lay ahead of me, I wonder if I would have taken those steps.

# TANNER

**W**ELL. THIS IS NEW.

Boulder's not exactly a sprawling metropolis, but this fucking place? What's more rustic than rustic? What's more rural than rural?

Let me paint a picture. There are trees everywhere. Tall ones. Fat ones. Light ones. Dark ones. Above the canopy is a sky so blue it could give a smurf a complex. There are wildflowers, creeks, lazy butterflies, mayflies, horseflies, and just plain old filthy flies. And that's just the view from my damn window.

This morning I woke up to the most terrifying sound I've ever heard. Honestly, if I didn't know better, I would have thought it was a witch. I'm serious. Have you ever heard the godawful sound a mountain lion makes? You might think you know what they sound like, but I'm telling you, you gotta google it.

There.

Now imagine *that* waking you up. It was still dark, and I scrabbled to grab my phone, to shed some light on the situation, but obviously, there's no power out here — except for a generator for emergencies — so there was no phone to be found.

So I lay in bed, breathing deep, chest heaving up and down until eventually I got back to sleep.

I've been at the Little Cabin for just over a week, and it's been a major shock to my system. To be honest, I still don't really understand how I managed to end up here. It's like I've been plucked from my old life and dropped straight into a new one.

I'm glad to be here though. After what I went through in Boulder, it feels like I've been given a lifeline. A chance to start again. Trouble is, since I got here, I've been feeling pretty damn directionless.

Still, that's not a problem for now. Right now, all I need to worry about is getting some damn breakfast.

I step out of my small guest cabin and take in the view. The vista is impressive. The early morning light is reflecting on the mirror-like surface of a lake in the distance. It's called Purple Lake, apparently, and I can see why. Not right now, but when the sun dips down behind the lake in the evening, the water does take on a kind of purple tint. I take a deep breath in. Man, you can taste the *health* in the air out here. It's like a fucking tonic.

'Something on your mind?'

I recognize the voice straight away — it's deep and resonant, but also has a strong European accent. It belongs to a friend of mine, Atlas. He's the reason I ended up at the Cabin. I met Atlas at my old place of work, a special type of BDSM club called Slappy's Funhouse.

You're cringing, aren't you? I get it.

Honestly though, Slappy's wasn't as bad as it sounds. It was just a place where Littles could come to express themselves. There was a full spectrum of experiences on offer at Slappy's. You could come and get treated real good, or — if you preferred — you could be treated *real* bad.

I was a kind of 'Professional Daddy.' I know, sounds like a dream job, right? Well, in a way, it kind of was.

'Good morning, Mr. Karandinis,' I say.

'Glad to see you're up.' He grins and gives me a quick fistbump. He's about the most Greek-looking guy I've ever seen. Short, thick, black hair. Sharp stubble. Deep brown almond eyes, and a super-cocky swagger in his step.

'Hard to keep sleeping with the noise of the fucking mountain lions around here.'

'Oh yeah, that was intense, wasn't it? Don't get used to that kinda wake-up call though, that almost never happens. Mia was terrified though, poor thing.'

Mia is Atlas' Little. When I'd known him at Slappy's, Atlas was a little promiscuous. Now though, he's strictly a one-Little guy.

'Poor thing,' I say. Mia's a sweetheart. Before she got together with Atlas, she had some kind of trouble with the mob, and it's left her a little highly-strung — understandably. 'She OK now?'

'Oh sure,' he says. 'She just needed some reassurance and a little time with her paci and she was good as gold.'

'Good.'

He motions to the path which leads to the other cabins. 'Joel's put together a kind of welcome breakfast for you in the main cabin.'

'A welcome breakfast? I feel honored.'

'You should. We got some of the early potatoes up too. Gabriel's particularly pleased with how well they're coming along.'

Gabriel seems like a good guy. He's not so talkative, but I get the impression that he's been through a lot. He's got that gentle giant thing going on.

Suddenly, there's a hint of something in the breeze.

'That's some pungent bacon,' I say.

'Fuck, Tanner, you've got a nose like a bloodhound.'

'That's why I'm always in trouble.' I grin. 'I sniff it out, wherever I go.'

*

You know, sitting here, eating breakfast with these people in this massive room, it kind of feels like I'm part of some huge, insane family.

Littles and their Bigs are all over the place. It's chaos. The girls are chatting loudly with each other. Bailey, Ella, and Mia. You can tell that they're great friends. They're laughing and joking, passing sauces and plates of food between each other. They're all sitting here in their diapers, with t-shirts that barely cover their tummies. They look so darn cute.

I guess this is kind of what I hoped that life at Slappy's might have been like. I've heard of places where Littles are free to be themselves 24/7. There's a place in New York — the Brooklyn Big Baby Bunch — which operates in the way I'd have run Slappy's. Shame that my boss, Lucile, didn't share my philosophy of treating Littles with tenderness rather than with contempt.

'Penny for your thoughts?' That's Joel, speaking from behind a heavy beard. From what I know of him, I like the guy. You can tell he's successful. He's got the confidence that wealth breeds, but he never comes across as arrogant.

'Honestly? I'm just still kinda gobsmacked to be here. A week ago, I was waking up in my tiny place in Boulder, getting ready for another day at work.' Six pairs of eyes on me, as everyone pauses their breakfast for a moment. 'Now I'm here, with you lovely people, and as nice as it is, I kinda feel a little bit lost.'

He nods. I'm sitting next to Bailey. She extends a hand and strokes my arm.

'Sorry if that sounds ungrateful,' I continue.

'Course not.' That's Gabriel. 'Everyone needs a purpose in life. Otherwise, all you're doing is existing.'

'Exactly,' agrees Joel. He flashes me a grin. 'And in fact, I kinda wanted to talk to you about that. About finding you a purpose.'

'Sounds ominous,' Atlas says, mouth full of bacon.

The Littles chuckle.

'Hey Gabe,' I say, keen to change the subject, 'these potatoes are awesome.'

He grins and nods. 'They're our first real crop. Glad we didn't get any blight.'

'What's blight, Daddy?' Bailey asks.

'Don't you worry about that,' he says, 'we'd have to get real unlucky to pick up blight out here. Not that it's typical farming land. To be honest, I'm surprised we managed to get anything to grow. Next challenge is tomatoes and lots of them.' Seems like, if you want to get Gabe talking, ask him about farming.

There's a brief discussion of the merits of various tomato strains, then breakfast is over. Joel beckons to me, and I follow him out of the room.

*

'Welcome to my office,' Joel says, sitting back behind a desk.

'Cute office,' I say.

'Well, I can only work with what I've got.' He smiles.

I can tell that Joel has tried to get some kind of semblance of professionalism in this place, but he's fighting a losing battle. Sure, there's a desk in here, but there's stacks of toys, piles of diapers, and shelves full of children's and young adult fiction.

'Feels more like a Little's store room'

He points at me. 'You're bang on, Tanner, that's exactly what it is. There are lots of challenges when it comes to looking after Littles, but I can honestly say that when I got into this game, I had no idea just how many toys and books the little tykes get through.'

I chuckle. 'You shoulda seen my old workplace. It was fit to burst with gear like this. I kinda loved it though.'

'I'm glad you brought your old workplace up. Atlas tells me it's quite a big deal in the Boulder age-play scene.'

I draw in a breath. 'Well, I guess that's true, to an extent. But it's not like Boulder had a super-vibrant age-play community.'

'Sure, sure. But you've had lots of experience with disciplining... trouble-makers?'

Hmm, I'm not sure I like where this is going.

'Joel, I've gotta level with you. I'm not so into the whole harsh discipline thing. That's kinda why I gave up my job at Slappy's. My boss kept giving me clients who just wanted me to kind of — and I'm aware how bad this sounds — abuse them. I don't want to yuck someone else's yum, and I think that kind of age-play exploration can definitely work as part of a loving relationship, it's just not what I'm into.'

'So what *are* you into?' he asks. His eyebrows are raised in question.

'It's simple. I want to nurture the Littles I work with. Help them with structure. I want to build them up, not degrade them.'

He nods. 'I think I might have the perfect project for you. Something that could be mutually beneficial for you, and for the young lady in question.'

I wrack my brains.

'You want me to help a Little who's already got a Daddy? I don't think I'd be comfortable doing that.'

He shakes his head. 'No, no, I'd never ask that. Look, we've got someone arriving later on today. She's had some bad luck recently, and she needs help. Always been a rebel, but it's got her into some hot water. I want you to teach her just how important and rewarding following the rules can be.'

I think this over. In the past, I worked with clients for money. It was never sexual with me — I kept myself professionally distant from everyone, regardless of how cute they were. I guess now, Joel's asking me to use my skills in exchange for shelter over my head. It feels like a fair deal, and in fact, I like the way he's asking me. Feels like he genuinely cares for this Little.

'OK,' I say, carefully. 'Maybe I can do this. I just want to ask one thing. You're not trying to set me up here, are you? You know, match-make me with her?'

He shakes his head. 'Absolutely not. That's why you're perfect for this job. I know you're a professional.' Is that a hint of something in his eye?

I ignore it. 'Good. When's she due in?'

*

I'm crackling with nervous energy for the rest of the day. I'm in my cabin running through rules and routines I might use to help the young lady I'm meeting later on. The woman I'm meeting is going to be staying here with me in the cabin, so I've spent some time cleaning up and setting up a guest bed. I'm just about to sit down and write my rules out when there's a knock on my door.

My throat goes dry. I'm so weirdly anxious, which is totally unlike me. But for some reason, I just can't stop running through what the next few days are gonna be like.

I walk up to the door and open it wide.

When I see who's there, I feel my eyes bulge with disbelief.

'Liv?' I say.

She looks at me like she's seen a ghost, her bright green eyes shining with shock.

'Tanner?' Her voice is small, almost scared.

Joel, who's standing next to her holds out his hand. 'Wait a minute, you two know each other?'

'Joel,' Liv says, her voice trembling, 'there's no way I can do this with Tanner.'

# LIV

No way. No freaking way. I come out into the middle of nowhere to try to escape my problems and build a new life, and I run into my ex-boyfriend's damn *brother*?

I knew it was too good to be true. I knew there had to be some kind of frickin catch. And here it is, the biggest, most drop-dead-gorgeous catch in the history of time.

Jackson's soulful, exciting brother. The golden child. The brother I *always* wished I was good enough for.

If Jackson is dark, Tanner is light. If Jackson is evil, then Tanner is good. The two of them couldn't be much more different. Jackson is skinny and dark, with intelligent blue eyes and a lean, angular look. Tanner on the other hand is a giant with golden hair and soulful hazel eyes. He's got the body of a God and the cheekbones of a model.

'So come on,' says Joel, 'what history do you and Tanner have?'

We're sitting in some kind of office. There's all kinds of weird stuff in here — books and toys and what looks like stacks of diapers. Diana tried to fill me in on the whole 'Little' thing on the way over here. I'm not totally on board with it, but I kind of get the idea that it's just a type of BDSM relationship. I can kind of understand the appeal of having a stern, powerful man look after you, too. I guess I just can't quite get my head around the idea of wearing diapers as a grown-up. Having a stuffie is one thing, but diapers?

I mean, what would they even feel like? Are they soft, crinkly? The thought of slipping one on is so taboo, so utterly unthinkable. It mig-

'You OK there?' He's looking at me with concerned patience. I just totally zoned out, lost in thoughts about diapers.

'Sorry,' I say. 'Everything feels kinda weird right now.'

'I get that.'

Joel's the leader of this little community, and he seems like a good guy. I know what Jackson thinks about good guys — they're easy to manipulate. That's the way I used to feel, too. But that's not who I am anymore. I'm trying to open my heart now. Because I know where that kind of thinking got me in the past, and I don't want to go back to that place.

'Tanner's my ex-boyfriend's brother,' I say. 'My ex, Jackson, was a bad guy.'

Joel pushes his fingertips together. 'Diana told me all about him. Said that he's basically a small-time crook. That he pushed you down a difficult path.'

'That's generous,' I say. 'The truth is I'm the cause of my own problems. Got no-one to blame but myself.'

'That's a big thing to say,' he says, 'but I can tell you're a good person, Liv.'

'Whatever.' I don't know why I always default to brat mode. Can't help but keep people at arm's length. And I hate myself for it.

'So, you think that Tanner's gonna tell Jackson that you're here?'

I snort. 'Tanner *hates* Jackson. I doubt he's even in contact with his brother.'

'So what's the problem with you working with Tanner? I think he could be a big help to you.'

'Look,' I say, sighing, 'I'm not super into this perverted Little/Big thing you've got going on here. I think that it'd just be better for everyone if I just got out of here. I'll head back to Little Creek and be out of everyone's life. You don't want someone like me in a place like this. I'm bad news. I hurt everyone eventually.'

'Liv, we're not giving up on you. Di believes in you. Carl believes in you. I believe in you.'

'You don't even know me.'

He stands up and starts to pace behind his desk. 'I've met plenty of people like you in the past, Liv. People who've made mistakes and who have struggled throughout their lives. You want to know the difference between the ones who made it and the ones who didn't?'

I roll my eyes. 'Go on then, tell me, guru.'

'Nothing mystical about it,' he says. 'The ones who made it just admitted that they needed help. That's all it is. And I know that by coming here with Di, you were admitting you need help.'

I shift uncomfortably in my seat, then look down at the floor. 'I'm scared,' I say. I barely recognize my own voice.

'Of course you are,' he says. 'Because you're gonna try to make things better. And when we try, there's always a chance that we'll fail. Makes you feel vulnerable, doesn't it?'

I nod, looking up at his intelligent eyes.

'But that feeling?' he says, 'That fear? That proves you care. Proves you're alive. Trust me, Tanner can help you. He's a good guy.'

I wish I could tell him the real reason that I don't want to spend time with Tanner — that I've got such a huge crush on the guy that I'm worried I won't be able to keep my hands off him — but there's no way I can.

'But I don't get why you think Tanner can help me. He's not a counselor or therapist. Didn't he used to work in some kind of sex club?'

'Not exactly,' Joel says. 'He actually has a lot of experience caring for young women who need structure and guidance. And I've seen the transformative power of age-play myself, first hand.'

'Will I have to dress up as a baby?' I ask, cringing slightly.

Joel laughs. 'Not if you don't want to.'

'What about...' I glance over at a stack of diapers in the corner.

'Well, we find that diapers really help to get the girls into Little Space, but, like I said, you don't have to do anything that you don't want to. Even though Tanner will be giving you direction, and asking you to follow certain rules, the truth is, you're going to be in control of the situation, and you can stop it whenever you want. It could be empowering for you.'

There's something about the thought of Tanner giving me orders and telling me what to do that I'm starting to find seriously exciting.

'OK,' I say. 'I'll try it.'

'Good,' he smiles. Then, he looks over at the door. 'Tanner, you can come in now.'

What the heck? Tanner's been eavesdropping this whole entire time? I feel my ears start to burn.

The door opens up and he walks in, stooping under the frame. He's so fricking massive — as tall and muscular as a damn bear.

'You sure you're up for this, Liv?'

Huh. No pleasantries from Tanner. Just straight down to business.

'Have you been listening this whole time?'

'Course I have. I want to make sure that you understand what you're getting into here. I'm not gonna work with someone who's not committed. Especially when we've got history. If my brother finds out about this little arrangement, he will be fucking furious. So if I'm gonna take that chance, I need to know you're serious about it.'

He seems so intense. This isn't how I remember him at all. I guess he must take all this stuff seriously.

Maybe this is crazy. Maybe it's stupid. He's right — if Jackson found out that I was Tanner's Little, he'd go berserk.

But looking up at Tanner, seeing how passionate he is about this, it's making me feel like I've got to at least give this a try.

'I'll do it.' I say the words as solemnly as I can.

Joel's about to say something, but Tanner cuts in. 'I'm gonna need you to follow my rules to the letter, Liv. I know that's something you've always struggled with. But with me, there are no ifs or buts. If you break the rules, you get punished, you understand?'

'Punished?' I wonder exactly what kind of punishment he's thinking about.

'That's right. I'll look after you, but I run a tight ship.'

'I don't know…' I start.

Tanner looks at Joel, clearly frustrated with my indecision. 'This is what I was talking about, Joel. This is typical of Liv. I can't do this. If she's not committed, it's too damn dangerous for me. I don't have the best relationship with my brother, but if she fucks around, it might be destroyed forever.'

'Don't be hasty,' Joel says, eyes pleading.

'No, it's OK, I've thought it through. I think this is a bad idea. I shouldn't even be here if she's gonna be staying. So I'll leave. Straight away.'

'But you don't have anywhere to stay, do you?' The question leaves my lips before I've even had the chance to think it through.

He pauses, just for a beat. 'That doesn't matter. I'll be fine. I'm always fine.'

'No,' I say, holding up my hand. 'Listen, I'll do it. I'll follow your rules to the letter. And if I slip up and break one, I'll deal with the consequences.'

I can't help but wonder if this is all some kind of big, convoluted test. Whatever's going on, I've just made a serious commitment, and for once, I feel certain I'm not gonna break my word.

'You're sure?' he says, his expression slightly more relaxed.

'I'm sure.'

'OK,' sighs Joel, clearly relieved. 'In that case, the training begins tomorrow.'

# TANNER

T HIS IS CRAZY. My head is telling me that I'm about to step into a world of drama. But I'm not listening to my head right now.

I've always had a soft spot for Liv. In truth, I've always had a *hard* spot for her too.

I keep telling myself that that's not the reason I've agreed to this scheme though. I keep telling myself that I didn't give in because of the soft sweep of her bust, because of the curve of her ass. I keep telling myself that my brother's ex is totally off-limits, that there's no way anything will ever happen between the two of us.

And I *half* believe it.

Yesterday, after the meeting with Joel and Liv, I took her up to my cabin and showed her where she's gonna be staying for the foreseeable future. She was typically Liv about it, teasing that it was a small space, barely enough for one person. She's not wrong, but I didn't like her attitude. From today, chat like that's gonna get her into hot water.

Speaking of which...

There's a basic camping stove in this cabin, and I'm trying to cook something half-decent up for our breakfast. I'm holding a bag of ground coffee, waiting for the kettle to boil. Then a thought strikes me — I don't even know if Liv likes coffee. Heck, I basically know nothing about her at all.

This is nothing like the kind of work I used to do at Slappy's. At the club, I had detailed instructions from each of my clients about what they expected from me. Some liked corporal punishment. Some liked lots of cuddles and playtime. Some just wanted me to change their diaper, over and over and over.

But Liv's a total enigma. She's not even a Little. Not really. She's just pretending to be interested in this lifestyle so that she gets free accommodation. I don't blame her for that, of course.

When Liv first got together with my brother, it was years ago. She was so sweet and innocent back then. That was before his corrupting influence twisted her, and made her mad at the world.

If I can just find some way to get her back to the person she was before he worked his sick magic on her, maybe I have a chance at helping her. I don't think traditional training is gonna work. I need a more subtle, tender approach. Less stick, more carrot.

I look down at the coffee, and I realize I'm squeezing it so tightly my knuckles have gone white. Fuck. Even thinking about my brother makes me mad. We used to be so close. Back at school, he was just my big brother, protecting me from bullies and being the tough guy on campus. Then he got involved with drugs and a bad crowd, and he was never the same again.

Things started to go missing from home. Little things, but I noticed. My folks didn't want to see it — that their boy was stealing from them — and when I spoke to them about it, they just brushed it under the carpet.

It got worse and worse. Then my dad discovered a gun in his room. And my dad *hates* guns. There was a huge argument, and Jackson left home. A few years later, I bumped into him in Boulder. He was running with a shady crew, and he'd just started dating Liv. I thought maybe he'd changed, but he hadn't. I watched him destroy that poor girl, as his own life swirled down the toilet.

At least now I've got the chance to help her out. Maybe I can do something to repair the damage that my bonehead brother did to her.

I ease my grip on the coffee. I've had an idea.

*

'You want me to write my own rules?' Liv is sitting at the breakfast table, looking at me as though I've gone mad.

'You got it. That way, you'll be the one deciding if they're fair or not. And then if you break one, you've only got yourself to be mad at.'

She grins a wicked grin, then starts to write.

*Rule 1: Liv must never do any chores.*

'Hmmm,' I growl, 'I don't know if that's exactly what I had in mind.'

Liv is looking absolutely gorgeous this morning. She's got that sleepy, just out-of-bed thing going on, and it's driving me wild. I never got what Liv saw in my brother, but I always knew what he saw in her. Those green eyes shine like the mischievous eyes of an alley cat. She's got jet-black hair and pale white skin, and altogether the effect is just overwhelming.

'Well sorry,' she says, using a Little voice, 'but Baby Livvy just wants to play.'

She's wearing a tiny top that shows off her slim, toned arms, and her generous bust. It's pulled in tight around the waist but doesn't quite cover her midriff. Just underneath, I can see a navel piercing — a shiny green and silver stud, perfectly matching the color of her eyes.

'So you're Baby Livvy now?' I ask.

'That's right,' she says. 'I thought I'd get into the spirit of things.'

'I guess that's good,' I say carefully. 'But why don't we cross that first one out? Because I happen to know that Gabriel is waiting for us on the farm today, and there's no way he's letting you get away without doing any chores at all.'

'Fine,' she huffs, angrily crossing through the first rule with her pen. She thinks for a moment, then gets a naughty look on her face. 'What about this?'

*Rule 1: Baby Livvy has to do whatever Tanner says.*

'Hmm,' I say. 'That's actually a very sensible rule. But you know what — since you're gonna be Baby Livvy, I think it's only fair that you call me Daddy, don't you?'

'I like that.' Her voice is dark and deep. Is something going on here? Are we flirting?

'OK, well, right it down,' I say, slightly awkwardly.

*Rule 2: Baby Livvy always calls Tanner 'Daddy.'*

'There,' she says. 'Is two rules enough?'

'Well, no,' I say. 'We need some basic stuff. Your daily routine. Bedtime. Toothbrushing, stuff like that.'

We write down a few simple rules, which we decide on together. An appropriate bedtime, and I make sure that she's going to wash herself and brush her teeth regularly.

'You know?' she says, chewing on the end of her pencil, 'this is starting to remind me of prison.'

I burst out laughing. 'Hopefully, it won't be that bad.' I sigh. 'I can't believe you were in prison, Liv. It's crazy. When I think back to that sweet girl I knew all those years ago, it just seems insane that you had such bad luck.'

She looks pissed. 'I wish people would stop saying it was bad luck, or that I'm not responsible for what happened. I stole. I sold drugs for Jackson. I did those things, no-one else. I wanna own it.'

I nod. 'I get that. I'm sorry.'

'It's OK.' She looks up at me with those big green eyes. 'Prison sucks, by the way. Zero out of ten. Would not recommend. I'm tempted to leave a really scathing Yelp review, but I don't think anyone reads those things when it comes to prison.'

'Probably not,' I grin.

'You know, I've got a pretty crappy attention span. Being in prison, with nothing to do except wait? It was torture for me. What really sucked was that we had chances for self-improvement, even some chances to earn some cash. But there was a hierarchy among the prisoners. In my first week, I was told — in no uncertain terms — that if I applied for any work at all, I'd get beaten. So I just sat around for six months. Doing absolutely nothing.'

'That must have been real tough for a little firecracker like you.'

'Firecracker, huh?' She smirks.

'I just mean that you always seemed smart and ambitious to me.'

'Ambitious? Only ambition I had when you knew me was to stop your brother smacking me around.'

I feel a surge of anger in my gut.

'He hit you?'

She nods and holds her left elbow in her right hand.

'I had no idea.' I'm gripping the table now, furious. 'That piece of shit. What a coward. I'm sorry he did that to you.'

'It's my own fault.'

I surge forward and grip Liv's forearm gently. 'No, Liv. The other things in your life — prison, the trouble you got into — those are on you. But not this. It's never a woman's fault if their partner hits them. Never.'

'Thank you,' she says.

'Don't,' I say. 'You don't need to thank me. I'm just glad you're here. I want to help you put all that behind you. I'll do my best, I promise.'

She nods.

'So what have you been doing the past few years? Not a sex club, by the sound of it.'

I grin. 'Well no. But I worked at a kind of BDSM club.'

'Bondage?' She looks genuinely shocked.

'Kinda, but not really.' I explain the kind of clients I worked with, the kind of jobs I did. I explained about punishments and treats, about how I'd help clients connect with their inner child.

'So you were kind of like, a playmate, but also, a super-hot sexy spank-meister?'

I burst out laughing again. 'I guess that's one way of putting it.'

She takes a long sip of coffee, then rests her chin in her hand. 'So I'm being trained by a professional butt-spanker? I better make sure that I don't break any of your rules.'

'Well,' I say, 'it's funny you should say that because I thought it was about time to put that to the test.'

She swallows. 'Oh? That sounds ominous.'

'Liv,' I say, my heart beating ever-so-slightly faster than it was a couple seconds ago, 'you trust me, right?'

She bites her lip. 'I think I do.'

'I'm glad to hear it. Wait here one second, because there's something I have to get.'

'OK, Daddy.' I know she's only saying it because of the rules we've just drawn up, but just hearing that word on her lips makes me instantly hard. She's so damn sexy. The fact that she's totally off-limits is just adding to the lust that's swirling around my brain.

There's no way anything can happen — and that's how things are gonna stay.

But these feelings I have are complicating everything. Especially with what I'm about to ask her to do. I grab something from the bedroom, and I come back into the kitchen, before dumping the item on the table.

'We're about to head to the farm, but I want you wearing this all day long. So, I want you to do what Daddy tells you, and go into the bathroom, and put this diaper on.'

The look on her face is one of confused horror.

Have I gone too far?

# LIV

'**I**'M NOT WEARING THAT.'

Tanner's face instantly hardens.

'It's right there in the rules,' he says. 'You have to do what Daddy tells you.'

'I know,' I say, holding my hands together and squirming in my seat, 'but Joel told me that I don't have to do anything I don't want to.'

My eyes are fixed on the diaper. It looks so innocent, resting there in his hand. In fact, it looks kinda cute. It's covered with all sorts of childish patterns, happy little cartoon hippos and crocodiles, all dancing around the puffy-looking thing.

'You don't,' he says, eyes softening, 'but I was kind of hoping that you might *want* to. The fact is, Liv, that I want to get you regressed and in Little Space as quickly as possible.'

'What's Little Space?' There are so many new terms swimming around my head that I'm struggling to keep up.

'It's hard to explain.' Tanner strokes his chin. 'It's different for everyone. It's like a state of mind. An innocent, carefree, child-like state. It means that you forget about all your responsibilities and your worries, and you can just *be*. Now, sometimes, wearing a diaper can be a kind of shortcut into Little space.'

'How come?'

'It takes away one tiny part of the adult world. It means that you don't need to worry about going potty. It's almost symbolic in a way. You don't even have to use it, if you don't want to. It's just there, in case you do.'

He's talking in such measured, caring tones, that I really do think he's interested in looking after me. Little Space sounds kinda cool. There's always thoughts buzzing around my head — worries about the future, about my past — I wonder if there's any way that wearing a diaper could actually help me with forgetting my anxiety.

'I'm not saying I'm gonna wear it,' I say, cautiously. 'But if I did, would *you* have to put it on for me?' As I ask the question, I realize that I don't really know what I want the answer to be. The thought of Tanner parting my legs, lifting my butt up, seeing my most private area — it's making me wet just imagining it. But at the same time, it would be so humiliating, having a big, strong man like him putting a diaper on me.

For some reason, even the idea of the humiliation is making me feel all fluttery down below. The tug of arousal is so strong I have to bite my lip.

'No,' he says, 'don't worry about that, you can put a diaper on by yourself. It's pretty straightforward. Of course, if you *wanted* me to put it on... well, let's just say that it's a service that I can definitely provide.' Is that a filthy glint in his eye? Is he as excited by the thought of strapping me tightly into a diaper as I am?

My throat's suddenly dry, then I remember who I'm talking to. This is Jackson's *brother* for crap's sake.

'No, it's OK, I'll do it.' My voice trembles. It's obvious that I sound unsure.

'So you're gonna wear it?' he asks, his own voice strange and soft.

'Mmmhmm. I'm gonna try it. Might as well throw myself into this weird new world.'

'Good girl,' he says. His smile is wide, and it makes his brown eyes shine with pride. He really is unbelievably handsome. There's a roguish quality to his face I've never really noticed before — a kind of wild, untamed cockiness that's so damn attractive it's not even fair. It's not that his face is perfectly symmetrical or anything, but it's his quirks that give him character, that make him so panty-burningly hot.

He holds the diaper out toward me, and I take it in my hand. It's light and crinkly. I turn it around a few times in my hands. 'Now, Daddy, how do I do this?'

'Head to the bathroom. You'll figure it out.'

The bathroom's small, but big enough for my purposes. I wriggle out of my pants. I'm wearing a pretty skimpy pair of panties today, actually — a little, black, lacy thong. The kind of thing that I'd normally consider sexy. I wonder if Tanner would find me sexier wearing the tiny panties, or this big, puffy diaper.

I tuck my thumbs under my panties' waistband and slip them down my legs. Then, I get to work on the diaper. It's actually a little more complicated than Tanner made out. First time I try to attach it, I realize it's back to front. I undo the tape and twist it around. I hold the front flap tight with one hand and then try to bring the wings around the side. It's a struggle, but after a few tries, I'm safely strapped in.

You know what? I think I get it. There's something reassuring about having this huge piece of fabric between my legs. It's not like I've ever struggled with incontinence or anything like that, but even so, I feel a little more relaxed. Just the knowledge that I haven't worn one of these things since I was a toddler (and with my mom, who even knows whether she used diapers or just stuck some TP down my panties?) makes me feel a little more childlike.

I'm about to pull up my pants when I decide to give Daddy a little treat.

When I swing open the door, he sees me. His jaw hits the floor.

'Did I do a good job, Daddy?' Even if I weren't trying to be sexy, there's no way I could say that sentence without a flirtatious undertone.

'That looks... satisfactory.' Watching him grope about for the right word is truly delicious.

'Good.'

'You know what though, you better put some pants on while we head to the farm. Wouldn't want any mosquitoes biting your tender parts.'

Oh my God. Is he blushing?

*

It's not that far to the farmland — just a walk through some trees, parallel to the bank of Purple Lake. Honestly, it doesn't really strike me as much of a farm. It's just a clearing between the trees where the sun can hit the ground. Gabriel and Bailey are already here, and by the looks of their soil-stained fingers, they've been working for quite some time.

'Liv!' Bailey squeals as she heads over. Her bright blue eyes shine in the morning sun. 'I'm so excited for you to be here. I've heard so much from Diana about you.'

'You have?'

'Sure. She's your biggest fan. She always talks about you when she comes to visit.'

This little piece of news takes me by surprise. I've always kinda thought that Diana was ashamed of me, or that — at the best — she was ambivalent toward me. To hear that she's been actively singing my praises makes my heart feel all warm and snuggly.

'I'm sure she's just being nice,' I say, scratching my head.

'Good to have you two here,' Gabe says, walking slowly across the field. 'We've got quite a few potatoes to get up. Then, we've gotta prepare the soil for tomato seedlings. Then-'

'Daddy,' says Bailey, 'let's not overload these two.'

That's when I remember that Tanner's new here too. Maybe this is his first time out on the farm. Feels kinda nice to be on the same level as him.

'Go on then,' Tanner says, 'show me how to get the potatoes up. I warn you though, I don't have green fingers. Every single plant I ever tried to grow at home died within a week.'

'Houseplants can be tricky,' Gabe concedes. 'Did you ever think to try a cactus?'

'Gabe, cacti are the only thing I ever tried.'

A grin. 'OK. Well. Just make sure you watch carefully.'

After a brief demonstration, we're handed a big fork each and are left to get going on the long rows of bushy potato plants. The whole time I work, I'm super-conscious of the fact that I'm wearing a diaper under my pants. I can feel the puffy fabric crinkle and bunch with every move, and when I bend over, I'm worried that someone's gonna catch sight of a cartoon animal.

I needn't have worried, though, because very quickly I realize Bailey's wearing a diaper too. Now I know what to look for, I can't help but wonder how many seemingly 'normal' people out there on the streets are wearing diapers. Way more than you'd expect, I bet.

There's something super-calming about getting up the potatoes. It's soothing to be doing a job that is so straightforward, but so important. I push the fork into the dirt, lean back, and lift out a bunch of gleaming potatoes. Then, I take the green part of the plant and dump it into a wheelbarrow for the compost bin. A simple loop, but really enjoyable. While I slowly work my way through the task, Tanner is doing more physical work with Gabe. They're using huge spades to turn over topsoil, before spreading old compost over it.

'How you getting on, Liv?' Bailey sidles up to me and gives me a squeeze. I'm not used to people cuddling me, but there's something so nice and disarming about Bailey that I don't mind.

'OK, I think. Getting a bit sweaty though.'

'Phew,' she wipes a hand across her brow. 'So you're human after all. With the way you were getting all those spuds up, I thought Joel might have bought a farmer-bot.'

'Ha. More like a fail-bot.'

Her brows knit together. 'I've noticed that about you.'

'What's that?'

'You always seem to belittle yourself.'

She's right, of course. 'I always struggled with self-esteem.'

'It's tough,' she says. 'I struggle with it too.'

'But you're gorgeous.' I know it's the wrong thing to say, but I can't help myself.

'Well thank you, that's sweet.' It's true too. Bailey's stupidly pretty. She smiles a sad smile. 'Things have been much better since I started living here. My ex-boyfriend was a little... well let's just say he was a jerk.'

'Aren't they all?'

'Yeah, but I think my story is a little unusual. Mine actually tried to kill me.'

I collect my jaw from the floor. 'OK. You win. You poor thing.'

'Whoop whoop, the winner!' She lifts her hands in little fists, pretending to celebrate.

We work quietly together for a while. It's a comfortable silence. Hearing Bailey's horror story makes me feel more at home. The girls here aren't simpering babies. They're fully-grown women with complicated pasts who needed a little help to get where they are today.

Eventually, I ask, 'Do you think Little Space can help someone like me?'

'I dunno,' she says, a naughty glint in her eye. 'Only one way to find out. Wanna come play in the mud?'

I glance over at Tanner. 'I think my Daddy might get mad.'

'That's half the fun.' She grabs my hand, and we run off together into the mud, whooping and cackling like a pair of hyenas.

*

'This kind of behavior is unacceptable, Liv, do you hear?'

I was expecting Tanner to be stern, but not this stern. We're back in our cabin, and I'm still covered in mud. Bailey and I got *really* into mud-pie making. It actually took about ten minutes before our daddies noticed that we were doing anything naughty, and by that time it was too late. My whole t-shirt is slick with mud, and it's so chilly that my nipples are clearly visible through the fabric. I can't help but notice that Tanner's eyes keep flicking to my chest. And each time he does it, I feel a throb of warmth between my legs.

'I don't mind that you wanted to play. I hope you understand that. It was the way you were doing cartwheels and slipping in the mud *on purpose*. That was dangerous. You could have easily fallen over and hurt yourself. When you're in Little Space, it can be hard to remember that falling over can hurt.'

I look up at him and pout. He's right. I had forgotten.

'And that kind of hurt can give you a boo-boo that even Daddy can't fix. We're a long way from hospital out here, so we've got to be careful. You understand.'

I nod, but I keep a bratty expression on my face. I wanna push him, wanna see how he's gonna react to me testing my boundaries.

His eyes narrow. 'You know what, Livvy, I think we're going to have to impose an early bedtime tonight.'

'No!' I cry out. 'I don't wanna!'

'Now, now,' he says, shaking his head, 'it's for your own good.' He looks so stern. So dominant. It's hard to argue with him while he's looking at me like this, but I have to try.

'I'm gonna stay up later than normal,' I sulk.

'One more chance, young lady, then we move on to a more serious punishment.'

I cross my arms and humph. 'No.'

His expression is ice.

'OK. Well, in that case, I'm going to have to escalate things. Time for you to have a bath.'

He gets up and heads into the bathroom. I hear water pouring into the tub, then Tanner emerges. 'I was hoping that I wouldn't need to wash you like a little baby, but I can see that's what it's going to take.'

He's gonna wash me? My skin starts to tingle, and my heart thumps in my chest.

Holy shit, he's gonna see me naked. *Holy holy holy shit.*

'In the bathroom.' He points at the door. Now's not the time to argue.

'Yes Daddy,' I say. As I walk over, I can feel my legs trembling beneath me. I could say no, I could tell him I'm not comfortable with this. But the truth is, I'm desperate to feel his touch on me.

He makes me stand by the bath while he drags a chair into the room, then he sits by the tub.

'Before we go any further, I want you to know that if you want to stop, we can stop. No fancy safe words, nothing like that. Just tell me to stop, and we'll stop. I'm grateful to you for obeying me, but I don't want you doing anything you don't want to do, you understand?'

I nod.

'Good. In that case: get undressed.'

The way he's talking, with such power and total confidence, is driving me wild.

'Yes, Daddy.'

I lift my filthy top up over my head, then let it drop to the floor.

'You're covered in mud, aren't you?' he says. 'It's caked onto you. What a dirty girl.'

I nod, then I reach behind me and unclip my bra. As I take it off, Tanner keeps his eyes on mine.

'Shall I take my pants off now, Daddy?'

He nods.

I can feel the tension between us. It's so thick and strong, it almost feels as though something's tugging us together. I unbutton my pants, and pull them down, yanking them past the diaper. The mud is soaked right through, and my legs are covered in thick, brown dirt.

'Diaper now,' he says in a deep voice.

'Can you do it?' I ask. I'm desperate to have him close to me, to have him touch me.

He sits for a moment, considers. Then he nods.

The first time he touches me, I feel like I'm gonna pass out. Those strong hands against my skin, gently holding my diaper in place as he undoes my straps. Then he simply lets it fall to the ground. I see him looking down at my pussy, with hunger in his eyes. Then, with so much effort it looks as though it's killing him, he turns his head away.

'In the tub.'

The water feels good against my skin. It's warm and full of bubbles.

'This punishment isn't so bad,' I say.

'It hasn't started yet,' he says.

He opens a cabinet and pulls out what looks like an ordinary bar of soap. He walks over to the tub and dunks the soap into the water.

'This might hurt a little bit,' he says, 'but it's good for your skin. It's the best way to get you nice and clean. And the pain will teach you not to disobey me again.'

He starts to drag the soap across my arm. As he does so, I notice that there are tiny little barbs protruding from the surface. They're not sharp — they're made out of some kind of bristly plastic — but as he scrubs more and more, it feels like a super-deep exfoliating scrub, and my skin does start to tingle with mild pain.

I wince a few times as I get used to the discomfort, then let out a couple tiny whimpers. But eventually, the unpleasant sensation starts to fade, until it starts to feel really damn good.

He starts to pull the soap across my shoulders, over my chest. He doesn't touch me with his fingers at all, but having the soap dragged across my nipples makes me moan softly — I hope he didn't hear. I can hear his breathing though — getting louder and louder, heavier and heavier. He has to be getting off on this, he just has to.

He scrubs my face now, carefully and tenderly. Everywhere this magic soap touches feels tingly and warm, like I've been gently rubbed with sandpaper. My legs are getting attention now, my calves and my knees, then underneath, up and round to my thighs. Then, slowly, carefully, he rubs my inner thighs. I'm groaning gently, and my head's thrown back in ecstasy, as finally, the slippery, bristly soap just grazes the outside of my pussy.

'There,' he says, pulling the soap away. 'I hope you've learned your lesson.'

He turns and leaves the room. When the door closes, I take the soap, and slip it up against my pussy, giving in to the pleasure I've been desperate for.

# TANNER

## ONE WEEK LATER

I 'VE BEEN THINKING ABOUT Liv, naked, in the tub for a solid week. I can't get the image out of my head. Can't forget the tiny sounds she made as I scrubbed her pink skin clean.

I've never used my special ex-foliating soap to punish a Little before, and I'm glad. It felt like something special, something that was just between the two of us. And I have to say, that as far as discipline goes, it really worked. In fact, it feels like it worked a little *too* well.

For the past week, Liv's been perfectly well-behaved. She's not made any fuss about going to bed on time. She's brushed her teeth twice a day. She hasn't done any more dangerous play whatsoever. Overall, she's been the model Little.

We're outside the cabin, hanging up laundry together.

'You know what Liv,' I say to her as I hold up one of my shirts to the line. 'I'm really proud of you. You've been so well-behaved this week.'

'Thank you, Daddy,' she says. Her smiles are so beautiful. I've been treated to more and more of them as the week's gone on. And there have been fewer and fewer scowls too. It's been wonderful to see her blossom. At my old workplace, I'd never really spend an extended period of time with each client. And if I did happen to see the same Little more than once, there wouldn't be any evidence of personal growth. I think working with Liv has been about the most satisfying, rewarding thing I've ever done.

The more I see her smile, the more I wanna see that smile. That's why I've got a little surprise for her today.

'You're welcome. You know what, I spoke to Gabe, and he's let us off farm chores for the day.'

'Awww, bums.'

'Well, that's not exactly the reaction I was hoping for.'

She reaches down into the laundry basket. 'Oh no, I'm grateful Daddy. It's just that Ella was on farming duty today. Me and her were gonna have a water fight over lunch.'

'I see,' I say. 'Well, there'll be plenty of time for water fights later. I had something special planned for today, you see. As a reward for you being such a good Little Girl.'

Her eyes light up. 'Is it ice cream? What flavor is it? Chocolate? It's chocolate, isn't it.'

I've always known Liv was sexy, but it's only recently that I've seen her cute side. And I absolutely love it.

'It's not ice cream. Although that could be on the cards for tomorrow if you're extra-specially super good.'

'So what is it?'

'Well, let's just say I got a special pack of swim diapers from Joel yesterday.'

She clasps her hands under her chin.

'Are we going to the lake?'

'We're going to the lake.'

*

Walking downhill, with sun shining through gaps in the tree canopy overhead, it really feels as though the two of us are on vacation. Liv's up ahead, wearing a pair of tight shorts over the top of her swim diaper. She's got a little shirt on, and it's tied up above her midriff so that when she turns around, I can see that bright green piercing glinting in the sun.

But nothing's as bright as that smile.

It's not that far down to Purple Lake, and before too long, I'm setting up a little base on the beach. I've brought down a picnic lunch — just some simple sandwiches and potato chips. I'm trying to downplay the idea that this could be a date in every way I can.

Oh, and by the way, I just want to let you know that the fact I'm going to get to see Liv in her swimsuit is definitely NOT the reason I chose this activity.

While I'm setting up some shade and towels for us to lie on, Liv's undoing her shorts. She wriggles out of them, and I see her in the swim diaper for the first time. It's so ridiculously cute. Unlike normal diapers, it's bright pink and covered with happy dolphins and super-cute sea anemones. Liv pulls her top over her head. Her bikini top is pink too.

'You're matching,' I say.

'Hey, are you checking me out?' she says. That naughty streak is back again.

'I can't help but notice that your diaper and top match, that's all,' I say, holding my hands up.

Obviously, I'm checking her out. I check out every square inch of her as she walks up to the edge of the water. I check out the slender shape of her legs, the soft curve of her back. I check out her tousled black hair and the tiny strap of her top. A strap that could so easily be undone...

'You think it's cold?' she asks, tentatively dipping a big toe into the surface of the water.

'Only one way to find out,' I say. I reach down and rip my own top off, then tug at my pants. I'm wearing my own swim outfit underneath, and in seconds, I'm ready for the lake. My approach to the water is a little different from Liv's. Instead of slowly making my way in, I charge.

'Daddy!' she shrieks as I barrel past her, before diving head-first into the chilly water.

Under the surface, it's like time stops. I open my eyes, see the ground beneath me, and I hang there for a moment. This is my life now — diving into lakes with a gorgeous woman. A woman who I can't have, but who I'm falling harder for every day.

When my head pops out of the lake, Liv's waiting.

'Get ready!' she shrieks, then she starts spraying me with water, splashing huge arcs of it over me.

'No fair!' I shout, and I wade through the lake, chasing her.

'No!' she says, turning away from me, laughing uncontrollably. 'You can't catch me!'

'We'll see about that,' I yell back.

Liv yelps then dives beneath the surface. I wait patiently, and a few seconds later, she emerges, like a mermaid, from beneath the surface.

Um. Something's wrong.

'Baby,' I say, my eyes politely averted. 'Where's your diapee?'

She wipes her eyes and looks down. There's a look of shock on her face. 'Oh my God!' she says, before covering her modesty with her hands. 'It must have come off in the water. I thought it felt a little bit loose.' She looks down, then a moment later dives under the surface again. When she comes up next, she's holding the diaper in her hand and she's got a goofy grin on her face. 'I can't believe that actually happened.' She's keeping her lower half under the water, but just knowing that she's skinny-dipping under there is getting me hot and bothered.

So hot and bothered, in fact, that I worry Liv might see.

'You're gonna need to put a new one on,' I say.

All of a sudden, there's a strange, dreamy look on Liv's face. 'You know what, Daddy?' she says. 'I think that I might need your help. You're so big and strong — I bet you could tie my diaper real tight for me. So tight it wouldn't ever come off under the water like that.'

My mouth is dry. 'I don't know, Liv. I don't know if that's a good idea.'

'Please, Daddy.' Her eyes are full of emotion.

The thing is, I'm desperate to do it. But not just that. I want to slip my tongue into that sweet little pussy. I want to show her what a strong, powerful lover I can be. I want to split her open, fill her up, make her shriek my name until her throat is sore from shouting.

I'm breathing heavily, and I'm struggling to keep my mind on anything but the growing hardness in my trunks.

'OK,' I say. 'I'll put a new one on for you.'

She rises up, out of the water. I see a carefully shaved strip of pubic hair above two soft, pouting lips. The most beautiful pussy I've ever seen. It feels like a crime to have to cover it up.

We head over to the towels I've set up. There's no awkwardness between the two of us. It feels natural to be here together, with my Baby Girl naked in front of me.

She lies down and I look over her gorgeous body. Her dark hair is wet and there are beads of water all over her. I think about bending over, licking up her thigh, tasting the freshness of the lake from her body. I open up my backpack and take out a thick swim diaper.

'Legs up,' I say, my voice guttural and commanding. She does as I ask, lifting them up. Liv won't take her eyes off me — they're fixed on my face.

'You look nice, Daddy,' she says.

I want to tell her that she looks nice too. I want to tell her that I've wanted her in front of me like this for years. But I don't. Instead, I take the diaper and slide it up under that perfect little ass. 'OK, legs down,' I say. They go down, and I pull the diaper tight, as tight as I can, so tight that she gasps. I look at her long neck as her mouth is open. It's insanely erotic, like the neck of some goddess.

Then, as I lean in close to fasten the tabs, I feel her hand, right on my cock.

'Baby-' I start.

'Daddy,' she finishes.

Then, before I can check myself, I'm on her, hungry and powerful, my lips finding hers, my hands pinning her down. She squirms and pushes up into me, meeting my passion with her own. Her tongue is hungry and she takes me by surprise, licking my lips as I push my erection down into her. She groans as she feels my hardness against her pussy, moaning as she grinds upwards into me.

Her hands dig into my back as the kisses get harder, more passionate, and then, just as I'm moving my wet mouth down her neck, over that sacred skin, toward the heaving mounds of her bosom, there's a noise, a distinct ringtone, coming straight from Liv's bag.

'Ignore it,' I say, kissing harder.

But Liv's gone stiff. I move back, sensing something's wrong. She looks as pale as a ghost.

'I can't ignore it,' she says. 'That's Jackson's ringtone.'

My fucking brother. He always has to ruin everything for me.

She reaches out her hand, grabs the phone, and looks at the screen. Somehow, she looks even more terrified, covering her mouth.

'Oh no,' she says, holding it out toward me.

*I know where you are, skank. And I know what you're doing. And I'm not fucking happy.*

# LIV

I'M TRYING TO RELAX, doing anything I can to get back into Little Space, when there's a heavy knock at the door. Tanner's been pacing up and down the living space for a couple minutes, but when he hears the knock, he goes straight for the door. I might be scared of Jackson, but he's not.

He opens the door. Joel's standing there, a grim expression on his face. 'Any luck?' Tanner asks.

Joel shakes his head. 'We've searched the whole surrounding area, and found no evidence of anyone nearby.'

'That's a good thing, right?' I ask. My voice is frail. I've not said much since I got the message from Jackson. I've been too busy freaking out, too busy worrying if he was lying, or if he really *does* know where I am and what I'm doing.

'I guess so,' Joel says, sighing. 'You know, this whole thing has really made me think that we should get someone out here who knows about security. A professional. The more people find out that there's a community of Littles and Bigs living out here in the wilderness, the more... unwanted attention we're gonna get.'

'Security is a good idea,' Tanner says.

'It's getting dark out,' says Joel, 'so we're gonna leave the search for now. Only a fool would trek out here at night. Besides the fact that you'd almost certainly get lost, there's all sorts of wildlife out there that likes to hunt at night.'

'Wildlife?' I try not to sound too scared.

'Don't worry, honey,' Tanner says, giving me a squeeze, 'we're safe inside.'

'Mountain lions can't pick locks,' Joel says, wryly.

Right now, I don't know whether I'd prefer to meet Jackson or a mountain lion. Being near Tanner makes me feel safe, but I'm more worried about what Jackson might do to his brother. Even though Tanner is a huge, imposing guy, I feel like he wouldn't hurt a fly.

'Joel,' says Tanner, scratching his head, 'did you bring over the receiver?'

'I sure did.' Joel holds up what looks like a black box. I wonder what it is. Some kind of infrared tracking system? Maybe sonar? 'I'm gonna need it back tomorrow, but for tonight, she's all yours.' He hands over the box to Tanner. 'Right, you two take care. I'm sorry about all this nastiness, Liv. This place is meant to be a sanctuary for people like you. I promise we're making it safe. I'll be letting Sheriff Carl know about the threatening message from Jackson, and no doubt he'll look into it for us.'

'Thank you,' I say. I feel so grateful for this community, doing everything they can to try and make me feel safe in all this madness. 'You don't have to do any of this for me, it's so nice that you're taking care of me.'

Tanner puts his hand on my shoulder. 'We *do* have to do this,' he says, his soulful brown eyes burning with sincerity. 'Because that's what Bigs do. We look after our Baby Girls, and there are no two ways about it.'

Maybe the only safe thing for me to do is to leave. Maybe I'm putting all these good people at risk, just by being here. They're risking so much. Jackson has connections to some very nasty people.

'Right you two,' Joel says, 'try to get some relaxation tonight. Mia's taking a group of us out to check out some animal habitats tomorrow. Should be a fun day, if you're game. Weather should be good too.'

'That sounds nice,' I say, but my mind's still whirring, trying to work out if there's any way I can get away from here tonight, stop putting everyone at risk. These are good people — they shouldn't have to suffer because of a fuck-up like me.

Joel gives a kind of half-salute, and then leaves our little cabin. It would be so sad to leave now — it really feels as though I'm building a little home here among the trees and the wildlife. Today at Purple Lake had been so perfect with Tanner, so natural and wonderful, that it had felt like the start of something new and exciting. Now though, it feels like everything's falling apart. All because of one stupid text.

'What's on your mind, Livvy? You freaking out?'

'How could you guess?' I ask, dryly laughing.

'A Daddy always knows,' he says. He puts the weird black box down on the table and walks behind me. I feel his strong hands on my neck as he starts to gently rub me.

'That feels nice.'

'Good. You deserve something nice after the day you've had today.'

'It's not so bad. Better than prison.'

He starts to push his fingers away from my spine firmly yet tenderly. It's a wonderful sensation, and in seconds, my body feels like warm butter.

'Liv, I'm sorry about what happened at the Lake today?'

My heart drops. 'You're sorry?'

'Not that it happened. Only because of the *way* it happened. The circumstances. You've gotta know that I've always had feelings for you, right?'

My heart skips a beat. 'No,' I say, in a tiny little voice.

'Sure,' he says. 'I felt so jealous of Jackson. That asshole didn't know what he had in you. I used to watch the way he treated you, getting you to do his dirty work for you, trying to make you into a bad girl — it used to drive me mad.' I close my eyes as his fingers grip a little more tightly, press a little more firmly. 'But I always knew the truth about you, Liv. You're not a bad girl — you're as good as a girl can be.'

I feel his lips on my shoulder as he lays a gentle kiss on my skin.

'You want to know how I thought of you?' I ask.

'So long as it's not too mean,' he laughs.

'You were like an angel. Someone I wasn't worthy of. With your warm smile and gorgeous golden hair. I used to wish that I could be good enough for someone like you one day.' I can feel hot tears pricking my cheeks. When I think back to those crazy times in Boulder and Little Creek, it makes me feel so sad. I let out a little sniff.

'Hey,' he says, 'no tears tonight. You know what that black box is?'

'A camera?'

'Nope, way cooler than that. That little thing is a satellite internet receiver. It's the only way that any of these cabins can get online out here. And tonight, Joel's letting me borrow it.'

'What for?'

He comes round in front of me, with a mischievous look in his eye. 'Tonight, Livvy, we're gonna Netflix and chill.'

*

I've never been cozier. Three hours of watching *My Crazy Ex-Girl-friend* on a tiny couch with a gorgeous man, and I almost feel human again. There's a fire in the hearth, and we've got a blanket pulled over us, and honestly, my fear and anxiety have all just washed away.

The credits roll on the fourth episode, and Tanner strokes my head.

'You know, it's actually really clever the way they work the songs into the story.'

'Holy heck, Daddy, have you never seen a musical before?'

He grins. 'Course I have, I just, well, you know, there's so many songs. And somehow this show doesn't feel corny.'

'Thanks for letting me choose what we watched,' I say.

'Are you kidding? You're a little princess tonight, darling. It's all about you.'

He feels so good, pressed against me like this. The whole time we've been wrapped around each other, I've been feeling low levels of arousal, tugging at me like an insistent dog on its lead.

'So,' I say, walking my fingers up Tanner's thick chest, 'what do you want to do now?'

'You had enough Netflix?'

'Uh-huh,' I say, pushing myself into Daddy. 'Now I think I just want to chill.'

'Is that right?'

I reach up for him, kissing his smile, and smiling back as I wrap my arms around him. He's so strong — in a second, he's gripping me tight and pushing his tongue against mine. My senses go into overdrive as he explores my body — I can smell his aroma, deep and woody and all man, I can feel his powerful hands grip me, I can hear his heartbeat somehow, resonant and loud as love.

'Today's all about you,' he says, as his fingers finally find my nipples, through my top. I gasp as he squeezes gently, then grabs handfuls of my breasts, kneading my flesh.

'Touch me, Daddy,' I pant, as he slips his hands under my top, exploring my bare flesh.

'I've wanted this for years,' he grunts, biting my throat gently.

His other hand glides down under my pants and finds the diaper I'm wearing. 'Take it off,' I moan.

Tanner moves back, down off the couch, and as he does, he tugs my pants down. I yelp in surprise, and he grins at me. 'I'm gonna make you come so damn hard, that you can't sleep all night.' His nimble fingers undo the tabs and yank the diaper off me. 'I'm gonna eat this pussy so fucking well that you squirt all over me.'

I can't believe how filthy he's being. Bad boy Tanner, ready to eat me all up.

'You're so wet,' he says, laying a single finger on my pussy lips. I tremble as he leaves it there, feeling the intent behind the digit as he looks up at me. 'So wet that it's like you're pulling me in.' His finger slowly slips inside me and I squirm.

'More,' I pant, 'please.'

'All in good time, Livvy,' he says, as his finger starts to make circles inside me, stretching my little pussy left and right, up and down. He leans down over me, kissing my stomach now. I feel my skin tingle as he takes control of my body. I can't move, can't breathe, can't do anything unless he tells me to. Already, I feel the rumblings of an orgasm deep inside me. With just one finger, this beast of a man is giving me so much pleasure I feel like I'm about to explode.

His stubble presses against my smooth skin as he drags his tongue down my body. The fire crackles somewhere in the background, but it feels like the rest of existence is far away, like it's some parallel world that Tanner's pulled me away from. Tanner's mouth comes to rest just above my opening, right next to my clit. I can feel the warmth of his breath, as his finger keeps working inside me, beckoning back and forth, slipping slowly in and out of my sex, wet with my lust.

'I can't take it,' I whine, grinding my butt down into the couch.

'That's OK. It's me that's doing the taking.'

A long, slow lick, all the way up my lips, from the base of my pussy to the tip of my pleasure. He pushes down firmly, and I can feel his slippery tongue as it starts to flick over my clit. At first, he's slow, and I can barely take it. But as he speeds up, as his tongue starts to circle my clit, then starts to push its way inside me, I start to see stars.

'Oh my God,' I whisper, grabbing the fabric of the couch so firmly my knuckles turn white. 'That's it, Daddy.'

He pushes in and out, rubbing my clit with a finger as he fucks me with his tongue. I'm so completely his, so totally lost in him that I forget where I am — I forget the fire, forget the trees. All I'm left with is this incredible man and his god-like tongue, as he takes me to the edge of orgasm, and then far beyond.

My body tenses, my legs go hard. My core trembles and I shake as I see rainbows of color even with my eyes closed. Then, I feel something I've never felt before — my pussy pulses and liquid sprays out of me, all over Tanner's hand.

'Good girl,' he says. I can feel sweat on my forehead, and I know that my cheeks must be super-red right now. But I don't care. Tanner joins me at the top of the couch and kisses my forehead. 'You're amazing,' he says, gently stroking my hair. Up close like this, his eyes are even more beautiful than ever. Like warm, hazel pools that I want to dip into over and over again.

'*You're* amazing, Daddy,' I say.

It's not the first time I've slept on a couch. But it's definitely the best time.

*

'Well, well, well. Looks like I caught you red-handed.' For the shortest second, I think it's Tanner's voice. But when I open my eyes, to my horror, I see that I couldn't be more wrong.

Cruel, ice-blue eyes. A lanky frame. Dark, short hair. Jackson's standing in front of me. Jackson. Instantly, there's ice in my veins.

My instinct is to lash out, but when I try to move my hands, to my horror, I realize that they're bound.

'Oh dear,' Jackson says, 'I think you'll find that this is even harder to get out of than prison.'

There's a funny smell in the air. Petrol.

Oh no. There's a canister of the stuff at Jackson's feet. And he's holding a lighter. He tosses it from hand to hand.

'Jackson, this is crazy.'

'Crazy, is it? You wanna know what I think's *crazy*, sweetheart? Fucking your boyfriend's brother.'

There are so many questions I want to ask, but only one I can voice. 'How did you find me?'

'Oh, that wasn't so tough. You know what though, originally, I wasn't even looking for you. I was after Tanner. Tracked him down to his old place of w-'

'Where is he?' I butt in, suddenly terrified for his safety.

'He's out of the way,' Jackson says. 'I'm going to have *words* with him. His old boss really doesn't like him much. Gave me all sorts of information about where he was headed. And then guess what? The tracker I had installed on your phone started beeping. And wouldn't you know, his location and your location just happened to be one and the same.' He flips the lighter on and watches the flame for a moment. 'I always knew you wanted him. Always knew that the two of you would betray me.'

'Jackson, we're not even dating, I haven't seen you-'

'You belong to me, bitch!' He roars. 'I made you. When we met, you were just some naive loser. Now, you're a cold-hearted criminal. I own you.'

I sob — a long, drawn-out sound. I can't believe it's come to this.

'And seeing as I own you, I get to choose how I'm gonna dispose of you.' He grins, a perverse, sadistic mirror of Tanner's noble smile. 'Only seems fair.'

# TANNER

THE INSTANT I WAKE, I know that something's wrong. Deeply wrong. I can hear voices nearby — Liv, sounding terrified, and a deeper voice, a voice I haven't heard for years. But it's a voice I'll never forget.

Jackson.

It takes me a moment to realize where I am — that I'm outside the guest cabin I've been staying with Liv. And it takes me a second more to realize that I've got both my hands and feet tied. He must have drugged me, used chloroform or something. Although that stuff doesn't knock you out in an instant, if it's held over the face for long enough, it can keep someone under.

Fuck. This is bad. Real bad. All I can think is how terrified Liv must be right now.

I test my bonds. They're tight — he's done a good job tying me. A professional job. For a moment, I wonder how on earth he could have found me, then I push those thoughts out of my head. I've got to think, and I've got to think fast.

It's dark, but I know there's a sharp stone around here — I pass it every day. Jackson's just dumped me out the front of the cabin. Obviously, he was looking to deal with Liv first. I find the stone after scrambling about in the dirt for a couple minutes, and start to rub the rope around my wrists against the pointed edge.

'This is so fucking ridiculous,' I say to myself, as I feel the thick bonds start to fray and weaken. As I finally break through the rope, something terrifying happens. A flickering light starts to emanate from inside the cabin. Then, Liv starts to scream — a wild, animal-like sound, primal and horrific and awful. I immediately think of the mountain lion.

In seconds I've got my feet untied, and just as I'm about to head into the cabin, I hear the sound of someone coming out. A moment later, Jackson is silhouetted in the front door — a lean, dark shadow against the orange glow inside.

'You fucking dog,' he says. He walks over to me and puts his hands on his hips. 'I always knew you wanted Liv. Always knew you thought she was too good for me.'

I can't move too soon, can't waste the opportunity he's given me. Right now, he doesn't know I'm free, and I want to make sure he doesn't work it out until he's face down in the dirt.

'What have you done, you maniac?' I shout at him. 'Are you seriously trying to kill Liv?'

He grins an insane grin. 'If I can't have her, no-one can. Who's gonna miss a loser like her, anyway? She'd be back in prison within six months.'

'Fuck you!' I spit.

'Oh, you're gonna regret that,' he snorts. He walks over to me. In the background, Liv's screaming for help. Surely some of the other guys can hear her. Surely someone's gonna come help. Jackson pulls his foot back and swings it toward my gut. There's no way I'm gonna let that kick connect.

Quick as lightning, I snap my hands in front of me and grab Jackson's leg. He's so surprised that he almost falls down without my help, but with a push and shove, I force him down onto the ground.

'What th-' he starts, before my fist shuts him up.

There's a blood-curdling scream from inside, and images of Liv, burning in flames flit through my mind.

'You gonna waste time on me?' Jackson asks, wiping his face. 'When your whore is in there, burning to a crisp?'

Damnit. He's right. I let out a furious roar and pound him once more in the face, before jumping off him. I shrug off my shirt, wrapping it around my face.

'You ever come back here again,' I shout, 'and I'll fucking kill you, you hear?'

He's already crawling away on his belly, like the snake he is.

I don't have time for this. I've never walked into a fire before, and I don't really want to do it ever again. Inside the little cabin which was fast becoming our home is a scene of carnage. Flames lick at every surface, smoke fills the air. I run through to the source of the screams. Liv's on a chair in the dining room and her eyes are wide with terror. She's tied up, struggling against her bonds.

'It's OK, Liv,' I shout, as I swoop down to pick her up. She pushes her body into mine. Poor thing, she's got ash all over her face. No time to worry about that though. I turn around and run out of the cabin as quick as I can. When I step out into the cool Colorado night, Jackson is nowhere to be seen.

*

'You sure you guys are gonna be alright in here?' Gabe hammers in the final peg of the tent.

'I'm sure,' I say.

'And you don't need a second tent putting up?'

Liv shakes her head wildly. 'No way. I don't want to be alone.'

'Don't blame you,' Gabe says.

In the distance, there's still an orange glow coming from the direction of our cabin. Atlas insisted on putting out the blaze, of course, but the embers are still glowing, a grim reminder of the madness that took place there tonight.

'You don't think he's gonna come back tonight, do you?' Liv asks. She hasn't let go of me since we left the cabin. I feel her need, like she can't bear to be apart from me. It's the same for me. I'm never letting this girl out of my sight.

'I think Joel was right,' Gabe says. 'Jackson will be back, but not tonight. Tanner beat him up pretty good, by all accounts. No doubt he'll want to regroup. We have to get ready for him.'

I nod. 'I'm thinking dogs. Lots of them.'

'We've got Brandy,' Gabe says. Brandy is his St. Bernard. She's as gentle as a dove, but so well-trained that I've no doubt she'd be an awesome guard dog. 'I keep thinking I should have let her sleep outside tonight. Maybe she would have picked up on a stranger's scent.'

'It's not your fault, Gabe. Jackson's the only one to blame here.'

'I can't believe the guest cabin's gone. That's gonna set us back a few weeks. Feels like someone's torn out a piece of my heart.' He sighs. 'We'll get that asshole, no doubt. You two better get some sleep. Lots of work to do in the morning. Plus I've got to check in on Bailey. She gets worried if I'm gone too long.' He gives a defeated-looking thumbs up and heads back along the trail to his cabin.

When Gabe is out of earshot, Liv says, 'I feel weirdly calm, Daddy.'

'Oh?'

'Yeah. I've been through so much recently. Prison. Homelessness. A near-death experience. And I should be feeling bad, you know. Or stressed. So why is it that I feel about the happiest I've ever felt?'

''Cause you're tough?'

'I don't think it's that,' she says. 'I think it's because I'm with you.'

In the dim light, her smile shines brightly.

'You know what? I think it might be nice to sleep outside tonight. What do you think? Under the stars?'

She nods.

I drag the travel mattress out from inside the tent and put it down on a clear patch of grass. Liv lies down and I cover her with a thick blanket.

'Need my Daddy in here to warm me up.'

'Now that's something I can do,' I reply.

It feels good to be lying next to her like this. We both stare up into the starry night. We're quiet for a moment, and I wonder what she's thinking, whether she's as weirdly happy at this moment as I am.

'I read a while ago that trauma brings people together,' I say, eventually. I take her hand in mine, kissing those cute fingers. 'Surviving stressful situations releases a kind of hormone storm. Oxytocin, dopamine, even a little shot of cortisol can help to bond people.'

'I didn't realize you were such a reader,' she says, almost purring with pleasure.

'There's lots about me you don't know,' I say.

'Like what?' she rolls over and lays her hand on my chest.

'Well,' I say, 'I guess you don't know that in high school, I was head of the debate team.'

She yanks her head up and bats my chest with a fist. 'Get out of here! You mean I'm dating a nerd?'

'We're dating, are we?' I chuckle.

'Well, I don't know, I me-'

'We're dating,' I say. 'If we weren't, it'd be pretty bad of me to do this, wouldn't it?' I take her hand and slowly move it down my body, until it comes to rest on the growing hardness of my crotch.

Her eyes widen.

'That would be totally unacceptable,' she gasps. 'One other thing I didn't know about you is how... big you are.'

'But you guessed, didn't you?' I grin a roguish grin.

'I guessed.'

She slips her hand down my pants, and I feel her warm skin against my smooth shaft.

'Fuck, you're sexy, Daddy.' Her hand starts to move up and down the length of me. 'There's so much of you. I don't know whether to be excited or nervous.'

'How bout both?' I say, starting to shift my crotch back and forth, rubbing my cock against her soft palm.

'You make me so wet,' she pants, 'no-one's ever done that to me. No one's ever made me come as hard as you did before. Right now, I'm seeping.'

I reach down, slip my hand down her diaper, and start to rub her delicate pussy. 'I guess nearly dying gets us both pretty fucking horny,' I say, kissing her shoulder, then biting her, harder than usual, so hard that she lets out a groan of pleasure.

'I want to show you how wet you make me,' she says. 'I want to feel you inside me, Daddy.' Her hand's moving more quickly now.

I don't really know how we both lose our clothes, but in seconds, we're naked under the sheets, naked under the stars. For a moment, I look up, tracing imaginary lines through the cosmos. I imagine Liv up there, her body spread out among the stars, her pussy twinkling with the heat of the sun, her eyes and breasts shining bright, guiding me in like a sailor coming home to port.

And then I'm in her.

We gasp, both of us, at the exact same moment. Our eyes are locked, our bodies engaged. My hand rests on her hip, hers is on my cheek. As I start to move, she bites her lip, and as we slowly move together, I watch her face melt into a mask of ecstasy.

'This is perfect,' she whispers in my ear. 'I can't believe we found each other.'

There's something incredible about the way we're moving right now. We're not just fucking. This is love-making, like our souls are singing to each other. She matches my every move, her slinky hips lashing back and forth as my hungry cock delves deeper and deeper into her, as my hands grab her back, pull her belly tighter into mine.

'You feel fucking perfect.' I grab her ass, squeeze her buttocks, then, in one swift movement, I flip her round so she's underneath me, hoist up her leg so that I can bury myself even deeper in her. She gasps, and I feel wetness pouring from her. 'You belong to me now, Liv,' I grunt, thrusting into her with all my power, grinding her down into the mattress. She closes her eyes, shoves her wrist into her mouth, and bites down hard, stopping herself from screaming out.

'It's so good,' she moans, 'too good.'

'You like it, huh? Like how my cock feels? What about the taste?' I grunt, pull out, shift up her body, so my glistening cock rests at the entrance to her mouth. She greedily opens her lips and takes me in, eyes widening as she tastes her own juices on me. 'Pussy tastes pretty good, doesn't it?' I lean back, find her pussy with my fingers, rub that tiny clit, make her buck and moan with my cock in her mouth. Her eyes roll back and I feel her body start to shake. I can sense she's about to come, and there's no way I'm missing that.

I wrench my cock from her mouth and stuff it back into that hot pussy, and as I do, she screams out, 'Daddy!' A second later, I feel her pussy contract around my dick, massaging me with the power of her orgasm. But I don't stop fucking, I keep going until the veins around her head are thick and her muscles grip even tighter, then I fuck her harder, and it feels so good, so impossible to resist that my own release builds, and in the tail end of her climax, I unload into her pink pussy, painting her insides with my cum.

We collapse down together, sweaty and hot. She rests on my chest and we look up at the stars.

'They belong to us,' I say, gesturing at the galaxy. 'Because love conquers all.'

# LIV

## THREE WEEKS LATER

'I'M SORRY I HAVEN'T been to visit you sooner,' Diana drinks juice from a sippy cup. 'I just wanted to give you time to get integrated into the community. Plus, I'm always cramping your style — not something I wanted to do here.'

I giggle. 'You never cramp my style, Di. I'm just happy that you've swung by now.'

It's been a crazy few weeks. Although I haven't seen much of Diana, I've seen her Daddy, Sheriff Carl, quite a bit. He's stopped by the cabin every couple days, to let me know how the investigation into Jackson is going. There's another reason too, he says. All the criminals in the Little Creek area follow his movements pretty carefully, and if they know he's spending time at the cabin, they're less likely to sniff around the place. And that means Jackson too.

'I'm so glad that you're fitting in so well!' she says.

We're sitting in the nursery of the main cabin at the moment, and the other Littles are in here too. Ella and Mia are playing a game of giant chutes and ladders in the corner, and all the Daddies are in the kitchen, having a beer.

'I know this is over the top,' I say, 'but I feel like this place has saved my life. It's not only given me a home, and a family, but I feel like I've finally found out who I am, and what I want from life.'

'And what is that?' she says, grinning widely.

'I guess I want to work on a farm and wear diapers all day.'

She bursts out laughing. 'Not something I would have expected to hear from you.'

'Believe me,' I say, 'I'm as surprised as you.'

'So is it true that Joel's hiring some kind of security guard?'

I nod and take a drink from my own sippy cup. I find it super-easy to get into Little Space these days. Having a load of toys and accessories around helps, but it's truly a state of mind that comes easy to moe.

'A big burly boy. I saw them interviewing him. He seems nice but *very* stern, even by Daddy standards.'

'Ooh, sounds exciting. What's his name?

'Blake.'

'Mysterious.'

'That's not all, though. Now that the boys finished building the new guest cabin, we're gonna start taking in more Littles. People who need help from all over the country. Apparently, the applications have been coming in thick and fast.'

'That's amazing!'

'I know. Only trouble is, there are so many, Joel's having to be really selective. Trying to make sure that we only take in people who really need help.'

Just that minute, Carl and Tanner appear in the doorway.

'Right sugar,' says Carl, 'I need to head back to the office now. Have you had a good chat with Liv?'

I've been amazed how well I've got on with Carl. He always seemed such a blowhard before I knew him. A by-the-book guy who cares about the rules and nothing else. But he's been super-sweet to me recently. Even gave me a little plant to look after. No doubt it'll be dead within days.

'You better get over here too, Trouble,' Tanner says to me. 'I've got a bath with your name on it. Gotta get rid of some of that juice.'

I glance down at my overalls. It's true, there's a damp patch over my chest.

'Whoops,' I say, twirling a finger in a ponytail. 'Sorry, Daddy.'

A couple minutes later, I'm soaking in the tub in our new home. It's even bigger and cozier than the last cabin. It's not plumbed in just yet — the water for this bath came from a huge communal boiler down by the lake — but it'll be sorted soon. With my brand new Daddy by my side, I think back to how different my life was, just a few weeks ago. I've gone from uncertainty to security. From madness to safety.

And as Tanner slips into the bath beside me and starts to gently scrub my body, I realize that I never want to get out. I want him to keep caring for me, keep training me, forever. No matter what the future brings.

* * *

**Read on for Blake and Delilah's story: *Guarded by Daddy*!**

## Chapter Six

# GUARDED BY DADDY

# DELILAH

I LOVE THE SMELL of baking pastry. Vanilla, butter, cream, and lots and lots of sugar. Whether I'm hard at work in my store, or in a more... exotic setting, like the kitchens at the Little Cabin, I just can't get enough.

'I'll never get my buns as soft and floury as yours.' Liv is looking at me like butter wouldn't melt in her mouth.

'Is that so?' I say. Liv and I hit it off almost as soon as we met each other. We've got the same cheeky attitude, and the same deadpan sense of humor. And weirdly, we've both had recent run-ins with criminals.

'Mmmhmm,' she smiles, then giggles. 'And if I can't get something like buns right, what chance have I got with apple pie?'

Bake Club is my favorite of all the weekly activities at the Little Cabin. I've been at this strange, exciting sanctuary for Littles for coming up to two months now, but even so, I don't think I'll ever get used to the sight of so many Littles in a kitchen, up to their elbows in flour and butter, and up to their butts in big, puffy diapers.

Aside from the fact that baking comes naturally to me, I'm actually kind of a professional.

*No, damn it, Delilah, you're an actual professional. You just don't have a store right now. But that's just a technicality.*

I'd been supplying the Little Cabin with cakes and pastries for a few months before my troubles started. But the first time that Mia's Daddy, Atlas, came into my store and bought a tray of chocolate eclairs, I never would have thought I'd end up living in some kooky commune for Littles and Bigs. And yet, here I am.

'Apple pie is honestly... a piece of cake,' I say. I'm slicing apples right now, using a sharp knife with a chunky orange handle. 'It's all about the spices you use. Obviously, you've *got* to use cinnamon, that's a given.'

'Oh sure,' Liv says, sarcastically, 'cinnamon's a given.'

I give her a look, narrowing my eyes.

'That's right, Liv,' I say. 'But the secret for me is a little pinch of nutmeg.'

'You know,' says Liv, 'sometimes you remind me more of a Big than a Little.'

People are actually really surprised when they find out I'm a Little. I think it's because I struggle to get into Little Space. Unless I feel perfectly comfortable with the people I'm with, unless I feel one hundred percent safe, I just can't do it. And I *can* be bossy, I'll be the first to admit that. I think that the Little inside me is more like a bossy ten-year-old than a toddler.

'If apple pie is so easy,' says Mia, one of the other Littles, 'then why do my efforts always turn out so... burny?'

It's true. Mia's struggled with her timings in Bake Club.

How can I put this without seeming mean? 'Cooking is an art,' I settle on. 'Baking, on the other hand, is a science. I love you, Mia, but I've never known anyone as easily distracted.'

As if to prove my point, Mia looks out the window. 'Oh look, Mr. Buzzkill's doing the rounds.'

'Mr. Buzzkill?' I ask, confused.

'Blake,' says Liv. 'You know, the strong but silent security guard?'

Oh I know exactly who Blake is. He's the one guy at the Little Cabin who I really don't get on with. You see, I can't handle people who don't ask questions. You know the type. They'll just sit opposite you, their eyes boring into your soul, expecting you to ask them question after question about their lives, while they don't ask a single thing in return.

When I talk to people like that, I tend to get a bit manic, trying to avoid silences at all costs. I still remember my first conversation with Blake like it was yesterday.

Well, 'conversation' is a generous term for it, really.

It was actually just me asking weird question after weird question until eventually, flustered to all hell, I asked him, 'So what type of underwear do you favor?'

Favor? What type of underwear do you *favor*? I mean, who talks like that?

Me, clearly.

He looked at me as if I was insane, and then politely told me that he had to feed his dogs.

Yeah, that's right. Dogs. Plural. Blake arrived at the Little Cabin with four Dobermans. All highly trained guard dogs.

Blake is the only guy at the Cabin who's not a Daddy. He's a staff member. He was hired by Joel — the guy who originally set this community up — as a security guard. Joel took him on after a local gangster burned down part of the complex and threatened Liv.

It makes me feel safer to have Blake around, but he doesn't half make me feel uncomfortable, too.

I wonder if there's some way to break the ice with Blake. Some way to loosen him up a bit.

Maybe it doesn't matter. I'm not gonna be at the Little Cabin much longer. As soon as my bakery in Boulder is refurbished, I'm heading right back.

'Hey,' says Liv, looking decidedly naughty, 'I've got an idea. A little trick we can play on Blake. Loosen him up a little bit.'

'What's that?' I ask, trying to keep my interest a little on the down-low. Because I've got a little secret about Blake. I've got just the teeniest, tiniest, smallest, most insignificant crush on him. Honestly, it's almost nothing. That's why I don't want anyone to know.

'Wellllllllll,' says Liv, extending the word so long it's practically elastic, 'I happened to get a special delivery last week.' She reaches into the front pocket of her denim overalls and takes out a little pouch. 'This is a Carolina Reaper chili pepper.'

'What's that?' I ask.

'Have you never heard of a Carolina Reaper?' Mia chips in, a look of genuine surprise on her cute face.

'Sorry,' I say. 'I'm not exactly a chili fan.

'The Carolina Reaper,' says Liv, with practiced theatricality, 'is the spiciest pepper on the face of the planet. It melts mouths, terrifies tongues, and thrashes throats.'

'So, it's spicy?'

She rolls her eyes. 'Yes, Mom, it's spicy. You know what a jalapeno is, right?'

I nod. A jalapeno is about as spicy as I go, really.

'Well, this tiny little pepper has as much spice as 880 jalapenos.'

My eyes widen. 'Can't that kill someone?' I ask.

'Nah,' she replies. 'I mean, I don't think so. Only one way to find out though, right? Why don't we make Blake a special apple pie? One with a little kick?'

My heart starts pounding. I love pushing boundaries, but this seems kinda crazy. What on earth will Blake think if I hand him a pie that's full of insane heat.

Hmm, maybe it'll warm up his icy exterior just enough to get him to crack a smile.

This is the kind of thing that I never normally do. Maybe that's why it seems like such an attractive idea.

'OK,' I say, grinning so wide I'm getting jaw ache, 'I'm in.'

Liv throws her head back and laughs like a cartoon villain. 'This is going to be fun.'

We slice the pepper as carefully as we can, washing our hands over and over again, making sure not to rub our eyes or touch any other sensitive parts. Then, when the bright orange thing is diced nice and small, we tip it into the appley innards of the pie. Thirty minutes and one hot oven later and the pie is ready for delivery.

'That looks amazing!' Mia says, her green eyes wide with hunger.

'Thanks,' I say. 'It's taken some getting used to, baking in a wood-fired oven, but I'm almost there!'

The cabins here are so off-grid they don't even have any electricity. Well, that's not entirely true — there's a couple solar panels that can charge up a cell phone in about fifty years, but other than that, it's just good old-fashioned fire and steam. I think about my sister, still back in Boulder, still running her own bakery a couple blocks away from mine. If Monica could see me now, she'd laugh her head off.

Monica loves convenience, and she'd never in a million years have agreed to come to a place like this with me. Believe me, I tried to convince her.

'Do you think he'll notice the heat?' I ask. I'm handling the pie like it's gonna explode.

'He'll notice,' Liv says. Her eyes dart to the window of the cabin. 'Look, he's coming round again. Go give him the pie, Dee!'

I feel crazy for a second, like I'm about to make a big mistake. Then, I panic in a different way — I don't even know what I look like. I haven't seen myself in a mirror for hours. And knowing what normally happens in Bake Club, I'm probably covered in flour and smeared with sugar syrup.

'I don't know if I can,' I say, suddenly terrified.

'Don't forget,' Liv says, 'the first rule of bake club.'

'Always double-prove bread so that it doesn't rise too quickly in the oven?'

Liv shakes her head in disgust.

'No, doofus. That's the third rule of Bake Club. The first rule is: Share our baked goods with anyone who'll eat them.'

'Hmmm,' I say. 'Not sure that-'

'Don't over-analyze, Dee, just act!'

So I take the pie and walk out of the cabin as innocently as I can.

*

It's a beautiful spring day. All around are the sounds of nature — the shrill call of birds, the creak of crickets, the rustle of pine needles in the wind. It's peaceful. Serene. And I'm about to break that serenity in the most ridiculous way imaginable.

'Hey, Blake.'

I see the hulking form of Blake from behind. He's wearing a tight white sleeveless top, and he's holding the leashes of two athletic-looking dogs. Even though he's silhouetted against the background, it's plain to see his strength, just in the way he moves.

On hearing his name, he turns back to look at me, and when he
does, it sends a jolt of electricity up my spine. He's got a gaze so
piercing it feels like I've been pinned to the wall of the cabin. For a
crazy second, I wonder if he somehow knows that I'm about to play a
trick on him.

His arms are thickly muscled, and his left is covered in ink — skulls,
guns, praying hands. It's the kind of thing that — if I didn't know him
— would terrify me. Even knowing him, I feel a little nervous.

'Dee.' His reply is curt and businesslike. His eyes flick down to the
pie in my hands, and then over my shoulder. It's like he's constantly
checking for danger, all the time.

'Um, I made this for you,' I say, holding the pie out to him.

He looks momentarily confused. 'For me?' His hard eyes look suddenly soft. 'What is it?'

'Apple pie,' I say.

His gorgeous blue eyes look full of happiness. 'Seriously? That's...
damn nice of you, Delilah.'

I can't believe I'm doing this. This is insane. He's being so nice. He
was meant to be mean and gruff, not appreciative and sweet.

'You like apple pie?'

'Who doesn't?' he says. 'Do you mind if I just take a bite, right
now?' He takes the pie from my outstretched arms.

'No,' I say, my voice strange and strangled-sounding.

God, he's gorgeous. Face thick with stubble, jaw hard and square
with a powerful chin. There are flecks of gray hair among his muddy
blond. He looks like a Viking warrior.

He lifts the pie up to his nose, takes a long sniff, then opens his
mouth.

'Wait!' I cry.

He stops, mouth open, looking at me with surprise.

'It's a trick,' I sigh. 'There's chili pepper in that pie. Liv put me up to it.'

'Chili?' he says with a shrug. 'I can handle heat.' And then, before I have time to stop him again, he takes a huge bite out of it.

At first, he seems unfazed. In fact, he seems to be enjoying it. 'That is delicious. Not too spicy eith-'

He pauses. His eyes widen. His jaw drops.

'Oh my God,' he gasps, his deep voice suddenly hoarse. 'What is happening to my mouth?'

'I'm sorry,' I say, 'I tried to warn you.'

He looks around desperately — I'm not sure what he's looking for until his eyes fix on a water barrel next to the cabin. Then, he drops the leash and grabs the barrel, before pouring gallons of rainwater up and over his head. He's half-drinking, half just washing his head.

'F-fucking hell,' he stutters, as the water pours over his body, 'this is the most intense p-pain I think I've ever experienced.'

He's soaking now, his shirt is stuck to his slick torso. It's time for my jaw to drop because I can see the body underneath that shirt, and it is incredible. Each individual muscle picked out, shifting as he moves. I get a sudden urge to reach out and touch him.

He catches me looking. There's something in his eye — a look of recognition. A look of lust? But it only lasts a moment. Because a second later, he's looking through me, straight past me, and there's horror in his expression.

I turn to look.

It's a dark shape, lying on the forest floor. A dog — not one of the two he's been walking. Its chest is heaving, its breathing is labored. Now that I'm focused on the dog, I can hear each painful wheeze of its breath.

Blake rushes straight past me, and crouches down by the dog.

'Maggie?' he says, stroking its fur. 'What's the matter, girl? W-who did this to you?' Another stutter. His voice is wracked with pain.

But the pain is only just beginning.

# BLAKE

I 'M DRIVING TOO FAST. I'm aware of that. But it feels like every fucking second in this car is a second closer Maggie gets to death. I shift the gear stick into fourth and push my foot down on the accelerator.

Sitting next to me, Delilah lets out a little yelp of shock.

I half expect her to say something about the fact I'm speeding, but to my surprise, she doesn't.

Instead, she leans in and says. 'She's gonna be OK.' I keep my eyes on the road, but I don't need to see her face to hear the concern in her voice. I feel her hand on my shoulder. I'm still wearing that dumb sleeveless top from earlier, and it's still soaked through.

When I saw Maggie like that, slumped on the floor, struggling to breathe, everything else left my mind. I couldn't think about anything but Maggie's safety. No time to change clothes. No time to ask why Delilah insisted on coming to the veterinarian. No time to do anything but get to the town of Little Creek as fast as humanly possible.

There's no road access at the Little Cabin, so I had to trek with Maggie in my arms and Delilah at my side through the forest before reaching my ride. Thankfully, Dee was pretty damn quick through the undergrowth.

'No guarantee of that.' I don't mean my words to come out as gruff as they do, but I can't help it. I'm seriously shaken up right now. Obviously, it's not Delilah's fault that Maggie's in this mess, but I can't help snapping.

'What do you think is wrong with her?' Her voice is so soft and fragile. She doesn't know my dog from Adam, but she seems to genuinely care.

'No idea. Couldn't find any wounds. Nothing on her body. If I didn't know better, I'd say it was her heart — that can make dogs breathe like this. But I had a scan two months ago — just a routine thing because Maggie's getting older — and she was in perfect health.'

'Maybe it's some kind of fit?'

'Maybe.'

The trees thin slightly as we approach civilization. Right up 'til the point I needed to get to the vet, I was finding living in the wilderness romantic. The peace, the quiet. It's a different world from my usual life in Phoenix. I'd been working security for a big biotech firm when I got the call from Joel. He's an old friend — we met at his old investment bank in Boulder. He's a good guy, and when he offered me work away from the hustle and bustle of the big city, I leaped at the chance. Phoenix has some bad memories for me, memories I was pleased to leave behind.

I was unsure at first, because of the whole *Little* angle. I wasn't sure how I'd feel, guarding a bunch of vulnerable women who like to act like kids. Turns out, it came pretty easy to me. I've always had a soft spot for cute girls, and the Littles at the cabin are about as cute as it gets.

But none of them are as cute as Delilah, mind you. The things I want to do to her would make a whore blush.

If it weren't for the fact that my favorite dog is on the verge of a medical emergency, I'd be feeling pretty damn uncomfortable being in this car alone with Dee. I've always been terrible around women I have a crush on. I'm not bad looking, and I've had plenty of chances with pretty women. And I've blown every single one.

See, I've got a stutter. I hate it. It's been eating away at my self-confidence my whole life. It's the main reason I come across as gruff sometimes — 'cause the less words I speak, the less likely I am to stutter. A simple equation, but the result is that throughout my whole life, everyone kind of ends up thinking I'm an asshole. And the trouble with everyone thinking you're an asshole is that sooner or later you start to act like one.

'I'm sorry about the pie.'

'You already apologized.'

She sighs. 'Does it still hurt?'

'Forget it.'

My mouth's still on fire, of course. I wasn't just posturing when I said that I can handle spice, but this pie was something else, believe me. It was like there was actual fire in my mouth — spreading all the way down my throat. Now it's sitting in my belly like a cozy dragon.

I've been through a lot — I've been shot for fuck's sake — but the feeling of that spice was the single most intense pain I've ever experienced.

'Sorry.' Her hand leaves my shoulder. I can hear the disappointment in her voice. I know she's trying her best to help. For a moment, I take my eyes off the road, looking at the perfect creature sitting next to me — she's got strawberry-blond hair like spun sugar, up in a little bun on top of her head, but a few strands frame her face. Her lips sit like a heart under a tiny button nose, and her pale blue eyes are framed by thick, expressive lashes. When she feels something, it's so obvious from her expression that she might as well have it written in huge letters on her forehead.

'Look, it's really OK. I'm not a-angry at you. Just want to make sure Maggie's OK.'

I feel the tension ease just a touch, and I can practically *hear* her smile.

Up ahead, a road-sign speeds past. *Little Creek 14.*

Maggie moans.

*

The waiting room smells of antiseptic. Delilah is standing up, pacing back and forth under the buzz of strip lights. My throat is dry. I keep running my hands through my hair. If I was more of a talker, I'd be chatting shit right now, trying to take our minds off the fact that in a room nearby, my oldest dog is getting her stomach pumped.

'Is there any way she could have drank bleach?' the vet had asked from behind a face mask.

'Fuck no,' I barked back. 'You saying I'd l-let my dog drink bleach?' I wish I didn't get angry like that. Normally I'm fine, but when someone I love is in danger, it brings out the animal in me. The protector. The guard.

'I'm sure she didn't mean that,' Dee had chipped in.

I wanted to bark something else, but I held my tongue. Obviously, Dee was right.

Now that we're waiting for Maggie to emerge though, the anger and adrenaline that had been surging around my body have been replaced by cold, creeping dread.

I keep thinking about stupid, unimportant shit. Like the fact that Ajax and Carla — my two other Doberman Pinschers — need feeding. Like the fact that no one has been patrolling the cabin since I left.

Honestly, I'm not even convinced that they need a security guard at that place. I mean come on, who wants to hurt a bunch of women who wear diapers and the men who look after them? Sure, there was some trouble with a small-time gangster who'd been romantically involved with one of the Littles, but I hadn't had a sniff of trouble since I arrived at the place. And obviously, I'm totally fine with being paid to do almost no work.

My thoughts are interrupted. 'Man, I'm so anxious right now. Feels like my heart is gonna burst any second.'

I look up at Delilah. She *does* look anxious, poor thing. I feel suddenly grateful to her — grateful for coming with me, grateful in helping to share the burden of my worry. I don't know Dee very well. She's been an exotic object of lust for me ever since I met her. But now I'm starting to see what she's like, that lust is developing, mutating into something much more dangerous: affection.

'Come sit down,' I grunt.

'Pacing helps.'

I consider this for a moment, then I decide to try something. I stand up and join Delilah. She watches as I walk up behind her. 'Go on then,' I say. 'Pace more. If it h-helps.'

She smiles and looks back, then takes a step forward. I mimic her, taking a step of my own. Her smile widens. She takes another step. I copy. Then she takes three steps, really quickly, shuffling along like a duck. I do exactly the same. Delilah lets out a snort of laughter, and it's about the loveliest sound I've ever heard.

'Nice technique,' I say before she takes more quick steps. I follow behind and then, without warning, she suddenly stops. I bump into her from behind — accidentally of course — but just for a moment, my crotch is pressed into her tush.

'Whoops!' she squeals, leaping forward.

'S-sorry,' I say, edging back from her, trying not to show how flustered I am.

'Hey,' she says, clearly blushing now, 'you mind if I ask you something?'

'Go for it,' I reply. To my shame, I can actually feel physical arousal spreading around my body like water seeping through a sponge.

'Do you have a stutter?'

Now it's me that's blushing. Damn. I thought she hadn't noticed. Not that it matters. Why should it matter that I've got a stutter? Who cares, right?

The answer, obviously, is that *I* care.

'Um,' I say. And then, before I can carry on, there's a click, and the door to the surgery opens up.

The vet appears and moves her mask down, revealing a serious mouth. 'I think you two better come through.'

*

Maggie is there, resting on a red pillow. There's a tube in her mouth and a machine nearby shows her vital signs.

I stand by her, running my hand through her fur, whispering to her. Delilah watches on, tears in her eyes, hands clasped under her chin.

'You're sure she's g-going to be OK?' I ask.

The vet nods. 'We've pumped her stomach and made sure that she's had plenty of fluids. She should be back to normal within a couple days. I'd like to keep her in overnight just to be doubly safe.'

'Of course. God. I always knew chocolate is toxic for dogs, but I had no idea that it can kill.'

'Now,' the vet says more grimly, 'mistakes happen, but Maggie's a big dog. She would have had to have eaten a *lot* of chocolate to get into this state. Bars and bars of the stuff.'

'What are you trying to say?' I bristle again.

'I'm saying that unless you've got a chocolate stash somewhere in your house that she somehow broke into, this could have been deliberate.'

Delilah butts in. 'But who would do something like that?'

'No-one at the Little Cabin,' I say. But as I do, I find myself thinking through everyone I live with. There's no way that anyone *could* have done this, is there? Absentmindedly, I scratch Maggie under her collar. And as I do, I feel something in there.

'What the—' I say, and take the item out. It's a folded piece of paper, fixed in place with Scotch tape. When I unfold it, what I see shocks me to the core.

*This is just the first bitch we're coming for. Delilah is next.*

'Blake? Blake, what's the matter? What have you found?'

My heart's pounding. Sweat beads on my forehead.

'It's a note,' I say.

'What does it all mean?'

I pull myself up to my full height. 'It means that you're my number one priority, Dee. I'm not going to let anyone hurt you. Ever.'

# DELILAH

SINCE BLAKE FOUND THAT message under Maggie's collar, it feels like life has been moving at a thousand miles an hour. We sped back to the cabin even more quickly than we'd made our way to the vets.

Just before we got called in to see Maggie, I felt like I'd been making a breakthrough with Blake, like I was actually managing to get through that tough exterior. Turns out, the way to do it wasn't to give him a super-spicy apple pie, it was to goof around with him and then just ask him about himself.

Even though I'm scared, there's a big part of me that's thrilled, because I know he was about to open up to me. And something else: when Blake started to goof around with me, I had a taste of freedom. A taste of real Little Space. Fleeting, but real.

Now, just a few hours later, we're back in the main living space of Joel and Ella's cabin. It's got a high ceiling and views from the windows across Purple Lake and the surrounding forest land. Everyone's in here, more than a dozen Littles and Bigs. But not one set of eyes is looking at the view.

No. Every eye in here is fixed on me.

'So tell us, Dee, who do you think is behind this attack?' Joel's a gruff-looking guy with a heart of gold. Behind his big bushy beard is a face that's quick to smile and slow to anger. But I'm learning today that when he does get angry, he gets super, super serious.

'Well,' I say, taking a deep breath. 'It's complicated.' I clutch Fluffkins to my chest. Fluffkin is my unicorn stuffie, and they've got magic powers.

When Blake showed me that note — scrawled in messy handwriting on a scrap of paper — I felt my blood freeze in my veins. I honestly thought that by leaving Boulder and coming out here to the wilderness, I'd escape the people tormenting me. Turns out that they have a longer reach than I would have ever thought.

'Break it down piece by piece.' That's Carl. He's the local Sheriff at Little Creek. He doesn't live out here at the cabin, but he is a Daddy. His Little is Diana, Liv's best friend. I get on well with Di, too, although I've only met her a couple times.

'Well, it all started about six months ago. It had always been my dream to run my own bakery ever since I was a kid.' I smile nervously. 'Always had a thing for donuts.'

'Who doesn't?' Mia — my distracted friend from earlier.

'My grandma was a seamstress,' I continue. 'And she worked all the way up til the day she died. She loved it. Almost all my clothes were made by her when she was alive.' I look down at my pastel pink overalls. 'She made these.'

'Granny got game!' Liv says.

There are a few nervous laughs, but reading the room isn't one of Liv's skills.

'Anyway, when she passed, she left me her old seamstress shop in her will. Even said that it was left to me on the condition that I bake there. Took a couple months for the store to be changed to a bakery, but the day I opened was the happiest of my life.'

'What name did you pick?' Liv says, a little sheepishly.

'Dee's Cakes and Bakes.' I shrug. 'Thought I'd keep it simple. My sister actually runs a bakery a few blocks away. Called Monicakes. She's called Monica, soooo...' There are a few giggles from around the room. 'I couldn't exactly compete with that. Now, at first, things were going well. Like, really well. My store's in a good part of Boulder, and I would get tons of passing trade. Anyway, after a couple months, this guy came in. Said that he worked for a local businessman who wanted to offer me protection services. To be honest, at first, I didn't even suspect him. He seemed like a nice guy, and I honestly thought that he was trying to warn me about other shady guys in the area.'

'That's a classic mob move,' says Carl. 'Plus, a lot of the time, they don't see themselves as bad guys.' He sighs. 'But they are. They really are.'

'When he told me that I had to pay $1000 a month for protection, I turned him down. He smiled, left, and I didn't think any more about it. Until I came into work two weeks later to a brick through the window. There was a note around it that just said: *This is just the start.*

'I called the police, but — no offense Carl — they were less than useless.'

'Big city police departments have lots of issues to deal with. A brick through a window is scary —sure — but not exactly high priority,' he reasons.

'The guy came back and was even more forceful this time. He heard about the brick, he said, and had been worried about the store. I think that's when I realized he was part of the gang that was targeting me.'

'I think that's when you must have spoken to me.' That's the Greek accent of Atlas, Mia's Big. He's leaning back in his chair in typical cocky Atlas fashion.

I nod. 'I couldn't believe it when you told me about this place, and I never thought for a second that I'd have to end up here. Of course, that was before they destroyed my store.'

The eyes of the Littles in the room widen.

'At first, I thought they'd just smashed the window again. When I realized what they'd done though, I just broke down.' There's a tremble in my voice. Even now, just thinking about what those thugs did to my grandma's store is making me tear up. 'They'd thrown paint all over everything inside. The counters, the walls, even inside the oven — which had been hit repeatedly with a hammer, by the way. All the electronic equipment was destroyed, and all the furniture had been obliterated.' It feels good to get all this off my chest. Only Joel really knew the details of my situation, and Atlas knew the broad strokes too. But seeing the rest of the Little Cabin community empathizing is really heartening.

'You poor thing,' comforts Mia.

'It just so happened that Atlas came by at opening time. The police were there, obviously, and they vowed to look into it. But I had no choice but to close the place down until I can get it fixed. That's when Atlas said that I could come live here until all my problems blew over.' I don't mention that Joel had offered to pay my rent on the place, too. He's been super-generous, but I know he wants to keep that detail between us. 'So that's the situation. I just left the store and came here.'

Carl stands up. 'I'm looking into the gang still. I actually got some interesting information just yesterday. It's taken me literally months, but I managed to get some stills from public CCTV of your street.' Carl holds up a brown envelope, then opens it up, before spreading out a bunch of big, glossy photos on the table in front of everyone. The shots are of men in bandanas, holding baseball bats. They're smashing the window to my store. The faces are all blurry. Suddenly, there's a gasp from across the table.

'Oh, my god. That's him. It's Jackson!' Liv's normally pale face is now so white that she looks like a sheet of paper.

Tanner — Liv's Daddy — holds her close. His eyes are fixed on the photograph.

'She's right,' he says. 'That's my fucking brother.' He catches himself. 'Sorry to swear guys, I'm just shaken.'

It takes me a moment to realize just how serious the situation is. Jackson isn't just Tanner's brother — he's Liv's ex. He forced her into a life of crime years before she ended up at the Cabin. He's the reason she ended up in prison.

'Well, well,' says Carl. For some reason, he's got a massive grin on his face. 'I know it doesn't seem this way, but this could be the best news I've had all week.'

Tanner looks furious. 'Are you kidding, Carl? This is a disaster. Jackson nearly burned this whole fucking place down. I thought he'd decided to leave us alone. And now that we find out that he's targeting one of our Littles again, you're over the moon about it?'

'Of course,' Carl says, 'because if we can track down Jackson, we'll have killed two birds with one stone. Our troubles will be a distant memory, and we can all get on with living our lives.'

'You know what?' Up til now, Blake's been totally silent. I've seen his eyes on me from time to time as I've been speaking. Now though, he sounds furious. 'T-there's been a lot of discussion of how we got to this point. Lots of speculation about who's behind all this nastiness. But you know what no-one's mentioned?'

Silence.

'No-one's suggested how we're going to keep Dee safe.' I feel my cheeks burn. Is that what he's been thinking about this whole time? My safety?

'Well obviously that's our main priority,' Joel responds, cool as ever. 'You're our head of security. What do you suggest we do? A generator for some security cameras?'

Blake shakes his head. 'I've got something a little more drastic in mind.'

'Go on.'

'We leave. Dee and I. These assholes know where the Little Cabin is. They could be here at any time. They must have gotten really close to poisoning Maggie. So we leave. I'll set up some traps around here in case they try anything.'

'Where are you going to go?'

'I can't tell you,' he replies. 'I'm not saying that I don't trust anyone — I do. I trust you all. In the time I've been here, it's become abundantly obvious that all of you are good people. It's just that we don't know if there are bugs around. People could be listening right now.'

'What about the rest of us?' says Liv, her voice unsure. 'Dee isn't the only one who Jackson's targeting.'

'The rest of you should head to Little Creek. Just for a while, til this is all sorted.'

'Good idea,' Carl says. 'I can put you guys up for a while — I know Robyn at the motel. Now that I've got some intel about Jackson's gang, it shouldn't take too long for us to draw a net around him.'

'Sounds like a plan,' Blake says.

'Not sure how I feel about leaving this Cabin.' Joel does look concerned.

'Don't worry,' Blake replies. 'I'll make sure it's well looked after.'

My heart's pounding in my chest. I'm going to be alone, with Blake, somewhere in the wilderness? Indefinitely?

A few people ask a few more questions. Gabriel asks about the crops. Atlas asks about a painting job he's halfway through. But I'm finding it difficult to concentrate because I can't take my mind off Blake.

The thing is, hearing him talk with such confidence and authority about protecting me was one hell of a turn-on. The thought of him sticking up for me the way he has is sexy as hell. Once again, I wish he was a Daddy. Just imagining snuggling up with him under the stars is making me feel all yummy inside.

Maybe there's a silver lining to this situation after all.

'So, Delilah, how do you feel about all this?'

Everyone's eyes are back on me again.

'Scared,' I say, truthfully. 'But I think Blake's plan is good.' I hold up Fluffkins. 'Plus it won't be just him and me. Fluffkins will look after us both.'

To my surprise, Blake cracks a smile. It's such a rare treat to see his face light up like that. Just for a moment, it looks as though his worries have evaporated. Then, a moment later, his face is serious again.

'There's only one problem,' Blake says.

'What's that?'

'My dog, Ajax, eats unicorns for breakfast.'

Just for a moment, the laughter echoes around the Little Cabin. It's the last time anyone will laugh here for quite some time.

# BLAKE

T HE NEXT DAY PASSES in a blur. In the morning, Joel did me a favor and picked Maggie up from the vet. While he was gone, everyone else made preparations to leave the Little Cabin. I stood guard the whole time, making sure that nothing untoward happened to anyone while we were at our most vulnerable. Plus I don't have much stuff of my own. Always travel light, that's my style.

Eventually, everyone but myself and Delilah started making their way through the surrounding forest. Joel booked a minivan at the pickup, so they could all travel together to the Motel in Little Creek. Even though these are less-than-ideal circumstances, everyone was in pretty good spirits. Lots of jokes and fun from the Littles. I could sort of tell that Delilah was a little disappointed not to be joining them. It kind of felt like some big road trip or vacation.

Eventually, when the gang is out of earshot, an eerie silence settles over the cabin. It's so strange to not hear the sounds of laughter and hard work that normally abound here.

I'm checking on the dogs in the kennel when I hear Delilah's voice.

'They're gonna be glad to have a break from Tina.'

Tina is Joel's cat, and she's got one hell of a personality. The first time Ajax met her, there was something of a Mexican standoff. I've never known Ajax to back down from a challenge before. The two of them growled and yowled at each other until eventually, much to my amazement, Ajax turned around and started whining.

'Ajax seems happier already,' I say, patting my dog on the head. 'Right, are you ready to get going? The sooner the better, I t-think.'

She smiles. She's looking gorgeous today. Overalls are kind of her signature look, I guess. She's wearing a pair of pale blue ones today, that bring out the beautiful color of her eyes. Underneath, she's got a tight, white sleeveless top, that accentuates the sweep of her bust. How am I going to keep my mind on the task of guarding her, when it's like she's been specifically designed to turn me on.

She clutches her little — what did she call it — stuffie to her chest. 'Fluffkins says we're good to go.'

'Fluffkins seems like a smart guy.'

'Silly,' says Dee, 'unicorns are genderless.'

I grin. 'Sorry. I should know to never assume a magical creature's gender.'

'That's right,' she smiles. Then, she gives a little yelp. 'Eeek! Didn't you say Ajax eats unicorns for breakfast?'

'Yep,' I grunt. 'Lucky it's lunchtime.'

*

An hour later, I feel seriously out of my depth. I have a plan — obviously, I have a plan — but how to actually put that plan into action is a little trickier.

It strikes me that I probably should have asked Joel for some information about the local area. My plan is to trek all the way around Purple Lake and make camp on the far shore. That way, we'll be able to see the Little Cabin from our camp. Obviously, we'll be a long way from the cabin in case of emergencies, but if I see anyone poking around, I'll be able to get in touch with Joel. There won't be power, so we'll only be turning our phones on once a day to check for messages. Other than that, we're going dark.

'Do you believe in monsters?'

I look back at Delilah. It's getting a little dark, and I guess she's feeling a touch scared.

'Of course not.' I don't mean to sound dismissive, but I think that's how I come across.

'What about bad people?' Her voice sounds small, almost like a little girl's. Much to my surprise, I don't find it irritating or grating. In fact, I just kinda feel like I want to look after her even more.

'W-well sure, I believe in bad people. But people aren't monsters. They're just... people.' Man, I sound dumb.

'What do you mean?' The way she's holding that stuffie, it's like she's using it as a shield.

I stop for a moment, then I move closer to her. I stoop a little, so that my head's at the same height as hers.

'Monsters are just evil, right? People are more complex than that.' As I talk, I realize that I'm thinking about Bud. Damn. That feels like a long time ago. 'Criminals have issues. And sometimes people do bad things for good reasons.'

'You mean you think that Jackson is attacking my business for a good reason?'

'No, course not.' I try not to scoff. 'But I doubt he thinks he's a bad guy. That's all.'

She considers this for a second, then nods in agreement.

'But, in answer to your original question, no, I don't think a banshee's gonna pop out the trees and squeal at us.'

'Phew,' she says.

We start walking again, and a few minutes later, we emerge from the undergrowth. It's gorgeous here. There's soft brown sand by Purple Lake, and dark pines all around. Above, the sun is starting to dip behind the mountain. The shadows are long and the first stars are twinkling up ahead, in defiance of the last few minutes of daylight.

Across the lake, in the murky evening light, I can just about make out the collection of timber buildings that make up the Little Cabin complex. There's still a plume of smoke coming up from the main chimney of Joel's cabin.

'Wow,' says Dee, 'you picked a gorgeous spot.'

'I'm just glad I managed to get us here.'

'We gonna camp on the sand?' she asks, unsure.

I shake my head. 'Nope. It'd be cold, and there would be a billion bugs. But I'll build us a fire here. Cook dinner on the beach. The smoke should keep the skeeters away.'

'Skeeters?'

'Mosquitoes. You know?'

'Oh don't worry, Fluffkins keeps those away. He's got anti-skeeter radar.'

'They're a useful camping buddy,' I snort.

'The best,' she grins.

'So,' I say, 'do you prefer pitching tents or starting fires?'

She grimaces. 'What's option three?'

'Option three is the most dangerous, difficult option of the bunch.'

Her grimace gets even more desperate.

'Option three,' I continue, 'is to look cute and help me with both.'

That smile. I swear it's gonna get me into a heap of trouble.

\*

'I love the smell of an open fire.'

We're sitting opposite each other, under the stars. Delilah looks wonderful, dusky, and calm. She's got a blanket from the tent, and she's wrapped it tightly around her. Her face is a wash of orange and red, as the light from the flames dances a tango across her smooth skin.

'Me too,' I reply.

'Makes me want to do some guerrilla baking,' she says with a wicked smile.

'You cook monkeys?'

'No, silly!' I wish I was next to her — I get this weird feeling she'd put her arms around me. There's something so sweet and innocent about her, and her sense of fun is infectious, too. Suddenly, she stands up. 'You know what?' she says, 'I actually brought something with me for you. I was going to wait until later, but I think that now could be the right time.'

She walks to the tent and returns a moment later with a mischievous look in her eye and something silvery in her hands.

'What's that?' I ask.

She doesn't say a thing, just walks up to the fire, and carefully places the silver parcel straight onto the embers. 'Hopefully, this won't just incinerate it,' she says.

'Incinerate what?'

'Patience!' she squeals.

'Huh, I always thought that you Littles were all about *impatience*.'

She thinks about this for a moment. 'You're right. Patience is something I struggle with a bit. But you're not a Little!'

'True enough.' I look at her standing there next to the fire, hands on her hips. There's definitely a bulge underneath the clean lines of her overalls. She's wearing a diaper. 'So Dee, tell me, when did you first know that you were a Little?'

'First know?' she muses. 'It's not like I had this sudden realization or anything. I was always into girlie things. Never really shook off that bossy, childish streak I had when I was a kid. I felt lost for years, like I just didn't fit in, like I wasn't being myself somehow.'

'Bossy, huh?'

'Mmmhmm. I always like being in charge of games.'

'But I thought that Littles liked to have someone else look after them. You know, a Daddy to take charge?'

'Never had a Daddy,' she says.

'Never?'

'Nope.' There's a look in her eye. I can't tell if it's sadness or desire, or something else. 'But I think if I did, I'd definitely like him to take charge of me. To look after me.' She looks down at her feet, clearly embarrassed. 'Kind of like the way you're looking after me.'

I feel it — this crackle of something between us. A dangerous spark. I need to ignore that spark. Can't afford to get distracted. We're both in danger out here.

'You deserve to be looked after,' I say. 'I hope you find someone who can look after you the way you need. I'm not a good person, Delilah. I've done some bad things. You wouldn't want a Daddy like me.'

She seems a little deflated. Could she really be interested in me? Could I really give her what she needs?

'What bad things have you done?'

'When I was younger,' I sigh. 'I ran with some bad people. Dangerous people.'

'What type?' Her questions are so innocent, but I feel like I can't sugarcoat this. I want her to know that I'm not good for her, that I'm bad news.

'A gang. A motorbike gang. Criminals, hustlers, drug dealers. Violent men.'

She looks genuinely shocked. 'No way! But you're so nice.'

I grunt a laugh. In truth, I didn't do much wrong when I was with the Filth Hogs. And I didn't stay in the club for long. Not after Bud died. But I don't want Dee to know that. I've got to put her off me, for both our sakes. 'You wouldn't have thought that about me if you'd met me a few years ago.'

Then, to my surprise, Delilah screams.

'No no no, it's burning!'

She grabs a stick I've been using to prod the fire and whacks the silver package out of the burning chunks of charcoal. It's steaming, whatever it is. Before it's had any time to cool at all, Dee swoops in and starts to tear at the silver, pulling it apart.

'Hey, that's hot!' I say, springing up from my seat.

'Asbestos fingers,' she replies. 'Professional baker, remember.'

'Even so, there's no rush. I don't want you burning yourself young lady.' My voice comes out so stern. It's like I'm really telling her off. For a moment, I worry that I've upset her. But she doesn't look upset, she looks excited.

'Don't you want to know what I brought for you?' She asks.

Silently, I pick the thing up from the ground. It's cooler now, and I un-peel the tin foil. Inside, is a steaming apple pie.

'No spice in this one,' she says, playfully.

I look at her, look at the pie. Then I lean in and sink my teeth into the buttery pastry. Inside is sweet and warm and good, and as I swallow a mouthful of the delicious filling, I can't help but imagine what it might be like to eat up the Little standing in front of me.

'You know,' she says, eyes lingering on my hungry face, 'I think I did hurt myself. My finger. Really, really hurts.' Her voice is different, like it's reacted to mine, like she's deferring to the brief moment of dominance I shared.

'You want me to take a look at it?'

She nods.

I step forward. She holds out her hand. Those slender fingers, that soft arm. I take her hand, holding it up in the light of the fire. 'Looks like you've got a bit of a blister here, darling. That's no good.'

'Kiss it better?' Her eyes are watery pools and her lip trembles.

Slowly, I raise her fingertip to my mouth, then I place the softest, lightest kiss I can possibly manage on that poor fingertip. 'You promise me you won't go touching stuff that's just come out the fire again?'

She nods, trembling.

'Good girl.'

'I like it when you talk to me like this, Blake.'

'I think I like talking to you like this.' Our breath hangs in the air. The stars shine above. I want her so badly, right here, right now, under the stars, damn the consequences.

I can smell her.

Then, from nearby, there's a terrible noise. The long, lonely howl of a single wolf. Dee's eyes bulge.

'Come on,' I say, 'let's get back to the tent. It's getting late.'

It's only as we start to walk back that I realize I haven't stuttered once this whole evening.

# DELILAH

T HE SUNRISE IS ABOUT the most beautiful thing I've ever seen — a giant, scintillating pink ball, lush and warm, yawning its way up into the sky, just starting to wake up the planet.

I can't believe I shared a tent with Blake last night. We slept apart from each other of course, but I could hear him gently breathing all night long. I could see his bulky form, shifting up and down with each breath. Dang, I could even smell him, a gorgeous, musky, masculine scent — all pine needles and lemon.

'I think I really fancy him,' I whispered to Fluffkins when I was sure that Blake was asleep.

This morning, as I wriggle out of my tight sleeping bag, it still feels as though my finger is tingling from the spot he kissed me last night. I mean, sure, it could just be the fact that I gave myself a nasty little burn from the embers of the fire, but I like to believe it's the magic of those soft lips and the memory of the tenderness we shared.

I can see the sunrise through a gap in the door-flap of the tent. I glance over at Blake, still snoozing in his bag. I wonder what time it is. I could check on my phone, but that would mean turning it on, and I'm trying to conserve as much battery as I can since neither of us knows how long we're gonna be out here.

I send off a quick message to Monica, my sister. She's still in Boulder

My diaper's feeling really full — I could definitely do with changing it, and I don't really want to do that with Blake in the tent with me, so once I escape from my snuggly cocoon, I crawl over to the door, and undo the zipper. 'What do you think?' I say to Fluffkins, 'You up for an early morning adventure?'

Probably, I shouldn't be off for a walk by myself. I mean, we definitely heard a wolf last night. I was a little panicked, and Blake had to speak to me while I fell asleep. He explained to me that wolves get really bad press, and wouldn't ever normally prey on humans.

'They're much more scared of us than we are of them,' he said.

It took me a while, but I did eventually calm down enough to get to sleep. He's got a lovely voice. Deep and rich and warm. Kinda makes me think of honey.

I pull on a jumper — it's a little chilly this morning — and a pair of boots. Until I joined the community at the Little Cabin, I don't think I ever really understood just how much variation there is in birdsong. Now that I'm at an even more isolated location, the dawn chorus is just amazing. Feels almost like I'm having a spiritual experience. It's just me and the birds, saying hello to the sun.

The dogs are sleeping in portable kennels next to our tent. I feel like they kept the wolves away last night, too. Probably the wolves could smell the Doberman Pinschers from miles away.

I walk away from the dogs and the tent, into the vibrant green of the forest enveloping me. My diaper is so full this morning that I'm almost having to waddle. I can feel the super-absorbent material collecting between my legs. I hope that I don't get any chafing — I should probably change it soon. Also, diaper rash definitely is something that I've struggled with in the past, and that is *not* fun. No, thank you, mister.

A Little, romping around the woods all by herself. I feel kinda naughty, and that feels kinda nice.

'What're we gonna find, Fluffkins?' I ask, making Fluffkins walk on my arm, as I swing past a thick-trunked pine tree. 'Do you think there could be treasure in the forest? Or maybe fairies? Shame it's not toadstool season — I bet we'd find a gnome or two. Or maybe a pixie or a brownie.'

I bet Blake wouldn't be happy with me exploring like this. He was so protective of me last night. When he saw that I'd burnt my finger, it was almost like he switched into Daddy mode, like he was telling me off. It was a real thrill. Not only that, it pushed me straight into Little Space. It's been such a long time since I really explored that part of myself, since I felt safe enough to make myself vulnerable. Pretty damn ironic that the person who got me there isn't even a Daddy.

Although...

What if he's a Daddy and doesn't even realize it? What if he just hasn't been with the right Babygirl? It's a delicious thought, that I could be the one to introduce him to the wonderful world of Age Play. I imagine what he'd be like as a stern protector, and it gives me a yummy, tickly feeling of over-excitement.

After five minutes of ducking in and out of the trees, I reach a little clearing. It's pretty here, with clouds of pink spring flowers sprouting in tufts between trunks of trees. Feeling free and close to nature, I pull my overalls down and reveal my diaper to the world. Even if I don't find it that easy to get into Little Space, I'm never without my diaper. I love the crinkly white things, and honestly, I just wouldn't feel like me if I didn't have one on. I feel like wearing a diaper is almost like a promise to myself. I'm saying, 'Dee, even if you can't get into Little Space, you're still a Little, and you're still trying. And that's OK.'

With expert skill, I undo the tabs of the Rearz Safari. It's really full, which can sometimes make it more difficult, but I manage just fine. I've never been naked in public like this before. There's something so freeing about it — so natural. I take a moment to enjoy the feeling of the breeze on my bottom, and on my front bottom. I let out a big sigh.

'Time to get Baby DeeDee in her diapee now, Fluffkins,' I say, my voice super little. I unfold a new diaper and carefully fasten it around my waist. Ah! There's nothing quite like the feeling of a brand-new, fresh diaper against the skin. So dry and reassuring. So tight and comforting. It's only really ever in these moments, when I'm totally alone, that I can feel myself.

I guess it's a matter of shame. Even though this is the person I am, and I'm surrounded by people who live the same lifestyle as me, I still feel ashamed of myself. I feel dirty, and like I'm a freak. Obviously, it had been much worse when I'd lived in Boulder. I only had one Little friend, and I barely ever got the chance to see her. So I felt like I was living a lie. All the customers coming into my bakery had no idea that the woman behind the counter was packing a diapee all day long.

I wonder if I'll ever get the chance to reopen my bakery. I'm hopeful that Carl can track down Jackson, but in reality, how likely is it? I mean, how often do you hear that an entire gang has been brought down? Not often.

I wrap my old diaper in a plastic bag and decide to just explore a tiny bit further into the forest. I don't know what I'm looking for exactly, but I'm enjoying the peace and quiet of this place immensely.

That's when I hear something a little strange. It's a buzzing hum. I decide to follow it. After a minute or so, I discover the source of the hum. Hanging up high in the branches of a tall tree, there's a shifting mass. It takes me a moment to realize that I'm looking at a wild beehive.

'Oh, my goodness!' I exclaim. I watch little black dots approach the mass, and other ones peel off. So many little bees, all working in harmony on their home. 'I wonder if they're honey bees,' I say under my breath.

For a moment, I imagine that I'm stranded in the wild, in a survival situation. Would I ever be brave enough to climb a tree and strip a hive of its honey? I'd be able to make honey cakes if I had all that honey. Mmmm. There's nothing more delicious than fresh, local honey. And nothing more hurty than a bee-sting.

Then, as I'm imagining the hundreds of thousands of stings I'd receive, something moves in the undergrowth. I freeze.

A bear. Oh my god. It's a bear.

A gnarled, dog-like maw sniffing the air. Shaggy brown hair, and dark, beady eyes. Huge paws, curled claws.

Obviously, I've never seen a bear in the wild like this. Heck, I've never seen a bear, period. There's something terrifying about the way this thing moves — it's so confident and uncaring. This thing doesn't give a crap about the buzz of the bees.

The bear lifts its paws up to the tree trunk and sinks its claws into the bark. It climbs the tree with an ease that's terrifying. I still haven't moved — I'm stuck to the spot as though my feet were caked with honey. Within seconds, the bear is on the honey branch. Even though I'm terrified, I can appreciate just how lucky I am that I'm getting to see this. How often has a human seen something like this happen?

Still, I wish I was safely back at the cabin with Blake.

The bear grabs the hive with both paws, and instantly the bees go berserk. The buzzing intensifies, and I see the tiny insects, valiantly fighting the massive bear. The bear is unfazed, and it takes a huge bite out of the hive. It's hard not to imagine those huge jaws biting into me.

Maybe I should leave right now, while this thing is busy with the hive.

*Come on, DeeDee, now's the time to take action.*

I lift my left foot slowly, carefully, but as I do, there's a crack from underneath me. Instantly, the head of the bear snaps straight toward me. Its eyes are on mine and I can feel it trying to work me out. Am I a threat? Am I a rival? Am I a meal?

The bear moves. Back to the tree trunk. I'm shaking, my knees knocking together, my arms trembling. What do I do? What *can* I do?

I should run. I should scream and run.

The bear's approaching me. Sniffing the air again. It moves slowly but then, suddenly, in a terrifying change, the bear starts to charge.

I scream. But it's not the sound I hear. Because from behind me comes a huge roar, an inhuman bellow of rage. I look around, expecting to see something worse than a bear, but instead, I see Blake. He's standing tall, high up on his tiptoes, yelling so loud and deep that I can hardly believe it's coming from his body. He lifts his arms up high in the air and shouts again.

'Back off, bear!' He shouts. 'You don't want this fight!'

The bear keeps coming, and then, just when it's almost close enough for me to smell, Blake steps in front of me and shouts again.

'Not today bear. Not my Girl!'

Somehow, amazingly, the bear stops. It thinks. Then, Blake takes another step towards it, and the bear turns and starts to run back into the undergrowth.

Blake waits a minute, unmoving, his hand raised up, willing me to remain silent. I feel tears streaming down my face. I've never been so scared in my whole life. Right now, I want nothing more than for Blake to hold me tight, to comfort me. But I know that he's doing everything he can to keep me safe.

The bees are still buzzing around frantically, but thankfully, they don't seem interested in stinging us.

Eventually, Blake says, 'Damn Dee, that was close.' He steps up to me and pulls me in close. 'You OK?'

I nod. 'How did you know what to do?'

He laughs. 'I didn't. Just... acted on instinct I guess.'

'You saved me,' I sniff.

'What were you doing out here by yourself?' he asks.

'Needed a diapee change,' I say, holding up the bag with my dirty diaper inside.

'You didn't need to leave for that,' he says. He feels so good with his big arms wrapped around me. I love his smell. Smells like safety. 'I don't mind if you change your diapee in the tent.'

'It's all my fault,' I say, still sniffing. 'I'm always so cocky. It gets me into so much trouble. Just like with the gangsters in Boulder. If I'd just had respect for them to begin with, I wouldn't be in this situation.'

'You're not cocky,' he says. 'You're brave. And why should you respect criminals? I love your bravery, Dee. It's who you are. I admire you.'

It's weird. I'd been expecting him to be angry with me. But he's being so calm, so loving. It's lovely to see this side of him.

'Thank you,' I say, looking up at his big blue eyes.

For a moment, he looks embarrassed. Then, he says, 'Come on. Let's get back to the tent. You need a treat.'

# BLAKE

I'M NOT EXACTLY A master chef at the best of times, but cooking links of sausage on a campfire is about the limit of my abilities.

'Smells delicious,' says Dee. I'm so glad that she's feeling less scared now. Seeing her with that bear was just about the most terrifying thing I've ever seen. And I wasn't even the one getting hunted. I'm kind of half worried that the bear might follow us to the camp, but the smell of the dogs should keep it away.

I realized something else when I saw Delilah so scared and needy. I want this woman. I want her more than anything I think I've ever wanted in my life. Seeing her life in danger crystallized it for me. My mind became hyper-focused, my emotions became certain. I had to save her life, then I *had* to make her mine.

Question is, how can I convince this woman who's looking for a Daddy that that man could be me?

'Hope these aren't too burnt,' I grunt.

I flip the sausage over in the pan. The heat from the fire is intense. I think back to Dee burning her hand yesterday and I wince. Poor thing. She's bold as thunder and bright as lightning.

'I've got bread here,' she says. She holds up a baguette that she baked the other day in the cabin — perfect for a sausage sub.

'OK, let's do this,' I say. I pull the pan out the flames and jiggle the sausages around a bit so that they come loose. Then, I tip the meaty treats into the fresh-sliced bread. The grease seeps into the soft white loaf.

I hear the whining of the dogs from nearby. 'Oh man, it's pretty unfair us eating this treat near the dogs. I'll have to save some for them.'

'You're generous,' she says. 'Not a greedy Little, like me. Sharing doesn't come naturally to us.' Her eyes light up as she bites into the sandwich. 'Oh, this is delicious!'

'Glad you like it,' I say. 'So, what's a Little's favorite food? You know, what's the food that you'd never want to share?'

She gives me a silly look. 'We're not aliens, dumb-dumb. And we don't all have the same favorite food.'

I can be such an idiot sometimes. 'Sorry,' I say. 'I'm just trying to work this stuff out.'

'It's OK,' she says, taking another bite out of her sandwich. 'I get that it's weird. Can I confess something to you?'

'Course.'

'When I first met you, I honestly thought that you were a Daddy.'

I let out a snort of surprise. 'Why?'

'I dunno. It's hard to explain. I just had this sense that, like, you'd make a great Big. I think it's because you're so confident and dominant. I can definitely imagine you looking after me. And punishing me.'

'Punishment? Like, spanking and stuff.'

'Maybe,' she says. 'But like, I sometimes struggle with having a potty mouth. And something I think that my Daddy would maybe like to wash my mouth out if I swear.'

'With soap?' I say, raising an eyebrow.

'Yuck!' she says, sticking her tongue out. 'Some Littles like that kind of thing, but I think I'd prefer water. At least to begin with. I'm not so big on humiliation. I know other people who like it, but not me. I just wanna be looked after.'

'So let me get this straight — you want to be looked after, but you want to be punished, too?'

'Only for my own good!' she squeals.

'I understand, I think,' I say, taking a bite of my own sandwich. Damn, this is tasty. Something about cooking on an open fire makes everything taste better. 'You feeling OK after your run-in with that bear?'

She purses her lips. 'I dunno,' she says. 'It was scary. A big grizzly like that.'

I shake my head. 'No Grizzlies round here, thank goodness. You had a run-in with a black bear. No less scary than a grizzly, but much less dangerous. Chances are, he just wanted to say hello. But you weren't to know that.'

Delilah looks suddenly ashamed of herself. 'You think I was silly for being scared?'

'No way.' I say. 'It was a bear, Dee.' I have a sudden idea. I wonder if it might actually help. 'Hey, a couple years ago, I went through some... trauma. Ended up going to a therapist about it. Most of the therapy didn't do much, but the one thing that worked was actually artist expression.'

'Like, drawing?'

'Well, for me it was actually writing that helped. I'm n-not much of a talker, but I like to write.'

She grins. 'Oooohhh what I wouldn't give to read that.'

I snort. 'You wouldn't like it. It was pretty heavy stuff. Not for anyone else but me.'

'Sorry,' she says, concerned. 'I didn't mean to make light of it.'

'No, don't worry, no offense taken. I was thinking that you might like to draw what happened with the bear? I've got some crayons — brought them from the cabin. Might help you process what happened.'

Her face lights up. 'Yes please, Daddy!' The way she called me that, so natural, so thoughtless. I feel a rush of pride. Am I acting like a Daddy now? Looking after my Little? If this is what it feels like, I think I want more.

It doesn't take long for us to get set up. Dee lies down on a rug next to the fire with a big sheet of card stock and some crayons. She grips the chunky crayon in a confident little fist and starts to drag it across the blank page. As she draws, she sticks her tongue out and waves her legs — she couldn't be any cuter.

As she draws, I treat myself to a coffee, boiled up in the fire, camp-style. It's a gorgeous day, and this has to be the most relaxed I've felt in a while. Despite the adrenaline spike of charging down that black bear, I feel calm. Like everything is just the way it's meant to be.

'I'm done!' she says, after twenty minutes or so of scribbling. She gets up, clearly excited to show me what she's done.

'Let's have a look,' I say, grabbing the drawing. When I see it, my eyes widen. 'Dee, this is amazing.'

She's produced a drawing that's full of color, expression, and vibrancy. Dark brown trunks, buzzing yellow bees, and a scary-looking bear. But there in front of the bear, clear as daylight, is me. And next to the picture of me, she's written, *Daddy Blake My Hero.*

'I feel better,' she says, giving me a look at that wonderful smile.

'I'm glad,' I reply warmly. 'You know, Dee, I think you're a very special person. You're brave, expressive, and cute as heck.'

She's blushing. 'Thank you, Daddy,' she says.

'It's time for part two of your treat,' I say, lying down next to her.

'What's part two?' she asks, her breath quickening.

'Let me show you.'

I rest a hand on her hip, feeling her warmth beneath me. She needs me, I can see that now. She needs my protection, but she needs something else, too. She needs my love. When she feels my touch, she wriggles closer, letting out a nervous chuckle. 'I've been thinking about getting close to you for a long time, Daddy,' she whispers. I stroke the hair off her face, revealing little pink lips.

'I've been thinking about this from the first time I ever saw you,' I say. I brush her lips with mine — tender and soft, but insistent, too.

As soon as I touch her, she whimpers quietly, yielding to the gentle pressure of my lips. She smells wonderful, like vanilla and honey, and as I push harder, I feel her press back toward me. I have to hold back — I want to just swallow her up — the last thing I want to do is overwhelm her. I slip my tongue into her mouth and she twists her own around mine.

'Mmm,' she moans. I wrap my arms around her, tugging her into my body, feeling the softness of her against my hardness. Instantly, she starts to grind into me, running her hands through my hair. 'You feel so strong,' she whispers into my ear, her hand shifting down my back, finding the firmness of my ass. I mirror her moves, exploring her incredible body — the swoop of her lower back, the tender mounds of her buttocks. My cock's going crazy — all I want to do is bury myself in her, open her up and plunder her. But I can't — not yet. First, I need to give her a treat she'll never forget.

'I'm gonna take your diaper off now, Babygirl,' I growl. 'Then Daddy's gonna give you a treat that you'll never forget.'

'I can't wait,' she groans. She unbuttons her overalls, and I tug them off, revealing her toned midriff, and below that, the puffy whiteness of a huge diaper. It's covered in cartoon animals and little flags. I'd been worried that I'd find the sight of a fully grown woman dressed in a diaper to be strange, or unsettling. But now that I know Dee a little bit, it seems like the most natural thing in the world.

She sees me looking at her, and I notice a look of worry in her eye. 'You think I'm a freak?' she asks, uncertain.

I can't help but smile. 'Darling, if you're a freak, that must make me king of the freaks.' She still looks a little unsure, so I kiss her forehead and say, 'No, baby, you're not a freak. You're wonderful.' Then, I slip my fingers under the tabs of her diaper and move it away from her. She bites her lip.

'We're safe, aren't we?' she asks.

'Nothing bad's ever gonna happen to you again,' I say, kissing my way down her tummy. 'You're safe with me, babygirl. Daddy's gonna take good care of you. I promise.'

She smiles a wonderful smile, and then I plant a big kiss on her stomach. I push my hands on her thighs, gently parting her legs and she sighs as I kiss the soft, smooth mound above her pussy.

'I'm your Babygirl now,' she moans. 'You own me, Daddy.'

'Damn right,' I growl. Then, I slip my wet tongue over her glistening pussy, and she shudders with pleasure as I start to delicately lick. She tastes so good, so sweet, that I can't believe my luck. 'I'm gonna eat you up, Baby,' I say, slowly sucking her pussy lips, then slipping my tongue all the way in. She whimpers and I push her legs further apart as she runs her fingers through my hair, tugging at me and grinding her crotch up into my face as I trace circles around her juicy little clit.

'Oh fuuuuu...' she moans, 'oh please...' I can feel her body start to tense up as I keep circling, and then, as I slip a finger right up into her tight little snatch, she arches her back and lets out a yelp, before biting her hand. 'I'm gonna scream,' she warns, 'it feels so good.'

'Let go, Babygirl,' I say, 'I want you to feel it all.' I see her hands grip the blanket beneath us, her knuckles white and her fingers straining. Then, as I gently suck her clit between my lips, she moans — quiet to begin with, but louder and louder until as her body bucks, she shouts out, 'Fuck Daddy!' She pushes her pussy into my mouth and then, in a silent moment of release, she slumps down.

'What a dirty mouth,' I say, making my way up her body until my face is next to hers. I've never seen her more beautiful: red, rosy cheeks, big eyes blinking, a warm flush of pink spreading out across her chest, eyes dancing with giddy pleasure.

'Not as dirty as yours,' she pants, smiling wide.

'Maybe you're right.' I put my arm around her shoulder and hold her tight to me. 'Now I just want to know if you're still excited for part three of your treat?'

She looks at me, wide-eyed, then nods fast and excited. That's the first time I feel it: that this Little is perfect for me, and I'm perfect for her. Nothing's gonna get between us. She's my Forever Girl.

# DELILAH

I'VE NEVER BEEN FURTHER from civilization, and I've never felt safer.

Wrapped up in blankets, by a roaring, crackling fire. Up above, stars twinkling in an ink-black sky. Next to me, my new Daddy. Someone I never thought I'd find.

'It's about time to show you the third part of your treat, Babygirl.'

I've been so amazed and impressed by how quickly Blake has fallen into the role of a Big. It was so obvious to me that he'd be good at it. But when he took control of my body, ripped my diaper off, and gave me the most intense orgasm of my life, everything just felt so right.

'I'm excited, Daddy!' I yelp. I've been in Little Space all day. It's such a wonderful feeling to be so free and happy. I've been needing this for so long. Ever since my store got destroyed, I've not been able to relax until this moment right now.

It's been an amazing day. Lots of drawing, playing with toys that Daddy brought from the Little Cabin, and yummy party food. Even though we're technically hiding out here, Blake's made this expedition into a kind of party. And it's been so much fun!

'First, we need to get these marshmallows toasted,' he says. He looks so gorgeous in the flickering light of the fire. His strong, stubble-frosted jaw and those big, pleasure-giving lips. His masculine nose and his big eyes, dark in the night light.

'We've got marshmallows?' I squeal, cuddling Fluffkins against my chest. 'Did you hear that Fluffkins? We're gonna get sticky lips.'

Blake raises an eyebrow at me.

'Daddy!' I say, fake-scandalized. 'You're so naughty!'

'Sticky lips?' he asks, with a wicked smile on his face. 'Come on, what am I *meant* to think of?'

'About s'mores, silly.' I giggle.

Blake pulls out a massive bag of marshmallows and rips the plastic open. As he does so, he lets out a playful roar. For a moment, he looks just like the bear I saw this morning.

'You better watch out,' he says, 'or Daddy Bear's gonna roar even louder.'

I let out a shriek. 'Not til after the marshmallows.'

Minutes later, there's a bunch of stick-skewered marshmallows blackening over the licking flames of the fire. I love the way they blister and melt. We sandwich the gooey things between some Graham crackers, with a generous chunk of chocolate in each one.

I'm expecting the taste to be divine — I mean, come on, who doesn't love s'mores? But I wasn't expecting the rush of nostalgia. I'm taken back to childhood camping trips, to all those times I've been cozy and happy by the fire. As a kid, my father would take me on fishing trips up and down the state. They're some of my happiest times. Once, my grandma went with us, and that's when she gave me Fluffkins. I cuddle my unicorn to my chest and think back to the good old days.

That's when it hits me: this *is* the good old days. Living in this moment.

'Is this the final part of my treat?' I ask, sighing with pleasure as he snuggles up to me. The fire's gently crackling.

'Well,' he says. 'It's part of it. But I was wondering whether you might like to do some stargazing?'

'Stargazing?' I ask.

'Yeah. You know, looking up at the stars. All the constellations? Those orbs of burning gas, thousands of light years away?'

'I know what a star is, dumb-dumb,' I say. I really like calling him dumb-dumb. I love it because he reacts with a smile. This big, powerful man, gleeful. Happy to be with me. Tolerant of my nonsense.

'Well sorry, Baby Girl,' he says. 'So, if you know about stars, I guess you can point out the big dipper to me, huh?'

We lie back, our heads on pillows. Above us, the cosmos is spread out like an ebony screen, studded with diamonds. Out here, with no real light pollution around, the stars are ridiculously bright and beautiful. Now that I take the time to really look, I can see that there are subtle shades of color up there. Faint greens and vague browns. The whole spectacle is incredible.

'Big dipper... big dipper...' I say, scanning the heavens, pretending to know what I'm looking for.

'It's that there,' he says, seeing through my weak deception. 'Those three stars, that's how you find it. Then you follow them round and then those four make a kind of box.'

Amazingly, I can see exactly the cluster of stars he means. They're shining so bright in the sky.

'I found them,' I say.

'Now isn't that amazing,' he says. 'Out of all the stars in the universe — billions — we're looking at exactly the same ones. We found them together. What are the chances?'

I sigh. 'Probably about the same as the chances of the two of us finding each other.'

My heart's pounding in my chest. I feel a pure, happy excitement. So content and glad to be here with my guardian, my protector.

My Daddy.

'It's nuts, isn't it?' he says. 'To think, I didn't even know I was a Daddy until I just started acting like one. Makes sense though. All I want to do is to look after you, to make sure that you have the safe, nurturing life that you need.'

He gives me a squeeze.

I've been thinking about bringing this up all day, and I'm nervous to ask, but I want to know more about Blake. I look into his gorgeous blue eyes, and I open my mouth to speak, but before I can, he says, 'I know what you're about to ask. You want to know why I was in therapy, don't you? And you probably want to know about my stutter. And my time in the motorcycle club.'

What the heck? Is he psychic or something?

'How did you know?'

He shakes his head, grinning. 'I don't know. I just felt it. We must be pretty in tune, huh? Must be looking up at the stars like that.' He sighs: a long, drawn-out sound. 'Well, obviously, it's all connected. Where do I start? The start, I guess. When I was a kid, I had a stutter, and it was bad. Not like now, when it's mainly only specific words that trip me up. Like *remember-ering*. Or if I'm nervous it can rear its head. Nope, back then. I could barely get through a sentence for the most part.'

'That must have been so tough on you,' I say, stroking his arm.

'Hey, I thought Daddies were meant to comfort their Littles, not the other way around.'

'I'm a person first, Little second.'

He pauses and looks at me. 'You're something special, Dee. I hope you know that.'

I blush, try to say something, but can't get a word out.'

'Anyway,' he continues, 'I got bullied a lot. I think that's why I joined the club. I wanted to seem tough. And what's tougher than a load of criminals, ridin' hogs, dressed in leather? That's how it seemed to me, anyway. For a while, I actually felt good about myself. The stutter went. I owed it all to the guy who sponsored me. Bud.'

'Bud? Doesn't sound so tough.'

He grins. In the firelight, he looks like some kind of Greek God — a living celebration of masculinity and tenderness. 'Bud was a sweetheart, but he was also the toughest guy I've ever known. That is, until he relapsed. Never seen a guy go from dominant alpha to basically a skeleton so fast. That's the dark side of MCs. The drugs. They sell a lot.'

'You didn't take drugs, did you, Daddy?'

He shakes his head. 'Those things always terrified me.' Somewhere nearby, I hear Ajax yawning. 'Bud had always had troubles though. He used to promise me that he'd quit. I loved that man like a father. Nothing prepares you to see someone you love... like that.'

I take his hand in mine. 'I'm sorry.'

'It's OK. It wasn't my fault. I know that now. When I found him, in the toilets of the club's private bar, I couldn't cope with the guilt.'

I try to imagine how I'd feel if I found someone like that. 'Was it an overdose?'

'Exactly. Still had the spike in his vein.'

'Oh no! Blake, I'm so sorry.'

'Anyway. After that, the stutter came back. It's taken me years of therapy and soul-searching, but I finally feel OK about myself.' He stops, pointing up. 'Look!'

I follow his finger up and see a strike of white light across the sky. It's thin and fast and unbelievably bright. And then, it's gone.

'Wow,' I sigh. 'A shooting star. So beautiful, but gone so quick.'

He nods. 'That's why I prefer the polestar.' He points straight up at the brightest star in the sky. 'It's not as flashy, but it's dependable. And it lasts a very, very long time.' He's squeezing my hand, gently rubbing me with a strong finger.

'Do you think,' I ask, 'that our love could last as long as the light from that star?' I hadn't even meant to say love — hadn't even thought about it before this moment. But it feels so right. And Blake doesn't even blink.

'Abso-fucking-lutely,' he growls. 'You and me, babygirl, we're gonna write our names up there, and the whole world's gonna know about how we feel. And other people will use the light from our love to find happiness of their own.'

As he takes me in his arms, I feel like I'm melting, swirling around in a warm pot of fuzzy feeling. His lips find mine and my chest starts to heave as he kisses me long and deep, devouring my mouth, making me sigh. I feel light-headed, I feel fluttery, like my soul's trying to burst out of my chest to get closer to him.

His fingers unloop my top and stroke my skin in the moonlight. I shake, quiver, and wriggle out of my clothes. My diaper's next — still fresh and clean against my skin. It's gone in a second, and my pale form is stark white against the dark blanket. My nipples harden, my pussy seeps. My body's buzzing — I need this man right now. I can't take it anymore.

His top comes off and I see the shape of his body beneath. Hard curves, the strong shape of his abs. Hip bones: prominent and sharp. It looks like the body of a predator, of a beast. But I know that I'm the only prey he's interested in.

'I'm gonna fuck you now, Babygirl,' he growls.

'Please Daddy,' I moan.

He tucks his fingers under his belt and tugs his blue jeans down. I see the bulge of his cock instantly underneath. Fuck, that thing looks dangerous.

'Be gentle,' I whisper.

'Don't worry,' he replies, tugging down his boxers, 'I'm going to give you exactly what you need.'

He leans down on top of me, pinning me down. Kisses on my breasts. Tongue on my nipples. Tiny bites, making me sigh. He's so strong, so soft, but so totally in control. As his hands squeeze my breasts, I feel like I'm his instrument and he's playing me.

His heavy, hot cock, pushes against my stomach. My breathing is ragged, desperate, hungry.

'You're so big,' I pant.

'I'm all yours,' he says. 'And you're all mine.' I feel the tip of his monstrous cock pushing against my pussy lips, gently, forcefully asking my flower to open for him. I'm so wet, so hungry, so ready for him that I can't help but open up.

'Fuucck,' he groans as he slides slowly into me. The pleasure is so intense I bite down on my lip. Then Blake's teeth sink gently into my shoulder and I moan, 'Daddy, that's it. Fuck me, Daddy.'

His hips start to shift, and his love moves into me, surging so powerfully, pushing me apart.

'You're fucking perfect,' he says, taking hold of my hips. He's plowing into me now, and as he does, I feel myself surrendering to him. To his desire, to his dominance, to his thick, incredible cock.

'Yes, Daddy,' I whimper as he hungrily kisses me, as he greedily grabs me as he deeply fucks me.

'You thought that orgasm before was something?' he says, slapping into me, making me moan and pant. 'Just you wait.' And he reaches down and finds my clit. As he looks into my eyes — into my soul — his fingers and his dick work together, whipping me into a frenzy. I feel myself being lifted up so high by my pleasure. So high that I start to see new stars, multi-colored smears of light, as he conquers my body. And at the peak of my ecstasy, I feel his cock surge inside me, and his pleasure mixes with my own, until we fall together, under the moon and stars, one creature, under the shining eyes of the heavens.

*

I don't know what time it is when I turn on my phone. I don't know why I do it. I'm so happy and drowsy and full of yumminess that I'm not even thinking straight.

But when I do, I'm surprised to see a message from my sister.

Except when I read it, I know instantly it's not from her.

If you ever want to see your bitch sister alive again, text back. It's time for us to meet and talk about your options.

My heart almost stops. But when I show Blake the text, he doesn't seem worried.

'Baby,' he says, stretching under the blue sky of a new day, 'it's time to sort out your problems, once and for all.'

'But how?'

He grins. 'Trust Daddy.'

# BLAKE

Back in Boulder. It's a city — one of the biggest in the state — but you can still feel the countryside all around. Wild mountains, trees, the wide blue sky. You can see it all in every direction. Normally I'd find it freeing. But today, I feel lost and lonely. Because somewhere out there is the Little Girl who just a few days ago I fell for so hard I thought I'd never get up.

I had to leave her with Joel in Little Creek. Had no choice. There was no way I was bringing her to this meeting. Not a chance in hell.

'You good?' Carl tilts his aviators down and looks over them at me. Apparently, years ago, Carl was a prizefighter. Bare-knuckle boxer. You can kind of tell by looking at him. His nose isn't wonky exactly, but it does look like he's been roughed up quite a lot. His body is still lithe and powerful, and even though he's shorter than me, I wouldn't like to square up to him.

'I'm good,' I say. 'Just nervous. Never done anything quite like this before. I'm used to standing guard, not taking the fight to a gang.'

'Don't worry,' Carl says, 'this is gonna be fine.'

'Remind me again why you're not just going in with the whole Boulder Police force.'

'There's no way my boss would ever agree to a plan as wild as this. Best to keep this as low-key as possible. Just us, Prince and Tanner.'

As if understanding exactly what Carl said, his dog Prince looks up and gives a small, quiet bark. Prince is a German Shepherd — a beautiful dog, and smart too. Carl reaches down and gives his muzzle a little stroke.

Tanner, Liv's Daddy is here too. He may be Jackson's brother, but there's no love lost between the two of them. He had a run-in with Jackson a couple months ago, and when he heard that Carl and I were planning to take him down, he insisted on coming along, too.

'Wish I could say it's good to be back in town,' Tanner says, looking around at the grimy street. 'But I never was much of a liar.'

We're in a neighborhood I'd never normally come to. The buildings here are run-down, and there's graffiti scrawled over every available surface. I'm not scared of course, but my senses are on high alert.

'Either of you know this place?' Carl asks. He's in civilian clothes, of course — there's no way that we want anyone knowing that he's a cop.

'Funny enough, yes,' says Tanner. 'My old club is a couple blocks away.'

I'm meeting Jackson in an abandoned warehouse just down the street. The plan is I go in, pretend to be Delilah's lawyer, and sign anything they want. The idea is that I trick them into thinking that Dee's happy to sell them her store, then, when their guards are down, Carl, Prince, and Tanner rush in and handcuff the fuckers. I'm wearing a wire to gather as much evidence as I possibly can.

My only worry is that I've got no idea how to act like a lawyer. Still, I'm sure I'll work it out. On-the-job training is how I learn best, anyway. Worked with Dee the other day. I feel like a fully-fledged Daddy now. Found it almost impossible to leave her. I left her a bunch of rules and tasks to complete while I'm gone, including working on her sourdough starter and completing a picture of each of the other

Littles she's staying with right now. I hope it's enough to keep her occupied. I don't want her worrying about me.

'Just remember,' says Carl, 'we can hear everything you'll be saying.' He motions to his earpiece. 'If anything bad goes down, use the codeword, and we'll get in there soon as we can.'

'Got it,' I say, nodding. It's a good thing Carl is licensed to conceal carry. Hopefully, the gangsters won't be packing heat.

The warehouse is right up ahead. Carl and Tanner hang back, waiting for me to approach the big building. It's eerily quiet around here. A stray dog hangs out at the front of the warehouse's front door — a poor, thin-looking mongrel. My immediate urge is to pet the dog and go find him a good meal. But I don't have time for that. As I pass the dog, he looks up at me with sad, brown eyes.

'Good boy,' I say, under my breath, patting his head.

'What was that?' Carl asks, his voice quiet in my tiny, hidden earpiece.

'Nothing, don't worry about it,' I whisper, before pressing the buzzer.

It's only a second before I hear a gruff voice. 'Who's that?'

'Anderson Clark. I'm Delilah's representative.'

I hear a brief, muffled conversation in the background, and then a different voice. 'Representative? Where's the fucking baker?'

'She's nearby, and she'll be coming to pick up her sister as soon as we've sorted the paperwork.'

There's a high-pitched voice in the background. It's a woman's voice, muffled. Sounds like she's gagged. Those monsters are gonna fucking pay if they've hurt a hair on my Girl's sister's head.

'Is that Monica?'

'Come in and see for yourself.' There's a cruel arrogance in that voice. When I hear it, I feel encouraged. Arrogance is weakness. I can use that.

I hear the clunk of the door as it unlocks. I step through. Luckily, there's no-one here. Need to make sure that Carl and Tanner can get in. I take a breeze block that was lying nearby and wedge the door open with it, that should do it.

As I make my way through the warehouse, I start to feel more and more nervous. Is this crazy? What if I end up getting Monica hurt, or worse? I'd never be able to live myself. I'm also getting crazy flashbacks to my days in the Motorcycle club. This is exactly the type of place where Bud would do drug deals and other shady shit.

'Keep focused, Blake,' I whisper under my breath, forgetting for a moment that Carl can hear me.

'Good advice,' he says, straight into my ear.

I see stairs ahead of me, and at the top, loitering by the entrance to another room is a tough-looking guy. He looks me up and down. I'm wearing a suit today, in an effort to try to look lawyerly, and he must be surprised because he's staring at me like I'm some kind of alien.

'In here,' he says, in a deep, resonant voice. I must look nervous, but that suits the story I'm trying to sell. I'm prepared to see something bizarre, but what I see when I step through the door shocks me to my core. A young woman, in tattered, ripped clothes is sitting in a hard wooden chair with her back to the wall of a small, dim-lit room. What have they done to her? She's got bruises over half her face, and her clothes look like they've been actively torn. There's a filthy rag in her mouth, pulled so tight that there's no way she'd be able to speak. To be honest, I'm kind of surprised she's managing to even make the whimpering, soft sound she is.

'Monica?' I ask, the concern plain in my voice.

'You two know each other?' It's that same cruel voice from before. It's coming from a cruel-looking face. Sunken blue eyes, above deep, dark bags. Sallow skin and unkempt stubble. There's an intelligence to this face, and a kind of lean, nasty pride. This has to be Jackson, just has to be. He's tall and lean, and I can see the vaguest family resemblance between him and Tanner. They both have the same face shape, although their hair and eyes couldn't be more different.

'No sir,' I say, trying to seem as meek as possible. 'Just assumed.'

There's another man next to Jackson, a short, powerfully built man with fat pink cheeks and a shaved head. In front of them is a table, covered in paperwork.

'I'm not happy that Delilah's not here,' says Jackson, pacing back and forth. His eyes are twitching — it's obvious he's on something.

'She'll be here soon enough, sir,' I say. 'Just wanted me to make sure everything's in order with the transfer of the property rights.'

'Whatever,' he says, then he looks me in the eye. 'You need to know mister...'

'Clark.'

'Mister Dipshit, that if you try anything funny, I'm gonna kill Monica. And her blood'll be on your hands.' Monica's eyes widen, pleading with me.'

'S-sure,' I say.

'O-OK then,' says Jackson, mocking my stutter. His goon of a friend laughs. Sounds like a fucking blocked drain. 'Well take a seat, Clark Kent. Time to sign some fucking forms.'

I do as he asks, sitting down at the table. I keep my eyes on Monica. She must be terrified. I wish there was some way I could let her know that everything's gonna be OK. She's a brave woman — staying in Boulder even after the mob was threatening her sister. I hope she won't pay the price for that bravery.

I start to look through the forms. They mean nothing to me. I better try to get some information out of these idiots. If any of the charges are going to stick in court, we're gonna need as much evidence as possible. 'S-so, if you don't mind me asking, why are you *so* keen on buying this particular store?' I look at a page, pretending I'm considering some clause or other.

'Simple. Revenge.'

'Against Delilah?'

He snorts. 'I don't give a fuck about Delilah. All I care about are those freaks out at the Little Cabin.'

I feel the hairs on the back of my neck tingle. So this isn't about Dee.

'At first, I just wanted to collect protection money. But when I found out that one of those perverted Daddies from the Little Cabin was buying fucking cakes from her bakery, I knew I wanted to shut it down.'

'Just for spite?' I ask, pretending to sign something.

'That's right, Sh-Sherlock,' he grins. 'But it's more than that. I'm going to take that place apart. Cut off their luxuries, then destroy the things they actually need. Ruin their fucking crops. Kill their animals.'

'But why?' I ask.

He raises an eyebrow. 'They took something that belongs to me.'

'Liv?' I say. Fuck fuck fuck. I've blown it.

Suddenly, there's recognition on his face. 'How do you know that name?' Shit. It's *go* time. I hope I got enough on tape to bury this piece of garbage.

'Mayday,' I whisper under my breath. Carl must have been ready to go because I immediately hear the snarl and bark of Prince, busting through the front door. But before anyone can make it to the room, Jackson jumps back. He pulls something from his pocket — a knife.

Less than a second later, he's standing right next to Monica. And the knife's by her throat. Monica screams through the rag.

*Think, Blake, think.*

'I knew there was something about you, Clark,' he says, pushing the wicked knife against Monica's pale throat. I'm too far from them to make a move. I can hear the sound of a tussle outside. I can't count on Carl and Tanner to help me out. I have to move now. But I don't have anything except...

Time to find out if the pen truly is mightier than the sword. I glance down at the fountain pen in my hand. It's the one I used to write poetry with — it's heavy, steel-tipped, solid enough to do some damage. If I can just hit the right spot.

I pause, looking straight into Jackson's eye. I feel the world slow down as my mind focuses, preparing to take the shot. And then, with a flick of the wrist and a snap of my arm, I fling the heavy pen as hard as I can straight into Jackson's eye.

The blunt end strikes his right eye hard and Jackson yelps. He flicks his own hand to his face, then moves to cut Monica, but he's too late. I'm already on top of him, knocking the knife from his flimsy hand, holding him down. A second later, Tanner is next to me.

'You idiot, Jackson,' he says Tanner. 'I knew it was only a matter of time before you'd fuck up.

I rush to Monica, undo her bonds, yank the rag from her mouth. She's crying, huge sobs. Now that I'm close, I can see the resemblance to Dee, and it's making me emotional. She throws her arms around my neck and sobs into my shoulder.

'Who are you?' she cries.

'I'm Blake,' I say. 'This isn't how I imagined meeting you, but I guess, in a way, I'm your sister's boyfriend.'

She moves back, looks confused, then passes out in my arms.

# DELILAH

## THREE WEEKS LATER

'I MAY BE STAYING with you guys,' says Monica, dryly, 'but there's no way that you're ever gonna get me to wear one of these.' She's holding up one of my Rearz diapers, with a look of confused amusement on her face.

'Good,' I say, grinning, 'that means there's all the more for me.'

Since Blake rescued Monica from Jackson's clutches, things have been insane at the Little Cabin. Things have changed a lot.

We've had people come around. Reporters. You see, the daring raid of the three Daddies on Jackson's gang has become quite famous. Jackson was working with one of the biggest, baddest, most dangerous gangs in the whole of Colorado.

At first, Joel was turning reporters away, even after they pleaded that they wanted to cover the story in a tasteful way. Eventually, though, Joel had an idea. He contacted his brother Caleb, who works in public relations in New York City. He's due to join us at the compound in a couple weeks to come up with a strategy to deal with the press.

'How long do you think you're gonna stay?' I ask.

'Well,' says Monica, thoughtfully, 'I think my customers are gonna be chomping at the bit to get some of my cake down their throats by now. I've had enough of a vacation I think.'

Monica is looking much better. The bruises have almost entirely gone. I can't believe that Jackson kidnapped her just to get to me. I don't think I'll ever be able to thank Blake for all he's done for me.

'What about you?' she asks. 'Have you thought about re-opening?'

'I have,' I nod. 'But I'm just not sure.'

'And this place? You gonna stay here.'

'Kinda. I think I'm gonna move to Little Creek. That way I'll be close enough to the compound here, without being totally isolated. Turns out that me and wood-fired ovens don't mix. So I think I'm gonna sell the store in Boulder and set up shop here.'

'Hmmmmm,' says Monica. 'Would you sell me the store? That way we keep grandma's place in the family, and I can expand Monicakes.'

'I'm gonna have to think abou— I'm only kidding, of course I will!'

She drops the diaper and gives me a squeeze.

Suddenly, there's a knock on the cabin door.

'Ah, that'll be Blake.'

'Have fun,' Monica says. 'Don't be naughty!'

'Impossible,' I say.

I open the door and sure enough, my Daddy's waiting for me. I still get a thrill every time I see him — that gorgeous, honest face, those beautiful eyes, and that hulking, powerful form. He smiles a soft smile. 'I got the juice. Have you got the cookies?'

I nod.

'Then let's get stargazing.'

*

We come out by the lake every Saturday night. Each week, Blake teaches me a new constellation, and I bake him some new confectionery. I know there's no such thing as the perfect relationship, but...

'I hope you don't mind,' he says, biting into a hazelnut choc-chip, 'but I made something for you.'

'Course I don't mind, Daddy,' I say.

The fire crackles in the background as the two of us curl up.

'Well, actually, Atlas made it for me. But I came up with the name.' He pulls out a little torch and unrolls a sheet of paper, before passing it over to me. When I see what it is, my heart melts into a pool of warm chocolate.

In beautifully written handwriting are the words Moon And Stars Bakery. Swirled around the words are glittering stars, including the big dipper and the pole star. It's a gorgeous composition.

'I love it.'

'How do you feel about going into business together?'

'Me and you?' My heart's reformed now, and it's pounding in my chest.

'Sure. First I'll do security. Then, when you've trained me up, I can help with the actual baking. I'm a quick study, and honestly, my days of fighting and guarding are over. Only person I want to look after now is you.'

'You'd move to Little Creek with me?'

'I'd move to fucking anywhere with you, Baba.' He grips me in those powerful arms, suddenly all lust and passion. 'I'd follow you to the ends of the earth — no — to the end of the universe.'

'Blake, I don't know what to s-'

'Just say yes.' His lips meet mine and I'm lost in him.

'Just promise me one thing,' he says, pulling away.

'What?' I ask, panting.

'No Carolina Reaper pie.'

I grin. I cry. We kiss again.

\* \* \*

**Read on for Caleb and Annika's story: *Claimed by Daddy*!**

# Chapter Seven

## CLAIMED BY DADDY

# ANNIKA

'Wow. That dress makes you look really.... mature, Annika.' Brenda gives me an acidic look, with a smile so sharp it could cut my dress to shreds. 'Do you need help with any of that stuff?'

I must look insane right now. I'm clutching a steaming cup of latte in my left hand, and I've got a stack of papers underneath my right shoulder. There's a pen clamped between my teeth and I'm got my handbag firmly wedged between my knees.

'Thank you, Brenda,' I answer curtly, past my pen. 'I'm fine, thank you.' I wish I could think of something equally back-handed to spit back at her, but I just can't. Especially before I've had any coffee.

I wish I didn't have to walk past Brenda Bryce's desk to get to my own workstation. Not only is she here before me every single fricking day, but she never, ever fails to make some kind of snarky comment about the way I look. I waddle past her with about as much dignity as I can muster (not much) and continue to my desk.

Truth is, the reason Brenda's so dang irritating is because of how perfect she is. Amazing at her job. Absolutely gorgeous. Immaculately dressed. If she wasn't so dang mean to me all the time, she'd actually be someone I might look up to.

I wonder what today will bring. No doubt, I'll be reporting on celebrity sightings and writing vacuous stories about fashion and sport. Ugh, I must sound so bitter.

Well, I guess I *am* bitter. Just a little bit.

See, back in the good old days, the days before Trent Linus became the editor of the Denver Chronicle, I was the lead crime reporter at the paper. It often happens that when a new editor takes over the running of a paper there's a reshuffle of the reporting staff. Trent brought Brenda across from his old paper in New York and installed her in my old job.

Technically, I was promoted. My new job title is *Features Editor*, but the truth is I just write up whatever crappy stories no one else wants to deal with.

Lost animals? Give it to the Features Editor.

D-list celeb spotted in a BBQ joint in town? Sounds like the perfect job for Annika.

Local news anchor suffered a wardrobe malfunction live on air? The Features Editor would *love* to hear about it.

I reach my desk and put my coffee down, before dumping the stack of old papers down next to my keyboard. There's a flashing red light on the phone next to my computer. A message. Already. Ugh. I wonder which of the disgruntled maniacs who call me on a regular basis to discuss insane conspiracy theories I'm going to have to speak to this morning. I part my legs and my handbag falls to the floor.

'OK, Annika, time to work.' Talking to myself is one of about a bazillion bad habits I have. I do it all the time, and have done ever since I was a kid. It's one of the reasons I've always struggled to get a boyfriend, although honestly, it's probably not the thing that's held me back the most.

I pick up the phone and press a couple buttons to access my voice-mail. I'm surprised to hear that it's not a disgruntled local's voice I hear, it's Trent.

'Annika, I want you in my office soon as you get in this morning. I've got something to talk to you about. Something exciting.'

That's it. How mysterious! Could it be that I'm actually going to be allowed to report on something worthwhile for once?

Brent's office is all the way across the news floor. A lot of newspaper offices around the country have downsized over the past decade or so. Print media is in decline, after all. Not the Denver Chronicle, though. Thanks to a robust early adoption of online journalism, we've managed to retain the vast majority of our staff. It means that we still have a huge, traditional news floor, with dozens of desks clustered around TV screens covered in rolling news coverage. I'm fairly young — only twenty-seven — but I get a sense of the history of this place. It was why I was so excited to join, straight out of college. Now though, I feel as though I'm adrift, with no hopes for the future.

I knock sharply on the door to Trent's office, and he responds almost immediately.

'Come in!'

The smell of the office is oppressive. Trent isn't meant to smoke in here, but it doesn't stop him. No one on the staff wants to challenge him on any of his behavior. He's always got a cigar on the go, and the acrid stench of the dark black smoke stinks out the entire place.

He's smoking right now, and fumes from his Cuban sting my eyes as soon as I step in.

'Annika, good to see you,' he says in his brash, perpetually impa-tient voice. 'Take a seat. I've got an exciting opportunity to discuss.' He gestures to the beat-up old chair in front of his desk. I sit down, a little awkward. I've not had much time alone with Trent since he joined the paper.

'That sounds good,' I say, but I sound unsure.

Trent smiles. He's got a strange face — leather skin and a short, bristly mustache under his thick, crooked nose. Whenever I see him smile, it never seems as though he's sincerely happy, and this smile is no exception. He just looks even more cynical than he did before.

'Trust me,' he says, 'this is gonna be right up your street.' He opens up a drawer in his desk and takes out a folder, then he throws it across the desk to me. I pick it up, but before I've even had a chance to read it, Trent says, 'Ever heard of Adult Babies?'

Oh crap. The blood in my veins feels like it's turned to ice. Does Trent know about me?

'Ugh, yeah, I've heard of them.'

'Remember a couple months ago, there was that story about the Jackal gang? Those two civilians and a country bumpkin sheriff brought down the head of the biggest criminal organization in Colorado?'

Oh, thank God. He doesn't know about me. 'Ah, I see what you're getting it. Those men are part of some kind of Adult Baby community out of Little Creek, right?'

'That's it,' he says, clearly happy to see that I know what he's talking about. I glance down at the papers in my hand now and see that it's the edition from the day of the gang bust. 'Imagine a group of perverts living in some kind of filthy sex cult in our state.'

I'm not surprised by Trent's take on the situation. He's a nasty man, and he's got no time for anyone he perceives as 'weird' or 'different'.

'Yeah, I guess maybe it might be a little worrying for our readers.' I try to be as diplomatic as I can.

'A *little worrying*? It's immoral, what they do. Grown women, wearing diapers? Men, pretending to be their fathers?'

'I don't think the men actually pretend to be the fathers, sir.'

He eyes me with suspicion. 'Course they do.'

'Right.'

Truth is, I actually know quite a bit about the Daddy Dom Little Girl subculture. I've done lots of research into it over the years. And not just out of professional curiosity. See, I've never found a man dominant enough for me, and for a while, I wondered whether I might be happier in a sub/Caregiver relationship. And if it weren't for my shame, I might have taken the research a little bit further...

'Anyway, I got a call from one of the freaks. Apparently, ever since we published our story, they've been having trouble. Local people — understandably concerned — have been making their concerns known.'

'You mean people have been harassing them?'

'I don't know the details,' he waves his hand dismissively. 'Anyway, he suggested that we send a reporter to get the real story of their community. So I thought I'd send you.'

My heart pounds in my chest. 'Me?'

'Yeah. You like stories about sex and crime, don't you? You miss your life on the crime desk?'

'Well, I guess so, bu-'

'Then this is perfect. You go there, uncover all the filthy secrets, dish the dirt on all the perverts living in sin together, then you write the story of the century!' He looks so excited he's virtually foaming at the mouth.

'You want me to write a hit-piece?'

'Exactly!' He grins that joyless grin of his again.

This all feels so off to me. I know that people would lap up an article like this — exposing the 'freaks' in our midst. Scandal and fear sells. But I don't want to be that kind of reporter. I don't want to whip people up into a frenzy, especially when innocent Littles could get hurt.

'I don't think I can do it,' I say.

Trent looks at me with so much confusion I might as well have just said I'm a giant floating dog. 'What the fuck do you mean?'

'I mean, I don't want to do it. I don't think those people are the freaks you think they are. I think they're just normal people trying to live normal lives.'

'Bullshit,' he says. 'You're honestly telling me that you don't find the thought of grown people wearing diapers and pretending to be children to be fucked-up?'

'I don't,' I say. 'In fact, I can kind of understand it. Modern life is so weird and relentless and miserable, I can totally relate to the idea of wanting to relive your childhood. And I don't even think that age-play has to be sexual. It can just be a relaxation thing.'

He snorts. 'Of course it's sexual. It's degenerate. It's an abomination.' He sighs, then draws air sharply between his teeth. 'Well, I guess I'm just gonna have send Brenda to cover it. She'll do a good job for me.'

Oh crap. If he sends Brenda, she'll tear those people apart. His little lap dog will do exactly what Trent tells her.

'Fine,' I say, quickly, 'I'll do it. I'll go.'

He grins a sickly grin. 'Lovely.'

As I walk back to my desk, I see Brenda looking over her computer at me. A thought hits me: why did Trent ask me to do this at all? Why didn't he just ask Brenda to do it in the first place?

Thing is, though, if I knew the real truth behind it, I would never have agreed to the story.

# CALEB

'**F**UCK, JOEL, DON'T YOU just go crazy out here with nothing to do?'

I'm looking out across a field of bushy green crops. In the distance, smoky mountains rise up above a clean, clear lake. A lot of people would look at this view and see a paradise. Me? I just see a wasteland.

'You know I love it, brother,' Joel says, grinning. He's changed so much since the last time I saw him. Gone is the city banker with pale skin and a lithe body. In his place is a rugged mountain man — bearded and thickly muscled. His skin is deeply tanned now, and he has laughter lines dancing at the corner of his eyes. 'There's no way I'd go back to the city now. My life out here is all I ever wanted.'

'Until the hate mail started, right?'

Joel looks suddenly serious. 'That's right. Not just hate mail, either. Recently, we've been getting threats, too. After all the crazy stuff that happened with Jackson and the stories the papers wrote about us, I knew I had to get you in to change the public perception of this place.'

Joel runs a kind of commune for Littles and Bigs in the Colorado wilderness. For the longest time, he ran this place under the radar and off-grid. No-one really knew about the slowly growing collection of log cabins, and the quirky age play community they house. Now, though, ever since some of the Bigs of this place took down an evil criminal gang operating out of Boulder, the Little Cabin has been under the glare of a harsh media spotlight.

'This is meant to be a vacation for me,' I grin at my brother. I work for a Public Relations firm in New York. We handle the accounts of a wide variety of people who operate in the public eye, as well as a couple large companies. Our clients span the gamut of human experience. Everything from NBA players to artisan bakeries. 'But I've got a feeling that I'm gonna be doing more work than play.'

One thing I've got zero experience with, however, is improving the reputation of a DDlg community.

'Hey, you can get some swimming in the lake done, if you have time between your duties.' My brother smiles his wicked smile. I've known that smile for years — ever since we were kids. Normally it means that we're about to do something that'll get us into trouble. This time, though, it's kinda the opposite.

'Why do I feel like I've been duped?' I sigh, thrusting my hands into my pockets.

'Come on, you knew what you were getting into.'

I snort. 'Hardly. What was the subject line of your email? Free vacation alert? Something like that.'

He chuckles. 'I can draw up a bill if you don't feel comfortable staying here for free.'

It's my turn to laugh. 'If anything, I think I've gonna be the one drawing up an invoice for my expertise.'

He looks a little more serious. 'Look, Caleb, I'm sorry I brought you here under false pretenses. The fact is that I need your help, and I didn't know where else to turn. Plus, I know you're already sympathetic to the type of place I'm trying to run here. I can't imagine anyone who's not living the DDlg lifestyle managing PR for this place.'

It's true. Like my brother, I'm a Daddy. We have slightly different styles, but the same basic belief: women deserve to be coddled and protected, and anyone who wants to live as a Little should be given the opportunity to do so without questions being asked.

'I'm just busting your balls, Joel,' I say. 'Of course I'm gonna help. I can't have maniacs threatening this place without you guys having the chance to set the record straight.'

The look of relief and gratitude on his face is instant and heart-warming.

'Plus,' I continue, 'at least I've got an excuse not to do *real* work on vacation now. So in a way, you're making me take a break after all.'

'That's the spirit,' says my big brother with a smirk. 'Reluctant acceptance.'

'OK,' I say, switching effortlessly into work mode. 'First thing we need to do is get in touch with some local, friendly media outlets. I'd stay away from whichever paper wrote that hit piece on you — what did you say it was called? The Denver Carbuncle?'

'Chronicle,' he says, looking a little uncertain.

'What?' I narrow my eyes.

'Let's head back to my office. I've made some... arrangements.'

'What kind of arrangements?'

*

'What's the point in bringing in an expert if you're just gonna do your own, insane plan?'

I'm pacing up and down Joel's diaper-stuffed office, furious with my big brother — not for the first time.

'I didn't know you were definitely coming,' he replies. 'And I couldn't afford to wait around. Things have been getting worse and worse around here. People are so freaked out at the thought of a DDlg community that they've actually been trekking out here to spy.'

'I get that,' I say, 'but contacting the Chronicle is insane. I guarantee, no matter what they might have told you, that the only reason they're sending a journalist out here is to write the most damning, incriminating hatchet job you can imagine.'

Joel shakes his head. 'No, the editor was very clear. A fresh start, he said. Totally objective.'

'Joel,' I say, clutching my forehead, 'how can someone as smart as you be this dumb. Sometimes I have to remind myself that you're a billionaire.'

'What?' He looks genuinely confused.

'Journalists lie. Every last one of them. They don't care about being objective, they don't care about the truth. All they care about is clicks and sales. They want the juiciest, weirdest, most shocking content they can publish. And let's just say that an exposé about a bunch of age play freaks is gonna sell a fuck-ton more papers than a measured report on the activities of consenting adults who've had enough of a society that's rejected them.'

He looks grim. 'You really think so?'

'I know so, bro.'

It's not like my brother to be anxious, but the signs of stress are clear on his face. 'Have I made a huge mistake? Put everyone here in even more danger?

*Come on Caleb, think. This is what you do every day. Turn problems into opportunities.*

That's when it hits me. 'What if there was a way to give them exactly what they want, but do it in such a way that they *have* to be sympathetic?'

'You've had an idea?'

'It's pretty extreme,' I say. 'And there's no guarantee that it'll work.
It totally depends on the type of journalist they're sending. She's a
woman, right?'

He nods. 'I did some research into her. She seems to be quite a
serious person. Used to do a lot of work on crime and vice, but now
she does more of a variety of reporting. What's your idea?'

'My idea,' I say, stroking my chin, 'is that we regress her.'

Joel's eyes widen and his jaw drops. 'Without her knowledge?'

'Of course not!' I reply. 'You really think I'd do that to someone
without their consent?'

'No... I just, I dunno, this is all so tough to get my head around. So
we have to convince her?'

I lean back in my chair. 'We have to convince her.'

*

It's not that much later when Atlas comes by. He's one of the
Daddies here, a big Greek guy who's a firefighter by trade.

'There's a journalist here,' he says, with suspicion in his eyes. 'Says
she has a meeting with you, Joel? That she's staying here? I thought
we were turning journalists away.'

'It's OK,' says Joel, 'tell her I'll be out to meet her in a second. She's
an exception.'

Atlas doesn't look entirely convinced, but he heads back out. Joel
hadn't told me that the other Bigs and Littles didn't know about
Annika coming to stay. I wonder if he's trying to protect them, or if
there's something else going on.

'Right, Caleb, it's all up to you. I'll go out and introduce myself,
then send her in here to talk to you. I know you can do it.'

'And if I can't convince her?'

'Then we do what we can.' He leans in and takes my hand. 'I'm so grateful to you for giving this a shot, bro.' He claps his other hand on my shoulder. 'Hey, have you been working out?'

It's a joke, of course. Joel knows I'm obsessed with healthy eating and exercise. 'Ha ha,' I say sarcastically. 'Just get out there and don't say anything dumb.'

As soon as he leaves me in here alone, I start to feel something unfamiliar. It's nerves. Even though I'm about to try to coach a journalist, I feel miles out of my comfort zone. I've never actually told anyone other than my brother that I'm a Daddy, either, and it feels as though I'm about to come out to a stranger.

*Just remember, whoever she is, that she's a journalist, and she's not to be trusted.*

Why did I ever agree to come out here? I should have known that something weird would happen. Eventually, I hear the murmur of voices from the front of the cabin, then the door swings open. It's Joel, and there's a funny look on his face. What is that expression? Surprise? Delight? Something else entirely?

'So, Annika, this is my brother, Caleb.' As he says the words, a figure steps up beside him. She's tall, and she's slim, and she's unbelievably attractive. She's got flame-red hair, down to her shoulders. Her skin is pale, her eyes green as gemstones behind cute, round spectacles. She's used bright red lipstick on bow-shaped lips. This heavenly creature isn't just my type.

She's perfect. Nerdy, sexy, and elegant as hell. There's no way she's going to agree to what I'm about to suggest, no matter how delicately I frame my request.

'Hi,' I say. My voice comes out hoarse and guttural. I must sound like I'm angry or something.

'Pleased to meet you,' Annika replies. She's clearly on edge — being in this environment must be bizarre for her. Well, it's nothing compared to what's coming.

'I'll leave you two to discuss the ins and outs of your stay here,' Joel says, holding a hand up, sheepishly. Then, without another word, he turns and leaves.

Annika slides into the chair opposite the desk, then leans forward. I absolutely do not glance down at her generous cleavage — no siree. Doing that would be both creepy and unprofessional. Somehow, though, I feel bad looking at every single part of her, because there isn't a square inch of her that isn't making me feel super-fucking attracted to her.

'So,' she says in a surprisingly low-pitched voice, 'what have you got in store for me?'

I gulp.

# ANNIKA

**M**Y HEART'S RACING. I can feel sweat on my brow. I haven't been this anxious in years. And all it took was one question. My voice, when I reply, is more wobbly than jello.

'No, I haven't heard of regression before.'

The man in front of me is insanely attractive. Like, I can practically feel my panties melting off me as he stares at me with those cold blue eyes. Aside from the fact that he looks as though he rips trees out of the ground as a warm-up to a real work-out, he looks super-smart. And that's what really gets me going.

'I presume that you've done some research into the Daddy Dom/Little Girl lifestyle though?' Something about the way he talks makes me feel as though he's worked with the media before. He's so confident and knowledgeable, as though he's pre-empting every answer to each question that he's asking me.

'Sure,' I say. What I don't add is that I've been researching age play since I was about eighteen years old. 'I guess I know the basics. It's a particular kink, right? An element of BDSM. But the reason I'm here is to find out more. So that I can pass on that information to our readers.' I'm trying not to give anything away, but I'm super worried that he somehow knows, that he can somehow smell that I'm interested in his lifestyle.

'I guess some people think of it that way,' he says, ignoring my talk of the readers. 'But the truth is a little more elusive. You see, the BDSM subculture is, for the most part, focused on sexual intimacy. DDlg relationships are a little different.'

I scrabble around for my notepad. Feels like this is the kind of thing that I should be writing down. When Caleb sees that I'm starting to write, he stops and waits a moment. Then he says, 'You know, I think that really, I'd like to do something with you that's not your typical newspaper article. I want to try to make sure that you really understand what life is like here at the Little Cabin. And to do that, I want to regress you.'

My throat goes dry, and I feel so suddenly shocked that I almost drop my pen.

'You want to...'

'To regress you. To connect you with your inner child. To help you get to Little Space.'

I laugh nervously. 'That sounds a little... extreme to me. Don't you think a more traditional article would be more sympathetic towards your cause?'

He shakes his head. 'Nope. I know that the only way your readers will get the full picture is if you go through the process. I want you to learn why it is that people enjoy this lifestyle. I want you to see that it's not some freakish, sex-obsessed cult. We're real people here, with feelings and needs.'

There's a feeling of dread growing in my gut. I'm scared. Not of regression. Of liking it.

'No,' I stammer, 'I don't think it's appropriate.'

He gives me a smile. 'You know, you might be surprised by how much you enjoy it.'

Damn, he's cocky as well as smart. And those blue eyes are doing something strange to my insides. 'So you're saying what? That *you* want to be my Daddy? That's what it's called, right?'

He nods, not taking his eyes off mine for a moment. 'That's exactly right.'

I imagine what it might be like to be regressed by someone like Caleb. For him to teach me about Little Space. Would he make me wear a diaper? Would he spank me, punish me when I'm naughty? Just the thought of it is making me feel turned on, even though I'm doing everything I can to keep a lid on my arousal.

I shift in my chair.

'What exactly would it involve?' I wonder what Trent would say if he even knew that I was considering letting this beast of a man regress me. Actually, I know what he'd say. He'd call me a freak, a degenerate. Would he be right to call me that?

'Lots of play time,' Caleb answers. 'I would wash you, dress you, organize your daily routine. I'd feed you and make sure that all your needs are taken care of.'

'Like a nanny?'

He shakes his head. 'Like a Daddy.'

For some reason, I can't get over the idea that he said he'd wash me. I mean, that would involve seeing me naked, right? 'When you say wash do y-'

'Your face and your hands,' he says, quickly and decisively. 'And when I say I'd dress you, I'm only talking about choosing your clothes, not physically dressing you. I don't want to do anything that would make you feel uncomfortable.'

'Oh really?' I ask, sardonically. I instantly regret it, of course. He's being open and honest with me, and I'm doing my usual trick of snapping back like a petulant kid. I eye a stack of adult diapers in a colorful dresser next to the desk. 'What about Diapers?'

He gives me a quizzical look. 'There's no way you'd agree to wear a diaper, is there?'

I ask myself the question, and can't quite form a solid answer in my mind. I mean, there's no way I'd ever do anything as extreme as wear a diaper, right?

'No,' I say, laughing nervously. 'Course not.' I wonder if he's more convinced by my tone of voice than I am.

'Look,' he says, leaning in close, 'I know that to you, this might all be some big joke. Weirdos in the woods playing dress-up and baby talk. But this is our life, and it means something to us.'

'I get that,' I say, trying to soothe his fiery reaction. 'I'm not here to judge.'

He snorts and kicks back in his chair. 'Of course not,' he says, his voice dripping with sarcasm. 'Of course the journalist from the big city is here to write a fair, balanced article about the joys of the age play lifestyle.'

'Hey,' I say, firing back. 'There's a reason I was picked for this job, you know. I'm a serious person, and I plan to write a fair article, whether you believe it or not.'

'I don't.' His voice is cold as ice. Obviously, this guy hates me. Journalists in general, too, but me in particular.

'You're not doing a very good job of convincing me to do this regression thing.'

'I know journalists,' he spits. 'I know the kind of lies you guys will print if it means you'll sell a few more papers.' So he *does* have a problem with journalists.

There's electricity in the air — a crackle of tension that seems to come from a deeper place than just animosity.

Now that I think about it, I know that Trent would be delighted to hear I was being regressed. I'm sure he'd think it would make for a lurid story, exactly the kind of story that gets clicks and shares.

'Listen,' I say, trying to clear the air, 'I think we got off on the wrong foot here.' My smile must be nervous as hell right now. 'How about this for an idea? I'm not saying I *won't* be regressed by you. I agree that it would make for a pretty interesting story. But for now, why don't you just show me around the place? Let me see the set-up here.'

For a moment, he looks unsure. Then, seemingly with some effort, his expression softens. Finally, a curt, tense nod.

*

I'm amazed by the beauty and peace of the place. It's set among some of the most pristine mountain woodland that I've ever seen. There's a view across a shimmering lake, and the dark green firs crowd around like eager friends, chatting and gossiping as gentle breezes make their needles rustle.

It seems like there's a couple different log cabins out here, all centered around a communal outdoor area. The cabins all have cute plaques over them, named after — I presume — the people who live in them. There's Ella's and Joel's, Gabe's and Bailey's, and Atlas' and Mia's. The only thing that seems a little off about the situation, is that I haven't seen a single other person. I thought this was meant to be a community.

'No-one about?' I ask.

He looks down at his watch. 'Oh, they're here alright. It's playtime right now.'

'Playtime?'

'That's right. Like I said before, part of being a good Daddy is making sure that your Little follows a pretty set-in-stone routine. Thing about Littles is that they crave structure and need guidance. So every day between ten and midday, everyone plays together.'

It actually sounds pretty good. I'm terrible at organizing my own time, and I've often wished that I had someone to tell me exactly what to do, and when to do it. 'So where do they play?' I ask, jotting down some notes in my pad.

'Depends on the day, and the weather. Even though it's a pretty day today, I think the girls are in the Nursery?'

'The Nursery?' For some reason, the word catches in my throat.

'Just up ahead,' Caleb says, motioning down a dirt track which winds its way between the trees. As if to confirm his story, I hear a shriek of excitement from up ahead.

'Can I see it?' I ask.

'Course.' He smiles, and I think it's the first truly sincere smile I've seen of his all day. 'Where d'you think I was taking you?'

As we walk, I take the opportunity to probe a little. 'You don't sound like you're from Colorado.'

'No?'

'Nope. You've got the look, but you sound more like a city boy.'

'What's my look?' He's giving me the most mischievous expression, making his blue eyes shine.

'You know,' I say, nervously, 'rugged. Strong. I can see you out here, chopping logs and wrestling bears.'

He chuckles. 'Only wrestling I've done recently is with a set of weights at the gym. I'm from New York. I do public relations there.'

That makes perfect sense. He doesn't seem like your typical PR guy though. 'You seem a little too... honest for PR.'

Another snort of laughter. 'I wonder if you're more honest than the typical journalist.'

Before I have time to throw a comeback his way, there's another shriek of excitement from up ahead.

'Now,' he says, 'the girls don't know there's a journalist coming. It'd freak them out. So if you don't mind, I'm going to tell them that you're a Little, looking round to see if you want to join.'

My heart skips a beat. 'Weren't you just having a go at journalists for dishonesty?'

'You'd be doing me a huge favor.'

'What about your Little? Are you going to tell her the truth?'

'I don't have a Little.'

Somehow, it's what I knew he was going to say.

'Fine,' I sigh. 'I'll do it.'

He opens the door to the Nursery. Inside is about the most fun-looking place I've ever seen. It's a big log cabin — the biggest one at the community. Honestly, calling it a log cabin is a little unfair — this place has been beautifully constructed. There are huge windows which overlook the lake, and the interior has been meticulously designed. There seem to be different play stations around the room. Each station has different toys and a different theme. There's a place for plushies, a place for board games, a place for videogames, and a place for craft materials. Dotted around the spacious interior are young women, who look happier and more at ease than any person I've ever seen before. All of them have wide smiles, naughty expressions, cute demeanors. There's people of all colors and creeds in here, but the one thing that they have in common is that they're wearing a variety of puffy, white, diapers.

'Oh my,' I gasp.

A cute, short woman with big blue eyes spots me by the door and waddles up to us.

'Hi!' she says in a sweet voice, 'I'm Bailey. What's your name, cutie?'

I'm so taken aback to be called cutie that I can barely open my mouth to reply. She must have taken it as nerves, because a second later, she says, 'I love your glasses by the way. They really suit you.' She's holding a lollipop and takes a long lick.

'Hey Bailey, does Gabe know that you're having candy before lunchtime?' Caleb says, sternly. Bailey blushes.

'Um, no,' she says, looking down at the ground.

'Well, don't you think it might be a good idea to save that for later?'

'Yeah,' she admits, kicking her feet.

'Good girl. Now go play with the others. I'm showing Annika around.'

'Annika,' Bailey says, smiling at me. 'That's a lovely name.'

'Thanks, Bailey,' I reply.

After she runs off to join in with some painting, I say to Caleb. 'So you look after all the Littles, in a way?'

'Pretty much,' he says, as we walk around the edge of the nursery. 'They need a firm hand sometimes, but only a Little's Daddy can hand out punishments. It's a special relationship.'

I don't know what exactly I was expecting, but it definitely wasn't this. A group of young women, freely exploring their child-like side under the supervision of tender but firm, dominant men? It kind of sounds like heaven. I feel a rising flutter of excitement in my tummy. Maybe it wouldn't hurt to let Caleb regress me. I'd only be doing it for the story, after all. At least, that's what I could tell everyone...

I open my mouth, and for a moment, I feel like I'm about to ask him to do it, but then, last minute, I chicken out. 'Caleb, could I talk to some of the other girls?'

Then, he asks me a question I'm not expecting. 'You want to play with them?'

# CALEB

THIS IS NOT GOING the way I thought. I mean, Annika said she didn't want to be regressed. And here we are, barely an hour later, and she's strapping on a plastic overall, getting ready to paint with the other Littles.

'Is there like, a right and wrong way to do this?' she asks, as she ties the strap of the overall around her front. Is it me, or is her voice a little softer than before?

'Nope,' I say, still wary of her. 'You just have to do what feels right to you, what comes naturally. Main thing to remember — most important thing of all — is that playtime is meant to be fun.'

She smiles and it lights up her face. It looks like a genuine smile. But I've been tricked in the past. She has to be faking it. There's no way I'm letting my guard down. Not after what happened with Bethan. No, I have to keep reminding myself why Annika's here, to make the community look predatory and freakish.

Auburn-haired Mia and funny little Ella are here, along with Bailey. The girls are firing question after question at Annika, and to be fair to her, she's coping really well with their curiosity.

'What's your favorite color?' That's Ella's sing-song voice.

'Um, green, I think.' There's no mistaking it, Annika's voice is most definitely softer. Higher pitched, too. It's like she's subconsciously matching the speech patterns of the Littles around her. Kind of like she's a natural submissive...

'My favorite's Red, like your hair,' giggles Bailey, lightly tugging at Annika's fiery locks.

'Don't pull hair, Bailey!' Mia says. She's only really pretending to be angry, but she does a good job of it.

'S'OK,' shrugs Annika, 'she didn't hurt me. No booboos!'

The girls giggle.

'Once,' says Bailey, 'my daddy spanked me so hard I got a booboo on my butt!'

All the girls fall about laughing. 'Ahem,' I grunt, 'I think that kind of talk is private, don't you Bailey? We've got to remember our boundaries.

'Booboo butt,' says Mia.

'Ohhhhhh!' Ella squeals, 'I know what I'm gonna paint. A booboo butt!' She grabs her palette enthusiastically and pours out a slug of bright pink paint.

'Hey! No fair! You can't paint my butt!' Bailey protests.

'Just watch me,' says Ella, defiantly. Then she holds up a thumb and sticks her tongue out, as though pretending to measure Bailey's butt.

I decide not to step in. The girls seem to be having fun, and it actually feels as though Annika is starting to relax. So I watch them paint. Between them, they all decide to paint Bailey's butt. Except for Bailey of course, who paints a grotesque caricature of Ella's face. When they show each other the finished pictures, a good-natured paint-throwing fight breaks out.

As a rule, the Daddies at the Little Cabin don't really step in to stop the Littles having fun unless what they're doing is actually dangerous. A crowd gathers to watch, and pretty soon, every Little in the place is involved. I watch from the sidelines with some of the guys.

'Damn,' Atlas says, 'I'm gonna have to discipline Mia later. I've told her about paint before.'

'Don't be too hard on her,' says Joel, grinning. 'It's the reason we put the plastic sheets down. They've not done any harm.'

'It's not about the damage done to this room,' Atlas replies in his strong Greek accent, 'it's about the fact that I know I'm gonna have to scrub down our bathroom for hours tonight.'

There are laughs all around. 'You know,' Joel says, his eyes still on the Littles as they play, 'Annika seems to be actually enjoying herself.'

I glance over at her. She's got paint in her hair and smudged over her glasses.

'Don't let her fool you,' I say. 'She's just pretending so that she can infiltrate our little group.'

Joel gives me a wary look. 'You sure?'

My eyes flick down to her firm, full breasts, as a splat of white paint sprays across them. I flick my eyes up again, hoping no-one noticed my wandering eyes.

'Positive.'

*

'You nearly done in there?' The sound of the shower stopped a few seconds ago. I'm in the guest cabin with Annika, waiting for her to finish cleaning up.

'Yeah,' she calls through. Her voice still has that more high-pitched quality to it. It's like she's letting this place get to her.

A moment later, the door from the bathroom swings open. To my surprise, Annika's just wearing a towel. Well, two white towels to be precise. One of them is twisted around her gorgeous red hair, and the other is looped around her body, over her bust.

She looks incredible — it's the first time I've seen her without her glasses, but her eyes look so big and beautiful now. She's got an incredibly expressive face, but now that I can see the full shape of it, it's hard not to feel stunned into silence.

'You know what,' she says. 'I really had fun with the girls.'

'I got that impression,' I say, trying to sound gruff.

'Can I ask you something?' she says, her voice suddenly vulnerable. 'Have you got a problem with journalists?'

'What gave it away?' I grunt, with wry humor.

'Just a hunch,' she says, wrinkling her nose up. Damn, she looks cute like that.

I sigh. 'Look. The love of my life was a journalist. She worked for the New York Times. I was only with her for six months, but they changed my life.'

'What happened?' she says, with genuine concern in her voice.

'Turns out, she was writing an exposé of my PR firm. My boss wasn't exactly a nice guy. Turns out, he was funneling money away from investors. Anyway, Bethan was only with me to get close to my boss. Soon as the story broke, she dumped me. She'd even been acting like a Little for me.'

'That's unbelievable,' she says.

'I know, it's wild.'

'I can see why you don't trust us.' She rests a hand on my shoulder. 'And it's true — some journalists have no scruples, no qualms at all. But we're not all like that.'

It feels good to have her hand on my shoulder like this.

'I want to prove it to you. It's so important that you know that I want to be fair to this community,' she continues. 'So I want to be regressed. For real. Fully.'

I can feel my eyebrow rise up. It's not a conscious thing, but I can't help myself. I'm about to say something like *I don't believe you* or *Sure you do, buttercup*. But I stop myself. Maybe I should try to humor her instead. But I'm not going to let her off easily.

'OK then,' I say. 'I guess we better get started.'

Her look of hope is replaced by one of apprehension.

'What are we going to do?' She looks really worried. I have a sudden urge to lean over and give her a cuddle. It's the Daddy in me coming out. I hate to see a young woman distressed — just can't abide it.

When I next speak, my voice is soft and soothing. 'Don't worry, baby. Everything's gonna be alright.'

\*

We're outside the guest cabin. Annika sits in a large, adult-sized swing that hangs from a sturdy branch of a nearby cottonleaf tree. She's swaying gently in the seat, and kicking her legs a little. It's the afternoon and the light is gorgeous — shafts of sun illuminate floating motes, seeds twirl round and down in crazy corkscrews. Looks like a scene from a painting.

'I've never been good at interviews,' says Annika. She curls a lock of hair around a finger, then uncurls it.

'This won't be like any kind of interview you've ever had.' I'm sitting nearby with a pad of paper in my hands.

'OK,' she says, trying a nervous smile on for size, 'I'm ready to begin, I think.'

'Great.'

Question is, am I ready? I've never tried anything like this before. I'm just gonna have to wing it. Come on, Caleb, concentrate, you can do this.

'Annika, I'm going to call you Anni from now on. OK?'

'MMhmm,' she nods, gently kicking back from the ground, swinging slowly back and forth.

'Anni, I want you to tell me your first memory.'

She scrunches up her mouth. 'That's a tough one.' She thinks for a second, then says, 'Oh no, wait, it's easy peasy. I remember! It's sad. My momma leaving me at playgroup. I cried and cried.'

'That must be hard to think about.'

She sighs. 'Nah. There's much worse things to remember.'

'Oh?' There's genuine concern in my voice.

'Sure. My momma wasn't exactly a good parent. And honestly, her leaving me at playgroup was a good thing to do. Trouble is, she couldn't afford to have me in there much. And when we were together, she kinda neglected me.'

'I'm sorry to hear that, Anni. What about your pops?'

She looks down. 'He died.' She looks slightly uncomfortable.

'Oh Anni, I'm so sorry to hear that. So sorry for your loss. We don't have to talk about this if it's painful. I want you relaxed and receptive, sweetie.'

Is that a sniff? 'No, it's fine. Never really felt like a loss to me. How can you lose something you don't even know you have?'

Damn. That hits me hard. 'You felt like you never had a dad?'

She nods, then I see a shift in her expression. She looks a little angry. 'So you get lots of women with daddy issues here?' It's a challenge.

'Truthfully Anni, we get all sorts of people. And honestly, most of the people out there in the world have daddy issues of some kind. So it's not that straightforward.'

She nods. 'Sorry, that was a prejudiced question.'

'It's always OK to ask questions,' I say. 'And I've got one for you. How would you like to be looked after?'

She seems genuinely stumped by this. 'You mean...'

'I mean, if there was someone in your life who could help you, who could support you in any way possible, what would that person look like? What would they do? How would you want them to make you feel?'

She stops swinging and draws a small shape in the ground with the tip of her foot. Looks like she's carefully considering the question. Then, finally, she says, 'You know what? That's actually really straightforward. I just want someone to make me feel like I'm good enough.'

'Good enough?'

'Yeah. Like I don't need to try hard to prove myself. Like I don't need to be someone I'm not.'

'And who are you?'

'I'm just Anni,' she shrugs. That's when I truly feel it for the first time. She's a Little. I'm sure of it. It kind of takes me by surprise — this deep well of feeling that I've stumbled into.

'Anni,' I say, 'I've got a choice for you. Just wait here.'

She nods and I head into the cabin. My brain's fizzing all over the place. I can't believe this is happening to me again. I've got feelings for this Little Girl. It's not just lust, it's more than that. I can't believe I've fallen for another journalist. I pick up a package and come back out, my heart pounding in my chest.

'You OK?' she says, looking me up and down.

'Fine,' I say. But I'm not. I'm winded, like I've been running a marathon. And when I catch sight of the concern in those bright green eyes, I feel like I'm back at the starting line, and I've got another 26 miles to go. 'Look, Anni, I've got a present for you. I just want you to choose.' I hold up the box.

'They're so cute!' she coos. She lifts up both the stuffies I chose for her. One happy little cat, and a fierce — but super-cute — grizzly bear. 'But it's got to be a bear. There's no way I can cope with how haughty cats are.'

'You want to stay away from Tina then.' I say, desperately trying to make conversation, desperate to not let her know that there's a hormone storm going on in my heart right now.

'Tina?'

'Joel's cat. She's got issues.'

Anni takes the bear and cuddles him up close to her chest. For a moment, I can't help but wish that I was that bear.

'Anni, I think you're ready,' I say.

'Ready?'

'For the next three days, I'm going to be your Daddy. I want you to call me Daddy all the time. No ifs, no buts.' She nods. 'I'm going to pick your clothes. I'm going to pick your meals. I'm going to set you tasks.' She looks nervous. 'But I want you to know, whatever happens, you are good enough. Not just that, you're perfect. Don't worry, you can't fuck this up. Just be yourself. Just be Anni.'

She smiles.

# ANNIKA

I CALL HIM BEARTIE. My teddy stuffie that is. Ever since Daddy gave me Beartie, it's like a whole new person's been unleashed from inside me. A person who's not clumsy, who's not afraid of making mistakes. A person who's just happy to be themselves, even if I am sillier than the average grown-up.

'You ready for breakfast, Baba?'

I'm sitting on the floor in the guest cabin. I've got my legs spread wide and between them is a big pad Daddy's given me to write in. The best thing is that I haven't been writing actual news stories. Pah! Yuck! No way. Daddy said that I can write whatever I want. So every day I've been writing fairy tales. Stories of sprites and goblins in the woods, setting up a little community for other forest-folk.

And guess what? Daddy says they're good stories! He even said that the other Littles might like them.

'I'm always ready for breakfast, Daddy!' I say. I spring up from my seat and stretch a little. I can't believe I've been writing before breakfast. The me from a couple weeks ago would be stunned at how productive I've been.

'I made us huevos rancheros.' He's got such a lovely deep voice. Makes my special place tingle whenever I hear him talk.

'What's that?'

'Like Mexican eggs.' He carries a pan over to the table. The smell is incredible — this smoky, rich scent that's making me salivate. 'Chorizo, beans, avocado. You name it, it's in this bowl.'

'Candy?'

He pauses and gives me a look. 'Surprisingly enough, I forgot to add the candy.'

I join him up at the table. I have a special chair that Daddy has to strap me into. It's a little higher up than a standard chair, and it's got a tray in front of it so that I don't drop any of my food down. I've been getting pretty excited when I eat since arriving at the cabin.

Living in a cabin with Caleb has taken some getting used to.

First, there's the cabin itself. It's pretty basic, with no electricity and no running water. All the water comes from Purple Lake, or at least from a well that Joel built months ago. Even though it's spring, it still gets pretty cool in the evenings, and Caleb has to light the fire every day to make sure that we're warm.

It's also strange to be in a place with so much age play stuff. There's so many toys, which are a constant distraction, especially when I've got such a specific daily routine to follow. Then there's the other stuff. Stacks of diapers. A changing station. I'm reminded all the time that other people have stayed here before me. And all those people were Littles. It's kind of exciting.

I wonder if I really *am* a Little. I mean, it's not like you need a certificate to prove it. I feel like if I decide I am, then I am. But at the same time, there's a niggling doubt in the back of my mind. Maybe I am just doing this to make Trent happy. Maybe I am just doing this for a story.

Aside from the cabin, I'm not used to living with a guy — especially a guy I'm so ridiculously attracted to. There's something about the fact that he sleeps in a room next to mine which is — to put it mildly

— a little exciting for me. I find it hard to get to sleep, imagining the gorgeous man who's just a couple feet away from me. I wonder if he wears anything while he's in bed, or whether his body is naked under the bearskin which keeps him warm.

In an attempt to take my mind off Caleb's hot, naked form, I turn my attention back to the food. From the very first mouthful, I know that this is something special. 'Mmmmm!' I moan. 'This is INSANE-LY delicious!' I shovel more and more of the incredible dish into my mouth, not worrying about the mess I'm making. As usual, Daddy doesn't look angry with me. In fact, he looks positively delighted.

'I can't get over how much you love your food,' he says, grinning. He looks handsome this morning. He hasn't shaved since we started sharing the guest cabin, and his stubble is getting so thick it practically looks as though he's starting to grow a beard.

'Where did you learn how to make this?' I ask, still engrossed in the flavors swirling around my mouth.

'A friend of mine runs a Mexican cantina in NYC.'

'Huh. Sometimes I forget that you're from New York. You seem to fit in so perfectly to the environment here, Daddy. Like you're part of the mountains and the trees.'

He snorts. 'You're just saying that because this is the only place we've spent time together. Maybe one day you can come to New York, and I'll show you just how boring my life really is.'

Before I have time to consider what I'm saying, I come out with: 'I'd never be bored around you.'

There's a moment between us. Our eyes are locked and it almost feels like we're breathing in time with each other. Then, Caleb glances down, and the moment's gone.

'So how's your article coming along?' It's so jarring to be wrenched out of Little Space like this, feels like I've been plucked out of a warm bath and plunged into a pool of ice. Suddenly my anxiety is back. That feeling of having something hanging over me that I don't want to do.

'Oh,' I say, 'it's OK.'

'Haven't seen you working on it much. Yesterday, after dinner, when you were meant to be writing your article, I had the distinct impression that you were writing more of your fairy tales.'

'Yeah,' I admit. I can't lie to Daddy, the thought doesn't even cross my mind. 'I guess I haven't really felt like doing it.'

'That's no bad thing,' Daddy says. 'Anni, while you're here, I want you to be free to express yourself however you want. We only agreed that after dinner would be time to write, anyway. So technically, you were sticking to the schedule.'

'Yeah!' I say, feeling immediately better. 'I can write that stinky article later.'

'Exactly. First, you have to live this life before you can write about it, baba.'

And just like that, I'm back in Little Space. 'What are we doing today, Daddy?'

'Well, I had something special planned. I wanted to give you a taste of what it was like at this cabin back in the old days, before it got so crowded. You know Gabe and Bailey?'

'Uh-huh.'

'They didn't actually meet right here at the Little Cabin. Gabe was a Mountain Rescue officer, working at an even more remote cabin near a place called Hiker's Foe.'

'Sounds dangerous.'

'The place is dangerous, but the cabin isn't. Before you arrived here, Gabe took me out there to give me a real taste of the wilderness. And I thought you might like to trek there together. Get some time away from the other Littles, and get a feel for what we're trying to offer here.'

A romantic trip into the woods just with Daddy? Sounds perfect.

'I'm up for it!' I say.

'OK, let me just get the bear spray and we can head off.'

'Eeek! Will Beartie be scared of the bear spray?'

Daddy shakes his head. 'Don't worry, bear spray doesn't work on magical bears.'

He heads into the other room to prepare his bag, and while he's gone, I pack my own. Then, as I'm throwing clothes in, I decide that I'm gonna take something special with me. I bite my lip, and look at the door to make sure he's not about to come back through. Then I grab something secret and stuff it into my rucksack.

*

This is the real wilderness. The further we trek from the Little Cabin, the more and more my wonder grows. As we get deeper into the trees, I feel like I'm seeing things for the very first time. The birds, hopping between branches, the cold, icy water of mountain streams.

Daddy's with me, guiding me carefully around obstacles and danger. He's got a map that Gabe made for him, a compass, and some fancy binoculars he keeps looking through. If I were by myself, I'd be freaking out so hard right now, but with my Daddy next to me, I feel as though I could do anything, no matter how scary or challenging.

'You enjoying the trek, darling?' Daddy says, looking back at me. His cold blue eyes catch the spring sun.

'Uh-huh,' I say. I keep thinking about the thing I've got in my bag, about whether I'm going to be brave enough to show Daddy what I brought with me.

'What's on your mind, sugar?' he says.

'Nothing. Just in a good mood, that's all.'

'You prefer it out here than in the big city?'

I nod. 'What about you, Daddy? Do you miss the city?'

'I dunno. Truth is, I was kinda dreading coming out here. I *do* love the city. The hustle, the bustle, the endless possibilities. In the past, whenever I thought about coming to visit my brother out here, I kind of imagined that it would be boring and bleak. You know, trees are all the same, right?'

I find it so weird to think that Caleb wasn't born out here in the woods, wasn't hunting his own food from infancy. He seems so natural, so at ease here.

'Turns out,' he continues, 'that not all trees are the same. In fact, no two trees are the same.' He pauses and walks up to two thick-trunked firs. I join him.

'You're right,' I say, looking at the trunks with the wondrous perspective of a child. I run my hand over the bark, really *feeling* the sensation under my fingers. So much warmer than the air around it, but still cool. The bark is rough, but almost crumbly. 'The colors are different, the pattern of the bark.'

'You're right,' he says. 'When you live in the city, it's like a million things happen to you every day, so you don't have time to really experience any of it. But here, I've got as long as I want to just feel a tree, to really *see* it.'

I nod.

'Same with people,' he says, looking down at the ground. 'In my normal life, I don't have time to really get to know people. But here...'

'You can form connections very quickly,' I say, finishing his sentence. He nods and looks me in the eye.

He steps forward toward me. 'I'm glad you're here with me, Anni,' he says. He takes my hand. It's such a simple, innocent thing, but it fills me with warmth and tenderness.

'Hey,' I say, 'do you think that trees can see us?'

He looks amazed by my question. 'I mean... not in the traditional sense, but, maybe they can sense us, somehow.'

'Do you think that to trees, we look alike?' It's a crazy question. There's no way that we look alike, not him with his hard body and me with my softness.

'You know what, I do.' He's close to me now, so close I can smell his clean, cool scent. 'And I think we are alike, Anni. The more time I spend with you, the more I feel like we're two halves of the same whole.'

'Like those,' I say, pointing behind him. He turns around and sees what I'm pointing at — two trees whose trunks have twisted around each other, whose branches are fused in a permanent embrace.

'Like those.' He says. For a moment, we're standing together, looking at the trees. Then, as if shrugging off some strange dream, Caleb snaps out of it. 'Hey,' he says. 'There's the cabin. We're here!'

'Hooray!' I squeal. But I don't mean it. I could have stayed here, close to Daddy, forever.

# CALEB

A S SOON AS WE get inside Gabe's old cabin, it's obvious that no-one's been in here for quite a while. There are cobwebs all over the place, and there's a damp smell which only a roaring fire has any chance of dispersing.

My heart's still going nuts. Outside, just a moment ago, I came about as close as you can possibly imagine to kissing Annika. That would be a mistake for so many reasons. Thank fuck I saw the cabin behind her. If I hadn't managed to distract us, who knows what might have happened?

'Smells funny in here, Daddy,' Annika says. She wrinkles her nose up, then heads over to the couch. She's about to dump her rucksack down onto the old thing but gives it a sniff before thinking again.

'I better get the fire going, huh?' I ask.

'That sounds good,' she replies.

'Hey, you could start writing up some of your notes, if you want? Just while I'm preparing the stove.' I gesture over to the cast-iron box which I'm about to start feeding with wood.

'Awwww,' she sulks, pouting her bottom lip out. 'Do I have to?'

'Course not,' I reply, shrugging. 'You can do what you want, Baby Girl. I just thought that in the long run, it might cause you a little less stress. If you do some of the work now, you won't have to do it later.'

'You're right,' she admits, before slamming her butt down on the hard pine chair by the dining table. 'Ouch!' She says. 'I think *I* just gave myself a butt booboo.'

'I didn't know they were contagious,' I reply. I probe the pile of logs by the stove. They're not perfectly dry, but they should definitely do. I hope. I'm not exactly an expert fire-starter, even if Joel has talked me through it a couple hundred times. Honestly, if I have to hear him say: '*It's all about the structure of your logs,*' one more time I swear I'll scream.

Still, though, I guess I better think about the structure of my fucking logs.

As I start to arrange them in triangles inside the ancient stove, I hear the scratch of pen on paper as Annika starts to write something or other. I wonder what she's writing. She could be saying anything. About me, about the Little community. Heck, she could be painting me as some kind of pervert who gets off on the idea of forcing a young woman to do whatever I tell her.

Maybe she's writing a story about how she fell for a rugged, mountain man who treated her right and looked after her in the wilderness.

Yeah, right.

There's so much wrong with that that I can't help but smile. Me, a mountain man? Get real. I'm just a fucking PR consultant. I'm about as fake as a three-dollar bill.

I reach for the matches and strike one, then hold the wavering flame up to a scrunched-up ball of newspaper inside the stove. Just before the paper lights, I notice that it's a front page from the Denver Chronicle. A few moments later and it looks like the fire is actually gonna take. I can't believe I've done it first time.

'Good job, Daddy!' Anni cries happily. 'We'll be warm in no time.'

'I hope so,' I grunt. 'I'm gonna stuff this stove full of fuel to make sure that we get as hot as possible in here, as soon as possible.' I push another thick, dry log into the front hatch of the burner, then close it. 'So,' I say, 'this has to be the furthest I've ever been from civilization. How about you?'

She looks up for a moment and chews the end of her pen thoughtfully. 'Yep, I think so. I mean, there was the time I was in Afghanistan, but other than th-'

'You were in Afghanistan?' Damn, I didn't mean to sound so surprised.

'Yeah,' she giggles. 'It was a college assignment if you can believe it. When I was a kid, I always wanted to do like, the most worthy, impressive jobs. Nothing was ever good enough for my mom. So I got it into my head that I wanted to be a war reporter.' She lets out a snort. 'Can you imagine that? Me, reporting from the frontline?'

'I bet you could do it if you wanted to.'

She smiles at me. 'You know, considering you hate journalists so much, you've been pretty damn nice to me, Daddy.'

'Hey,' I say, 'no cussing young lady.'

'Whoops,' she says. 'Sorry.'

'It's OK. First time you get a pass.'

The flames start to crackle inside the burner, and already it's starting to feel warmer in here.

'Oooh,' Anni says, 'I'm gonna come snuggle up.' She leaves her writing on the table and comes up to me, holding her hands out towards the fire. 'That feels goooood,' she coos.

'Nothing like a warm fire on a chilly day,' I agree. 'So, when did you realize that war reporting wasn't your bag?'

There's a far-off look in her eye. 'Probably when I saw my first body.'

Oh shit.

'I'm so sorry.' The things this woman has been through are crazy. No dad, next-to-no mom, a job so tough it can break your heart in half. I don't want her to ever suffer again.

'What really sucked,' she says, staring into the flames, 'was that it was a kid. Totally innocent. Her life had been taken away from her. No chance to grow up, no chance to get out of her crappy situation, just snuffed out like a birthday candle.'

'Poor thing,' I say.

'Sometimes I feel selfish for complaining about my childhood,' Annika says. 'At least I had the chance to grow up.'

Without thinking, I put my arm around her shoulders. She's a skinny little thing, but I love the way she feels against me. Warm and soft and small and perfect. 'Other people suffer, it's true. But that doesn't reduce your suffering.'

Her hand's in mine again. It's like we keep getting drawn together, no matter what we do.

'Wait,' she says.

'What's the matter?' I whisper.

'I have to go potty,' she whispers back. Then, a dumb grin breaks out on her face.

'You know what,' I say, smiling like an idiot, 'I think you really are a Little. Deep down. Otherwise, this regression wouldn't have taken hold the way it has.'

She bites her lip. 'I dunno,' she says, but I can tell that she agrees with me. 'Back in a sec.' She seems suddenly nervous, like something big is happening, then she grabs her bag. 'Where's the bathroom?' she says.

'Uh, I don't think there is one. You might have to head out into the woods.'

'Eeeek! What about bears.'

'I'm sure you'll be fine,' I say.

'You know what,' she says, 'I think I have a better idea.'

'No holding in,' I say, sternly. 'It's no good for you.'

'Not that, silly Daddy! I actually brought something with me. I wasn't sure that I was brave enough to wear it, but maybe I am after all.'

Then she reaches into her bag and takes out something big and puffy and white. It's a Tykables overnight diaper. My jaw hits the floor.

'Where did you get that, you little sneak thief?'

'From the guest cabin,' she says, giggling her head off. 'Do you think I was naughty?'

'Well, yes, but I can see why you did it. So you're really going to wear a diaper?'

She nods, biting her lip so hard, she practically chews it. Now it's heating up in here, her little cheeks are getting all rosy.

'You even know how to put it on?'

'I want you to help me, Daddy.' She sounds cute and flirtatious at the same time. This Girl is dangerous as they come.

'Are you sure?' I say. 'This isn't part of the regression. And you may find that once you put the diaper on, there won't be any turning back.'

She purses her lips. 'You know, I haven't been totally honest with you.'

Instantly, my heart sinks. I knew it. Knew that there had to be a catch to this weird situation. Of course she hasn't been honest with me. 'Go on,' I grunt.

'I've actually suspected that I was a Little for a long, long time.'

This takes me by surprise. 'Seriously?'

She nods. 'Ever since puberty, really. I looked into it for a long time. Before my brief deployment as a war reporter. I've always been a little childish. I think that might be why my boss hates me so much.'

'He sounds like a jerk.'

She sighs. 'He is a jerk. A major-league asshole, in truth. He sent me here to ditch the dirt on you guys, to write something damaging. He doesn't care about the truth. All he cares about is his stinky paper.'

'But that's not your plan?' My heart's beating like crazy, and it's getting warmer and warmer in here.

'Of course not, Daddy. All I want to do is help you guys out. Make sure people know that nothing bad is going on at the Little Cabin. I want to teach people that Littles aren't anything to be scared of. They're not freaks, they're just normal people. Like me and you.'

I consider what she's saying. It feels like it's coming from the heart. The fire is raging now, and the whole room is getting warmer and warmer. 'Think I overdid it with the logs,' I say, wiping sweat from my brow.

'I hope you can believe me,' she says. 'I think that's another reason I want to put the diaper on. I want to prove myself to you.'

I stop and look her in the eye. 'Anni, when are you gonna figure it out? You don't need to prove yourself to anyone. You're good enough.'

Maybe she's blushing. Maybe it's the heat.

'I'm really hot, Daddy.' Her hand reaches up to her blouse. 'I need to cool down.'

Before I have the chance to even react, she's started to undo the buttons, then, her blouse is tugged up and over her head. I can't help but look at her heaving bosom, pushing against her powder-pink bra.

'Damn, Anni.'

'No cussing, Daddy,' she says. She pushes her finger up to my lips. I kiss it.

'Take your pants off,' I say, my hunger suddenly urgent.

'Yes Daddy,' she says, breathlessly yanking her sweatpants down. Her legs are slim and toned, and she's wearing a tiny little pink thong that barely covers any of her skin. She's pale next to the pink, and I'm desperate to rip those dumb little panties away from her. 'You gonna help me with these?' she asks, looking down at the thong. She lies down on the thick bearskin in front of the fire. She looks so gorgeous spread out like this.

'You don't need to ask me twice,' I grunt, then I crouch down over her like a hungry animal. Seconds later, I grip the tiny piece of fabric between my teeth and tug it back.

'You're so strong,' she says. 'I've been thinking about what you're gonna do to me since the first time I saw you.'

'Baby girl,' I say, 'I'm gonna make you mine.'

Just then, as I'm about to dip my tongue into her hot, pink pussy, there's a flash from the window. We both look up. There's a face there, hidden behind a camera. For a second, I can't make out who it is. Then, a second later, she moves the camera down, and in a moment of horror, the realization hits me.

'Betha-?' I start to say.

But before I can finish, Annika says, 'Brenda?'

Then, a moment later, she's gone into the dark of the evening. I look at the photo she must have caught. Me, leaning over a young woman, pulling her panties off with my teeth. Next to us, on the floor, casual as anything, is an open, adult diaper.

'Oh no,' I say.

# ANNIKA

'**S**HE MUST HAVE CHANGED her name.' I'm back in my clothes, pacing around the little cabin. Thoughts are buzzing around my head and I can't think straight. The atmosphere in here couldn't be any more different. Anxiety has replaced happiness, worry has replaced lust.

'I can't believe it's her.' Caleb seems even more shocked than I am. Could it really be that Trent sent Brenda to follow me out here? Did he somehow know that I'd have more than a professional interest in what's going on at the community? I wrack my brain, trying to think about anything I could have done at work to give the game away. 'I haven't seen her for years and then she just shows up out here? Last I heard she was still in New York.'

'That's where she and Trent came from,' I say. 'When he took over as editor at the Chronicle, he brought over his best reporter.'

'You know what,' Caleb says, pointing his finger at me, ' I bet you Brenda is her real name. Even though I was dating her for six months, I bet she just used a fake identity the whole time.'

'That's evil,' I say. 'How could anyone do something like that?'

Now that this is all sinking in, it's hard not to feel jealous. Brenda is one of the most gorgeous women I've ever met. I can't help but imagine my new Daddy with his hands over her tight body, I can't help but imagine her ruby-red lips on his.

'Truth is,' Caleb says, 'I don't think I ever got to know her. Not for real. She just showed me a persona, designed to trick me into trusting her. When I told her about my interest in age play, it must have felt like she'd won the fucking lottery. She realized I was vulnerable, and then just honed in on it like a guided missile.'

It's so weird to think of someone as confident and strong as Caleb being vulnerable, but I guess that in a way, he was. He was looking for a Little. And when he thought he'd found one, it was his kryptonite.

'What are we gonna do?' I ask. Without realizing, I've got my thumb in my mouth, with a finger curled over my nose. Caleb looks over at me, and the anxiety on his face just melts away.

'First thing I'm gonna do is my duty as your Daddy.' He grabs his rucksack and pulls out a familiar dark brown shape.

'Beartie!' I shout, 'I can't believe I forgot you.'

Caleb smiles as he hands me my stuffie. I cuddle Beartie hard, holding him close to my chest. I feel my heart rate come down straight away.

'You mind if I give you a cuddle, sweetheart?'

'You don't need to ask, Daddy.'

'Sure I do,' he says. 'I gotta make sure that my Little Girl is happy. You must be hurting right now, and I want to reduce that pain as much as possible.'

He leans in, wraps his thick arms around me, and squeezes me gently. He's so strong, so *big,* that I feel like I'm being held in Beartie's arms, my big Daddy Bear, making me feel all cozy and loved. It's a feeling I haven't felt for a very, very long time. I let out a long sigh.

'Does that feel good, baba?' he asks, kissing my hair.

'Uh-huh,' is all I can manage in response.

'Good.' He says. 'Now, I don't want you to worry about this nastiness with Brenda. Or Bethan. Or whatever she's called. Daddy's gonna
make it all go away.'

'How?' I whisper. 'People are going to see that picture of me.
They're going to know that I'm a Little. And I don't even know it for
sure myself.' As I talk, emotion bubbles up in me, and before I even
know how I really feel, tears start welling up in my eyes.

'It's not fair, is it?' he says. 'Being outed like this. Well hopefully, I've
got a way of stopping anything coming out.'

'Daddy?' I say, in a tiny little voice. 'Do you think I really am a
Little?'

'Only you know the answer to that,' he says, warmly. 'But there's
one thing that I *do* know. You're totally adorable.'

I look up at him and even with how vulnerable and scared about
Brenda I feel, right now, in this moment, there's nowhere else I'd rather
be.

'I don't mind people knowing what am I,' I say. 'I think I *am* a
Little. I think I've always known. I just needed to meet someone to
help bring it out of me.'

'You just needed some confidence, didn't you?' he says.

'Yeah. I just hate the thought of having that power taken away from
me. The power to stand up and say, *My name's Annika and I'm a
Little.*'

'It sounds good when you say it like that,' he says. Then, he sighs.
'You know, when I saw her at the window, my first instinct was to run
out and shout, but I'm glad I didn't. Let her think that she's got some
crazy scoop. She deserves to have it taken away from her.'

Dang, he really sounds like he has a plan.

'So what are we gonna do tonight?' I say.

'Well, I kinda figure, since a journalist took a photo of you next to a diaper, we might as well get you diapered up for the night.'

My heart starts to pound. How should I be feeling right now? Should I feel guilty for just wanting to enjoy my time with Caleb? Should I be trapped in anxiety? Struggling to fight my way out?

The truth is, I feel strangely fine. Things can't get any worse. Which means they can only get better.

'I think I'd like that, Daddy,' I say.

'Well then, let's get your little touche back on that bearskin.'

As I lie down this time, I almost feel as though I'm in a dream. It's so warm and cozy and nice in this cabin, and Daddy says that everything's gonna be OK, so maybe everything really is going to be OK.

It doesn't feel real when Daddy leans down and tugs down my sweatpants. How could something this wonderful really be happening to someone like me? I don't deserve happiness, do I? He tenderly strokes down my leg, from thigh to knee.

'You know what, this is still perfect,' he says. 'You're still perfect.'

The last time he pulled down my thong it was with lust and passion. This time, he's moving with true feeling. It almost feels like there's love in his movements. He slips his thumbs under my thong, and gently tugs.

'Cute color panties,' he says.

'You don't think they're silly?'

'Course they're silly,' he says with a wicked smile. 'That's why they suit you so much. I know that you're a serious journalist, and you're a smart cookie, too. But underneath it all, I can just tell that you're a silly little noodle.'

I let out a chortle. It's so nice for him to talk about me like this. I feel so close to him, and so far away from my responsibilities. Daddy's making everything better.

My panties are off now, and Daddy's looking down at me with tenderness in his eyes.

'I'm gonna lift up your butt now, sweetheart, then I'll pop the diaper under you.'

The anticipation is killing me. I've thought about wearing a diaper so many times over the years. I've wondered how it might feel — whether I'd feel straight-up disgusted and humiliated, or whether I'd find it comforting and yummy.

Now I'm about to find out.

The first thing I notice when I lower my butt down onto the white fabric is just how unlike panties it feels. It's so crinkly and thick. I can just tell that this is super-absorbent. My journalist's brain is ticking away like crazy as I think about how I'd describe this experience to someone.

'OK, I'm gonna do this up for you now, Baby. Will you tell Daddy if it's too tight for you?'

'How will I know?' I ask, quietly.

'You'll know sugar, don't worry. You're a clever girl.'

I love hearing him compliment me. It's such a treat to feel comfortable and empowered like this. He grips the tabs on either side of the diaper and pulls it tight around my tummy. For a moment I worry that he's going to squeeze really hard, but he doesn't. In fact, he's pulled it perfectly tight — I feel reassured and happy.

'Thank you, Daddy,' I say.

'Now, why don't we get ready for bed? I'm gonna make you a cup of hot cocoa on the stove, and then — if you like — I can read you a bedtime story. I brought some board books. Do you like *The Gruffalo*?'

'I've never read it,' I admit. I look up at Daddy's handsome face, and I can't believe the attention he's lavishing on me.

His eyes widen and for a moment, he's the one with a look of childlike excitement. 'Oh Anni, you're gonna love *The Gruffalo*.'

\*

I never much cared for bedtime until today. With Caleb, my new Daddy, it's a magical experience. I guess staying the night in a gorgeous, fire-lit cabin in the middle of nowhere might have something to do with it.

There's something magical about the smell of cocoa when you know it's being warmed by logs your Daddy chopped a couple hours ago. There's something indescribable about hearing one of the most magical stories I've ever heard for the first time.

'You seemed like you really enjoyed that.' Daddy closes the board book and sits back in an old armchair.

'I loved it! The mouse was so mischievous. And *The Gruffalo* was so scary!'

He smiles. 'Hope it wasn't too scary for you. Especially after today.'

'Nope,' I say. 'It was perfect.'

'OK, now it's time for sleep, I think, Anni.' He walks over to me and carefully tucks me in, pulling blankets all the way up to my chin.

'But where are you going to sleep, Daddy?' I ask.

He points to the couch. 'Over there, Baby Girl. You'll have plenty of space to stretch out.'

I stick out my lower lip, pouting. 'But I'll get scared. I want you in my bed with me.'

'You do?'

'Uh-huh. In case the Gruffalo comes to get me.'

He grins again. 'Cutie-pie, the Gruffalo isn't coming here. You're totally safe.'

'Please Daddy,' I whimper. 'I don't want to be alone in here tonight.'

He stops for a moment. Somewhere nearby I can hear the crackle of the fire as the last few logs burn to embers. Through the window, there's a hunter's moon up high in the sky, painting the mountainside silver. My Daddy looks incredible, silhouetted against the night sky.

'How am I meant to say no to that?' he says, shaking his head.

When my big, strong daddy slips into bed next to me, it's like having a wonderful hot-water bottle. Being this close to him is hard, and I'm desperate to slide my hands over his warm skin. But he holds back.

'Let's just lie together tonight,' he whispers in my ear. 'This is all new for both of us, and we've got all the time in the world.'

'But aren't you gonna go back to New York when this is all over?' I ask, dreading the reply.

'We'll work something out,' he says. I feel his arms loop around me, and just a second later, I'm his little spoon, pushing my diaper back into him, feeling his body rise and fall as he breathes.

As I drift off to sleep, just for a moment, I remember that Brenda is gonna post a picture of me, is gonna out me publicly. But then I remind myself that I'm safe with Daddy, and he promised to fix the problem, so I've got nothing to worry about. I sigh, close my eyes, and dream.

# CALEB

WAKING UP NEXT TO my Baby Girl is about the sweetest moment of my life. She looks so gorgeous while she sleeps, that dark auburn hair, strewn across her pale cheeks. I don't want to wake her, but I need to sort this shit with Brenda out before she's up. I don't want her to have to worry about anything now that I'm looking after her.

So I carefully, slowly, pick my way out of bed. I feel like I'm playing Jenga, and if I make one wrong move, she's gonna come tumbling down. I slide my arm out from under her torso, and move my leg out from under her leg. I'm moving so slowly, and she grumbles a couple times, but eventually, I manage to extricate myself from the embrace and I'm safely out of bed.

I pull the blanket up to her chin again, and she sighs before snuggling down.

I can't believe I'm about to do this. After two years, I'm going to ring the person who broke my heart. She probably won't even pick up. Mind you, if she doesn't, I'm going to make sure she does.

Outside, the sun is high up above. The longer I've stayed out here in Colorado, the more I've started to appreciate just how clear and blue the sky is. Between the dark fronds of the trees, I can see the heavens.

I breathe in deeply. Here goes nothing.

Thankfully, I've got one bar of reception. According to Gabe, Mountain Rescue have set up an actual camp near here, which means they boosted the signal of a nearby cell phone tower. I flick through my phone and find it. Her number isn't under Bethan anymore. I renamed her: Never Under Any Circumstance Ring This Number No Matter What.

I hit call.

Unsurprisingly, it rings out, straight to voicemail. She's got one of those generic voicemail messages, but I'm not gonna leave a message. I don't have time for that. So I open up my pictures folder. I scroll back in time. I find the picture, and I send it through. It takes a while — my phone connection is sketchy at best — but after around five minutes, I see a little tick next to the message. It's been sent. A moment later and a second tick appears next to it. She's read it.

Then, before I even have time for my heart to skip a beat, my phone starts to buzz.

Well, that worked even more quickly than I hoped.

I take the call, but before I have a chance to even say hello, an angry, low, women's voice snarls: 'I should have known you'd be out there with those fucking perverts, Caleb.'

'I should have known you'd be the asshole journalist making Anni's life hell.'

She snorts. 'Anni? Is that what you're calling that scrawny runt?'

'Watch your mouth,' I say, raising my voice more than I mean to. 'I'm not going to have you speak about her like that.'

'Whatever,' she says. 'I know that you still want me, anyway.'

I know that if I reply to that, or even acknowledge it, she'll have won. 'So anyway,' I say, 'how come you're calling me?'

I can hear her rage before she says anything. 'You know exactly why. I want you to delete that photo from your phone right now.'

'That won't help,' I say.

'What?'

'I've got lots more photos where that one came from. And some of them are much, much worse.'

'How?' she asks. 'How did you get photos of me dressed as a baby?'

'I took them, idiot? Do you honestly not remember?'

I had her consent to take the photos. At the time, I thought she was cute. So, during some of our age-play sessions — which she pretended to enjoy — I took some snaps.

'I thought that you just used that Polaroid. I didn't know you had files.'

'I digitized them. I was gonna make you an album of them as a present. But after you confessed that you weren't the person you said you were, I kind of lost enthusiasm.'

'Please, Caleb, you can't show anyone those photos.'

'I won't,' I say. 'Provided you don't use that photo of Anni in the paper. Or anywhere else. You don't get to take away someone else's power like that, Bethan. Or Brenda, or whatever your goofy-ass name is.'

'Ugh,' she sighs. 'This is so fucking annoying. I was gonna do a whole thing on the fact that freakish adult babies are everywhere in society. It was so perfect that Annika worked for the paper, it would have been amazing.'

'How did you know?' I ask. 'How did you know to come out here and try to catch Anni in the act?'

She laughs — it's a sick, mockery of a laugh really. So different to Anni's wonderful, innocent giggle. 'Oh well, turns out Trent gets access to everyone's internet browser history. Little Annika has been searching for a lot of very fruity shit, including lots and lots of adult baby stuff.'

There's proof positive — Anni isn't lying to me. She really is a Little, and she really has been interested in the age play lifestyle for years. I never really doubted her, but hearing it from Brenda definitely makes me feel more secure in my feelings.

'I promise you,' I say, 'if I find out that you post that photo anywhere, I'll expose you. Not just the many photos I have of you in diapers, but ones of you with binkies, holding stuffies, all of it.

'OK!' she stresses, 'I won't print the photo. But I warn you, Trent's gonna print a story about her. I don't think I can stop him. And he doesn't give a shit about anything but the paper.'

'Just do your part. Don't print the picture.'

Even though she's lied to me countless times in the past, I feel sure this time that Brenda is telling the truth. When her own reputation is on the line, she's a coward.

'So,' she says, her voice softening slightly, 'you don't love me anymore?'

I shake my head. There was a time, not that long ago, when a question like that would have sent me into a confused spin. Now though, I feel so clear-headed and totally over her. 'I'm afraid not. In fact, I think I've found real love this time.'

I know it's a crazy thing to say, but in truth, I haven't even thought about it until this point. But as the words leave my mouth, I know that it's true. For sure. I'm falling for her. Maybe I've already fallen for her.

'Well good luck with your freak,' says Brenda, before hanging up. I hope it's the last time I ever hear her voice.

Suddenly, there's a rustle from the direction of the cabin. I turn around, on full alert mode. But there's no bear. No cougar. Just one heck of a cute Little, and her lower lip is trembling.

'You've found love?'

I gulp. 'I mean, I...' But I decide that I can't lie to her. Ever. So I nod. 'I found *you*. I know it's crazy, but it's how I feel. Obviously, I didn't mean for you to hear. Not so soon at least.'

She looks down at the ground. 'Do you wish I hadn't heard?'

'Nope,' I say. 'Honestly, I'm glad you did.'

She looks up at me, lower lip trembling. 'I'm glad I heard it, too.' Then she's running to me. Just a couple of steps, but she takes them quickly, before she pushes her body into mine. I felt her push up against me last night, felt the curves of her squeeze into me. But this is different. Last night she wanted comfort. Today, she wants me.

'The first time I saw you,' I say, gripping her tight, 'I wanted you. Now I'm gonna show you just how much. I'm gonna make you mine.'

She threads her fingers between mine and holds my hands. 'I'm already yours, Daddy,' she moans. 'You've owned me ever since the first time I called you Daddy.'

And then I taste her for the very first time. Her lips are sweet, her tongue warm. I feel her hands on my back, moving up and down, as my own explore her body: the sweep of her lower back, the fleshy hump of her tight little ass. She must have taken her diaper off because I can feel the smoothness of her skin under her sweatpants. I feel myself harden instantly as her breasts push into my chest.

'I'm gonna destroy you,' I growl into her ear, squeezing her butt hard.

'Yes please, Daddy,' she moans, gently biting my neck, 'I'm desperate for you too.'

I grab her top, tugging it up and over her head. I see her naked breasts, pale in the morning light, her light pink nipples hard and small.

'Damn you're fucking perfect,' I grunt, taking huge handfuls of her body. She moans as I kiss her, yielding to the demands of my hands and mouth. I squeeze her nipples gently, then take them in my mouth, biting, teasing, cupping her breasts. She's wriggling out of her pants, and then grabs hold of mine. I feel like a horny teenager, stumbling out of my clothes, desperate to bury myself in my partner. 'You taste of strawberries,' I say, mouth full of breast. Anni giggles.

'You're silly.'

'Nothing silly about what we're about to do,' I growl in response.

I push my fingers between her naked thighs, finding the warm wetness down there. She gasps as I push into her, then slides herself further onto me, forcing more of my finger into her, trying to swallow me up entirely.

'Hungry girl,' I whisper, as I pull my fingers out, starting to trace lines up down the soft lips of her opening. 'And you're so wet.'

'You made me wet,' she moans. 'You did it to me, Daddy. I'm dripping for you.'

I can feel her lust coating my fingers, a warm river of desire that I'm desperate to taste. 'Don't move, Baby,' I say as I crouch down between her legs. I push her knees apart, looking at her perfect pussy for just a moment.

'Do you like the way I look, Daddy?' she asks, suddenly vulnerable.

'I've never seen anything as beautiful in my life.' I don't wait for her to reply, I move close, right next to her sex, and then I kiss her. I move my lips and tongue down the length of her pink lips, feeling her shudder and tremble in reaction, feeling her hands as they find my hair.

'Oh Daddy,' she sighs, 'I don't know if I can take it, I don't know how lo— '

'You're gonna take it until I say it's over,' I say, looking up at her. 'You have to trust Daddy. You can take it.'

She pauses, bites her lip, nods. Then she pulls me in close again.

I eat her up. From the base of her pussy to its tip, up and down, and then I dart my tongue in. She yelps and I feel her push into me. Then I start to slowly push my tongue in and out, hard but slow. She moans as I fill her up, pushing myself into her, flexing my tongue in and out then slipping it up over her moist little clit, making her shake and quiver.

'I'm gonna fall,' she gasps, 'I can't keep standing like this Daddy.'

'You can rest after you cum,' I growl, then push my fingers back into her, flicking my tongue over her clit. I look up at her, see her mouth make a little 'o', see her eyes roll back and up. Her knees push together, gripping me, and she lets out a long, low moan, until she's bucking and shaking and I know she's in the grip of ecstasy.

I wait with her, holding her tight, supporting her as she slumps down into my arms. There's sweat on her brow, her cheeks are flushed. She's never looked more gorgeous.

'Can you take any more?' I ask, wiping my hand across her brow.

'I can take whatever you want to give me, Daddy.'

Her hand drapes down onto my crotch, and as she feels my hardness there, her eyes widen. 'Looks like you've got a lot to give me,' she says, biting her lip again.

'It's all for you.'

She undoes my fly, and like a spring, my cock shoots out. She lazily folds over and puts her ruby lips against the tip. A moment later, she swallows it up. Seeing her lips around my shaft makes me so insanely hard that my cock strains against the confines of her mouth.

'I need to fuck you right now,' I say.

She nods with a dream look, then she slowly rises up, as if in a trance. She leans against the cabin, turning round. Her beautiful ass is there, and like a split peach, her perfect pussy waits for me, glistening in the morning light.

'Be gentle, Daddy,' she says.

'I dunno,' I say, 'way I'm feeling, that might not be on the cards.'

When I enter her for the first time, I feel instantly like I'm gonna explode. She's so tight, so hot, so fucking wet, that I never want to leave.

'Fuuuuuccckkkk,' she breathes, as I start to move in and out of her. It's heaven — pure, unbelievable pleasure. She's shaking, and I don't feel so different. I have to grab her back as I slump over, then I compose myself and start to pound her. She responds to my pace, moving back and forth with me, intensifying my sensation, making me grunt with passion.

I don't know how long we're here, moving like animals together. I move her around like she weighs nothing, lifting her against trees and impaling her as she rides above me like a goddess. I rub my cock on her clit, slip it once more into her mouth — she grinds her pussy into my lips, squeezing my ass, tracing her hands over my abs, my pecs, my cock once more.

We're loud, shouting and grunting until finally, lost in sensation, I reach round, put my thumb in her mouth — she sucks, bites, kisses me — then I grab her breasts, part her buttocks, drag my nails over her skin. She's bucking and squirming and then a moment later I feel her come again, her pussy gripping my cock so tight that I can't contain myself.

'Come in me,' she pants, 'I want it, I need it, please Daddy.'

And as she says my name, I give in to the pleasure and I spray my seed thick and strong inside her, grabbing her body so hard we're almost the same person.

'Oh, Daddy,' she says, panting, 'that was the best, you're the best.'

'No,' I say, kissing her forehead, 'we're the best. Me and you. Together.'

# ANNIKA

## THREE WEEKS LATER

*M*Y NAME'S *ANNIKA AND I'm a Little*. That's what I decided to call my blog. It took a huge amount of bravery, but now I'm pretty much the official chronicler of the community here at the Little Cabin.

Today, I'm writing a report of this week's water fight. It was Bigs vs Littles and it was *epic*. Ella took photos as we all frolicked in the water. The shots are amazing: lots of laughing Littles and surprisingly wet Bigs.

'I can't believe you're going to publish that picture of me.'

Caleb's looking over at me from the kitchen. Our cabin hasn't been built yet, so we're still waiting in the guest cabin, but I already feel totally at home. Quitting your job and leaving your home is surprisingly easy when you've got a dreamy life lined up with a man you love in an idyllic setting.

'What's wrong with it?' I ask, innocently. I open the picture bigger on the screen of the laptop. It's a close-up of Caleb's face as a huge water balloon collides with his cheek.

'Oh, you know, the focus is slightly off.'

I laugh, 'I think it's close enough.'

'Did I ever tell you that you're a very naughty girl?' he asks, with laughter in his voice.

'Once or twice.'

'Come on, finish up, I need your help to carry this over to the Nursery.'

Once a week at the Little Cabin, we all have dinner together in the Nursery. Each week, a different Daddy takes it in turns to cook. This week is Caleb's turn. He's been nervous about it all day because all the other Daddies are such good cooks. But he's no slouch either, especially when it comes to Mexican food.

All afternoon, he's been preparing tacos. When he decided to give up his life in New York to handle all the PR at the Little Cabin, he brought some of his personal possessions over from his place. He didn't bring much, but I was surprised to see that one of the few things he did bring was his tortilla press.

'Couldn't live without it,' he said when I asked him about it. 'Nothing like home-cooked corn tortillas.'

Now that I've experienced them finished over an open fire, I have to agree.

I put the finishing touches to the water-fight report and hit publish. My blog is already doing way better than I expected. I set it up to get our side of the story out there, to fight against the misinformation being spread by the Chronicle, but it's done so much more than that. Littles from across the country have got in touch with me, inspired by my story, and the story of the Cabin. I've got interviews lined up with all the Daddies and the Littles, as well as how-to guides and general information about the Caregiver/Little lifestyle. I'm not an expert, but I kind of think that people appreciate that.

And the article from the Chronicle, when it dropped, hasn't seemed to make anything worse for us. In fact, we've been getting way less hate mail, and many, many more messages of support.

As we pack up the carnitas, roast pineapple, salsa, and tacos, Caleb says, 'I'm so proud of you, sweetheart.'

'You are?'

'Of course. You're a real force for good in the world.'

I don't think I've ever smiled as wide in my whole life.

The evening is magical. The Littles and the Bigs, all tucking into Caleb's amazing food. As I look around at all the happy faces, all the people living fulfilled, good lives, for the first time in years I actually feel proud of myself. Finally, I'm doing something I really believe in. Sure, it might not be as worthy as being a crime reporter, but in my own little way, I'm changing the world for the better.

And there's nowhere I'd rather be.

* * *

Thank you so much for reading this box set!

Hungry for more Lucky Moon box sets? Check out Little Ranch: The Complete Collection!

If you're after more mountain men, take a look at Daddies of Pine Peak, a new novel series, as well as my Daddies Mountain Rescue novella series!

And finally, if you enjoyed this box set, please leave a review to help others find and enjoy my work too. Have a fantastic day, and don't forget to sign up for my newsletter for a free box set and all the Lucky

Moon fun and games you could ever wish for: competitions, giggles, bonus content, news, and soooo much more!

A full display of my books can be found at:
www.luckymoonbooks.com.

Join me on Facebook:
www.facebook.com/groups/luckyslovelyreaders.

Hugs and positivity!

Lucky x o x

# Also By Lucky Moon

**BAD BOY DADDIES**

DADDY MEANS BUSINESS

DADDY MEANS TROUBLE

DADDY MEANS SUBMISSION

DADDY MEANS DOMINATION

DADDY MEANS HALLOWEEN

DADDY MEANS DISCIPLINE

**LIBERTY LITTLES**

TAMED BY HER DADDIES

FAKE DADDY

DADDY SAVES CHRISTMAS (IN A LITTLE COUNTRY CHRISTMAS)

SECOND CHANCE DADDIES

DADDY'S GAME

THE DADDY CONTEST

DADDY'S ORDERS

**DRIFTERS MC**

DADDY DEMANDS

DADDY COMMANDS

DADDY DEFENDS

**DADDIES INC**

BOSS DADDY

YES DADDY

MORE DADDY

**COLORADO DADDIES**

HER WILD COLORADO DADDY

FIERCE DADDIES

**THE DADDIES MC SERIES**

DANE

ROCK

HAWK

**DADDIES MOUNTAIN RESCUE**

MISTER PROTECTIVE

MISTER DEMANDING

MISTER RELENTLESS

**SUGAR DADDY CLUB SERIES**

PLATINUM DADDY

CELEBRITY DADDY

DIAMOND DADDY

CHAMPAGNE DADDY

**LITTLE RANCH SERIES**

DADDY'S FOREVER GIRL

DADDY'S SWEET GIRL

DADDY'S PERFECT GIRL

DADDY'S DARLING GIRL

DADDY'S REBEL GIRL

**MOUNTAIN DADDIES SERIES**

TRAPPED WITH DADDY

LOST WITH DADDY

SAVED BY DADDY

STUCK WITH DADDY

TRAINED BY DADDY

GUARDED BY DADDY

**STANDALONE NOVELS**

PLEASE DADDY

## DDLG MATCHMAKER SERIES

### DADDY'S LITTLE BRIDE

### DADDY'S LITTLE REBEL

### DADDY'S LITTLE DREAM

## VIGILANTE DADDIES

### BLAZE

### DRAKE

### PHOENIX

# Copyright

Content copyright © Lucky Moon. All rights reserved. First published in 2023.

This book may not be reproduced or used in any manner without the express written permission of the copyright holder, except for brief quotations used in reviews or promotions. This book is licensed for your personal use only. Thanks!

Disclaimer: This is a work of fiction. Names, characters, businesses, places, events, locales, and incidents are either the products of the author's imagination or used in a fictitious manner. Any resemblance to actual persons, living or dead, or actual events is purely coincidental.

Cover Image © Curaphotography, Fotolia. Cover Design, Lucky Moon.

Printed in Great Britain
by Amazon

23596114R00255